WHEN
I
WAS
BETTER

RITA BOZI

atmosphere press

To my beloved parents, Ethel and Steve

And to my beloved husband, Ken

And my dear friend, Adrienne K.

Hungary 1945

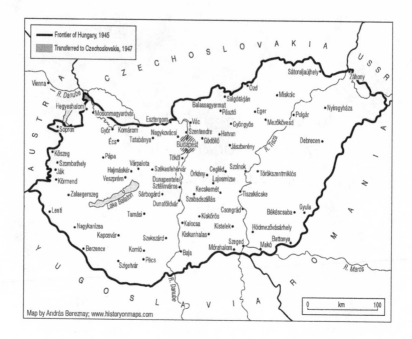

Map by András Bereznay; www.historyonmaps.com

The Hungarian Revolution 1956

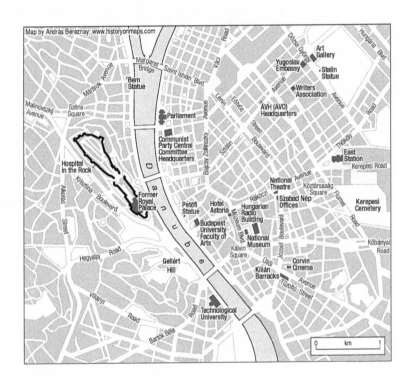

Map by András Bereznay; www.historyonmaps.com

CHARACTER LIST

Teréza
István (her husband)
Zolti (their son)

Pista (István's best friend, also a voice in his head)

Anna, Gyuri (Teréza's parents)
Klára (Teréza's eldest sister, living in Budapest)
Elek (Klára's husband)
Ági, Juli, Kati (Teréza's sisters)
András (Teréza's brother)

Feri (István's stepfather)
Zsuzsa (István's mother)
Tamás, Lali (István's brothers)

Sándor, Péter, Laci (István's co-workers)
Barna (István's roommate in the refugee camp)
Varga (István's childhood enemy, later a turncoat)
Csoki (Hungarian soldier, István's friend)
Yvan, Bolochka (soldiers)
Németh (Arrow Cross commander, secret police officer, Varga's uncle)

János (Teréza's uncle)
Hermina (Uncle János' wife)
Hermus/Mrs. Stalin (Hermina's mother)
Anikó (old woman, distant relative)

Bela, Marika (István's friends, fellow refugees)
Ackermann (István's boss in Canada)

TABLE OF CONTENTS

SEPARATION

REUNIFICATION

"We forget that we are history. We have kept the left hand from knowing the right...We are not used to associating our private lives with public events. Yet the histories of families cannot be separate from the histories of nations. To divide them is part of our denial."

Susan Griffin, *A Chorus of Stones*

PROLOGUE

1964

THIS IS WHAT DYING FEELS LIKE

1964, February 28.

Sign language. If Teréza missed a signal or a cue she would be lost. Her heart raced, and she clutched her passport to her chest. The last person she and her eight-year-old son had spoken with was the unfriendly *Malév* stewardess from the substandard Hungarian airline. Here, in the bustling Brussels airport Teréza felt like a speechless toddler. Her world had transformed into a place of gestures and facial expressions, making her feel more vigilant now than she had ever been under Communism. No one understood her but Zolti. Already she ached for her language and the family she left behind.

In her bewilderment, Teréza felt energized and diminished at once. The representative from Sabena, the Belgian airline, beckoned to them with long thin arms sheathed in white gloves as she ushered them through the terminal to customs. Lush plants stretched skyward to the sunshine pouring in through the glass ceiling. Pastel colours fused pleasantly with the scent of croissants and café au lait.

3

Everything in the West seemed bright and cheerful. If only István had chosen to settle in Brussels instead of Winnipeg when he fled Hungary without them. But he was always such a contrarian.

Teréza kept pace with the woman's long stride and pulled Zolti along as they passed by boutiques where well-to-do women shopped for diamonds and lace, items that were impossibly out of her reach. But here in the midst of the indecipherable announcements Teréza could hear only one thing: their last conversation in person, hers and István's.

"I'm going today," he'd said one morning seven years ago.

"How can you do this to us? We could have escaped, together! As a family."

"They're coming to arrest me."

"Why didn't you tell me sooner?"

That was the last day she saw him, when his son Zolti was but a babe-in-arms.

István woke at dawn, with a new set of worries. What if Teréza wasn't on the flight? What if the authorities didn't let her out of Hungary? What if she had decided not to leave?

He lay on the sofa bed in his friends' Montreal living room and through the window watched it snow again. He tried for hours to fall back to sleep, but his tossing and turning kept twisting the sheets around his ankles, pulling him down into nightmares.

In fits of lucidness, he thought of the day he fled seven and a half years ago – thirty-two years old – the last time he set eyes on his baby boy, lying motionless on the day bed.

He'd asked Teréza, "What's wrong with him?"

She replied, "What's wrong with you?" He had no answer.

István reached over to his neatly folded pile of clothing on the chair, and from his overcoat pocket pulled a tinted photograph taken a half-year ago. Mother and son. The last one she'd sent from Hungary. She was almost thirty-four now and István was pushing forty. Such a pretty woman, with a warm smile and skin that always looked clear and bright. When Teréza posed for photos she had a habit of tilting her head to the right, as if trying to improve her appearance, to make life more pleasant somehow. But photos betrayed appearances. This benign bearing couldn't hide the side of her personality that believed existence was beyond repair. She often said, even of good photos, "I hate this picture of myself."

Studying the photo, István was fascinated by his son's features. Something troubled him about the boy. He leaned against his mother like an unstable shack, the walls and roof sliding one way, its base clinging to the earth. Years ago, after István reached the refugee camp, Teréza had sent him a picture, taken when Zolti was just fourteen months old. In it, the toddler's eyes were fixed on something or someone, off camera, much taller and bigger than him. He looked worried, startled even, with his button mouth turned downwards. This most recent photograph showed his son's eyes fixed in exactly the same direction with the same startled look. The boy was almost eight, but his expression hadn't changed.

Put it all behind you, István. Begin again.

"Pista! Back from the dead!" István laughed aloud. "My dear friend, are you speaking to me from heaven? When you died you stopped being my advisor."

Everything comes to end, Pista replied. *Have you reason-*

able regret?

"I do. I do," István replied.

Well then?

István closed his eyes. The image of wife and son burned itself into the backs of his eyelids. Once he opened them, he would fit back into their lives again.

In a cozy corner, a businessman dictated a letter to a typist attired in a pale pink pullover and green pumps. Teréza wanted that job in this important glass palace. Mesmerized by the glamour in the terminal, Teréza barely paid attention to her son who rushed to keep up with his mother.

"Come, Zolti. We can't fall behind," she said, turning to look at the *Chanel* perfume counter they passed. It was only then that she realized she had no money in her wallet. Nothing. Even if the Hungarian security officials hadn't relieved her of her forints, they would have been worthless here.

"But I want to look at the telephones." Zolti locked his knees in the middle of the bustle and refused to move.

"You'll have one in Canada. Please?" Teréza's expression was a mixture of pleading and apology. She glanced towards the Sabena representative who was well ahead of them now.

Zolti quickly conceded, sensing his mother's anxiety.

The stewardess motioned for them to take a seat.

The waiting lounge was full of French businessmen. There were very few families and less than a handful of couples. Teréza was the only single woman with a child. She was troubled to see a very large group of Turkish men in the terminal carrying rucksacks. Rural men who wore old, loose-fitting clothing. *The conquerors*, she thought, her mind taught to remember the hundred and fifty-year occupation of her people. A Sabena stewardess politely ushered the group to the waiting area. Wasn't she afraid of them? One of them – likely the same age as Teréza's father – pulled a colorful prayer rug from his bag and with a gracious gesture handed it to the stewardess. She declined until he lightheartedly tucked the rug into the creases of her arms, playfully bending her forearms and hands inwards as if wrapping the rug in a package.

Zolti watched them. "That's a kind man. Is my father kind too?"

"Yes, he is," Teréza heard herself say through the lump in her throat. She thought of all the times István had forged ahead and created a home for her. Other men thought it the job of the woman to make the nest. It was another way he was different.

A new world was changing her view of the old one, for the third time in her life.

An announcement crackled over the public address system in French. Some passengers stood. Teréza looked around, worried, understanding only one word.

"Come Zolti. We're going to Canada." She felt disembodied, as if part of her was floating in reverse, homeward.

Two hours before the flight's arrival, István paced the spacious corridors of Montréal-Dorval International Airport, retracing his steps when he hit dead ends. He was familiar with the terminal; he'd landed here the day before, from Winnipeg.

He'd kept alive the hope that there would be one moment in life when his best intentions and deepest desires aligned. When fear and failure transformed into love and acceptance and these new states remained effortlessly balanced within him. He yearned for the miraculous transition when fate switched over from loss to triumph, that distant region that held freedom, and promised him immunity from pain. István had no proof this place existed, but he had hope. He convinced himself that day would be today.

At arrivals, he watched the automatic doors swoosh open, swoosh closed. Shortly after, a small dog outsmarted its owner, darted straight for István's legs and ran frantic circles around him, binding him in the leash. The mutt nipped at his ankles. Close to losing his balance or swearing at the thing – he hated yappy little dogs – István summoned his composure when he realized, to his amazement, that the dog belonged to a very important-looking woman wearing a snow leopard coat. Elizabeth Taylor! She was waving to a tense looking man to *get the dog*! All István could do was marvel at Ms. Taylor while the dog choked itself trying to get loose. The man, presumably her assistant, apologized for the mishap and unwound the hysterical animal from István's legs.

"It's no trouble," István lied.

Surrounded by bodyguards, Ms. Taylor offered her lips and the dog obliged, licking them. She had been married four times; one of her marriages caused a scandal when she stole another woman's husband. If she had done this in the East bloc no one would have cared. Thievery was to be expected. He wondered if she couldn't be loved enough, if they shared the same affliction. In the blink of an eye, the movie star disappeared through some secret door.

István found a newsagent and read front-page captions of

English language newspapers. "U.S. President Announces New Jet Airplane." He tried to sound out impossible words in the French journals. He imagined how he would greet his wife and son. He didn't know how best to prepare for this. He'd never hugged his boy before. Who should he embrace first? Would his son run at him and jump into his arms? What if his son didn't recognize him? He remembered his wife's fantastic reversals. At first she offered understanding, then later, unexpectedly and with unabashed fury came her real feelings. Anger always came after forgiveness. He wondered how long it would take this time.

On the second flight, from Brussels to Montreal, Teréza reclined in her seat, her stomach uneasy, her head spinning. She steeled herself. With her head thrown back against the headrest, eyes closed, she placed a hand on her forehead and a narrow white paper bag on her lap.

The woman in row eight continued to gag. In solidarity, Teréza vomited too; her Hungarian anti-nausea pills proved useless. When the plane reached cruising altitude, the stewardess gave her real ones.

Her son pressed his face against the window, his fingers suctioned to the glass, white with fear. She smoothed Zolti's hair, brushing it off his forehead. His skin was moist, his cheeks were flushed and he looked like a shiny plum. The world didn't appear to move, and the roar of the engines scared him. "We're going to fall out of the sky! We're going to fall out of the sky!" Zolti shrieked.

"Please don't be silly, Zolti. The plane's not going to fall out of the sky."

When she wasn't calming him with fairytales or dozing in and out of a medicated sleep, Teréza prayed. When she ran out of fairytales, she told him the joke about the fox, the wolf and the rabbit, something she would never have shared with him in the homeland.

Zolti made Teréza tell it over and over again. "But why do the fox and the wolf keep beating up the little rabbit?" he asked every time.

"Because under an oppressor there is never a right answer," Teréza whispered. "Without God, men are animals. And Soviets don't believe in God."

"Will there be Soviets in Canada?" Zolti asked.

"No, my darling. But there will be Liberals."

It continued this way for the next seven hours, her son in a state of mild terror, pressing her with questions, while Teréza's head bobbed helplessly back and forth between the past and the future.

Teréza imagined her István. Remembered how soft his skin was, pure white, almost translucent. She knew he had been working hard to prepare a home for them, that he had promised to be a different man upon their arrival. 'I have the freedom here to be a good man for you,' he wrote in his last letter.

The edge of the Atlantic Ocean came within reach. Vast, unmoving blue. The white noise of the airplane sedated and aggravated Teréza in equal measure. As she dozed, her mind grappled with complex thoughts. What use was life if everyone lived in their own reality as her husband did? Wasn't that the loneliest place on earth? The isolation of the mind? She'd never had this thought before, and now she grew anxious from the anticipation of seeing István. She didn't know what his life was like anymore. She didn't know his mind anymore. What if he'd grown more taciturn over the years? What if he could express himself only through letters? Would they be passing notes to each other in a soundless house? What a ridiculous idea, she thought. He spoke not one but two languages now. Four if she counted the Russian he resented and the German he admired. But whom did he talk to in the seclusion of his Winnipeg home?

Teréza finally dozed as the plane began its descent. It was in her dreams that she heard her son's ceaseless cries. "We're falling out of the sky!"

"We're not falling out of the sky." Her words were drowsy, her mouth dry.

"Look, Mama! Fields! The ground is rushing up!"

"My sweet child." Teréza put her hand gently on his. "Planes don't just fall out of the sky. It's our spirits that can fall at any moment."

She closed her eyes and leaned her head against the back of her seat. "Be a good, brave boy for your father. Worlds have collapsed for him," Teréza said, already sleeping. The plane plunged. Zolti screamed.

István rechecked the arrivals board. On time. Only forty-three minutes were left of the seven years they had spent apart. Last minute he decided to re-park the car so it would be closer to the door. Along the way he found a flower shop.

"When I was better I didn't brag," István answered the French Canadian shop girl who asked him how he was. She'd looked as perplexed as most people did when István answered this way.

He chose white carnations. Swiping the coins off the counter, he pocketed his change. He observed a tall, lean, older gentleman with spectacles, a tidy suit and a cane, walking from the arrivals area, making his way towards a taxi exit. The gentleman had the look of someone who either by choice or by circumstance had been without a spouse for an arduous length of time. Resignation and indifference, that could have been me, thought István.

The first passengers trickled out as István quickened his pace back towards the waiting area. More passengers emerged in clumps, staring dumbfounded and bleary-eyed into the crowd. Were they from the Brussels flight? Or from a previous flight? The waiting made him somber. The doors opened, then closed halfway, then opened again, but no one walked through them. A long pause ensued. The doors closed. A few people around him lit cigarettes. Then no one came for what seemed like twenty minutes. He stopped checking his watch. A few last passengers surfaced and then he found himself alone in the waiting area holding the carnations upside down by his side.

Did he miss them? Did they not make it out? He'd have felt reprehensible if, after coming out to the airport so far in advance, his wife and son had walked out searching for his face, and found nothing.

Like a magic act, the doors swooshed open again, and no one was there. The doors closed again.

He thought, this is what dying feels like.

TRAPPED

1956-1957

SON OF THE REVOLUTION

On the day Teréza hated most, May Day, her first child was born. It began like any other celebration of the Hungarian Workers Party. The country turned red with decorations, banners and furbelows.

The Sunday previous, István had announced that he would have to take leave for two days on either side of the May Day celebrations and could not disclose his whereabouts. Nor could he come home during that time. Four years of this secrecy and Teréza was getting bored. Who would she possibly tell? And why?

"Do they take me for an idiot?!" Teréza railed. Everyone knew that firemen were recruited as reinforcements and stationed near the border in case anyone tried to escape or invade on Communism's most important holiday. She consoled herself that István's mandated secret missions allowed him to learn all the areas along the border where citizens could possibly escape to the west.

"Fine. Go wherever they send you," she seethed. "Are they

15

really such idiots? Do they actually think the Americans will attack? Who the hell wants in here?!" With her large belly she looked like an angry hen.

"You know how I feel about this!" István erupted. He ran his hands through his hair several times, unable to tolerate the suggestion that he was somehow complicit with the enemy.

The next day István kissed his wife on the cheek as he was leaving. She let him and said nothing. He then slipped through the garden gate and reported for duty.

"Get back in time for your son," she had yelled after him. A male presence grew inside her, she was sure, the way it kicked, insisted and pushed against her pubic bone. The baby fought confinement in exactly the same way her husband did.

Monday early evening she lay in bed, on her side, staring at the chalk-white wall, dreading the following day's festivities. She thought about how in Mays past, in early childhood, together with her eldest sister, she used to follow the delicate scent of violets, diminutive blooms that hid under bushes or sprang up through the cracks in sidewalks. They collected tiny bouquets of these aromatic flowers and brought them home to their mother. The thought made her feel incurably lonely. She pushed her reflections onward to the tulip petals she collected in a basket for Easter Sunday, which she gently sprinkled at the feet of priests walking the route to the resurrected Jesus, on the grounds of the old church in her village. The contractions began. She was gripped with the fear that her child might be breach; arriving the wrong way in retaliation to the brutality her body had suffered. Or that the child's face might already bear the marks of the ugliness she'd lived. She wanted nothing more than to give this child a life free of violence.

She walked herself to the Socialist hospital built exclusively for childbirth. She saw the high-quality natal management as another ploy by the socialist government to ensure the best care for its new seed, the purpose of which was already set out for it: to sprout into another worker.

There were moments when she wondered if she could make it to the hospital or if she would lie down somewhere in a park and let the seed return to God. During her painful yet dignified walk she remembered her pact with God. She would bring forth a child of the Almighty and teach her son to be a gentleman.

To soothe the pain, she grabbed hold of a wrought-iron fence and breathed in the aroma of lilacs. She adored the enormous bushes that burst through gates and intruded onto the sidewalk, their petals white and mauve. She preferred the white ones, and she wouldn't look at any red flowers, not today.

By dusk, Teréza underwent labour alone with a nurse. Terrified of scaring the child, she did not yell out. Instead she bore her pain as impassively as she could muster.

She wanted to deliver the child into a semblance of quiet beauty; a response to the violence simmering around her.

At quarter to one in the morning, she couldn't bear it any longer. The pain accumulated into a searing ball of sound. Teréza cried out just once in a last final push. She regretted it immediately. She had brought him into this world hearing agony. Everything bad that happened to her son from this moment forth would be her fault. She couldn't protect him, even from herself.

Baby Zolti arrived without his father. He cried in great distress and presented himself underweight, weighing in just less than 2.5 kilograms. A small bag of flour. Once Teréza finally held him in her arms, it was morning, and his shrieking had turned him crimson and electric. Teréza had infected him. She begged him to eat. When he finally took to her breast it was as if he would never let go. In return, she vowed to never let him go either. The daylight portended a warm and sunny day with everything in full bloom. From her window she could see flowering trees and cherry blossoms. May Day. She thanked her infant for sparing her from the festivities she hated most.

I'M GOING TODAY

1957, January 30. Szombathely, Hungary

Teréza finished ironing the shirt and a numbing wave of unease flooded her thighs. She looked up and examined István's eyes; these days her husband perpetually wore the frightened look of someone fleeing. The reprisals had been going on for months now.

Standing with his arms crossed, wearing only his singlet and trousers, István looked leaner. She opened the shirt and held it against his back. "Here you go, it's still warm."

Pressed cotton blended with the smell of bitter coffee rising in the stovetop espresso maker. She could tell from his softening expression the warmth felt soothing. She offered to button his shirt.

"I'm not a child," he said, with mischief in his voice.

She adjusted his collar. "And if you were, I might spank you," she said, surprising them both.

She placed his espresso on the table and pulled a skirt onto the narrow end of the ironing board as he sat down in front of his breakfast. She gazed towards the single window of their kitchen, a presentiment rising in her. It was still dark outside, and she saw her reflection in the glass.

"The ice crystals remind me of my childhood bedroom," he said, gulping his coffee.

"Wait for it to cool. I don't know how you drink it scalding."

"I like popping the blister I get on the roof of my mouth when it's this hot. And then I like rolling the torn tissue around with my tongue."

Teréza shook her head and re-positioned the skirt on the ironing board. "You're a strange man."

"Our kitchen cabinets look butter-coloured in this light," he said.

"They need painting," she answered, moving the iron back and forth.

He took another swig of coffee and said, "I'm going today."

"What did you say?" She looked at him with the startled expression baby Zolti had inherited.

"You heard me."

It was nearly impossible to leave Hungary without being captured or shot. By the New Year, the exodus to Austria had come to a grinding halt. Single shoes, bits of clothing, discarded dolls and teddy bears littered the eastern border near Szombathely, a stillborn testament of the impregnability of the border. Teréza heard the rumors at the County Council where she worked. A few trusted co-workers whispered in the Ladies Room about someone who had been caught, jailed or deported to the Soviet Union since the failed revolution. The new Soviet-installed government, headed by Kádár – whom Teréza secretly called "the traitor" – had successfully smothered all public opposition ordering hundreds of executions in Budapest. A heavily guarded border was the punishment for those who stayed.

Now the insides of Teréza's legs were on fire.

Her female colleagues at work suggested the rash might be from the cold, since temperatures had plummeted well below zero. "No," Teréza had said, "it's fear. It affects us all differently. For some women, it's their liver that goes, for others it's their womb. For me, it's my skin."

Teréza waited for the prickle of heat to fade and exhaled slowly.

István glanced into her eyes. "They're coming to arrest me."

"How do you know?"

"I know."

"Why didn't you tell me sooner?"

He didn't answer and she didn't wait for one. "Blast you! I begged you to leave while we had the opportunity! Say something!" She wanted to throw the iron at his head.

István's eyes lost focus, looking nowhere.

She threw the iron in the sink. The terrible clatter startled the baby, who quieted again immediately. "How can you do this to us?" she cried. "We could have escaped together. Weeks ago! As a family!"

He looked down at his empty cup.

"István!" she cried. Teréza loathed István's hesitancy, his weakness, his talent for self-preservation.

"No, we couldn't have!" István slammed his fist on the table. His cup danced on his saucer.

Teréza's heart fell to her knees. Her soul into a dark hole. Her mouth couldn't bear to say the word betrayal. Saying it aloud would have meant the end of them – instead she allowed herself to feel like an animal left for dead. After a long and painful intermission, she tired of looking at the top of her husband's head. "So, you've made a plan?"

"Not exactly. I'm going to drive –"

"Don't tell me. I don't want to know." She leaned against the sink. Teréza wanted to unleash one last raillery, but she controlled herself. Her goading and accusations would solve nothing. What would be the point? To prove that she was right? That she should never have trusted him? This was her fault. Her son was being abandoned because she cried out during his birth. She'd cursed him.

"Where are you?" István asked. It was in moments like these, his wife embittered and remote, that he wanted to disappear. To be left alone forever in a safe, quiet place without people. Only him and the earth. He imagined an outpost in the Arctic.

"I'm nowhere," Teréza said to the iron.

Behind them, Zolti lay on the day bed, swaddled in blankets, motionless and staring. István turned to look at the baby. "What's wrong with him?"

"What's wrong with you?" Teréza shot back.

"Why doesn't he look like me?" István searched his wife's face.

Teréza shrugged. "If he did, would you stay?"

Their separation began here. A tattoo that read, *You left us.*

István knew his time would come that day in November when Péter his rookie was executed. When István had gotten to the fire hall, Sándor, his nemesis, remarked on the torn books in the library. "The Revolution's over," Sándor said with sarcasm in his voice, "and someone's got a mess to clean up." His black hair looked blacker today, as though he'd dipped his head in a vat of tar.

"Then clean them up. Burn them," István barked, as he plodded down the hallway towards his office.

"The hand that tore them should burn them," Sándor called to him.

A prickly feeling shot up István's spine.

István sorted requisition orders on his desk. The truck needed new parts, and who knew how long it would take to get anything done in the aftermath. He worked undisturbed until Péter bust into his office, his pipe tight between his teeth, yelling, "The tanks are coming!"

Outside, István heard shouting. He rushed to the window. Russian tanks were aiming their guns towards the fire hall, encircling the building. When István gave the evacuation order Péter stopped him. "There's no use. They're out back too."

"How did I not hear them coming?" István hissed, ducking low, moving through the hallways to round up his men.

Péter followed. "Sir, get that thing off your arm." István was still wearing his Hungarian brassard. He tore it off and shoved it in his inside pocket.

A dozen Russian soldiers entered the building carrying rifles. "*Vylezat'! Vylezat*!" they shouted. With nowhere to hide, István walked out into the main foyer, his arms raised high above his head. Péter followed, the pipe still tight between his teeth. "Get that pipe out of your mouth," István yelled.

Péter shoved his pipe into his upper coat pocket, still lit.

A soldier smacked István across the face, "*Net govorit*!

István was forced outside with the butt end of a rifle to his back. His men were pushed and shoved and forced to kneel with their arms up. István couldn't see Sándor.

They stayed that way for a long time. István's knees and shoulders ached; his arms went numb and beside him Péter's pocket began to smolder. The tank drivers trained their cannons on the firemen. All twenty of them. The soldiers yelled in Russian and István understood every degrading word.

When the soldiers readied their weapons István waited for the bullet. Who would be the first to go? He didn't care if it was him. He didn't want to live to see the world returned to its former pre-Revolution state. Beside him, he could smell Péter's pipe burning through his uniform. Before István could say, "Don't," Péter reached for his pipe. The next moment, his blood splattered István's cheek. Péter dropped in front of him, face first in the mud. When Péter's best buddy Laci howled, he was shoved to the ground and kicked in the kidneys.

István didn't move and didn't react when the Russian soldier asked, "Haven't you taught your men to stay in line?" Instead, he hoped Pista's voice would drive him to say, "Shoot me too." But it didn't. Pista didn't speak to him anymore.

The downpour came out of nowhere. It soaked through István's uniform in a matter of minutes, as though the Russians had commanded it. His men shivered from cold. The rain and Péter's blood pooled around his knees. Pushing down every last feeling inside himself, István hardened his heart. So he felt nothing when he, along with the rest of his men, were ordered to their feet and marched back inside the fire hall to resume their duties in this latest Soviet era.

Since then, István and Teréza had lived in fear. The mood at the fire station reverted to the time before Stalin was dead. Citizens made last-ditch efforts to flee Hungary. Nearly two hundred thousand had left since the uprising. A little wooden bridge at the otherwise insignificant border crossing of Andau, Austria, became famous for supporting the flood of refugees over a marsh. And now the Soviets had destroyed that too, making the journey that much more perilous.

István waited, wondering what would happen next. He and Teréza slid into melancholy: neither talked much in the days and weeks following Péter's death. The same pointless feeling returned, the one István had felt when he lost his brother Lali.

At night, they whispered about Kádár and Nagy, even though such talk could have them jailed. How the newly installed Party leader, Kádár János had betrayed his friend Nagy Imre and several other colleagues, first by going to Moscow with instructions to broker a peace deal and returning with two thousand tanks and a new job for himself. Secondly by promising Nagy and Rajk's widow Julia safe passage home from the Yugoslav embassy in Budapest where they took refuge. Instead, Kádár, under the instruction of the Soviets, deported Nagy to Romania where he was being jailed and tortured.

"How can he live with himself?" Teréza rubbed her forehead as though she was scrubbing tarnish off silver.

"They've all become soulless. Every last one of them."

István turned towards Teréza and touched her cheek. An uprising had come and gone since they'd last made love.

István walked to work carrying the heavy load of his secret. Soviet tanks still surrounded the fire hall. The snow reflected the brilliance of the sun and the blankness of his mind. White blindness induced peacefulness until he thought about what he had yet to pull off. When he reviewed it in too much detail his muscles started to twitch. His body was coiled and tight by the time he reached the door of the fire station.

Yesterday, Sándor had pointed a gun at István and said, "I feel like shooting someone." István knocked the revolver to the ground. Sándor laughed heartily, swiped up his revolver, and shoved it in his holster. Shortly afterward, István joined the lineup to collect his monthly salary. The secretary slid the envelope over the counter, but when his fingers touched it, she refused to let go. "They're coming to arrest you," she whispered while pretending to busy herself with paperwork. "I saw the list."

Their eyes met.

"Thank you." He didn't dare say more. He had turned and slid the envelope into his coat pocket, and there it stayed. No matter how the next few hours played out, one way or the other, he wouldn't be needing it where he was going.

Now, the fire station gleamed in the early morning light. István took a breath and opened the door. In the meeting room, eight firemen in uniforms, hard as cardboard, sat at a round table. Smoke circled, wafted in front of the red star in the centre of their caps. He took the seat farthest from Sándor and felt sick.

Sándor blew smoke towards István's face.

It didn't reach him, but István coughed anyway. "Good morning."

"Try smoking. It's good for your nerves."

Fuck you, thought István. He nodded and smiled instead.

"Number one on today's agenda…" Sándor spoke with his usual self-importance, though he was reading from his notes, "discuss preparation plans to welcome our Soviet comrades who arrive next week for friendship building."

After his recent demotion – an edifying gesture bestowed on him by the powers that be – István was no longer permitted to chair meetings. He bugged his eyes out at Laci, his protégé, who had to look away. As long as tanks surrounded the fire hall, the Russians had no intention of amicable camaraderie. They'd increased their surveillance and were searching for signs of dissent.

"Maybe we could organize a game of cards for our Soviet comrades," István quipped. He couldn't help himself. It was the kind of thing Pista would have urged him to say.

Laci put the wrong end of the cigarette in his mouth, lit it, and sucked in the foul taste of filter.

István pressed his lips together, trying not to laugh.

The morning passed slowly. Every movement seemed magnified: how the secretary adjusted her cat eye glasses before scratching notes on paper, how Sándor stumbled over his notes and cocked his head when he wanted agreement, how Laci tapped the underside of the table nervously while the rest of the firemen sat still in their starched uniforms. Mostly new faces. Sándor had replaced several firemen, all of István's friends, and brought in five new recruits, all Party members. István couldn't trust any one of them. He had only Laci now.

After his humour wore off, István felt like a butterfly pinned under a microscope. They knew that he wouldn't be around by next week. In this society built on informants, word travelled fast. He was certain they'd been discussing his fate before he'd arrived that morning, speculating that he'd rot in prison, maybe a gulag in the Soviet Union, or be summarily shot.

"Stop," István cried.

"What?" Sándor said, looking insulted.

"Stop tapping your fingers, Laci, it's driving me nuts," István said.

"I'm running this meeting now. I'll decide what's making you nuts," Sándor replied drily.

"Please, go ahead. In fact, I would be pleased if you determined what makes me nuts."

Sándor exhaled. "My guess is...ideological confusion. To believe or not to believe, that is the question."

When István was asked to weigh in on the condition of the fire trucks he sounded clear, organized and obedient. Cheerful even when he pointed out that if the Soviets ran into any vehicle trouble, he could only do so much to help them. "Question is, will they camp out for the six to eight weeks it'll take for parts to arrive? I have about twenty forms to fill out for one air filter."

"Comrade," Sándor said, slowly, "I would hardly suggest that someone in your position point out –"

"Point out what? Comrade?" István smiled like he'd won the lottery. "What position?"

A thin smile formed on Sándor's lips, a look of contempt that the new recruits mimicked. They were a pack of hungry dogs, ravenous for István's flesh. István knew one of them would be reporting his behaviour to the "behaviour department" by day's end. He was relieved it didn't matter anymore.

When the meeting adjourned, István left the fire hall and walked down the icy boulevard to the County Council building. As he stood facing the building, he felt the acid from his morning coffee rise up. He pushed open the imposing doors, and with his stride resolute, approached the front desk. His stomach growled; it was almost lunchtime. He asked for his wife and swallowed hard as he waited for her to come down from the third floor.

The click of her shoes preceded her petite form. She wore her chestnut brown skirt and an olive pullover that accentuated the fullness of her nursing breasts. She was dainty and nimble as she approached him, so pretty.

"You'll need your coat," he said.

"We'll only be a minute," she said politely to the receptionist.

They walked outside into the crisp sunlight where trees were brittle from the cold and frost glittered on the ground. Their breath infused the air between them with apprehension. Her body began to shake. Her fingers went white, like chalk. She tucked them under her armpits. He wanted to reach out and hold her, but it would have felt too final. They couldn't let on that they were saying good-bye.

"You're freezing." He handed her the envelope that he'd forgotten to give her this morning, after their fight.

"I'm worse than that." She tucked the money into her ivory clutch purse. "Thank you."

"It's nothing." He looked down at his boots.

"I hope it works." She looked around, nowhere in particular. The wind picked up and blew her coiffed hair.

"Go inside." Even as he said the words, he knew he didn't mean them. He wanted to collapse onto her and sob. He wanted her to reassure him it was just a nightmare he'd wake from. That he didn't have to leave the only woman who had ever loved him.

Their lips turned bluish and their heads turned in opposite directions. As they stood, a clutch of crows came to roost in the large bare sycamore above their heads. The sound was astounding, a concert of mockery above their heads, teasing them as they gathered close. The birds grew louder.

"Ugly birds. What a horrible sound." Teréza spoke with such disdain István was surprised. He thought he'd already seen her most unseemly sides.

"They're socializing their young," he explained.

"Is that right?" She gently challenged, then dropped her tone lower. "I love you. Go already."

He didn't move.

Her body shaking, Teréza said, "Remember, the border is still open. You have only bullets to dodge. No wire to climb, no mines to avoid. All you have to do is run. Fast."

István swallowed the lump forming in his throat. "Thank you. That's what I needed to hear."

Teréza looked into his eyes. "Be careful." Without embracing him, she turned and hurried back to work. Her knees nearly buckled as she reached the door of the County Council.

"I love you too!" he called to her as she yanked open the door and the wind danced her skirt about her shapely calves.

An hour after Teréza left him under the sycamore, István was travelling toward the Austrian border. Sándor laid out the ground rules before they got in the truck.

"I'm in charge now. I'll do the talking and deliver the paperwork. You're only here to inspect government vehicles in case they're pressed into service. Remember your place."

István had counted on the fact that none of the new recruits had sufficient mechanical experience to do the inspections. Sándor would be forced to bring him along on this assignment. István had recommended Laci to chaffeur, knowing that Sándor liked to angle smokes from the junior who wouldn't protest.

The click of her heels on the stone stairs to the third floor struck Teréza's eardrums until each step irritated. The tension of a tightly held secret pressed on Teréza's sternum like an attacker pushing her to the ground. Unable to meet the inquisitive stares of her colleagues she sat down. Her hands were ice-cold and stiff, poised over the keys of her typewriter. She hit a key. Pain shot up to her temples. She started typing gibberish to look busy while her mind and body split into a thousand sharp fragments, like shrapnel.

She had no idea how long it would be until she heard news of her husband, and that made the minutes since their farewell agonizing. Teréza knew it was pure luck that the wire and the landmines had not yet been reinstalled, that István only had to outrun bullets. She caught herself thinking, in what terrible world did that constitute luck?

Before her stretched an indeterminable waiting, unless of course, she was branded an accomplice to a defector. Her legs jittered violently under her desk. She clenched her thighs tightly. Pain flared. Documents strewn around the surface of her desk blurred through unshed tears. She felt transparent as her mind spun with possibilities of the worst kind: István's body pierced with bullets, his stunned eyes left open to the sky. What if Kádár's border guards caught him alive? How long would they jail him? How long would they beat him? What if they deported him? What if they came for her? What would happen to her son?

She shook herself loose from her nightmarish daydreams and began to type. She typed the same sentence three times before noticing the error. She tore the paper from the carriage, crumpled it and tossed it in the garbage. Her stomach heaved and her mouth flooded with saliva. She covered her lips, hurried to the bathroom and threw up.

Faint and trembling, Teréza returned from the bathroom and caught her stockings on a nail sticking out of her chair. "Damn it," she swore, fingering a long thin run up the back of her leg. A few heads turned. She wouldn't look at her colleagues, not even the ones she trusted.

She checked her drawer for her purse. To her horror the drawer was empty. The money! Where was the money? She felt her nerves fraying at the edges and grew frantic. One month of her husband's salary gone. She didn't see her purse anywhere. Not beside her chair, not under her desk. Did she leave it in the bathroom? She didn't remember taking it with her. She stood and hurried back, aware of the eyes watching her odd behaviour. Normally she never left her desk: she worked from the minute she sat down to the minute she took lunch. She'd been away from it three times already this morning. Even her trusted colleagues looked at her askance.

The ivory clutch was on the counter next to the sink. She reached inside and felt the envelope, but the money hardly mattered now. How would she explain a missing husband? She was complicit, even if it wasn't her idea. All her actions felt illicit, more than they had since the Communists took over. Even reclaiming her purse in a washroom felt criminal.

Her fingers grasped another object: smooth and round with a little textured cap. She'd forgotten to give István András' lucky acorn. She laughed miserably at the memory; what had ever been lucky about it? There was no luck in

Hungary. Never had been.

She looked at her pale, gloomy face in the mirror and regretted every hurtful word she'd ever spoken to her husband.

The heater was broken in the government vehicle. István could see his own breath; he detested being cold. When he sensed they were getting close he said from the back seat, "Let me drive a little." He caught Laci's eyes in the rearview mirror.

Hesitantly, Laci slowed the jeep, brought it to a stop, then climbed out and walked around to the passenger side while István crawled over the seats and settled in front of the wheel.

From the backseat, Sándor complained with undisguised disgust at the liberties István took. "What is this? A jungle?" he said to Laci. "Some of us, it seems, haven't yet evolved from the ape. Star Man one week, Ape Man the next. Give me a cigarette."

István glanced at Laci. He looked tractable. István repositioned the rearview mirror, adjusted his cap just above eye level and started driving. Laci wouldn't look at him. István knew he suspected what was coming.

Soon the air inside the cab grew stuffy with smoke. István wanted to shove the burning cigarette up Sándor's nose, instead he cranked open his window.

"That wife of yours, Teréza," Sándor said, "Pretty little thing. Does she really think that God can deliver her from the evils of this world?"

István tightened his fingers around the wheel. Since the failed uprising, Teréza had resumed her clandestine worship, following other women on nightly excursions to cathedrals, their heads covered with scarves.

"It's not your business what my wife does." István took the curve abruptly. Laci hit his head against the window and Sándor lost his cigarette.

"Jesus Christ!" Sándor cursed, his head down, searching the floor and under his coat. "Who the fuck taught you to drive? Aren't you supposed to be a mechanic?"

István's opportunity was closing in.

After Sándor had recovered his cigarette he resumed his declamation. "In this world of comradeship, everything is everyone's business, or have you forgotten? Maybe you are so self-interested, so Western-minded that you care not for the affairs of your fellow countrymen? Has Radio Free Europe infected your mind? Have you forgotten what it takes to get ahead in this system?"

"From what I know," said István, "in a system of equals there's no ladder to climb, only basements to purge."

"Ah, you've learned well. Let me tell you a joke."

"In Hungary it's always a good time for a joke!" Laci said, relieved.

"A party agitator talks about the future of Communism. In Communism, he says, everyone will have an airplane. 'And why does everyone need an airplane?' asks his comrade. 'Well,' says the party agitator, 'because if you hear that in Vladivostok stores you can get potatoes, you can fly your own plane to get in the lineup.'" Sándor grinned in the back.

István saw the tree ahead that marked the path.

Laci laughed and slapped his knee. István faked a sudden swerve and straightened out the vehicle. Sándor cursed as he bumped his head against the window.

"There's something wrong with the jeep," István said, as

casually as he could. He drove a few metres more, slowed down and parked on the shoulder. "I need to check under the hood."

"You can't even keep these vehicles in half decent shape. What kind of a mechanic are you?" asked Sándor.

Laci sat poker straight and offered Sándor another smoke. He accepted.

István stepped out of the driver's seat and raised the hood. His body surged with adrenaline. Breathing heavily onto the hot engine, the smell of radiator fluid soothed him. Half amused, he saw the jeep did in fact need some repairs. Not now, he thought, don't get caught up, you have no time. He loosened both spark plugs, just enough.

"What the hell is our dear comrade doing?" Sándor yelled from inside the jeep.

István's legs weakened. He needed to piss. He looked to the left. He looked to the right.

Just run.

"Go see what he's doing!" Sándor ordered Laci out of the vehicle.

Laci opened the passenger door and made his way around the hood to the grille where István hesitated. Paralyzed, he looked Laci square in the eyes and nodded.

He reminded himself of Teréza's parting words: the border is still open. (At least it was in May, when he last helped patrol it, the day his son was born. He'd made a point in checking in case he'd ever need this route.) You have only bullets to dodge. No wire to climb, no mines to avoid. All you need to do is run fast.

Just run, Pista's voice urged.

"Farewell," István said and took off like a shot. He darted between trees while Laci bowed his head and looked at the ground.

Run! "You're back," István yelled as he ran, rejoicing in the sweet sound of his friend's voice.

Last time. Just to make sure you don't do something foolish like get yourself shot.

"God I've missed you, Pista," he panted. His legs pumped underneath him, propelled him like they knew where to carry him. But the snow was deep, and he stumbled. He stumbled again. After a long smooth stretch he stumbled again, this time slamming into the frozen earth, face first, as if a giant hand had pushed him down. The crack of gunfire whistled over his head and through the trees. He winced and swallowed snow.

He tried to rise but the pressure on his back pinned him down.

Wait.

Instinct took over; his eyes wide open to the horizontal world. Lying on the ground he waited and counted. Another bullet followed.

The pressure on his back was gone.

Sándor could never catch you in a race, but he's a great shot.

István cursed mightily, then scrambled to his feet and ran full tilt through the trees. *Left.*

Bullets marked his path and punctuated the spaces he had fled only moments before.

Right.

His heart pounded in his throat and his torso heaved from the weight of his overcoat. His sweat chilled quickly under the heavy wet wool.

Straight.

He ran through a white field and heard someone calling

his name, yet there was no one around. No sound but the suck of his boots punching holes through the snow. And gunshots.

And Pista's instructions: *Faster.*

Frigid air burned his throat, the cold cut his lungs and his vision blurred. Bullets sprayed the snow behind him.

István bolted between birch trees, zigzagging, trying to throw them off. But he didn't know exactly who he was throwing off. Sándor? Hungarian border guards? There was no path, no direction, just dead white branches, barbed wire and thirty-foot watchtowers.

"Damn it, there weren't any guard towers when I was here in May!"

Well there are now. Keep running.

Snarls echoed across the field. Black dogs. He couldn't go on.

You have to. You have a family. Think of their future.

He saw the open border. Wooden guard towers, armed patrols and prowling dogs. His body flailed and pitched forward like a man at the end of a marathon. Bile oozed up his throat. He couldn't remember when he had eaten last.

Whatever were you thinking, escaping without a good lunch?

His legs and feet burned. His veins felt like they would soon burst. His scalp sizzled.

This is why an athlete's face expresses agony as their body throws itself towards a finish line.

István laughed. He wanted to cross that finish line. To tangle himself in streamers and swallow confetti. He wanted his victory splashed across the front page.

Rifles met his blood-shot eyes. He heard a command. "*Stop! Oder wir schießen.*" Border guards surrounded him. Dogs snapped at his ankles.

I'm done for, he thought and started blubbering like a child. He got control of himself and raised his arms. He heard words but couldn't make out their meaning. He saw only green-grey wool. Hungarian green. Soon enough they'd grab his wrists and lock them in handcuffs. Next, they'd throw him to the ground and kick him in the kidneys. Then they'd haul him to his feet, drag him along to a dark cell and give him the beating of his life. Game over.

The barrel end of a rifle approached and grew larger." *Wie heißt du?*" a voice bellowed.

In a moment of lucidity his mind corrected the confusion. The guards were yelling in German; they wore Austrian green uniforms. His confusion felt like a partial stroke. He floated in the current of an adrenaline overdose.

"*Deustshe?*" he asked aloud.

"*Ja Deustshe!*" one of the men replied. The border guards, four of them, patted him down.

He'd crossed the border. He'd made it.

"Pista!" he yelled.

No. You're István.

His name came as an eruption. "István. Kiss István," an uncontrollable expression burst from his mouth. "Kiss! István!"

Like a water-filled balloon pricked with a pin, his throat burst open and his eyes flooded with emotion. His teeth chattered uncontrollably. He looked to the sky. Nothing could have been more beautiful than the sun, blinding him with relief and ecstasy. He cradled this sensation in his heart, like water in the palm of his hand.

"My name is István."

SEPARATION

1957

THAT'S THE LADY'S PROBLEM

1957. January 31 – March 31

"What was your job in Hungary?" asked the large stocky officer, in German. He had a thick phlegmy cough. The interpreter, a bespectacled man in his forties, translated quickly without missing a word.

"Chief mechanic in the fire department." Dressed in his uniform, István saw himself as an unwelcome refugee. He removed his cap, and placed it on the floor beneath his chair, the Soviet star facing away from the authorities.

"I thought you were a fireman." The interpreter stifled a yawn.

"I was an officer in the fire department. I repaired and maintained all the vehicles," István replied, straining to hear himself over the other man's coughing. He knew he was being tested on the accuracy and authenticity of his story.

At Traiskirchen Refugee Camp, two stern officers questioned István twice daily for a week. Based in the centre of the small town of the same name, the former Imperial Artillery Cadet School was imprinted with the presence of the Soviet troops that had occupied the utilitarian building in Allied-

41

occupied Austria up until just a year ago. István could make out Russian names carved into the walls. The Soviets still felt too close. Each day brought different officers but the same sequence of questions. After two days István knew them by heart. Today the sequence was different. After years of living under Communist rule, this interrogation was child's play. He was always one step ahead.

The bored one continued perfunctorily, while the other one coughed, the sound like a rough file scraping over wood. "What I want to know is, what did you do to get your name on the list? Don't make me ask again." The meek interpreter translated for István, fighting his way in between the wheezes and inquiries, nervous sweat beading at his hairline. He looked like a prudish professor.

István looked at him. Why did the interpreter have to use that tone?

For the duration of a week, István was restricted from leaving the Isolation Unit, except for meals. The silence inside him grew starker. He discovered he had a life full of secrets that began to torment him once he had only walls to stare at. By now his stepfather Feri would have heard that István was gone, and that he left without saying goodbye. He pictured Feri in his shoe repair shop, his head drooping like a wilted flower, forehead pressed against his thick hands stacked one on top of the other on the worktable, his eyes stinging from tears. A strong smell of glue in the air. Surrounded by worn shoes, Feri asked, "Why didn't István come to me first? I could have helped him." He imagined Feri shoving aside the next pair waiting for a sole, too heartbroken to work.

Guilt plagued István when he should have been thinking about his wife and child.

In the cavernous cafeteria, the afternoon sun poured in through the Georgian windows, casting long golden boxes on the floor. Women wearing traditional headscarves distributed food to their families. The lineups for meals were lengthy, but the refugees behaved patiently; István saw thankfulness in people's eyes.

He'd been instructed not to talk to anyone. A more bellicose officer had relayed the instructions with a kind of impudence that triggered in István a need to flout the rules, at least in fantasy. He resisted the urge to have in his pocket a note he could pull out at any time with a message saying I am mute.

I dare you. That might be fun.

Standing in the doorway, István recognized the smell immediately. Grenadir. Flat egg noodles with potatoes and paprika. Foolproof, filling food.

When as a child, István refused to eat the pale pink dish, Feri hauled his small adopted boy onto his lap, stabbed a fork into the noodles, twirled them around and held up a mouthful as a prize.

"During Europe's Napoleonic Wars, field kitchen cooks devised *Grenadir* to feed Austrian foot soldiers, *Grenadiers*," Feri recounted.

It had never occurred to little István that people made up dishes. He'd always thought that meals were like national holidays. They just existed. He looked at Feri, then back at the noodles.

"Because food got scarce between deliveries soldiers carried small quantities of pasta, herbs and potatoes in their backpacks. The cooks made Grenadir out of whatever ingredients they had. So, boys who eat Grenadir are soldiers."

Feri's tactic worked. István grabbed the forkful, ate it, then dug into the rest of his meal. The memory formed a lump in István's throat starchier than the noodles themselves.

Forbidden to talk, István grew aware of the tremendous gap in his being, an emptiness he'd experienced around his mother when she coddled his brother Tamás. The feeling came upon him when he was prohibited from engaging with the rangy single men who huddled together at tables in the far end of the room. His forced silence meant no laughing, whistling, humming or commenting. He felt defenseless. Anyone could comment on him, judge him or speculate about him, out loud, and he couldn't defend himself, correct their story or interject with his own version. The thought upset him, and he wondered how much of his own life he had made up. What stories he told himself to keep going. Like the time Tamás, growing into his blonde manhood, punched István in the gut as he snuck a morsel of dried bacon from the pantry one winter evening. The kitchen was lit by the flame of a single candle when István coughed up a stream of spice and bile. His mother had stood by, leaning on the doorframe, her arms and ankles crossed, a prideful smile upon her face. She congratulated Tamás for his aim in the dark.

As István turned inward he began to attune to something else. His heart. He heard it beating. He began to cherish small gestures, a smile from a child, a gentle nudge from a woman to move ahead a little in line. In the vacuum of his enforced silence, tiny expressions loomed large.

A woman handed him a plateful of noodles, and he found somewhere to sit at the end of long wooden table, thinking of Feri as he ate. How Feri had what he called a "trick ear" that would on occasion bleed, like someone's nose might. Or how Feri got intensely irritated by the sound of folding paper. The only sound that could soothe his eccentric ears was the whirring of the shoe-stitching machine. These reflections made István smile, just a little.

From around crowded tables, István picked out juicy bits from the stories he overheard. Some of tragic journeys, others updates on families or politics. He listened to the beauty of his language, rare and isolated with uncertain origins. Juxtaposed with the guttural strains of German, Hungarian sounded like singing. "*Testvér*," one young boy said to another. Sibling, made of two words, body and blood. Bodyblood.

Another woman nearby shared a harrowing account of a newborn being passed from hand to hand above the frigid waters of a marsh. When someone lost their footing, the baby was dropped. It took too long to find her in the dark and she drowned. Consumed with grief, the mother held herself under water, pushing away help, refusing to let anyone save her. The story had left István feeling disturbed for days.

It had never occurred to him that he would see so many children who had escaped on their own. He thought he recognized some of their faces, those who had been involved in the street fighting in Budapest. István listened to stories of entire classrooms of children who up and left with their teachers, including children brought up in state orphanages, young industrial apprentices, poor peasant children and a class of students training to be Forestry Technicians from Sopron. Rumour had it they were on their way to Canada, along with their professors. István suspected that the interrogation translator was one of those professors. Students in the mess hall frequently surrounded him.

While others encouraged and guided entire groups to freedom, he had thought only of himself. István's decision to escape alone ate like acid at his guts.

As he chewed his plate of noodles – how unsatisfying it was to eat the salty dish without pickles – twenty or so refugees gathered around a scruffy fifteen-year-old orphan seated in front of him.

"I crossed with an old woman. We waded through the marsh together. She wore a fur coat and with only a satin slip underneath. But still she had brought with her an entire smoked duck wrapped in paper and string."

The detail elicited an uneasy round of laughter.

"The old lady buried the duck under the snow when she took rest stops on her walk across Hungary. She planned to bribe border guards with it to let her cross into Austria. She wouldn't listen when I told her the duck wouldn't make a difference. It had been a major feat for her to keep it preserved along the way because she figured she had only seven days until it spoiled. On the seventh day, she made it to the border carrying nothing but the duck."

István and the refugees stared blankly while the teenager continued.

"When we crossed the border, she clutched the duck to her chest. The guards didn't want it and pushed us through. Finally safe across the border, the old lady swore a blue streak condemning the 'savage destruction of Budapest' by the 'Russian destroyers.' She was furious that first night in the camp. I mean who could argue with her? We had little other than guns and Molotov cocktails to ignite the uprising."

István heard pride in his voice. He was a child fighter, and István felt a strange sense of envy.

"The old lady yelled from her bed, 'How many pigs had they tried to take from me over the years?! The swine! At least ten! But they never found my duck!'" The teenager bent himself over like an old woman and waved his fist in mock rage.

"When we arrived here, an Austrian soldier asked to look at the contents of her package. She wouldn't let go of the duck. She played tug of war. Like this!" He demonstrated with grandiose theatricality. "So they moved her into a solitary room in the Isolation Unit. The next morning, she was found dead with the duck on her chest!"

István, including all the boys and men around the table stared dumfounded. No one knew what to say. Was this true? Was Duck Woman made up? István swore he would memorize it for Teréza and write it in a letter once he was allowed to send one.

Every day István replied to his interrogators' questions with immaculate consistency. He kept his story as straight as a line of marching soldiers. After a week, the officials, convinced that he was who he said he was, proclaimed István an authentic refugee. This man is not a spy, they wrote in his file.

The officer who'd spent the week yawning livened up. "*Glückwunsch!*" He was impressed that István had managed to escape alive and told him that by early January, few refugees, if any, were making it across the border, and that's why they interrogated István with extra diligence. By the time István fled, almost the entire western border was riddled with layers of defense: trip flares followed by deadly explosive mines culminating in a barbed wire fence with a "V" shaped wire on top. The Hungarian border guards, who during the previous months had waved on refugees by the thousands, had been imprisoned and replaced with the vigilant eyes of new guards, anxious to shoot.

★

István was given a small narrow room in the dormitory, another change of clothing, toiletries, pocket money, cigarettes, a small mailbox outside his door, and a roommate – the boy from the cafeteria.

"Papa," said the rambunctious teen.

"I'm not your father," said István as he sat down on his cot. The boy in front of him looked like an aggressive weed: his black hair stuck out wildly in all directions, and his lanky frame made him look leggy and overgrown.

"Barna." The teen extended his wide, thick hand.

"István." They shook. An excellent handshake, he thought. "Barnabas, son of exhortation."

"My nickname. I earned it during the fighting. In my gang, I led the charge with the Molotov cocktails. I blew up two Russian tanks singlehandedly and together with my buddies took out three more."

István laid down, tested his bed. The white wrought iron bunk bed sagged like the one in Feri's house. The one his littlest brother Lali liked to bounce on. The brother who had died in his arms.

"You can have mine," said Barna trying out his own mattress. "It's firmer and you'll need it. You're an old man."

"I'm only thirty-two."

"In Hungary, that means you're an old man. I'm fifteen. And I've already seen everything."

They smiled at each other.

"You look like you smoke." István handed Barna the pack of cigarettes.

Barna grabbed them. "Papa! You're the best!"

★

"Will there be KGB agents in a Communist utopia?" Barna asked, sitting on the edge of his bed the next day. His elbows rested on his knees. He rocked a little. It was late afternoon.

Ten days a refugee, István lay on his bed, his forearm draped over his forehead, staring at the yellowing ceiling. "I don't know," he answered, watching the slanting snow rush down their window.

"There won't be." Barna grinned wide. "By then, people's intelligence will have reached such high levels, that each person will be arresting themselves."

István smiled.

"How do youth play dangerous games in the rest of the world?"

"Fuck if I know." István sat up on the edge of his bed.

"In the USA three young men get into three race cars, and organize huge races, all the while knowing that the brakes in one of the cars doesn't work. In France, three young men spend passionate nights, each with a woman all the while knowing that one of them has a sexually transmittable disease, but they don't know which. In the Soviet Union, three young men tell political jokes all the while knowing that one of them is a canary." Barna paused dramatically. "Those sick fucks in France!" he snorted.

In spite of himself, István laughed. Then he leaned in towards Barna. "A very old mummy is discovered. No one can determine its age. They send it to America. It is there for a week, but no one can determine its age. America sends it back. They send it to England. No one there can come up with anything either and they send it back. Finally, the mummy is sent to the Soviet Union. After a week the Soviets declare that the mummy is 238,000,000 years, 6 months and 5 days old. The world is in awe. How did they figure it out?! The Soviet Union replies, 'It confessed.'"

Barna wiped his eyes. "That's funny. But not as funny as mine." He rubbed his hands together. "I want to make lots of money in the west. I'm going to England," Barna announced in English with an implausibly British accent. "Where you headed?"

István stared at the bare stained walls of their room. It dawned on István that in his thirty-some years he'd never travelled outside of Hungary. He'd never wanted to leave. How could he possibly know where he wanted to go?

"To safety. To freedom. To where I have purpose. Is there such place on a map?"

"Take me with you. I'll be your son." Barna grabbed his arm.

István shook him loose; the boy was starting to look a little crazy. "I can't just take you with me. You're not my son." István couldn't believe he was having this conversation.

"If you adopt me you can."

"That's ridiculous. I don't even know you."

"Now you do."

István wondered how many Russians this boy had killed. "I have a son of my own."

Barna exaggerated a sad face. "I can keep you company. I can mend your socks."

"I told you. I already have a son."

"Can he mend socks?"

"He's an infant. Besides, it's my wife who mends my socks."

"I don't see them anywhere." Barna looked under the bed, under the chair, under his blanket.

"You're a goddam monkey, aren't you?"

Barna batted his eyelashes and played coy.

István felt himself warming towards this clown. He reminded him of his former self, the self he was when he horsed around with Pista.

"What's wrong, old man? You're not having a heart attack, are you? You can't leave me now." Barna playfully positioned his ear near István's chest. "It's still beating!"

Six days after István's arrival, a woman from Szombathely had visited the camp. She'd come to retrieve her twelve-year-old son who escaped a week before István. The boy had befriended Barna, which allowed István to come in contact with this woman. He'd pressed a note in the woman's hand and whispered in her ear. "I beg of you, mail this to my wife so she can know my address." The woman nodded and left with her son.

On February 13th, two weeks after his escape, István received a reply from Teréza.

The small, pale green, onion-thin envelope rescued him from unhappiness. He tore open the envelope almost thoughtlessly, then shut the door of his room. He sat on the edge of his bed and waited before removing the letter. If he waited long enough he could prolong his relief and break up the monotony. When his heart raced sufficiently he unfolded the delicate thin paper and saw a short, typed sentence in black ink.

Dearest István,   *1957. II. 8*

I write this from work. We are eating and

*we are safe. More soon. Please let me know
you got this.*

> *With kisses and love, Teréza*

He held the letter to his chest for a spell, then folded it, returned it to the onion thin envelope, placed it in his inside jacket pocket, and dabbed a few tears from his eyes. He'd wanted to read pages and pages of her longings for him. A love letter. The paper in his pocket made him sad and panicky. Two weeks of ennui had found no resolution. Straightening himself out, he decided to leave his room, look for something with which to occupy himself.

The natural thing was to write back. How safe would that be for Teréza? What could he write exactly, when the Hungarian authorities wanted to know what was happening in the camps? Later that evening he could think of only one thing.

Dearest Teréza,　　　　　*1957. február. 13*

> *My heart aches without you. I'm also eat-
> ing. But there are no pickles. I think of our
> son.*

> *With kisses and love, István*

The Monday after István fled, Teréza walked down to the cafeteria to eat a large bowl of potato stew. She made a pact with herself to present her best face each day as not to arouse the suspicions of the authorities. She vowed to look and perform impeccably. The clothing her Uncle János had given her she kept immaculate. She'd not allow herself to be reduced to dressing like the rude, cantankerous, and sullen women with manly haircuts and swollen ankles that Socialism bred.

Since István fled she never once slept through the night and took to standing at the window, pressing her face to the glass, checking for informants in the darkness.

Had she better known the nature of this state – disconnect and shock – she could have accepted why her breast milk suddenly dried up, leaving Zolti grasping with tiny fingernails for her flesh, and peevishly pushing his bottle of formula away.

It was the sheer force of her baby, the anguished pain of his glottal cry that roused her from her crumpled state and pulled her to her feet to embrace him, soothe him and coo to him. His existence kept her up till midnight, picking out a series of decent outfits for the workweek that she'd iron meticulously.

At the end of the workday she hurried to the market but found only shrunken apples. She would cook them into a sauce, she decided; her son had been without a bowel movement for days and his little belly was sticking out. The dour-faced fruit seller picked the apples for Teréza, several bad ones with bruises. Teréza pointed to the slightly nicer ones on display in the front.

"Couldn't you kindly give me–"

"All apples are equal," interrupted the seller.

Teréza tucked her hands into her pockets and retrieved some coins.

She took the bag of apples and rushed to the butcher who had only chicken heads left. Even if he had a thigh or a neck she could only afford the head, she reminded herself, and felt her spirit sag.

Without István's salary, and with the consistent food

shortages, it was her childhood all over again; daring not waste the black spots on the potatoes or the bruises on the apples, and a persistent, gnawing hunger. The benefit to scarcity, of course, was a slender figure.

Like her sisters and girlfriends, Teréza preferred to eat less in order to look good, not that they had much to choose from as everyone looked the same. Department stores carried only five styles of everything. Five styles of shoes, five styles of skirts, five styles of blouses. Like the five-pointed star. Like the five-year plan. Dressing stylishly was its own form of resistance.

She returned to the County Council, entering quietly through a side door. She was greeted by the dulcet sounds of playing children. Dressed in regulation white cotton dresses with little slacks, the girls had red bows in their hair and the boys sported little red scarves round their necks. Zolti, like the other baby boys, resembled an overstuffed butcher's sausage tied with string. She spied him sitting in a high chair facing the wall, eye-level to a framed picture of Kádár, Hungary's new leader. Zolti was reaching forward with chubby fingers to touch the man's pockmarked face.

A youthful daycare attendant noticed Teréza standing by the door. She looked admiringly at Zolti and said approvingly, "There's hope for him, you know. He knows who his real father is."

It took every ounce of Teréza's control not to slap the woman.

Teréza's skirt hung loose around her waist as she marched home, carrying groceries in one hand and Zolti in the other. She walked at a furious clip. "His real father!" she said into the wind that penetrated her coat and made her skin shiver over her bones.

Ahead, the bus pulled over and stopped for passengers. She didn't run, deciding it would be cheaper for her to re-heel her pumps instead of taking the bus. Besides, the baby needed fresh air after breathing in Socialist indoctrination all day. The bus's doors squeezed shut. The vehicle plodded ahead and belched a puff of exhaust in Teréza's direction, putting a large period at the end of her thought.

She felt placid and pacified as she walked, thinking about how István had made do with used parts to repair his fire trucks. "The newer used parts outperform other older used parts," he told her once, "and start a chain reaction throughout the entire vehicle."

"So new parts are even worse?" she'd asked him.

"That's the wrong question. What we need is a whole new system. All new parts." This thought brought a smile to her lips, and she longed to see and feel him again.

From under the clear plastic bag the chicken's baleful eye monitored her baby all the way home. Chickens had become Communists too, she thought, climbing the steps to the house and unlocking the door. She slammed the bagged head on the kitchen counter, then twice more for good measure. She tossed it in water with paprika and salt, added an onion and brought it to a boil. The weak broth would feed Zolti while she waited till the next day to eat again. Her stomach turned over and over, waiting for a decent meal.

She forgot to check the mail, which she did obsessively; the chicken eye had thrown her off. Back outside, her hunger flipped to nervousness as she lifted a foreign envelope from the mailbox marked with a handwritten return address from Szombathely she didn't recognize. Her fingers tore open its contents.

*I am safe. There is a hole in my heart. Not
from a bullet. I love you.*

Teréza let go the tension she'd been holding for days.
Eight days. István's first sign of life granted Teréza a few
hours of euphoria that evening. They could correspond now!
Over and over she repeated his poetic line "a hole in my
heart." She felt into his hole. Had it not been for his admission
of pain she would not have felt these great surges of adoration
for him. His agony made their love real to her. It was proof of
attachment. She wrote back.

Late into the night, while Zolti slept soundly with a full belly,
Teréza counted and re-counted her forints at the kitchen
table. When she grew weary and her eyelids grew heavy from
the heat from the hearth, she stumbled to the cold of the
bedroom where she tried to sleep, blanketed by several fluffy
layers. Most nights she wondered if she had slept at all,
hovering somewhere between worry, nightmares and
exhaustion. Her son's breathing seemed almost
imperceptible as he slept cocooned in his crib. It seemed as
though he'd stopped growing in the past month. Was it only
her imagination? Had he used up his energy just coming into
the world?

Before daybreak, she awoke to someone pounding at the
door. She threw off the covers, and ran to Zolti who had
started to whimper. She covered herself and her baby with her
housecoat and found two police officers standing at her door.
She opened it.

"Good morning," she said, the cold air rushing in under

her nightgown.

"Good morning," said the taller of the two.

"What seems to be the problem?" she asked.

"Your husband's defection." The tall man thrust an envelope towards her. "He is to show up for trial on February 10th, at eight-thirty in the morning at the City Courts."

"Sign here that you have received the summons," said a scrappy looking man with nostrils so wide they almost met his his cheekbones.

She signed the document, her handwriting barely discernable. "But he's not here, so how should I get it to him?"

"That's the lady's problem."

"Good day."

They stomped off into the inclement morning.

"What happens if he doesn't appear?" she called after them.

They didn't answer.

She'd refuse to attend his sham trial, she resolved. Slamming the door closed she plunked herself down in a chair and bounced Zolti in her lap.

Zolti hiccupped then vomited on Teréza's housecoat. It startled him and made him cry. As she cleaned him up she touched his forehead. He was burning up. She couldn't afford to miss a day of work, but neither could she bear the thought of leaving her son at the nursery with Kádár papa.

After she bathed and dressed for work, she carried him upstairs to the neighbour's.

The solid woman named Emi opened the door, wearing an apron.

"My husband's gone," Teréza said, starting to cry. The exhaustion and hunger had weakened her. She felt a little unhinged.

"We heard on the radio," said Emi with a soft expression.

She lovingly took Zolti in her arms. "Hello, my little fellow."

"Then everyone's heard," Teréza said sadly.

István could never come back to Hungary.

She fretted all day and barely ate. Wrapped in a rough brown paper napkin were two salty pastries she'd hidden in her desk. Swallowing them, they were dried out and she nearly choked. As Teréza typed, her colleague with the fluffy white dandelion hair placed her large hand on Teréza's stiff shoulder and murmured in her ear. "Please let us know if there is any way we can help."

"God helped me already," Teréza said, assuring her of her gratitude. "They could have fired me by now, left me dependent on my parents. They make a pittance farming their puny plot. So far I've been spared. Twelve days have passed, and no one's come for me. What possible harm can I do? A single mother with a nine-month-old?"

"Your child is still useful to the Communists," her colleague said with irony.

At day's end, Teréza ran all the way home, praying Zolti hadn't died. When she reached the neighbour's she found Emi's daughter holding Zolti on her lap. The girl had a perfectly round face, short-cropped brown hair and coral lips. She wore ecru ankle socks, even in winter, and a boat neck, burgundy wool dress that zipped up the back and accentuated her budding breasts. Her baby fat gave her an awkward part-child-part-teenager appearance. She covered Zolti's face with kisses, making him squeal with delight, and handed him over.

"He's a good, good boy," the girl said as she skipped downstairs. She was on her way to the weekly meeting of the

Young Pioneers. The girl gave Teréza a niggling feeling, though she was adept with the baby. Children raised with a Communist education were different, Teréza decided. Cannier than she cared for.

Emi emerged from the kitchen wiping her hands on her apron. "Teréza, thank goodness you're back. Zolti's temperature shot up, so I drenched his body in cold wet rags. He wailed so hard he made himself sick and threw up. Seems much better now." Her soft blue eyes reassured Teréza who felt, for the first time in weeks, that she had someone to trust. Teréza made arrangements. From now on she'd pay Emi one hundred *forint* a month to care for her son so he'd never again reach for Kádár.

That Sunday evening after she'd put Zolti down, she thought of István. In fact she always thought of István. A moment didn't go by that she didn't wonder what he was doing. He meant more to her now that he was gone. And in her comparison, his freedom was surely exhilarating compared to her prison.

At one time István and Teréza marked life before and after Stalin. For Teréza, life was now before and after István. On the last Sunday in March, for their first wedding anniversary apart, Teréza crafted a card. Prudently, she cut a rectangle from the cardboard packaging that came with her new stockings, making sure to leave leftovers for future cards. At work she'd lifted the heavy metal scissors from the top drawer of her desk and slipped them in her purse when no one was looking. It was time to take back what the state had stolen from her.

The cutting took some time. She snipped slowly, precisely, careful not to slip off the pencil line. She could smell the paper pulp as she cut. Her wedding photo sat in front of her on the table. István looked expressionless. She stopped cutting for a moment as the photo disclosed something it hadn't before. She realized just then that he never smiled for photos. Not even their wedding day prompted hope for István. She wished he'd have smiled just that once. She finished cutting out the shape of the card and erased her fine pencil lines. From the pages of *Petőfi Love Poems*, the book he'd left on her pillow, she removed a pressed flower. She tied the dried stems of the dwarfed bouquet with a white cotton ribbon edged with silver thread and positioned the flower on the cardboard. The glue held. In the tiny right margin of the card she wrote in cursive:

With love we think of you on our anniversary. Szombathely. 1957.III.17 Zolti sends kisses. Teréza.

She touched her lips to the card and sealed her creation in see-through plastic wrap, taped its edges to the cardboard and fashioned strips of paper into a foldout stand.

István spent the next several weeks in the refugee camp learning German and discovering his facility for languages. Speaking Russian had always been such a hateful chore that he hadn't tried to be any more than passable, but now the officers praised him for his capable Austrian dialect and put him to work as part-time camp translator.

He allayed the worries of refugees who couldn't understand why and where they were being transported next. Couples, families with children, and minors without parents or guardians took priority over single men like him. Strangely, Barna had fallen through the cracks. There was no information about where Barna would be transported. Secretly, István didn't mind. He'd grown accustomed to the wild boy. He kept István up at night with stories of the revolution on the front lines.

"…and then, when I got here at the end of November, a repatriation commission consisting of secret police showed up one day. The assholes barely walked through the gate when a bunch of us stoned the motherfuckers. I got one of the jerks in the eye." Barna demonstrated his shot. "It was fantastic!"

"Let me guess," István teased. "You'd had practice with Molotov cocktails."

"Very funny."

"You remind me of a film I once saw with my wife. About a Russian athlete throwing a javelin."

Barna looked at him blankly. "May I continue?"

"Be my guest."

"We got the Austrian soldiers all worked up, you should have seen them, running around like scared chickens." He flapped his arms and squawked like a bird. "You don't screw with a Hungarian. What other country has risen up against the Soviets?"

"Don't you dare get wrapped up in any political movements," István advised him. "We're not allowed to do that here. The Austrian Ministry of the Interior issued a statement saying they won't tolerate any activities by foreigners that disturbs their peaceful relations with any other states. You'll lay low if you know what's good for you."

Barna looked away.

"I know you're up to something. You've been spending time with those young activists in the camp. Listen to me," István leaned in close and placed a fatherly hand on his shoulder. "The Revolution is over. American intelligence organizations are trying to hire freedom fighters to go back to Hungary and serve as agents. The ÁVO are trying to recruit the very same youth to stay informed about developments within Austria. The scum are among us, boy. Liberate us by showing everyone that Hungarians won't be puppets for anyone."

As he counselled Barna, his own inconsistencies surfaced. Hadn't he always been up to something himself? But not enough to satisfy Pista or his own conscience, however. His feelings of remorse wouldn't let him look Barna in the eye.

Barna plopped himself down on his cot. "Give me something to do," said Barna, picking dirt from under his nails.

István taught Barna about cars.

István began to repair and maintain vehicles for the Austrian border control. After he'd put a vehicle up on a hoist he proudly exclaimed, "See that! That brake cable is about to snap!" When he wasn't blowing cigarette smoke into the tail end of a muffler, Barna hovered over István's shoulder, learning to perform an oil change.

"There, you don't need me for this now, you know how to do it yourself," he said proudly, stepping out of the way.

Some nights the brandy flowed freely in the camp. Stuffed in hastily packed suitcases, a precious bottle would emerge, and refugees took turns sharing their last remaining stash. Passing Barna the bottle, István whispered in his ear, "Keep sane boy, not too much."

He watched over Barna who preferred the company of adults. Together they sat in the cafeteria where their evenings consisted of serious conversations, word games and storytelling. Families wrapped themselves around long wooden tables like soft, warm pretzels; the young and old spilled over each other's chairs and leaned over tables to catch snippets of information. A sheet-white teenage boy with fingers like tentacles banged out folksongs on the upright piano. He repeatedly played the one dead key giving his performance a dishevelled sound. Middle-aged ladies sang *The Song of Kossuth's Camp*, the revolutionary ballad about Hungary's 1848 struggle for independence from Austria.

"Good thing the Austrians can't understand Hungarian," István remarked to Barna.

How strange it was to see the Austrian guards smiling like that. The song's melody could rouse anyone.

Barna elbowed István and gave him an incredulous look. "Should we say something?"

"Absolutely not."

They burst out laughing.

"I have no idea why they haven't sent you to England yet," István said to Barna, while consuming yet another plateful of noodles. He quickly tired of food at the camp – the limited selection rotated every three days – and his pants, held in place by a belt he'd pulled one notch tighter, sat well below his waistline. Most days he no longer felt like finishing his meal. Flus and colds spread throughout the camp and his guts had been troubling him for a week. Barna handed István a banana, the first he'd ever seen, Communism's example of Western decadence.

"This will help your guts," he said in a doctorly tone. "Peel it. Rip the top and pull."

István liked a fruit whose peel obeyed.

"That's it," said Barna, nodding.

István liked the taste of the West.

Despite his recurring ailment, he dreamed of food. "What I wouldn't give for a morsel of well-browned pork fat with some good bread. Want this?" He shoved his plate of pink noodles over to Barna who, without answering, dug in. Even though Barna ate everything put in front of him, he too had lost weight. And at night, the teen had nightmares. He swore in his sleep and had taken to pounding his face into his pillow. Sometimes István slept through the commotion, and at other times he ran the risk of getting clobbered when he tried to rouse Barna from his nocturnal fits.

Nearly five months after the initial refugee exodus, both their cases were stalled. Each foreign government had its own processing timeline and criteria for accepting refugees. The UK, Germany and Australia had been stepping up. "Back in November, a week after my arrival," said Barna, "the Hungarian government demanded that Austria return all minors. They'd announced an amnesty for all Hungarian citizens who'd left the country illegally. If they returned to Hungary by the end of March."

"And here it is," István noted, "two days before the deadline."

Barna shovelled the remaining noodles into his mouth. He spoke while he chewed. "England isn't ready for me yet. Families, the elderly and children go first. I don't fall into any of those categories." A pink paste filled his overflowing mouth.

The sight revolted István, though he knew he had the

same habit of chewing with his mouth open. Was this what fathering would be like? Staring into the face of the most repulsive parts of oneself?

"Besides," Barna said, finally swallowing, wrestling the paste down his throat, "I wouldn't have met you, Papa."

"I told you I'm not your father."

"So you still won't adopt me?" He picked up his empty plate and began licking it clean.

As Barna washed down the last bite with milk, something familiar flashed out of the corner of István's eye. A figure standing by the door of the cafeteria. Varga.

At first István couldn't believe it. The bastard hadn't changed. He looked like he'd aged in reverse. A hefty government salary kept him well-fed, well-housed, and content. As an AVÓ man he would live nicely, making twenty times the national average. Before István's escape he learned from Pista that Varga, his childhood nemesis, had moved to Sopron. With its proximity to the Austrian border, Varga probably made a living out of brutalizing those who attempted to escape.

He stood at the door calling out a list of names, all children, all under the ages of fourteen. Some thirty names had been called when István heard Barna's name, the very last on the list.

"There must be some mistake. The boy's sixteen," István yelled on his behalf.

"The children named on this list shall be repatriated to Hungary as they have no legal guardianship and are considered minors fourteen years of age and under. I shall be back in two days to complete the transfer. We have consent from the Austrian government."

"I said there's a mistake!" István stood up to press his

point.

If Varga was surprised to see István he didn't show it. The roomful of refugees grew silent and curious.

"At sixteen he does not belong on your list," István asserted.

Varga smiled like he was posing for an election poster. "Have we met before?"

"May it be our last," István said. "How many more people's lives are you going to ruin?"

Barna looked up, conspiratorially. Those were fighting words, and he was always ready for a scrap.

"I don't see here anywhere that this boy has a guardian," said Varga pretending to re-check his notes. "Is he yours then?"

István remembered it, that self-righteous, contemptuous attitude, the way Varga assumed full power. His tentacles of cruelty crept deep beneath the surface of the earth like the roots of an invasive species ensuring that nothing else had space to thrive. It made István want to thrust himself at Varga's neck and choke the life out of him. "No he's not. But neither is he yours."

István couldn't look at Barna. István walked out of the cafeteria, remembering the chills that crawled up his spine when Varga taunted him with "Jew nose," as the Germans were invading. How could two tiny words exert such control over István, changing the course of his life?

Later, in their room, Barna grew agitated and wouldn't talk when István suggested they play cards.

"Just leave me alone," Barna yelled at István. "You know

what help I need."

"It doesn't make sense. Legally they can't send you back. How the hell did your name get on the list? Why hasn't England taken you yet?"

"I don't know. I petitioned to go there, but nothing's materialized."

"The UN High Commissioner should have dealt with your case by now. You're sixteen. Aren't you?"

"Yes."

István pressed his forefingers into his aching forehead trying to come up with a plan. He knew there would be no amnesty for kids like Barna. They'd throw him in prison or send him off to a labour camp. He came from a state orphanage – maybe they'd recruit him for the secret police.

"I'm getting the hell out of here before they come for me."

"You can't just run. The Austrians will catch up with you, and then you'll be in bigger trouble."

"To hell with everyone. I can take care of myself. Just leave me alone!"

Cigarette smoke hung in the room. István thought of all the times he'd berated Pista for smoking. Now he didn't dare say a thing. Barna looked mad and lost. His stubborn confidence was gone, and he looked like he might cry.

"You know what help I need."

István paced. "Why me? Why have you chosen me? You could have asked countless others in this camp before I ever arrived."

"Leave me!" Barna shrieked. His voice sounded like a child's, raging and helpless. István left the room and walked slowly down the hall towards the common area where every third male had his head buried in a newspaper or reading over someone's shoulder. If he adopted Barna, would his own son grow up feeling as unwanted as István had when his brother Tamás was born? There had never been enough love to go around in his household, his mother saw to that. István was the bastard son born of a Jewish landowner, and his half-brother Tamás her golden boy, Feri's boy.

A lingering sense of incompleteness marked each day and manifested as an inability – or an unwillingness – to fully love another. His selfishness was a method of survival. István never wrote to Teréza about any of this. Instead, he blamed her for it because he believed she left him no choice. He had to devote what love he had to his own son, Zolti, because he'd left the baby in the crib. He couldn't believe that even at a distance they had disagreements that happened only in his mind.

This incontestable conclusion, that adopting Barna would do more harm than good, finally brought István succor, and he decided to sit down and enjoy the night's activities best he could. He didn't have a paper and didn't want to get to close to anyone; it was beneath him to read over someone's shoulder.

Instead, he parked himself near the piano, with the women, where the sheet-white boy with tentacle fingers played *Gloomy Sunday*. István recognized the tune immediately. The famous song, composed in 1935 by Seress Rezső when István was just ten, supposedly set off a rash of suicides in Hungary. István had heard the hit song only twice before. He was puzzled. What the hell was a child doing playing such a morose song this early in the evening? Didn't anyone supervise the entertainment in this place? Still, István listened as a young, blond girl sang the song, the melody and lyrics making him infinitely sad.

With the last note, the roomful of refugees applauded.

When the applause subsided István called out a request. "*Tiszán innen, Dunán túl.*"

The boy at the piano was conferring with the blond when another little girl skipped up to link elbows with her. She wanted to sing it too.

A woman rushed into the common area, breathless, her face horror-stricken. "Your son!"

István turned to look behind him.

"You sir," said the shapely woman, imploring him. "Please come quickly, there might still be hope."

István jumped to his feet and rushed along behind her, down the long corridor. Already he knew. When he arrived at his room the male nurses were taking down Barna's body, undoing the sheet from around his neck.

"They might be able to resuscitate your son." The woman touched István's forearm as he looked on in alarm.

"He's not mine," István said weakly as the nurses carried Barna past him to a stretcher. "He could never have been mine." István broke into sobs as the woman put her arm around his shoulder. "He had courage. I d-d-don't," he stuttered.

"He's gone," said a nurse.

REVOLUTION

1956

ASSEMBLING ASSEMBLY

1956, Tuesday, October 23. Hungary

At the Fire Department, István paused at the *Szabad Nép* newspaper left on his desk by his assistant, Laci.

That damned Communist mouthpiece.

"Yes, Pista, I hear you," István said aloud. He was worried he was starting to look crazy talking aloud to himself, but Pista was a formidable force. István was sure there was a name for this affliction, when a best friend lodged himself into the crevices of the mind, commenting on every thought and observation, but he couldn't recollect it.

István scoured the newspaper's pages in search of asinine propaganda on industrial development to regurgitate at a Political Training Meeting. Today's tardiness demanded extra indemnity.

Earlier at home, Teréza had been curt with him. "Can't you hold your son for once?" She had a run in her pantyhose that needed a quick stitch. He cussed, not because he didn't want to hold Zolti, but because he was tired of her making him late. It had been going on like this for years.

Doesn't she realize you use punctuality as a weapon against the powers that be? Pista didn't miss a beat; he never thought it would work between the two of them.

"Can't I leave him in the crib while you do that? I'm going to be late for work." He used a tone that made Teréza prick herself.

"Damn it," she winced, "there's more to life than your bloody work." She took the baby from his arms, the sewing needle still dangling on a thread from her stocking. "Go." She turned away from him coldly. Whatever joy their new son brought her, she reserved for the baby.

"I don't understand how siblings come out so differently," said István.

She glared at him with cold eyes. "I don't know if I should be taking that as a compliment or an insult."

"You decide."

"By your tone of voice, I can only guess that you're repelled by me."

"Klára. She went through the siege, and yet she shows kindness to her husband."

He could tell by the fury on Teréza's face that had she been holding anything other than her baby, she would have hurled it at him. "How dare you decide who's suffered more! Klára didn't have to work for years on end for a wretched woman like I did. She didn't have to witness what our parents went through after the war! How the Russians defiled our mother, and the Communists wore them down to the bone. What's your excuse for being so miserable?" Teréza took the baby to the other room. He watched her unbutton her blouse to breastfeed.

István stood in the sparse dayroom, trying to forgive himself. He'd been an ass. He had just enough fortitude left to remember that it was their corrosive political and social system that had eroded her desire to thrive, not him.

He tried to apologize, but his pride prevented him from saying what would have brought her back. Instead he left for work, wishing for a fire or other natural disaster that would keep him out late.

The secretary with the heart-shaped face had been absent when he walked into work five minutes late. He'd missed seeing her sympathetic expression at the front desk by the main entrance. He assumed she had in her a good dose of Jewish blood. He liked her intellect, her curvy shape and inviting voice.

Laci and his cohort Péter had been engrossed in conversation, their morning salutations less than enthusiastic as they washed the fire truck.

"Spotless, please," István said in response to their lack of interest.

His colleague, Sándor, had a penchant for repeating Communist maxims. "Only delinquent activity makes people late."

Without acknowledging him, István passed him in the hall. He disliked Sándor's wide face, his almond eyes.

Must have some Russian blood in him, Pista commented before István could say it.

István slipped into his office. One day, Pista's inductions would spill out like water from a ruptured dam and flood what safety he had left.

He glanced at the front page of the *Szabad Nép* newspaper.

Assembling assembly. University students, college students, engineers, art students, legal experts in Budapest, Szeged and Pécs are coming together in a fervent and stormy mood. More like a torrential river than an artful channel or creek. Is this a good storm? Is it good this fiery spirit? Let's confess, that in these past years we have gotten unused to mass declarations.

He had to re-read the first paragraph. Couldn't believe what he was reading.

Sectarianism, Stalin's mistakes have blunted our disposition and even today there are those who are wired to look upon these student demonstrations with alarm. Szabad Nép stands behind these youth and approves the demonstration to come.

He paused, combed his fingers through his hair and skipped to the end.

...Students have announced their solidarity with their counterparts revolting against the Soviet occupiers in Poznan, Poland. We wish them success with their astute and constructive deliberations.

"I'll be damned," István said aloud. *Well they can plan whatever they want, but the government will never allow a demonstration to begin.* "What if just this once you're wrong,

Pista."

A gloomy semidarkness filled the sky outside his office window, and the fire station felt unusually quiet, subduing his feeling of elation. Focusing on his duties behind the desk – preparing requisitions for parts to repair the fire truck which would take months to arrive – proved pointless.

Why are you even bothering with this bullshit? What could be more important than this front-page news?

The knock on his door he dismissed with a brush of his hand; it was his rookie Péter smoking his goddamn pipe and Laci with his low elephant ears and stunned expression. He wanted to be left alone, let his mind run wild at the implications. The feeling was almost sublime.

He turned on the radio and fiddled with the dials until he found Kossuth Rádió.

At seven minutes to one o'clock, István heard it – the Ministry of the Interior banning the demonstration.

Of course.

Then the station stopped reporting altogether and switched to music. He kept the radio on.

Another hour passed. Once again Laci knocked on his door, and this time he let himself in. István was turning dials; on every station he could find only somber classical music. No reporting anywhere. "What is it, Laci?" István said impatiently.

"That's pretty serious music you're listening to," Laci said.

"If you have nothing better to do than pester me, how about you lead the hose inspection and supervise cross and reverse lays practice."

Laci raised his eyebrows.

"Do it," István barked. "Tell everyone those are my orders." Laci lingered a moment. A concerto was interrupted by an announcement. "The Ministry of the Interior is allowing demonstrations to go ahead."

István's heart skipped. "There's going to be trouble in Budapest."

Laci's low ears moved upward as he smiled. He turned and left. István locked his office door. His only thought was to get to Budapest.

In case a fire breaks out?

"Bugger off, Pista. You know why."

He gathered his ID booklet, coat and cap, marched out to the staging area and whistled sharply. He waved Laci and Péter over. "Come with me," he said to his two subordinates, and instructed Sándor to oversee hose inspections. Sándor lowered his chin, crossed his arms and gave István a baleful look.

"Where are we going?" Péter asked, chewing the end of this pipe.

"To Budapest. We're taking the transport truck."

The drive lasted three hours, but István said practically nothing to Laci or Péter. The farther he drove the less he was able to turn back. When he predicted how panicked Teréza would be if he didn't return home at six he felt slightly satisfied.

They were stopped several times by Russian soldiers ensconced at checkpoints, asked for ID and questioned. Speaking passable Russian, István appealed to what made Russian soldiers tick: he slipped them some money and said, "We're visiting ladies in Budapest. A night off for my young firemen." István winked.

They waved him on.

A risky move István. Last I heard prostitution was banned under Socialist law.

"At heart Russian men are pigs," István said to Pista in the rearview mirror.

"Whatever you say boss," Péter chuckled.

"What did I say?"

"You're kidding, right?" Péter looked at him bemused.

He noticed Laci and Péter looking at each other making faces, giving each other incredulous looks.

Darkness enveloped the streets of Budapest. Thick mist hung in the air. Far from downtown the streets were practically deserted. István turned off Üllői Avenue, pulled the truck into a small dirt lot behind the Kilián Barracks and ordered his boys out. At the front office he asked for Sergeant Rigó.

Rigó, also known as Csoki, ambled down the hallway. His swagger well practiced, he greeted István with disbelief. "What the devil are you doing in Budapest, you son of a bitch?"

István had met Csoki, the soldier with the perpetual tan, six years earlier during his wedding to Teréza. He slapped Csoki on the shoulder and introduced his underlings who were giddy with excitement. "Farm boys. Neither have been to Budapest. You know where we can find them some girls?"

"I got some ideas." Csoki's smile spread across his face.

István pulled him aside, walked him down the hall a little. "I heard about student demonstrations. I figured there might be some trouble brewing."

"Trouble? That's an understatement. Is that why you're

really here?"

"Of course. What's happened?"

"Thousands of students gathered in Március 15 Square, at the Petőfi Statue. Along with their professors. The students read a list of demands."

"Demands?"

"Sixteen of them. Pretty ballsy. They called for the Soviets to get out. And to stop forcing us to learn Russian."

At last.

"They went as far as to ask why they can't earn enough to live on and petitioned for improved living conditions. And get this, they want the old flag back!" Csoki clicked his tongue.

Imagine what our teachers would have done to us to even think such things, István thought, but didn't dare say out loud. "That's only four."

"I know. Memory's not my strong suit."

"Were you there?"

"No, I just heard it."

"What else did you hear?" István tried not to sound too excited.

"Let me think…"

István kept an eye on his boys, who were looking restive.

"The students demanded to know why the ÁVO are persecuting us."

"You're talking about revolution," István said coolly.

Csoki's face darkened. "You son of a bitch. You're testing me to see if I'm on board. Aren't you?"

István could forgive Csoki for being suspicious. He could not know what side István was on. Even mentioning the ÁVO aloud was either a death sentence or a prescription for torture. The barbaric Hungarian arm of the KGB had for over a decade brutalized the innocent who objected to Moscow's rule over Hungary. But when the ÁVO tortured, paraded and purged good loyal Communist leaders whose only crime was wanting independence from Moscow, the ÁVO sent a terrifying message that no one was immune. István was just beginning to thaw from his own frozen terror – the immobolization of the jaw that everyone felt, the crippling tension every time they opened their mouths to speak a thought. Sometimes István's thoughts were so loud he was sure the ÁVO had heard them and they were going to drag him away, face scraping in gravel, in the middle of the night.

Csoki grabbed István by the shoulders and looked him piercingly in the eyes. Pressed his forehead to István's. "By four o'clock, a crowd of about ten thousand crossed Széchenyi Bridge and walked to Bem Square. Some students and professors from the Technical University. They were joined by factory workers. Thousands of them."

"Incredible." It was like drinking brandy. Each shot got better, more exhilarating. István cast a glance towards Péter who was filling his pipe and Laci who was chewing on his thumbnail.

Csoki asserted more pressure, forehead to forehead with István, and continued. "Then came military officers and members of the intelligentsia."

"And the government let this happen? They didn't send in the army? The ÁVO?"

"By some strange coincidence, most everyone's on leave. The soldiers, the officers. Anyway, the gathering was peaceful. They sang Kossuth songs and recited poems. And professed their solidarity with Poland. You heard about the strikes?"

"I have." István was on the brink of mental ejaculation.

"They chanted 'Long live Poland,' which later turned into 'Russians Go Home.' By that time the crowd was enormous. A group of people cut a hole into the flag and removed the hammer and sickle."

István made a whistling sound like a grenade falling. "And they still didn't call you guys out?"

"No. I took a nap. There was no violence. Listen, you want to see for yourself?" Csoki clicked his heels. "I'm off duty tonight. Maybe we can find these guys some girls while we're at it."

Go, Pista prodded.

István nodded. They headed for the Parliament Building, a thirty-minute walk.

István led the pack. Nervous tension electrified his legs. He wanted to sprint and work off his excess energy.

"For an old man you sure move fast," Csoki called after him.

István had forgotten about eating for the first time in his life, though it was well past dinnertime. More and more people poured out of their homes, running in the same direction as he, along wide roads empty of cars. They came out of their homes. Civilians. Men, women and children. In the past ten years he'd not seen confidence on the faces of his compatriots, let alone people pouring out of their homes heading towards a demonstration. He passed Juli's apartment on Múzeum Street where she lived with Ági, near the Magyar Rádió building, but there wasn't time to stop in and fetch Teréza's sisters. The spirit moved him like a powerful wind pushing his back.

István heard peels of laughter from behind. Péter and Laci had buddied up with Csoki, telling him the latest in the series of Aggressive Little Pigs jokes, a favourite Hungarian pastime. István led them along Nádor Street, heading straight for the Parliament Building. Along the way he caught snippets of news, disconnected jagged bits. Every so often he stopped and asked someone, "What do you know?"

A shrunken old man standing in a doorway told him that a massive group had made their way to Stalin's statue in Dózsa György Square. His bluish lips quivered as he spoke. He had a mouthful of nothing. "The welders from Csepel cut Stalin off at the lower legs, leaving only his empty boots."

"Csepel?" István marvelled. The purpose-built industrial enclave on an island north of Budapest was a notorious Communist stronghold. It was almost inconceivable that these hard-core party members were participating in a demonstration.

"His body's lying face up, missing its right hand." The man leaned in to István's ear. "I'd piss in his boots if I were there, but my old lady won't let me go in case I get a heart attack. God be with you." He tapped István's face with tender fingers.

István took off again, nearly losing sight of Laci, Péter and Csoki who ambled with arms around each other's shoulders.

As he neared Kossuth Square István gathered more news. A third group had splintered off, marching to Magyar Rádió to have the sixteen demands read off. Drunk on happiness, István lost himself in the good-natured mood. A decade of mistrust and alienation vanished with the daylight, and a city united in hope blushed in the fading light of dusk.

Demonstrators held homemade torches made of newspaper, illuminating the night sky since the government had ordered the street lighting turned off. In front of the Parliament Building on Kossuth Square and the surrounding streets the demonstrators had swelled to a quarter of Budapest's population, a crowd in the hundreds of thousands. István had never seen anything like it, not even on May Day. He had expected to hear fulminations or rowdy agitators but instead he was overcome by the peacefulness of the crowd. How could hundreds of thousands be so quiet?

They've practiced this silence for the past eleven years, and now they're using that skill to their own ends.

Women walking in procession, their faces serene as they carried green candles, the sincere innocence of all these young people standing, waiting, hoping, made joy shoot through István's heart.

A girl of no more than seventeen looked up at him as he pressed himself into the crowd. He watched her purposeful eyes taking in his uniform. She smiled and István caught her sense of pleasure. He wanted to kiss her. He'd waited his entire life for this moment.

Some generations live for the day they marry or hold their first child; this one lives only to realize independence.

He checked his watch but could not see its hands in the dark. Thinking of his wife and son, István was distracted with regret. He still had a three-hour drive ahead of him, in the dark, and Péter and Laci were punch drunk.

The crowd began calling for Nagy Imre. The slogans turned radical. "Russians go home! If you are Hungarian, you are with us! Nagy Imre to government, Rákosi to the riverbed!"

Say it. Say it.

"Rákosi to the riverbed!" István joined in. "Rákosi to the riverbed! Rákosi to the riverbed!" The release of his voice sparked a flame in István's body. He tingled with rebellion and thought about Teréza. He could bring her the news that would restore sparkle to her soul and heat between her legs.

Reports on the activities of the other groups began travelling through the crowd, and István gathered that the students never made it into the radio building. A military presence fended them off.

He turned to Péter and Laci. "They must have called in the reinforcements. Come on. Things are about to turn."

"We can't leave now." Péter drew on his pipe.

Stay. Stay.

"I have to get us back to Szombathely. I didn't tell my wife where I was going."

Coward.

"Look, I promised her father I would never leave her."

"Do you always hear voices in your head when you're in trouble?" Laci joked.

"I said I have to go back to my wife."

Csoki looked revved. "Things are about to get interesting at the radio station. Let's head back that way."

As István led the way out of the pressing masses, Nagy appeared on the balcony of the Parliament Building to address the demonstrators. The quiet turned to roars of enthusiasm. István stopped. The temptation to turn back was enormous, but his guilt was so considerable that he had no choice but to forfeit this extraordinary moment. His obligations overshadowed every possibility.

Had you been courageous enough to tell her of your heart's desires – to protect your country – she might have supported you. Maybe you underestimated her. In this political upheaval, is there a chance she could have been altruistic enough to absolve you of the promise you made to her father? You could have been a part of creating history. But you'll never know.

"Go to hell," István said aloud. He pushed ahead, out of the crowd, defying Pista's voice, his constant inner critic. István would never again see a day like this.

BUDAPEST IS READY, ARE YOU

1956, Tuesday, October 23. Hungary

If Teréza had been a bomb she would have exploded by now; the pressure in her skull was so great she squeezed her temples with her free hand. She turned off the radio. Official Party Leader for only three months, Gerő was just another mouthpiece for the demoted leader, Rákosi. He smeared the protests in Budapest as "nationalistic, patriotic and anti-semitic." An absurd declaration, Teréza thought, fuming. Of course, he called it antisemitic, because the majority of the heads of government were secular Jews who had embraced Communism after the Soviets liberated them from concentration camps. They were loyal to Soviet Stalinism, which discouraged nationalism and patriotism. She was emphatic with the audience in her head.

Baby Zolti couldn't sleep. He'd been unsettled and colicky the entire evening. Bouncing him gently in one arm Teréza paced the length of the dayroom.

Earlier, she had run from the office to the nursery, retrieved her baby and had run back home. She'd heard something momentous was happening in Budapest. She prepared egg noodles with cottage cheese, fried them slightly so they were sticky and browned on the bottom, just the way István liked them and then started pacing and cursing when he'd not shown up for dinner. She breastfed Zolti then bathed him. And still her husband hadn't arrived or sent word. By the time she heard Gerő on the radio at eight p.m., Teréza was beside herself with agitation and hadn't eaten dinner. István's impetuosity had always troubled her, but now she condemned him for his impulsive ways. Her body shook from nervous tension. There would be reprisals against demonstrators. Gerő had only been Party Leader since the ousting of Rákosi in July, after Khrushchev's speech denouncing Stalinism. But Teréza hated Gerő, Chairman Nagy's counterpoint to reform. On the radio, Gerő gave a flat-out "no" in response to the people's requests for change. She was furious with this Soviet puppet and her husband.

István had still not been able to find a shaft of light to read the hands of his watch. The streetlights in most districts of Budapest were out, and he'd lost all sense of time. Csoki led them towards Múzeum Park, convincing István to stay another thirty minutes so the young lads could meet some girls before they left the city. A single streetlight lit the entire neighbourhood as they walked. The atmosphere was charged; those they met in the park were engrossed in conversation. Csoki talked up some attractive girls. István was restless, lost in thought when the first gunshots rang out from the direction of Magyar Rádió, around the block from the park.

Csoki took off, leaving the girls stranded mid-conversation. Laci and Péter gave chase, and István followed in haste. As they turned the corner onto Brody Street, a second volley of shots pinned them to the door of a building.

"Jesus Christ!" István yelled out, caught in the violence he'd feared all day. The ÁVO started firing into the crowd in front of Magyar Rádió, shooting at unarmed students. He could taste ash and smell gunpowder. Deceiving warmth surrounded him like a campfire – teargas.

Csoki didn't waste a second. "Come! Let's get some guns!"

In the crowd, women gasped and shrieked. Their beautiful eyes were glassy, reflecting the flames of their torches. A few people had fallen. In his mind István saw Lali dying before him in the long grass. He blinked and rubbed his eyes. He saw men and women grab guns out of the hands of the military who were as paralyzed as István. They started shooting at the ÁVO men in the second story windows of the radio building as the crowd began to chant, "Death to the ÁVO!"

It's happening. It's finally happening. Pista sounded excited for once.

"Follow me!" Csoki yanked István away.

They set off running back towards the Kilián barracks. It would take at least fifteen minutes to get there, if not more. More shots were fired. István heard screams. He fell in behind Csoki and his rookies. He sped up, determined to never lose, never to be last. He began to overtake them, fighting for his own freedom. What he glimpsed over his shoulder fuelled his excitement: dozens of people following them to the barracks. Some had stopped, pushing their bodies against abandoned trams, rocking them, overturning them. More just kept coming. The energy had a terrifying edge.

Budapest is ready, are you? Pista needled him.

"Yes, you asshole. I'm ready!"

Csoki pulled ahead. "I'll race you," he yelled back at István. Péter and Laci ran with ecstasy on their faces. Csoki stuck his thumbs in his ears and wiggled his fingers mockingly.

Nearing the barracks, István fell behind. With a battle about to erupt, he was dressed in a uniform with red stars on his epaulettes. How could he fight for Hungary without recriminations from the Communists? He fought familiar feelings of ineptitude and shame, ones he'd not experienced since his teens.

Minutes before István reached the Kilián Barracks, a grenade exploded, blasting out several front windows. As the dust settled, he saw the damage as he approached, his lungs on fire from running. Csoki emerged out of the main doors of the barracks. "I got the son of a bitch!" he yelled, pumping his arms in the air. "An ÁVO vermin was walking down the hallway."

István stopped twenty metres from Csoki, bent over, resting his hands on his knees, catching his breath when Csoki yelled again. "Behind you!" Csoki tossed a grenade, right over István's head.

"Christ!" István crouched and spun. He saw scores of ÁVO men on the road charging towards him. They'd somehow cut in front of those coming from the radio building. Péter and Laci scattered, diving out of the way.

István heard a whistling sound. Then felt the blinding blast and burning red flash.

The explosion threw István to the ground and smashed his body into the concrete. Disoriented, he couldn't hear anything and felt only heat. Scrambling to his feet, he stumbled towards the lot behind the barracks, yelling for Laci and Péter to follow. Another grenade went off. He managed to escape the fragments showering the air.

How do you always get so lucky? How is it you never get hurt?

Péter moved his lips but István still couldn't hear a thing but Pista's voice. He fought with his balance.

"Where's Laci?!" István yelled.

Through the smoke Laci appeared, staggering, bleeding from his scalp. István ran towards him, threw his jacket over his head, rushed him towards the truck, and hoisted him into the passenger seat.

Péter found the first-aid kit and pressed a cloth hard against Laci's wound.

Laci joked, "I stood up the girls. Do you suppose they'll ever forgive me?"

István stuck the key in the ignition and reversed from his spot adjacent to the barracks, narrowly missing debris. He turned sharply, hitting the curb, and barrelled down the street, scattering the surviving ÁVO men. As he drove through the streets, he saw civilians, even children, setting up roadblocks. He heard the trailing echo of gunshots while legions of civilians concocted firebombs and secured strategic positions around the city.

Are you seriously leaving Budapest now? Are you really such chicken shit?

"I lost my fucking pipe," Péter said.

"You can buy a new one tomorrow." István gripped the wheel, trying to keep his anger at bay. In his mind, he was drowning out Pista's protestations by rehearsing an explanation to Teréza, imagining the stripping down he would receive when he got home.

"It was my grandfather's." Péter started to cry.

When he saw a checkpoint in the distance, István switched off his lights and swerved from the main road. He had no more money for bribes. István knew a much longer route home that would likely have no military presence.

"We have to come back with supplies. Budapest will need food, guns and first-aid supplies," István planned aloud.

That's it, my little bug. Be brave. Contribute.

In his half sleep, Laci mumbled something about fondling girls, his head wrapped thick in bandages.

"Do you know what you're saying?" Péter laced and unlaced his fingers repetitively, trying to find something to do with his hands.

"I know exactly what I'm saying." István kept his eyes on the road.

Think about Csoki back in Budapest. About all the young men and women who are fighting against the ÁVO. Csoki will be ordering his men to make Molotov cocktails all night. What will you be doing, safe in your bed?

István focused on the road. He had no answer for Pista.

Her angst evolved into a mild fever, then sweat, then resignation. Beside her, baby Zolti lay sleeping in his crib. Teréza felt limp. Even when she heard the gate open and close, she didn't move nor run to the door, she lay there on top of the covers, shivering and spent. Only when she heard the key in the door did she move and only then to remove her hand from her forehead. The sky was still dark though it felt like the crack of dawn. She had left the outside light on for István. The air that followed her husband inside had a drizzly feel, and she could hear him remove his shoes, set them on the mat and unbutton his coat. She turned her head towards the door, aware he was breathing rapidly. She waited for him to come to her.

At the doorway of their bedroom he said, "I'll never do that again."

She turned her head back towards the ceiling and said nothing.

"I don't know what possessed me." István remained standing at the door, his arms hanging by his sides like drooping flags, his ears still ringing from the grenade blast. "I don't know if you've been following the news."

Teréza felt the tears roll into her ears, pool there. She didn't wipe them away.

"Great things are happening in Budapest."

"Your favourite cottage cheese noodles are still in the pan. On the stove. Browned and stuck together. The way you like them."

István felt awful. After a long pause, he asked, "May I come in?"

She didn't answer.

He sat down on the bed beside her, her small body hidden in a nightgown, and looked over at their baby. Barely perceptible in the shadows, a tiny chest moved up and down. He felt Teréza shivering. "Why aren't you under the blankets?"

"You went to Budapest?" she asked.

He kept his voice soft, unexcited, but he wanted to bare his heart, divulge every precious moment of what he had witnessed. "There were hundreds of thousands of people at the Parliament." He paused. "Students, factory workers and everyday people. Women with green candles."

Teréza nodded.

"The quiet..." he whispered and reached for her hand, "the quiet was remarkable."

She let out a sob and sucked it back in. He stroked her hand. They continued to whisper.

"And then Nagy finally came out on the balcony to greet us."

"What did he say?" She felt something like wonder and joy rising up.

"I didn't wait to listen to him. I was anxious to get back to you. So I left. When we got to Magyar Rádió –"

"We?"

"Péter, Laci and Csoki –"

"Csoki?"

"An army friend I met at the barracks the weekend we got married."

"Péter and Laci went with you?" she asked, trying to cover the envy in her voice.

"I needed a cover. We went through checkpoints on the way."

Baby Zolti stirred and made babbling sounds.

"Keep your voice down," Teréza said.

He told Teréza how the ÁVO started shooting into the crowd and she gasped. How the welders had severed Stalin from his bronze boots. Cut off his head. He retold the incident with the grenades and the hundred charging ÁVO men and how the citizens of Budapest were mobilizing. The young, the intellectuals, the artists and the army were all rising up against the Communists.

"The army?" she asked. In the dimness he could feel her face light up. He touched her cheek. "Even the men from Csepel came out. All fifteen thousand of them, they say."

"From Csepel? The staunch Communist factory

workers?!"

"Yes! I heard the men from Csepel were stripping the barracks of weapons and were holing themselves up in the Corvin Cinema, blocks away." István squeezed her hand. "They're preparing themselves for the tanks."

Teréza covered her mouth.

"Something very big is happening."

"Promise me you won't go back to Budapest."

You can't promise that.

When he tried to curl into her body, she stiffened.

After two hours, she woke him. István had overslept. Teréza turned on the radio, which had set up a temporary broadcasting station in the Parliament Building. The message was the same over the course of the morning: fascist, reactionary groups had made a counter-revolutionary attack against the state.

"Bullshit." István pulled on a clean white shirt and raised his voice at the radio, "There were no fascists. It was a native Hungarian protest against the AVÓ and the Soviet occupation!"

"Shhh–" Teréza handed him the baby. "Hold him," she said. "He loves you. Look at how he observes you."

István opened his arms. His baby blinked and smiled, stuck his fingers in his mouth.

They listened to the morning broadcast as Teréza prepared their coffee and bread, uncertain of what the day held for their country. Well before nine o'clock Nagy Imre had been appointed Prime Minister. Martial law was imposed, curfews were put in place and assemblies banned. Schools and offices were declared closed.

"Remarkable!" Teréza said as she poured them thick black coffees and added milk. "My prayers are answered."

István brushed her cheek with his lips. He touched her hair, turned and left.

Teréza rushed all the way to the centre of town where she dropped baby Zolti at the nursery, only steps from the County Council building across the park from City Hall. Offices and schools were closed in Budapest but not yet in Szombathely. When Teréza walked into the large foyer of the County Council, the mood crackled, and a sedate hopefulness pervaded interactions. Employees greeted each other politely, with added courteousness.

"A very fine morning to you," said one woman whom Teréza suspected of being an informant.

"No finer than yesterday," Teréza replied, beelining it to her desk.

The woman raised her eyebrows. "Have you not heard of the events in Budapest?"

"You would have had to be born without ears not to hear about the events in Budapest." Teréza replied. Like her colleagues, Teréza wasn't prepared to express outright support in either direction.

Someone had brought in a radio and played it on low.

A few employees in the office welcomed Nagy's twelve o'clock speech, in which the four-hour-old Prime Minister scolded the people and ordered them to cease fighting. Teréza saw the informant nodding. Communist. Others silently lauded the rebellion with knowing looks. A colleague winked and smiled at Teréza, but she looked down and continued to shuffle papers.

FREEDOM SEIZED THE NATION

1956, Thursday, October 25. Hungary

Heavy ground fog settled over the streets. István felt naked in his vehicle – a sole moving target, even with Péter sucking on a new pipe next to him in the passenger seat. All public transportation had ceased in Budapest since the outbreak of the revolt. After a dubious drive along a wide abandoned boulevard, István pulled up to the Kilián Barracks.

Ah, the scene of your ignominious flight from danger.

In the murky daylight, the building displayed its wounds. The front door was off its hinges and shards of glass poked through the debris left by the blast. Several bodies were sprawled out front.

ÁVO men, shot to death?

"Who else would they be?"

"You talking to me, boss?" Péter shifted his pipe to the side of his mouth, looked out the side window and squinted.

István pulled on the parking brake. "No, to my conscience."

"You know, sir, there's an affliction called shell shock. Might you have it? I don't remember you telling me about serving in the war."

István stepped over a corpse. "Does it take a war?"

In the front foyer, sitting on a long bench, Csoki swigged brandy. His black hair was impressively thick, like a fur hat, but it was dusted white. Fallen plaster surrounded him and covered the floor. The barracks was as quiet as Csoki, its armories stripped of its munitions.

"The last time I saw you two, you were backing over a squadron of ÁVO thugs in a delivery truck."

See, even he knows you were fleeing.

"The last time I saw you," said István, "you were throwing a grenade at me."

Csoki cracked a grin. "I told you to duck." He passed István the bottle. "What have you got for me in that truck?"

István took a few sips and ordered Péter to unload the supplies. Csoki shouted down the hallway and delegated two of his underlings to help. A pair of brawny, young soldiers dawdled out of an office and followed Péter outside.

Debris crunched under István's boots. Through the blasted windows, he saw dismembered corpses of the ÁVO scattered like garbage.

"Let the crows pick out their eyes," said Csoki, seeing István staring.

"I wasn't made for the army," said István. "The worst injuries I can bare to look at are burns."

"Surely you don't feel sympathy? They got what they deserved, the goddamn torturers. I wish they felt the same measure of pain they inflicted on the rest of us."

István nodded, remembering his own transgressions.

Are you too afraid to kill one yourself?

After István left Csoki to his bottle, he headed to the 5th District. Beside the National Museum on Múzeum Street, István found his sisters-in-law, Juli and Ági, holed up in their apartment. Juli quickly drew the door closed. Her hair resembled Teréza's, fine light brown strands scarcely able to hold a curl for long. Ági sat at the kitchen table, her legs tightly crossed, looking thin in a grey pencil skirt and tight red pullover. István sat down next to her while Juli moved about the kitchen, putting water on for tea.

"We didn't sleep at all. The sound was unbearable. Like the end of the world," Juli said.

"It went on all night," Ági said miserably.

"Must have been hundreds of tanks in our streets." Juli set cups on the table. "How is Teréza? And the baby? Are they well?"

"More or less." István felt Juli's eyes searching his, but he had nothing to add.

"Well, at least you're sheltered in Szombathely. You don't have to go through what we're going through here," said Ági.

"Shame on you, Ági. That's a terrible thing to say." Juli opened the sugar container, a turquoise tin with a red star and smiling children.

István wondered how they could be so different. How could sisters be so different, born of the same parents? Didn't they have the same mother?

Juli poured boiling water into the teapot. "We realized early this morning that we had no bread. We went to the bakery before seven, and there was nothing left. Bless her heart, the attendant, Rozsi, told us to wait. When the others cleared out of the shop, Rozsi pulled out her last two loaves.

She gave them to us!" Juli's eyes brightened. "I tried to get one to Klára by calling her neighbour – that's how we get messages to her – but there was no answer. They're too close to the Party Headquarters. It's dangerous." Juli placed a brown package on the table, the shape of a loaf. She sat down next to István and scooted closer. Her body felt like his wife's: small and sturdy. "Her little ones also need to eat something."

Come on, my little bug. Take the hint.

István hesitated. "You want me to deliver the bread?"

"Would you please?"

Ági sulked in the corner.

An hour later, with the loaf in hand, István darted along the quieter side streets making his way to the other end of District V.

The people he met – most carrying arms – young men, women, even children, seemed exhilarated, jubilant, free.

He'd just entered Kossuth Square when István felt a different current. He knew something had gone wrong from the faces that rushed toward him. The faces were panic-stricken, and they rushed away from the Parliament Building. He tried to ask what had happened, but no one would stop for him.

Whatever it is, the situation's fresh.

István pressed forward against the surging crowd and looked for something to climb up onto, but there wasn't a corner of building that wasn't already jammed with people. A handful of Soviet tanks flew Hungarian flags. Protestors clambered on top of them, forty or fifty to a tank. The crowd in front of the Parliament Building was as massive as the first night, but the mood had transformed from hope to horror.

A man in a beret, smelling of sour sweat, talked nervously: "The ÁVO fired into the crowd from those rooftops from that direction, I think." He pointed over his shoulder. "The Soviets are shooting back – they think they're being targeted. Maybe some of the protestors are shooting too?" The man removed his beret and placed it over his heart.

The pop of guns filled István's ears. He heard screams and thunderous footfalls. He'd never seen anything like it and was unable to look away. He watched people crumple to the ground; he watched a massacre unfold in Kossuth Square. His need to witness the horror satisfied some dark impulse, even as it turned his stomach.

Is this what you came to see?

It wasn't until he was all the way back in Múzeum Street that István realized he'd been gripping the bread so tightly he'd put his fingers through the crust. He'd been arguing with Pista the whole time: "I have a wife and son! I can't risk my life for a loaf of bread!"

But try as he might to justify his actions, he understood that he was too afraid to deliver the bread to Klára.

In the truck, Péter had fallen asleep with the pipe between his teeth. He woke with a start when István slammed the door shut. "How can you sleep at a time like this?!" István looked at him, incredulous. "Eat some fucking bread. Maybe it will keep you awake." He threw the loaf in his lap.

Péter pulled off a chunk and started munching. "It could use some duck fat."

On their way out of town István pulled over when he saw a young Russian soldier, no more than twenty, lying face up, dead on the tram tracks. His eyes stared straight up to the sky, the way Lali's had, so blue and warm. István felt cold. How could you hate a stranger enough to want to kill him?

It's Rákosi you and I want dead. And Vargas.

István agreed. He'd seen enough of those faces for the past ten years.

Back in Szombathely, no matter how he conveyed the story, István couldn't reassure Teréza enough. "There was no way to get through. Hundreds of thousands filled Kossuth Square. I can't even count how many died in that hour. I can only guess it was hundreds."

"Couldn't you go around? Take a side street?" she asked, warming milk for the baby.

"It was impossible to get through. I'm sure Klára's safe in her apartment. She survived the war. She'll survive this."

"Safe? Blocks from the massacre? How is everyone else getting through?"

"You weren't there! How would you know? What did you want me to do? Fucking die for the sake of a loaf of bread and leave you here alone with the baby?" Why did he always feel like he was pleading or apologizing for something?

He excused himself, said he had business at the fire department.

Teréza rocked the baby in her arms. "You're leaving again? Do you have to go?"

"I have to check on things. I've been away." István stood by the door.

"Why do I feel you're about to get yourself in trouble?"

István resented Teréza's predictions, interpreting them as veiled judgments. Why couldn't she ever predict that he would do something outstanding?

As he walked down the quiet halls of the fire station, everything appeared normal in his absence, clean and orderly. The revolution had not yet touched Hungary's oldest city. Sándor played cards with another young fireman on the overnight shift. István muttered a few words to them about having to do some paperwork. Inspired, he stole to a meeting room where he smelled opportunity.

Pista gave the instructions, István carried out the orders.

Switch on the desk lamp, rather than the overhead light.

István held the lamp by its wiry neck. His hands took over, reaching for several books on the shelf. He pulled books from their slots, like secret policemen pulled people off trams. He emptied an entire shelf. Falling to his knees, they went at them. In rage, his hands ripped through paragraphs and chapters, tore away footnotes and severed indexes. Sweating, he mangled hundreds and hundreds of pages.

There's more up there, get those.

Sensual rapture flooded István's body. Olive green bindings lay strewn across the floor, their pages scattered over the library floor. Communist manuals. Their covers torn away from their influential notions. Marx and Engels' *The Communist Manifesto*, extolling the virtues of scientific socialism, mangled. On the floor, a portrait lay torn in thirds: beady eyes with a full forehead and receding hair, another section with a mustachioed lip, and another with a deformed goatee. Lenin's *What Is to Be Done* ripped apart and demolished.

Sensing something behind his back, István turned and caught a glimpse of Sándor surreptitiously slipping away from the window in the door. He saw what István had done. Stalin stared back at István from the cover of a ravaged volume long enough to warn to him from the grave: "I'll punish you yet."

★

The following morning István jolted awake to someone banging on the front door. It wasn't even six. Teréza bolted upright, gasping. The baby started crying. It was Laci, looking apologetic. "You're being requested at the police station."

Teréza pulled on her robe and came to the door of the bedroom. "What on earth happened to you?" She looked at his bandaged head with concern.

"Didn't István tell you about our night in Budapest?" he asked, surprised.

"Shut up, Laci. What's this about the police station?"

"What the hell have you done now?" Teréza searched her husband's face. Zolti cried louder.

István ignored her. He was panicking. Laci looked to him, hesitant to disclose too much. "It's okay, Laci," said István, "you can tell us."

Laci whispered. "Students have broken into the police station. They've started burning citizen dossiers. Sándor wants us to make sure the fire doesn't spread out of control."

The revolution had reached Szombathely overnight. "Incredible!" István gathered his coat, his keys, his wallet, then looked at Laci. "Let's move it."

Well done István, you've managed to wiggle out of this one too.

Seated behind the wheel of the fire truck, Laci brought István up to date. "The police encouraged the students. They gave them access to the Soviet dossiers."

On the lawn in front of the red brick fire station, the flames licked the morning mist and warmed all those who stood round, requited smiles on their faces, young men and women, students from the university. Péter and Laci sat in the vehicle whistling in amazement. "Everything they know about us –" Péter said, dancing.

"– is going up in flames," Laci finished his sentence.

"Stay with the truck," István instructed. He walked into the police station. No one stopped him. The police stood by, watching, smoking, as dozens of students went on a rampage, relieving the station of thousands of dossiers. The students worked quickly, removing document after document, laughing and shouting as they worked.

It didn't take long. The files were meticulously organized.

István read his file cover to cover, as he fed each page into the flames: that he'd been a member of the Arrow Cross; that he had buried Jews, a mother and two children, and that he had participated in cataloguing Jews for deportation; that he registered as a Jew after the war but that his paternity was uncertain and his ethnicity was unverifiable; that he married the sister of an Enemy of the Party; that he was sent home from Communist training camp and relocated. It even said his best friend was Pista from Ják. There was a special note that he was to be watched closely for signs of dissent. Everything he'd ever done was there, even things he was predicted to do, that was the most astounding part. "Uncooperative. Noncompliant," he read out loud, proudly, as students shoved past him.

He went back and searched for Teréza's dossier, a thin folder, filled with her activities as a "religious deviant" attending secret Mass.

Outside, the fire crackled and shot sparks upwards as he tossed Teréza's dossier on the flames. He recognized several men walking along the periphery of the police station's grounds, ÁVO men, wearing civilian clothing. They didn't wear their brown shoes or their uniforms, which would give them away to the zealous student mob. Still, István shot them a long disgusted look. He turned away from the fire, headed to the truck and ordered Péter and Laci to go find their dossiers. "I can't deprive you of the pleasure."

The two ran inside like gangly puppies chasing a stick.

Teréza packed her basket with provisions and set out with the baby. She travelled to Ják to see Kati and their parents, relieved to catch the last bus before the general strike spreading throughout the country reached Szombathely. Never in her life had Teréza not left a note for her husband, not shown up for work. But the possibility of freedom seized her as it had the nation. As the bus made its way down muddy roads, Teréza saw green candles in the windowsills of the farmhouses. Green was the colour of the Peasants' Party and had become the symbol of freedom, protest and revolt. She saw slaps of fresh green paint on white adobe walls, on barns and on the Town Council building in Ják at *Fő* Square, the village's main plaza.

Before long, she was at her parents' kitchen table, eating a slice of thick bread with potato stew made with dill, sour cream and paprika. Anna cuddled her grandson while Gyuri revelled in the news from Budapest and pressed for more information. Teréza was running out of inspiring news. Amidst their genuine excitement, they feared for Klára and her family living so close to the violence.

"Our Klára has a way of being right in the thick of things," said Gyuri proudly. "Our first born leads the way."

His words stung and made Teréza feel she was tagging along for the ride. She'd not done anything significant to contribute to the uprising, hadn't put herself in danger and readily chose safety over defiance. Spooning stew into her mouth, she didn't want to admit she had István on the same leash and that it made her hate him at times.

Her youngest sister reported on the developments in the village. Kati had just turned twenty, but still looked sixteen and was as winsome as ever. She worked in the accounts department at the State Farming Collective.

"The first news we got in the office was that a 'counter-revolution' had broken out in Budapest," Kati reported. "My boss gathered us together. I was incredibly nervous, but too enthused not to follow his lead. We hopped into the tractor trailer, and I held the Hungarian flag." Kati gestured with her hands. "Can you believe we rolled into the centre of Ják? You should have seen Varga's face."

"Hammer-chin Varga was there? Didn't he move to Sopron?"

"He did," Kati said, clapping her hands together, giggling. "His mother has gallstones. He comes back to visit her."

"Serves her right. Raising a son like that."

"The strangest feeling gripped me," Kati continued. "All around us it was peaceful. But still we were getting pulled into a political movement very far away from us. Then within a day, half the workers in the department decided that because the border was open, they were going to leave Socialism behind. They up and left. Just like that."

An idea took root in Teréza. She had never even considered the prospect before then. Something in the way Kati told the story made it seem so simple, that existence on the other side could be thinkable. It was possible to get across the border for the first time since 1945. Eleven years.

"When the bookkeeper up and left, that's when I asked if I could have his job. The office is only six kilometres from here and easier for me to get to on my bike. Especially as winter sets in. I guess you could say I'm an opportunist."

At the word "opportunist" Teréza's urge to leave Hungary grew stronger.

"You're not thinking of crossing that border, are you?" Gyuri asked, sadness pressed into the lines around his eyes. "This past spring, we when got wind that the government started dismantling a section of minefields and barbed wire near the Austrian border, I thought, that's the one thing I can thank Stalin for, that he died. They completed the tear-down of a three-hundred-kilometre stretch of it a few weeks ago. The government must be regretting that now!" Gyuri looked at Teréza and then at his grandson.

She wondered if he was giving her permission to go.

STAR MAN

1956, October 28-30. Hungary

On the fifth day of the revolution, István conscripted Péter and Laci, his two underlings, and drove the fire truck right up to the steps of the Szombathely County Council. The front tires grazed the first step as he pulled on the parking brake.

"What are we doing now?" Péter asked, sounding reluctant, biting down on his pipe.

"I don't know what *you're* worried about," Laci remarked, his head still fat with bandages. "I haven't recovered from last time."

Péter sized him up. "It's an improvement. You look like one of the Turks that scaled the wall of the Eger Fort during the invasion."

"Come on, boys, watch how it's done." With the help of his crew, István extended the truck's long ladder as long as it would go, high enough for him to reach the large red star positioned on the peak of the cornice. A crowd began to form as he climbed swiftly to the top, with crowbar and hammer in hand. Up here, the wind was fierce but refreshing.

Would you look at that.

"Which of you idiots can climb up here and bring me a screwdriver?" István yelled to his crew. "We've got a slapdash Soviet job up here."

Laci volunteered. István watched him ascend with the screwdriver between his teeth.

Your rookie Laci looks like one of the Turks that scaled the wall of the Eger Fort during the Turkish invasion.

"That's what Péter just said," István said aloud.

"Still talking to yourself, sir?" Laci mused.

"What?" István looked confused.

Laci reached up and handed István the screwdriver.

István took it. "You can return to Constantinople now."

"You forget we Turks stayed around for centuries," Laci quipped, climbing back down, "and did less damage than the Russians in eleven years."

"That hardly reassures me, Laci. I can't tell you I would choose a Turkish jail over a Russian one." But Laci was already down at the bottom of the ladder and didn't hear him.

The star had seemed omnipotent from afar, but now that István examined it up close, he saw it was as poorly made. If only the system was as easy to dismantle. He removed the star, pocketed its screws, and held it high in the air. He felt giddy. Péter lead a cheer, and the crowd below joined in. Then István let the red enamelled metal drop several stories to the ground where it sustained dents to two of its sharp points. After a pause, the crowd cheered again.

People were already talking about Star Man like he was a local folk hero when Teréza dismounted the bus from Ják, with Zolti drooling in her arms. She walked to the City Council office.

At the back of the ever-growing crowd, one of her colleagues, the oldest typist in the department, a rotund lady with thinning hair like the white circular seed head of a dandelion, was taking in the amusing developments. She sidled up to Teréza and said, "A gift from your husband."

"What is?"

"That!" she said, pointing to the fallen star below Teréza's office window.

"Your István is Star Man." Her colleague winked and smiled.

In spite of her training to stifle expressions that betrayed her emotions, Teréza allowed herself to smile. Her handsome, rebellious husband had done this wondrous thing.

Later that night, when she returned home with Zolti, he was waiting for her. He'd bought beer, a bag of onions and fresh-baked bread and was preparing the one and only meal he knew how to cook – onions sautéed in bacon fat and beer.

Teréza smelled the caramelizing onions outside the house. "It must be a special occasion, Star Man," she said as she opened the door. "You never cook."

"Well, I do tonight." István waggled his eyebrows at her as he stirred the onions. Teréza put Zolti in his bassinette and hugged her husband from behind, pressing herself into his buttocks, holding him around the waist. She rested her cheek on his upper back and thanked God for her small family.

★

That night they listened to Rákóczi Rádió. The station – broadcasting from a migrating bus – had been created and organized by revolutionaries and continuously moved around Budapest to avoid detection. The announcer spoke excitedly. "Children as young as twelve are involved in the battle, throwing Molotov cocktails at oncoming Soviet tanks..." Teréza and István fell silent as they listened. He worried about his buddy Csoki. Was he still alive?

When Teréza suggested István drive to Budapest to bring her news of her siblings, he jumped at the chance. He'd got wind that the Austrian Red Cross had unloaded medical supplies at the border, and he decided he'd stop there first to stock up. This time he went alone, putting Péter and Laci in charge at the Fire Station. He took with him a tin of *kifli.* "Please deliver them to my sisters," Teréza had said upon his departure. Legend had it that the tiny pastries, shaped like a Turkish crescent, had been invented by bakers in the late 1500s, after the Turks were repulsed at Eger.

Are you sure the kifli isn't jinxing a premature victory?

"Must you always cast doubt on everything?" István shoved the tin under the passenger seat.

Warm and eager Austrian Red Cross workers greeted him at the border. Complimented for his excellent accent, István practiced his limited German, conveying what he could about recent victories. The workers handed him food and medical supplies and helped him load his truck. He spotted a large group of Austrian students and Boy Scouts looking at maps. They'd just crossed the border into Hungary with the purpose of hand-delivering supplies to the wounded in Budapest. They couldn't have been older than eighteen. István wasn't convinced their orienteering skills were up to the task, so he volunteered to lead them in a convoy.

The makeshift convoy followed him to the centre of the city. He pulled over, gave the Boy Scouts directions to the Kilián Barracks and told them to ask for Sergeant Rigó. When they looked like they wouldn't be able to pronounce his name, he made it easier for them. "*Fragen Sie nach Csoki. Schokolade,*" István explained in German. "Csoki," he said again. "It means chocolate. *Schokolade.*"

István surveyed the crews of fighters he saw patrolling the streets: thousands of them, the majority no older than eighteen, many still involved in skirmishes with the ÁVO. The bulk of the fighters were tough, disadvantaged industrial workers, the very workers the Rákosi regime claimed to represent. By now, soldiers, policemen, writers and intellectuals joined their ranks, and with them, boys as young as eight. Some fought in trench coats and berets, some in blazers, while others had acquired Soviet-style padded jackets and bits and pieces of military uniforms. The ubiquitous Hungarian armbands unified them all. Some women wore blue light-weight workers' coats and carried rifles and holstered pistols while others wore skirts and sported padded jackets, belted at the waist, their hair perfectly coiffed. Many others wore headscarves and heavy boots. Red, white and green cockades replaced the red star on men's caps.

His eyes sweeping the street, István wanted to take up arms with his brothers and sisters, but felt bound by the duty of fatherhood. He couldn't bear the thought of dying in battle and leaving behind his wife with an infant.

He had almost reached Republic Square when a familiar shape leapt out at him: András, bent over, vomiting at the edge of the sidewalk.

"Brother!" István yelled. He bounded out of the driver's seat, grabbed András, held his forehead and said, "Didn't anyone tell you the meat was off?"

"My good God help us. You can't even imagine the scene over there!" András righted himself. He had nothing left inside. "My apologies brother, I have never had a strong stomach and what I've just seen I will never forget as long as I live." András pulled a handkerchief from his inside pocket and wiped his mouth. They heard the sound of women crying out. "They've hung them upside down from lampposts, gutted them like swine."

István couldn't believe his ears. "Who?"

"The ÁVO."

"The ÁVO did this to whom?"

"The citizens did it to the ÁVO," András exclaimed. "It's too much! It's indefensible! If the West learns of this we'll be seen as murderers. It will give the revolution a bad name."

When they arrived at the square, István saw at least twenty bodies hanging from trees and lampposts. He saw many more stacked like logs, four to a row, a metre high. They were covered in honey.

"To avoid the spread of bacteria," István said aloud to himself, aghast at what he saw. Women spat on the bodies on they passed.

A familiar pop sound pressed István to the nearest wall. By now his ears were attuned to the danger, but it took András several seconds to seek cover.

"That's an ÁVO administration building." András pointed to a non-descript edifice fronting the square. "There's a bunch of them holed up inside. They weren't shooting before."

"Well, they are now." István saw commotion at the front of the building. Three ÁVO men emerged, their arms raised in surrender. They took several steps into the open, their arms held high while five white-coated first-aid women helped wounded revolutionaries in the square. Across from István, a young boy raised his rifle and fired three shots. The three men fell in quick succession. From the rooftop, the ÁVO fired at the medics in retaliation. Their bodies fell to the ground and their white coats turned red in a blink of an eye.

You're always on the periphery of danger, looking in while others die. How do you do it?

István started forward. For an instant he wasn't certain if he was headed for the first-aid women or the open door to the ÁVO building.

He felt András grab his shoulder. "You have a wife. And an infant."

"So do others." His body was caught in a rocking motion – moving forward, staying back. András squeezed his shoulder firmly. István could have broken free, shook him off and surged forward.

If you really wanted to.

"András, you have to help me get the supplies to the wounded."

They ran back to the truck. István drove to the Hospital in the Rock, dodging massive holes in the road, swerving around burned out tanks and streetcars lying on their sides. András looked out the window at the wrecked city, at gaping holes in buildings where Soviet tanks had fired at anything that moved.

István felt utterly distraught, but he couldn't understand why. The country was on the verge of victory, and yet he felt inexplicably lonely. Duty had robbed him of his autonomy. Who was he without his conviction, without his courage?

"Under the seat. Teréza made some *kifli*," István said.

"Isn't it a little premature?"

"That's what Pista thought."

"When did you see Pista?"

"1955."

András looked puzzled. He reached under the seat and opened the tin. In spite of himself he laughed and bit into one. "Apricot jam. I don't even have enough self-restraint to abstain at a time like this. I hate myself."

"Where are your pithy aphorisms now? Don't you have a saying about eating pastries during a revolution?"

András laughed with his mouth full. "Actually yes. But I have another joke for you: The devil seduced Eve in Italian. Eve mislead Adam in Bohemian. The Lord scolded them both in German. And the angel drove them from paradise in Hungarian." András bit into another *kifli*.

"I knew you'd deliver."

István passed through the iron gates guarding the Hospital in the Rock, parked in front of the secret door, knocked using the code Csoki gave him and waited. András stayed in the vehicle. The hallways of the underground medical complex some fifteen metres below the surface of the city were difficult to navigate because of the wounded, lying wherever there was space. Women and children were now among the injured. The stench was halting. Doctors and nurses raced about nonstop. In front of him, a young nurse with red hair squeezed István's hand as he started handing her packages of food and supplies.

"Thank you." Her breasts heaved with gratitude. "Please keep the supplies coming," said the young nurse, as though she was certain of more bloodshed.

At home, Teréza's mood had turned to elation as she breastfed her baby. She'd spent several days alone with him while daycare, schools, offices and stores remained closed. Nagy had become Chairman of the Council of Ministers, declared his intent to remove Hungary from the Warsaw Pact and begun his appeal to the UN to recognize Hungary as a neutral state. Teréza listened, astonished at Nagy's pronouncement that the recent past was a "rigid dogmatism of the Stalinist monopoly." Could this spontaneous transformation hold? Why had it taken so long? Or were his attempts at reform some sort of trick?

It was well after seven in the evening and pitch black by the time István returned home. Teréza couldn't understand why he wore such a long face. "What happened?" she asked.

"I'm tired. I need a beer."

Why couldn't he talk about what he'd seen that day? "Did you get the *kifli* to my sisters?" she asked.

"I saw András."

"And?"

"He's doing well."

"Is that it?"

"The city's a wreck. András said he'd deliver them to Klára and save some for Juli and Ági as well."

"How about Uncle János and Hermina? And the twins?"

"I don't know anything."

"Why don't you know anything? Weren't you in Budapest?"

"Of course I was in Budapest! Do you have any idea of the carnage, of the fucking destruction? You're safe near your radio, you and your family. Holed up in your safe little rooms. Your sisters haven't even attended a fucking demonstration, and there's András stuffing his face with *kifli*. None of you have any balls. I'm the one who drove up there."

Teréza turned without a word, went into the bedroom with the baby and shut the door behind her.

The following evening as Kossuth Rádió resumed broadcasts, Teréza and István stayed close to the wireless, amazed by what they heard. The baby slept in her arms. Nagy Imre was no longer calling the uprising a "counter-revolution," declaring it instead, "a great national and democratic movement."

Teréza laid the baby in his crib. "Zolti will have good dreams tonight," she said and returned to sit next to István. She reached for István's hand and held it as Nagy guaranteed impunity for insurgents and confirmed the Soviets agreed to a ceasefire after their thwarted attacks on Corvin Alley.

"Unbelievable!" István shook his head.

He pulled Teréza even closer. Her body gave way and rested under his arm.

They listened, in suspense, as Nagy announced the disbanding of the AVÓ and withdrawal of Soviet troops.

By the end of his speech, Teréza's cheeks were wet with tears. She cried softly in István's arms. The revolution had triumphed in a few short days. "We have our country back," she said into his chest.

"Yes, but the Russians are still here," he reminded her.

"Nagy just said they're leaving. Didn't you hear that?"

"Of course I heard it. I'm not deaf. But the Turks were here for centuries."

"I can't tell if your caution is wise or if it's blowing out what tiny flame of optimism I've managed to keep burning.

It doesn't take much to blow it out."

He blew gently on her neck. "Air feeds fire. It takes just a subtle wind to keep it going and make it stronger."

The anticipation of freedom opened their bodies and she let him touch her. He asked her to lie naked on the bed, by candlelight, without covering herself up. "Let me look at you," he said. He pulled up a chair and sat with grateful eyes.

"Hurry up," she said, "I'm getting shy."

"Just one more minute, I need to remember this." Then he crawled onto the bed. "Don't move."

She felt nervous and exhilarated. With one open palm he brushed her nipples, with the other he caressed her inner folds. It didn't take long until her body produced a quiet miracle.

NO ONE'S COMING

1956, Saturday, November 3. Hungary

At the border, István watched his fellow Hungarians decamp by the thousands into Austria. Fog turned to drizzle then freezing rain, pelting the refugees. István wondered what propelled these people to depart in trucks, tractors and carts, on foot, and walk hundreds of kilometres from Budapest carrying only a suitcase or a cloth grocery bag. Some women wore muddied pumps and fur coats, matted like drenched animals. Children whimpered, their legs tired and listless. Elderly men wept openly, their faces a confusion of dread and wonder, dragging their feet. Even so, István envied their courage. Why were they leaving and not he? Did they know something he didn't? Was it fear or stubbornness that prevented him from agreeing with Teréza, to pack their few possessions and run?

Underneath the foodstuffs provided by the peasantry and the first-aid supplies donated by the Austrians, István hid munitions in the truck bed. Their original source remained undisclosed. He covered the cache with heavy woollen blankets given to him by the Red Cross workers. Before departing he bid them farewell with firm handshakes.

"*Danke*," and, "*Auf Wiedersehen*," he replied with a well-copied accent, endeavouring to be precise in everything he did. Someday he might need to speak German again. Reversing his vehicle, István girded himself for another trip into the heart of the Revolution. He'd made this trip half a dozen times over the past two weeks, but now was not the time to take anything for granted. He could smell dank smoke on his fireman's uniform. It needed a wash, but he'd spent precious time early in the morning servicing the cargo truck. Nothing mattered but that it ran smoothly for the journey. He knew from his years of training as a fireman that disaster could come from only one moment of inattention.

Arriving in Budapest in the late afternoon, István recalled the familiar scent of destruction from the first time he had entered the capital, nine years earlier, then in his early twenties. Now as then, the city smelled wet, clay-like and stannic. Buildings still slated for repair were knocked down to their knees. Some trees stood, reaching for a sun banished behind clouds, their branches prickly from winter's harsh winds, while other trees were broken at the waist, folded in half, their limbs dangling.

As the wind picked up, forcing puddles and pedestrians onward, István drove into Buda Castle District. Once again he passed through the iron gates of the Hospital in the Rock and parked at the secret door. István knocked in code. Minutes later he was greeted by the red-headed nurse who no longer bothered to fix her hair. Every time he made a delivery, she looked at him through strawberry strands like a hero with the power to transform her predicament. He wanted her. He could feel his appetite rise; the need for food, safety and sex in times of danger sent blood pulsing to his loins.

His previous visit did little to prepare him; the hallways were littered with the wounded, and the smell was ghastly. After handing off the bulk of his legitimate supplies to the hospital, he drove the secret munitions to the Kilián Barracks. The corner of the building was lobbed off; an arrested avalanche of bricks spilled into the intersection. Several hundred windows were entirely shattered. Csoki stood smoking at the front entrance, like he owned the joint. He looked as battle-worn as the building itself. "We seem to have lost our front door," he called out cheerily.

"Should I let myself in through the back?" István joked.

"Only if you plan on staying and picking up a gun."

István looked away.

"A promise to family is always cursed," Csoki said, smiling wide.

"You have a memory like a steel trap."

"We aren't done yet; you know that?" Csoki tapped his foot.

"How would I know that?"

"Something's in the air." Csoki drew on his cigarette. "We could sure use more of what you've got in the back of your truck."

"I'll do everything in my power." They unloaded the munitions. István bid Csoki farewell, climbed into his vehicle and headed for home.

It had been thirteen days since two hundred thousand Hungarian protesters had taken to the streets of Budapest demanding a democratic system and the withdrawal of the Russians. Thirteen days since István read the astonishing headline in the morning paper.

He waved to friends and fighters on his way out of

Budapest as he returned to Szombathely to his wife and son. Now that he knew the faces behind the rebellion he felt a rekindled grudge towards the constraints of family.

And you still want to fuck that red-haired nurse, don't you?

Through his windscreen, an alarming image grew on the horizon. In the space between dusk and dawn, between light and dark, the forms came into focus. A row of Soviet tanks so long he couldn't even begin to count them. Hundreds and hundreds of them, in one long row. The sight was so spectacular, at first he didn't register the implications. They moved in the opposite direction, towards Budapest. It was really happening. A traditional military attack to quell the Revolution. "Jesus Christ!" He pressed the gas pedal to the floor. His palms grew hot on the steering wheel while the mist peeled off his windshield.

You're going the wrong way.

István's mind whirled as he sped farther away from the capital. Farther from Csoki and the Kilián Barracks, farther from Corvin Alley and the red-headed nurse, farther from the centre of the fighting. Farther from the young fighters who within hours would engage in the battle of their lives.

He screamed to the window, to the wind, to the road ahead of him.

When his vision was blurred by tears, he turned left onto a country road, away from the tanks that stippled the landscape. Pulling over, he wept, his forehead on the wheel.

Hours later, when he pulled quietly into Szombathely's sleeping streets, Soviet tanks already dominated the town square. With the Austrian border only kilometres away, Soviet special forces had moved quickly, securing this viable stretch of country. István knew to take precautions; he took back alleys the rest of the way home as the sunrise forced its way through the clouds. Steam lifted off the asphalt and the hood of his vehicle.

He walked the rest of the way, checking in all directions as he approached the pale yellow adobe house he and Teréza called home. The iron gate made a sound louder than he wanted when he shut it behind him.

When he entered the bedroom he sensed that Teréza was awake.

"You're safe," she said, as István entered the bedroom wearing only his briefs. "I've been up all night." Teréza pulled back the covers, inviting him in. "What's happening in Budapest?"

István curled into her diminutive body. She smelled fresh, like face cream. Lilac. She embraced his shoulders. He pressed his face into her soft breasts and let himself be held while overcome by an incredible fatigue and disquiet. He didn't want to tell her about the tanks, but she pulled it out of him anyways.

"Do you wish you were still in Budapest?" she asked.

He didn't know how to answer.

When morning broke and István stepped out onto the street in his uniform on Hungary's fourteenth day of freedom, the world had been transformed. From the kitchen, Teréza heard an elderly neighbour call out to him, "Take off your armband, István. The Russians have attacked Budapest."

He came back inside. "I'm turning on the radio," he said, as Teréza bathed the baby in the sink. The Communists had taken back the main radio station in Budapest. István fiddled with the dials and managed to find Rákóczi Rádió, still operating from the roving bus.

The reception was poor, but they heard that two thousand Russian tanks had penetrated Budapest at three o'clock in the morning, along the Pest side of the Danube River. The Soviet army had secured all bridges, and by five o'clock artillery fire rang throughout every district of Budapest. When he heard about the airstrikes, István dropped his head. When the announcer spoke of Prime Minister Nagy's final plea to the nation and to the world, declaring that his government would remain at its post while Soviet forces attacked, his voice was brittle and fatigued.

István changed the station. On another frequency Radio Free Europe continued encouraging, "Keep fighting, keep fighting. Freedom is afoot! The West is coming to help you. Hold out." István and Teréza couldn't look at each other. The news was unbearable.

"No one's coming," István said, turning to his wife. "They've raised our hopes while they sit on their hands. We're the ones covered in blood."

She opened her blouse and offered her breast to her baby. The little one latched on as they listened to Budapest being pounded from her hills. The young fighters were no match for the two thousand tanks that had been blasting the city since dawn.

"It's so pathetic to keep believing when you know it's all lost," said István. "I feel like I spent my whole life believing in what I can't have."

Of late, this was the most István had divulged to Teréza about his innermost feelings. She wondered, what were all those things that he couldn't have?

Rákóczi Rádió rebroadcast Kossuth Rádió's final plea:

"This is the last broadcast to the free world. Nations of

the world, the last flames of Hungary's thousand-year history are quickly being snuffed out. The Soviet army is attempting to batter us. Shells and tank destroyers are lumbering across Hungary. Our mothers, our women, our daughters are in danger. Save our souls. S.O.S.! S.O.S.! This could be the last time Free Hungarian Radio is heard in Hungary. Nations of the world, please listen to us! Help us. Not with advice. Not with words. But with bodies. Don't forget that we cannot stay the barbaric Soviet aggression. The next sacrifice will be you. Please help us! S.O.S. Nations of the world, in the name of truth and freedom. Our boats are sinking, our flames are being extinguished. Hour by hour the shadows will be darker in Hungary. Please listen to our cry! Extend your hand of friendship! Rescue us! Help! Help! S.O.S.! God be with you and with us!"

István held his head in his hands.

"Let's go." Teréza surprised herself.

"What do you mean?"

"Let's go to Austria." She popped her nipple from Zolti's little mouth. He looked up at her in surprise.

"Don't be ridiculous."

"We could go. Right now."

István laced his fingers. She knew the signs of opposition.

"We could have a life. Think about your son," Teréza began to plead. "Come. Right now!"

"Don't you love your motherland?"

Teréza laughed aloud. "Since when did you commit yourself to defence? You didn't want to fight before."

"What are you talking about?"

"When you hid."

"Hid? Hid what?" István kept his eyes down.

"Under a false identity. You registered as a Jew, no?

When the Germans were defeated and the Russians started rounding up the collaborators? The Arrow Cross."

István's face turned pink while she waited for him to reply.

"What the hell are you making up?"

"You mentioned something about it." She felt low bringing it up this way, but she needed fuel for action.

"I never did any such a thing." István looked confused, almost panicky. Like he was about to blow a fuse. "Where did you get this idea?"

"We can make it out if we go now," she persisted.

"I demand to know!"

"We can bring the rest of our families out in time. If we go now. Please." Something like hope was swelling in her breast. Zolti felt it and gurgled happily.

István turned off the radio, smoothed the hair on top of his head, got up and began to pace.

"Please," Teréza said weakly, losing confidence in her plan. "Let's go now. Let's leave Hungary."

He wouldn't look at her.

Neither Teréza nor István knew what to do with themselves, so Teréza started cooking onions and István took apart the radio. Teréza didn't ask why.

SEPARATION
1957

WAYFARER

1957, Summer.

István furtively admired the beautiful women. They'd curled
and backcombed their hair for the occasion, applied make-up
and dressed in their nicest frocks. None would be changing
their attire for the next two weeks. On August 5th, 1957,
István, along with all the others heading for Canada, donned
his best clothing. His only suit, donated by the Red Cross
upon his arrival in the camp, had pleated trousers, wide legs
and cuffs. The fabric, with threads of mustard and olive, had
sheen to it, and the blazer that came down to his mid-thigh
had only one button. With it he wore a toffee-coloured tie and
white shirt, which he had pressed himself. In his suitcase, no
bigger than a briefcase, he carried a casual change of clothing,
pyjamas and a few undergarments. With the small amount of
money he'd made in Austria repairing vehicles, he scraped
together enough to buy himself chic sunglasses with plastic
trapezoidal frames and sturdy arms.

He'd just seated himself on the train and slipped them on
when a young couple appeared across from him.

"Nice sunglasses," said the young man, several years his

junior.

István tried to pronounce the style in English, "Vayfayrer."

"*Wayfarer*. By Ray-Ban," said the man, offering István a cigar.

"No, thank you. I don't smoke," said István.

The man leaned forward extending his hand. "Bela."

"István."

Bela oozed sex appeal. Beside him was his slender and attractive wife. She smiled exquisitely and winked. She had short, cropped hair in the Communist style, but on this woman when paired with a stylish Western dress, it looked modern and alluring.

She extended her hand to István. "Marika."

"István." He took her graceful hand.

"Did you get them in Austria?" Marika said, examining the sunglasses.

"Yes. I want to take in the vastness of the ocean when it comes time to travel by ship. But if the sun blinds our vision every time we go on deck, it's going to be a long two weeks."

"That particular style came out only last year, in '56," said Bela. "They're revolutionary." Bela winked.

István felt an immediate kinship.

"How is it we did not run into you?" Bela said while kissing his wife's bare shoulder. She wore a sleeveless yellow sheath dress. Classic. And sling-back shoes, the kind that made István sweat under the collar.

"Were you not in the camp?" Marika crossed one leg over the other.

"I was in Traiskirchen for six months."

"That explains it. We were in Kilmer."

"What's your final destination?" Bela inquired.

"I put in a request for Winnipeg," István replied.

Bela removed his fedora, hung it on a hook. Most every other Hungarian wore berets. Bela retained some sense of individuality in the midst of the Socialist conformity, or István figured, he had someone from the West sending him clothing.

"We're heading there too," Bela said. "If it's in the centre of the country, it must be the most important city. We have no idea what we'll find, but we –"

"– can head either east or west easily enough if we don't like it there," Marika finished his sentence.

"My wife has an uncle in Winnipeg. Left Hungary in 1909." István smoothed his hair. He felt burdened and had to erase Teréza, Pista and Feri from his mind if he didn't want to come apart. Those three were his family and none of them by blood. The movement away from them brought on subtle states of panic, which he dampened with indifference.

The temperature soared by eight in the morning. István removed his suit jacket, rolled up his sleeves, stuck his tie in his pocket and loosened his top collar. He had time to neaten up again before his arrival in Canada: two weeks away.

Bela and Marika seemed utterly in love. István envied their state. Youthful and in their late twenties, their shared movements were complete sentences. She rubbed her leg against her husband's. He placed his cigar between her lips so she could take a pull off it. She had a husky laugh for someone so fine. They seemed to have left behind the trappings of their Socialist upbringing and were enjoying the liberated behaviour of the West.

István stirred as the train's whistle blew. Its carriages at full capacity lurched forward out of the Vienna Hauptbahnhof. Women sang Hungarian folksongs, and the men whistled in accompaniment. István joined in at whim, his passions selective. The joyous mood continued well into the day and across Austria to Sankt Pölten, Linz...István read the signs out loud. They were given ham and smoked cheese sandwiches and hot coffee with cream and sugar.

They were in Switzerland by midnight, and Marika had her head on Bela's shoulder, sinking into his body. István and Bela continued to cover every subject: war, death, religion, politics, brandy, war tunes, poetry, cars, world affairs, latest inventions, distances between places, populations. Censorship. Displacement. Real history, fabricated history. How they'd escaped Hungary. Neither man had ever talked so freely.

The carriage grew quiet. The lights had dimmed.

"I bet there are ÁVO on this train." Bela whispered, a tinge of intrigue to his voice.

"Likely," István said. "I'd like to murder them." He was wide awake, yet his watch read two-thirty. He didn't want to miss anything though there was not much to see of Switzerland in the pitch black. They were passing through mountains for all he knew.

Throughout the next day the train made its way through France. István saw it first: Versailles Palace with its gold decorated exterior.

"That's where they signed the Treaty of Trianon. That's where they destroyed us," Marika stated, matter of factly.

Within seconds the outrage spread throughout the carriage and the length of the train. Transformed from sleeping mummies to hysterical hyenas, the refugees began booing. They opened their windows, shook their fists, hollering at the top of their lungs. "*Nem. Soha!*" No. Never! Soldiers accompanying the refugees stood watch but didn't intervene. "*Nem. Soha!*" No Never! Bela joined in.

How sorry István felt to witness elderly refugees crying. They had lost countless relatives to Romania, Czechoslovakia, Yugoslavia and Austria when the treaty had carved up Hungary after the First World War. What a painful reminder it must have been for them to view the scene of the Trianon crime at a time when the Soviets had once again squashed them. Now they were fleeing their homeland. Salt in a wound.

"*Nem. Soha! Nem. Soha! Nem. Soha!*" It could have turned into a riot, but the passengers did nothing more than yell their protest until the palace was but a golden speck in the distance. The rest of the trip lost its festive mood; they were heading for the unknown, for Canada. For a country István assumed had known nothing but freedom. The idea was almost unimaginable to him.

"I want to meet your wife someday," said Bela.

István felt a lump form in his throat. How easily he cried, sometimes. Was he crying out of sadness or for strength? Or because some part of him shed tears for his unworthiness? The train rocked him from side to side. After a long pause, he replied, "She's pretty. And fiery."

"I can imagine. And your son?"

The lights went out in the carriage. "I can't remember what he looks like," said István.

"Already?"

"Already."

István was now eight months gone and Teréza felt gratifyingly reckless. She no longer cared who watched her, in spite of the fact that there was an entire department at the County Council dedicated to spying on workers and she knew they knew she'd begun to attend church. She could do what she wanted, disobey resolutely because nothing could hurt more than the break-up of her small family.

At fifteen months Zolti walked eagerly by Teréza's side. They held hands and together kicked at stones and walked around puddles. He ran into her open arms and threw himself at her legs with the force of a small cannonball.

She took Zolti to a different church every Sunday morning in various districts of Szombathely, to neighbourhoods where no one knew them. Taking the tram was adventurous for her son who even at such a tender age exhibited a level of curiousity akin to his father's. Like István, Zolti examined objects closely, staring at them as though they'd reveal a mystery. If forced to relinquish something before he had found every way to relate to it, he flew into a tantrum. His outbursts upset Teréza, and she took to using a stern tone at such times. She'd grab him by his upper arms, get down on her knees and look him straight in the eyes.

"Make a positive example of yourself," she'd say. "We have everyone to impress and no reputation left to lose. And remember, God is watching you."

Whether he understood this or not, Teréza induced his mind to play two parts: one that presented the perfect picture to the outer world, and the other to fight for autonomy in clandestine ways. Eventually she would need to explain to him that certain things he said outside of home could get them in trouble. She was aware that most parents had "the talk" when their children reached the age of eight, swearing the child to secrecy. It involved telling their youngsters that everything they'd learned in school about politics and history was a lie. That Stalin and Rákosi were both murderers and that the current Party Leader, Kádár, was but a milder version. Because the Revolution would never be taught or mentioned in school or in public, Teréza wondered if she could wait until Zolti was eight. If she couldn't talk about the Revolution, how could she explain to her son why his father had left?

Well into the summer, when Teréza was still receiving letters from Traiskirchen Camp, she wrote her responses on Saturdays during her lunch breaks at work.

Her fingers moved rapidly over the keys, barely keeping up with her thoughts, like a stream rushing over stones. At home she eagerly checked her mailbox every day, knowing full well that a letter came only every two weeks. The habit of checking made her a little crazy, but touching the lid of the mailbox, even if empty, connected her to him a little bit each day.

"Look at your father's beautiful handwriting," she said to Zolti, as though she'd never seen it before. Holding Zolti with one arm, she held up the letter with the other, far enough away from his curious, flailing grasp as not to let the precious letter tear. As she read, he made little grunts and sounds, as though giving instructions on how she should reply.

One day they received a package from Austria: a tin of cocoa, a pair of black and white two-toned patent leather shoes, and an infant sleeper in white cotton with pale blue piping and elastic around the legs. She adored the soft fabric of the little suit and the fine quality of the sewing.

She searched the package to see if István's letter had been tucked somewhere between the tissue paper. There was nothing there. Teréza found the absence of a note odd and unsettling, like István was paying a debt.

When András and Juli arrived that weekend, she dressed Zolti in the suit.

"What a handsome little devil," Juli remarked. "If I didn't know better I'd say he was fathered by a Gypsy – look at the mischief in his eye."

Teréza looked at her. "How dare you say such a thing! You can't make bacon out of a dog. You know very well István was just as mischievous as a child. He was the daredevil of the village."

"Let's not quarrel with our own shadows!" András dropped his parcels.

Her siblings surrounded her and Zolti with hugs and kisses and brought seeds, walnuts, cheese and salami from the Central Market in Budapest.

The same afternoon, Kati arrived from Györ in a playful mood, skipping up the walk as Teréza threw open the door. She greeted her youngest sibling with open arms. "How is it that nothing ever troubles you?"

"I don't take risks, hence trouble never follows."

"Why does this whole family talk in sayings?" Teréza shook her head.

Kati scrunched up her face and stuck out her tongue. "I have no ambition," she laughed at herself. "I'm no further ahead nor behind since the Revolution," she said, mocking the steps of the *Csárdás*, dancing with the verve of a wind-up toy. She broke into fits of laughter. Juli caught it too. Then Teréza, then András, till they all bent over at the waist, like old people, snorting and chortling, forgetting why they were laughing in the first place.

Teréza arranged a faded tablecloth on the kitchen table

and dusted the entire fabric with flour while her sisters set to making strudel. András ground poppy seeds for filling, his sturdy arms cranking the handle of the tabletop grinder faster and faster, the table wobbling in protest.

Teréza moved about the small kitchen efficiently, impishly bumping her body up against that of her siblings, pulling out knives, cutting boards and bowls. She smacked their bums with wooden spoons. She chopped walnuts and Kati pitted cherries, popping every third one in her mouth.

"Hey, hey!" András horned in. "Save some for the strudel!"

"Your tongue's already magenta!" Teréza swiped the cherry bowl from under Kati's hands. Kati tried grabbing it back, but Teréza ran circles around the table, Kati in hot pursuit. Juli yelled at them to stop while she stretched the paper-thin dough over the tablecloth, from corner to corner of the table, trying not to rip it.

Giggling, Teréza didn't notice Zolti tailing them clumsily; his baby limbs quickly gave out when he attempted to speed up. It was too late by the time Teréza reacted and Kati buffered him. His little head crashed into the table leg causing Juli to swear and rip the strudel dough. Teréza scooped him up, kissing the lump quickly forming on his forehead. Zolti wailed louder.

"He looks just like you when you cried as a baby!" András said to Teréza, positioning his face in front of Zolti's, mimicking the boy's pout. "In fact, I remember a horn on your forehead in exactly the same spot."

Zolti stopped crying.

"It never fails." András chuckled. "When I made the same face in front of you, Teréza, you stopped crying too. Your son's a carbon copy."

"I still want to know how he got such dark hair," added Juli, reassembling the torn strudel, her fingers pecking at thicker sections, removing excess dough, and filling new holes with motherly frustration.

"The walnuts are on the stale side," Teréza said, as she pulverized the last of the mound.

"I'm surprised you found any at all. You should have seen the lineups in Budapest," Juli said, dappling the dough with cherries and powdered walnuts. "There were barely any left by the time we made it to the front of the line."

"And yet, our glorious new leader says the shortage economy's over. Kádár's trying to show us how much better life is going to be under his leadership." András clapped his hands together theatrically, just once.

"They have to keep us happy now," Kati remarked, looking over Juli's shoulder as she carefully rolled the strudel into logs. "All those who voted with their feet are going to be writing home about what's available in the West."

"What can you tell us of István?" András asked.

"He says he's making pocket change repairing vehicles. He alluded to some terrible incident involving a young man in the refugee camp, but he gave me no details. You know the way he is. He sets me up to get curious and then withholds the meat of the information. Drives me crazy. But he wouldn't tell me how he's really feeling, not even if he was tortured." Teréza rolled her ankle.

"How are you managing without him?" Juli asked, wiping her floury hands on Teréza's borrowed apron.

"We're getting by. But I feel like a deflated balloon. I feel flat until I hear from him. It's a feeling I have never known."

While Zolti made vowel sounds and slapped the arms of his highchair and Teréza and her siblings sat quietly, the kitchen began to fill with the scent of baking cherries and caramelizing sugar seeping from the insides of the strudel.

András pulled out a camera. He'd found a colleague at work who owned one and was willing to part with it for a day. "Can you put Zolti by the doorway? We'll send István a photo of his son in his new suit. That should cheer him up."

The snapshot would catch Zolti snuck halfway out from behind the bedroom door, tentatively looking up at his mother, just out of the frame, with worry in his eyes. The corners of his mouth turned downwards.

Dearest István,   *1957. VII. 20.*

For your upcoming name day and thirty-second birthday (I know it isn't for a month, but in case it takes forever for this letter to find you) we are sending you a piece of yourself: your son's hair. This way you will always have him close. You can see in the enclosed photograph that his hair was getting so long he was starting to look like a girl. Strangers were asking after the name of my daughter. It was rather cute, it suited him, but a boy should look like a boy. Zolti cried so hard when I first pulled out the scissors. His chubby cheeks were as purple as plums. He thought it was going to hurt. I told him hair doesn't hurt when you cut it. I don't remember reacting that way when I was a child. Do you? I had at home 4 eggs and a tiny bit of sugar, so I mixed up a little treat for him. He forgot about his "hurting hair."

We wish you great health of mind and spirit. The future is so uncertain. But you can be certain of our love. I wish you a happy day, as happy as it can be.

I kiss you with love, Teréza

★

"This way, István!" Marika grabbed his arm. "Don't get left behind. We're travelling together. Remember?"

The last leg of the journey had dragged. István had slept five hours in two days and felt as though his brain was floating outside his cranium, somewhere out there on the sea, as though he was already on the ship, dizzy and disoriented. Thank goodness for hot coffee, he thought, and another sandwich as they disembarked in Le Havre.

The newness of it all, the lyricism of French, the contemporary, modern architecture, the massive group of them rounded up and directed onto buses, the crowd that had gathered to watch them, waving, all of it buoyed István. The sensation was a kind of amnesia to all that had come before. He couldn't feel Teréza anymore, only the weight of her disappointment.

They were bussed to the ocean liner, the *Ascania*, an Italian-style passenger ship. Hundreds of Hungarian refugees were escorted to the dock. The French were still waving and cheering. What had they done to deserve this? István marvelled at the sight.

Bela grabbed his other arm.

Climbing the gangplank, life surged through István again, unexpectedly.

"Someone looks happy," said Marika, turning to look at him.

"Come on, old man," Bela said with a cigar between his teeth.

"Why does everyone call me an old man?" István shook his head.

Once he found his cabin – he'd been assigned to bunk

with three other men – he met Marika and Bela on the uppermost deck of the ship.

The view of the war-destroyed city now rising from the ashes was astounding from this height. Le Harve was a new metropolis of reinforced concrete and polished structures, built with uniform regularity and interspersed with towers. Dozens of cranes rotated on their axes, their jigs extending outward, lowering their lifting hooks. István gazed at the large surviving pre-war avenues opening out onto the sparkling sea – it made him giddy. The main thoroughfares of the old city formed a triangle, each angle punctuated by a major building or another stellar tower. He could make out the town hall, several churches and a covered market.

"Fantastic," István said aloud.

"Impressive," Bela echoed his sentiments. "Somehow we got a room to ourselves. We're lucky sods."

At mealtimes, the three of them ate fresh baked bread and drank litres of red wine in the handsome, half-empty dining room, while the majority lay sick, vomiting day in and day out in their cabins. When they emerged days later, they were thin and worn out; attractive women with formerly perfect dos no longer bothered to coif their hair, their curls hung low, limp from exhaustion. Men's suits, once nicely pressed, looked rumpled and dishevelled. István, Bela and Marika didn't feel that much better. Still, they climbed the stairs to the uppermost deck and resolved to resist the nausea by laying recumbent in wooden lounge chairs, basking in the sun, István wearing his Wayfarers, Bela smoking cigars, while Marika crossed her knees. István thought it charming that she yelled messages out to sea, seeing how far her voice would travel.

"Tell me where you are?" she yelled, cupping her hands.

"Are you out there?"

István noticed tears streaming down her face as she turned into the wind. He thought it might have been the salty air stinging her eyes, but Bela, noticing István's quizzical look, leaned into him and said, "There are nine hundred and thirty-two of us on this ship," he said, butting out his cigar. He looked serious for the first time since they'd met. "There should have been one more. She miscarried."

"I'm terribly sorry." István couldn't understand why Bela's loss meant more to him than his own, more than what Teréza was experiencing, left alone with their son. István frequently thought there was something terribly wrong with him that he could feel more empathy for friends and strangers than his own family. He had to change the subject.

The thrum of the engine and the froth of the ocean filled the silence. István felt fatigue overtaking his body. "Have you noticed that there's only one funnel on this ship," he asked, looking up. He dropped his chin towards his chest. His eyelids began to droop.

Bela also looked skyward. "Apparently the ship was badly damaged in '41 in a collision with an aircraft carrier. That's when it lost its second funnel."

Slipping into sleep István remarked, "Fascinating."

He was already dreaming in the shade as the sun warmed his bare feet. In his dream, Lali, who was still alive, jumped from foot to foot on a wide balcony. István wanted to go to his brother but there was no staircase to access it. Out of the corner of his eye István saw Arrow Cross members weaving their way through an assembly below. Feri wept openly for Lali, and István started to panic. Uncle János and Hermina were there with Csoki, encouraging people to sign petitions to allow bananas into Hungary. Mrs. Stalin whispered something in their ears and pointed down at István. Mrs. Stalin was an informer! He couldn't locate Teréza and Zolti anywhere, and the twenty gendarmes who followed him on horseback carried out the orders of Hitler himself. He could hear their hooves beat the cobblestone as he dodged down a narrow alley full of metal lockers. He'd just managed to force himself into a tiny dented locker and was pulling the door shut when he felt Varga on the other side. Heard his breathing through the grate. István's heart pounded under his sternum. His guilt intensified; he hadn't stayed long enough to find his wife and son. He would never be free.

"Wake up, István, wake up!" Marika was shaking him. "There's a storm brewing."

"Come on my friend, time for the lower deck, we're in for a doozy." Bela grabbed him by the shoulders. "Looks like you were having a nightmare."

"And you're sweating." Marika touched his forehead.

"Come to our cabin," said Bela. "We can batten down the hatches and ride out the storm. I'll find a bottle of wine. Better if we're in good humour if we're about to be tossed around."

As the storm shoved the ocean liner from side to side its walls creaked; the ship slowed in submission to the forces. In a cabin deep in the vessel, István, Marika and Bela lay like matchsticks on the economical-sized bed, spooning. Humidity hung in the air and moistened their foreheads, their shirts wet against their backs. Marika's yellow dress clung to the dew on her breasts. They agreed to the comfort of lying together when so much had already been lost.

"You don't think like everyone else," Marika said, breaking the silence of their intimate world. The squalls outside grew intense.

"Because I don't believe in an afterlife," István said to the wall. It felt good to be held. He'd not felt so at peace in months.

"That, and you just think differently," she said stroking the nape of his neck.

"I think she means you're an upright kind of man," Bela said.

Marika lay in the middle, curled into István, her right arm around his waist. Bela lay curled into Marika, his right arm around her waist.

"How can you say that? My wife would divorce me if she saw me like this." István felt an upsurge in the storm. "Hang on everyone."

Bela squeezed his wife's breast. Marika laughed.

"For one, you never stole anything from your workplace in Hungary. Two, you wouldn't let us fetch another bottle of wine from the kitchen," offered Marika.

"I can't do it. Someone's paying for all of this," said István.

"The West took it all away from us decades ago," Bela said, kissing the back of his wife's neck. "What's another bottle of wine?"

"I always pay my way," István said, feeling Marika's hand moving across his belly and down under his pants.

"That's what I mean, you think differently," she said.

István grew tense, until her touch relaxed him, and released him.

When Teréza returned home that night and touched the mailbox she received a bitter reward. In his haste, István had forgotten to date the letter. Naturally this detail caught Teréza's eye. Only then did she read on, on a sunny Saturday

July afternoon, resting on the stoop outside her kitchen while Zolti napped inside. She wore a simple housedress, asymmetrical closing, with cap sleeves and indigo flowers on a white background. Around her the blue poppies had multiplied in recent weeks. The first line of the letter took her by surprise; her hands started to shake.

Dearest Teréza,

Canada has offered to take us in, all of us, and we are best to accept their offer. I must continue onward. This means I'll be farther away from you, which breaks my heart. But it also means I shall be able to earn money and within six months I'll have enough to bring you to Canada. Trust me, as I go farther afield.

I kiss you, István

A sickening sensation surged through her body as she reread the letter. By now, István was on a boat many days into a journey that would take her dream of love and togetherness a continent away. He'd made another decision without her. Folding the letter, she felt the sting of resentment but also the unwieldy longings for fulfillment. The thought that the photo and Zolti's lock of hair never made it to István before he left made her want to cry.

RESISTANCE

1951 - 1956

WE CAN'T STOP HERE FOR LONG

1951, March 21-25. Budapest, Hungary

István left Makó on the five o'clock morning train and disclosed his destination to no one. Only twenty-six and he felt old. He had with him a small suitcase. In it, his shaving kit, his pyjamas, a change of underwear, a clean pair of socks, and a book called *Fire Truck Maintenance*. As he boarded, the lights stopped working in his carriage and left the passengers silhouetted in the darkness of morning. *Fire Truck Maintenance* sat useless in his lap.

All the way up to Budapest, he nodded in and out of sleep. He felt unsettled each time he woke. He had managed to become invisible, except to the little blonde girl who, no more than six, kept her almond eyes pinned on István as though she'd discovered the father she'd lost to a work camp.

The train stopped at a poor forgotten village. István pressed his forehead against the cool glass of the window, looking down the platform at the bareness.

It was not even a year since András had been hauled away from their walk together at the Buda Hills, interrogated and beaten. In the shocking aftermath István had grown even more wary.

András later told him that during the beating the ÁVO Secret Police had pressed him for information. Was István opposed to rule by Moscow? Did he ever speak out against the Communists? Was he plotting an undergound overthrow of the government?

The event had triggered a reaction in István, similar to the one he had experienced when he heard about those Hungarians who had managed to escape the country: a sense of implosion, the regret of a missed opportunity, the anticipation of a failed future bound to confinement. But each time he visualized escape there were blank spots he couldn't fill in.

When András wouldn't answer, they gave him black eyes. István's status put his family and friends in danger, which is why he kept his whereabouts secret, just like his plans.

Hey István, can you ask that guy over in the next row for a smoke?

"No!" István said, waking from his lucid dream. Pista's voice followed him not only on trips but across unreal frontiers.

The little girl looked at him like he'd turned into a monster.

István's drowsy thoughts gliding in and out of sleep were nonsensical. If he ever had a boy, István would tell him that the two worst professions he could choose would be a fireman or a policeman. And if his son ever became an ÁVO man, he'd strangle him with his own bare hands. The girl frowned at him as though she knew what he was thinking and buried her face in her mother's armpit.

With mere seconds to spare, he made it from the station to City Hall where Teréza, dressed in a brand new white skirt suit, waited for him. István greeted Hermina, Teréza's aunt, dazzling in a lavender dress, by kissing her hand, and shook hands with her Uncle János, who was outfitted in a shiny grey suit.

István was out of breath when he delivered his apology. "The train had to stop for thirty minutes while a bunch of geese walked across the tracks."

News of the waddling geese put a smile on Teréza's face. He was grateful for it; he'd waited months to see it. A light in her eyes, a welcome benediction. He kissed her hand and her cheek and felt weightless with joy.

"We're up next," Teréza said, admiring him in his sand-coloured officer's uniform, which he wore with a white shirt and black tie. Flustered by his late arrival, István hadn't noticed Teréza's new apparel. He felt like a fool for not complimenting her on her wedding day.

The whole civil wedding transpired in a blur. His nervousness cancelled out everything but the lines he was asked to repeat: "I, Kiss István, take Édes Teréza to be my wife." Yet, fleetingly, he was aware of the scent of Teréza's hair, of wood polish, and the smell of the starched shirt worn by the Council Secretary who married them.

Behind the secretary hung the Rákosi flag, designed and self-named by Hungary's leader Rákosi, Stalin's best pupil.

István had promised Teréza a second real wedding on Sunday in a church, so he wasn't too worried that the first flew by. Church weddings were forbidden under the new system, but he'd prepared himself to take a risk and prove his loyalty to her.

After an uneventful dinner of bread and hen soup, István kissed his new wife goodbye. He left her at the apartment where Uncle János ran a small private tailor shop and she lived and worked as a maid for Aunt Hermina. Regretfully, István made his way to the Kilián Barracks. As a uniformed officer of the Makó Fire Brigade he was required to stay there when in Budapest. At the front office, the new man on duty introduced himself as Sergeant Rigó. "Call me Csoki."

Some years younger than himself, István immediately took to this outgoing soldier with the olive skin and cocksure swagger whose nickname meant "little chocolate."

"István," Csoki leaned in conspiratorially, "If you're here for three nights you're probably looking for girls."

"I've got one thanks, but maybe another time."

Quietly opening the door of a large room where he would bunk with seven other snoring men, István felt cheated. Mentioning to anyone he'd married today would have come across as pitiful; why wasn't he in the arms of his new bride? He pulled the military issue grey blanket over his head, warming his face with his own breath, making believe that Teréza was under the blanket with him. There was nothing he could do about the erection making a tent of his pyjama bottoms.

Teréza rose promptly the following day to meet her father at Nyugati Railway Station. He had travelled this way to attend her proper church wedding on Sunday. When Gyuri disembarked from the train, his palms open, tears sprung from her eyes.

"Come, my daughter," said Gyuri smiling widely. "You are my most beautiful one, Teréza. Like a small pony, you are graceful yet easily spooked."

His peasant dialect hit her ears harder now that she was

used to city speech.

An embrace that once would have felt natural in childhood now felt clumsy. She was conscious of her breasts against her father's body. "Don't say such things," Teréza laughed, taking his face in her hands. "I have always been the runt of the family."

"Well, the runt is our first one to marry. She is the prize."

Mrs. Stalin's mood improved with Gyuri's arrival. Hermina's elderly mother lived at the apartment too – her nickname, Mrs. Stalin, was secretly bestowed upon her by Teréza for her tyrannical behaviour. Perhaps it was the way Gyuri kissed her hand or complimented the shade of her cardigan – robin's egg blue – that the old woman decided to show some decency.

Emerging from the sewing room, Uncle János called out, "Little brother!" The two siblings wept when they saw each other. A German war and a Russian occupation had separated them for ten years. Teréza saw it all in their eyes and the delicate way they touched each other's skin to see if they were still human.

The next morning, Teréza awoke with the sun streaming in the sewing room window, the room that doubled as her quarters. She was marrying on Easter Sunday, the holiest day of the year, the day Jesus rose from the dead, a day of hand-painted eggs and sweet baked *kalács*. For the ceremony she chose the pale yellow cathedral on Nagymező Street with the tasteful grey-and-white interior. They could walk to this one separately, in groups of two, in less than a quarter of an hour. The ÁVO secret police systematically stopped groups, three or more people who journeyed or collected in any public place.

The priest at St. Teréz Church agreed to hold their wedding at eleven o'clock at a little side altar. He had not yet been arrested, so he continued to bless the unions, births and deaths of his flock.

Hermina's twins watched awestruck as Teréza slipped on her wedding dress in front of the long mirror in the sewing room. She pulled up the side zipper of the knee-length orchid pink dress Uncle János had made her. A fine narrow belt pulled in its A-line skirt. Decorative covered buttons ran down from the neckline to the sternum. Edging the cap sleeves and the neckline, the soft cotton lace added youthfulness to the dress. As she slipped on her shoes Teréza could hear András telling jokes in the hall. Her sheer stockings felt smooth inside her beige kitten heels as she raised herself up on her arches, just a little, to get some height.

She turned to face the twins. "What do you think?"

The girls squealed, jumping side to side, their blonde curls bobbing higgledy-piggledy.

Hermina peeked in the door. "Beautiful," she said. "András's here. It's time."

Her brother poked his round face in the door while Teréza buttoned up her coat.

"You must be a foreigner," he said.

She smiled at him. "Why?"

"Because your coat fits you. You didn't buy it in a state shop."

She laughed. "Or I have a very good tailor."

Hermina herded her squealing girls out of the room.

"Where's István?" András asked.

"He's meeting us at the church."

"He must really love you to take such a risk."

Teréza dropped her head and breathed in. "God will protect us. A miracle happened on Easter Sunday."

"Either it will be a miracle or else we'll land in prison for painting eggs."

In the hallway Uncle János outlined the plan: Teréza would walk with her father along Eötvös, turn right on Podmaninczky, left on Nagymező to Király. András and Uncle János would leave five minutes later and walk along Eötvös, Podmaninczky, turn left on Jokai, right on Andrássy, to Nagymező to Király. Hermina and Mrs. Stalin (each with a twin) would walk 50 paces apart along Eötvös to Andrássy, the ring road to Király, then to Nagymező. István would be waiting around the corner.

"Only Andrássy is no longer Andrássy, Uncle. It's Sztálin Street," András said. He was always the one to correct mistakes, Teréza thought, because only he could say things without scorn in his voice.

"It will always be Andrássy to me," Uncle János said, reaching for his fedora.

Mrs. Stalin scowled. "The corrupt money-hungry bankers, landowners and aristocrats who built Andrássy Boulevard can go to hell. They robbed us like the Communists are robbing us now. I'm leaving," Mrs. Stalin huffed. "It will take me the longest to get there." She grabbed the hand of the smaller twin and left.

"Are István's parents coming?" Gyuri asked.

"His mother wouldn't permit his stepfather to travel to Budapest. She said it would be too dangerous," Teréza said, resentment in her voice. Her father had made the trip; why couldn't Feri? Teréza admitted only to herself that she somehow willed the absence of István's family at the wedding.

When István griped that his family didn't give a damn about showing up, and that Pista had drunk all his money away and was incapable of affording a train ticket, she didn't offer István any reassurance. Her objective to separate István from his roots was twofold. First, he'd come from an ill-mannered, foul-mouthed mother. He hadn't learned all his vocabulary from Pista. Why did the world need more expletives? Secondly, she knew that his mother chose favourites, and that to this day it pained István. Teréza could never forgive a woman who chose one child over another.

Living in Budapest had taught Teréza the difference between rabble and the cultured class, and she couldn't imagine István's mother or maybe Feri and certainly not Pista in the city. Her criticisms of country bumpkins didn't extend to her own parents, though, whose love and goodness and generosity she felt exempted them.

Out on the sidewalk, arm in arm with her father, Teréza felt the signs of spring. The sun felt warm against her back this early in the morning, yet small mounds of snow still rested in shady areas. Like little Greenlands, she thought. She'd learned in school about this far-off undeveloped island. It captured her imagination how during the war Greenland declared its independence when Denmark fell under the control of the Nazis. She'd wondered how they could declare self-governance and Hungary could not. In her ten-year-old mind Hungary, with its isolated language, was just as much of an island.

As they passed by Russian soldiers, their ornery hangovers lingering from their Saturday-night drinking binges, she could sense her father's unease. Teréza spotted two ÁVO men, and her heart jumped to her throat.

"Look, father." Teréza pointed away from the ÁVO men.

"What?" Gyuri asked.

"Nothing. Just look that way at nothing," she whispered in his ear.

"Why would I look at nothing?"

"Because there's nothing there to look at."

"I understand now. You've become skillful at this, my daughter."

Teréza looked at her father's profile as they strolled and smiled up at him.

Gyuri's lip quivered. "You will be happy. István promised me he'd never leave you."

"When did he promise that?" Teréza nudged her father around a corner. "Turn this way."

"When he came to ask for your hand. He's in love with you. I can tell."

Her heart fluttered. "How do you know for certain?"

"A man can tell the way another man feels way down in his soul when he says the name of the woman he loves."

She wanted to believe it. In her life, there had been none other than István, yet she knew enough about how men behaved: the Russian soldiers that raped her mother and then her village, the ones in Budapest that had their way with Klára and the ÁVO police who nearly did the same with Teréza in the hills. Men were wild beasts in need of taming. And they ruled the world.

"Listen, my child," said Gyuri, pulling Teréza closer. "Before you promise your life to this man, I share with you something you must lay to rest. We are in a time when war makes every man choose a side and turns him into what he isn't."

Teréza hoped their footfalls would cover the sound of his voice.

"István was in the Arrow Cross. From what I know he never earned a uniform. But as you well know, we who silently backed the Germans out of necessity now have a dirty past. So forgive your husband many times over for the acts he has committed. War makes cowards of many. Not everyone can be a hero."

She wasn't sure why her father was speaking of these things on this morning. Had he picked up on her low niggling presentiment? Or had he recognized her fear and disdain for violence and sought to drown it with silence?

Her heart beat against the buttons of her dress as her father led her to the tree opposite St. Teréz Church. She scanned the street, waiting for several people to pass by.

"Now," whispered Gyuri.

They bolted across the street to the small side entrance. She held her father's thick, clammy hand. His neck was turning red, the flush rushing up to his chin. They heaved open the cumbrous wooden doors. Inside, the quiet was staggering. Teréza's body, flooded with anxiety, calmed as soon as she breathed in the aroma of rose. Incense. She passed beneath the ornate wrought iron inlay in the archway, still clutching her father's hand. Together they dipped their fingers in the cool holy water, crossed themselves and thanked God for delivering them safely. They walked under the three-tiered sparkling chandelier that had miraculously survived the war. Gyuri looked up in awe. Sun poured through the lofty windows and illuminated the main altar in white light. Teréza longed for this divine tranquility, present only in God's house.

Blessing the foreheads of the twins with holy water, the priest didn't notice Teréza arrive. Over by a small side altar, István stood smiling as he waited for her. She felt immense longing. So handsome, he glowed. With his thick ginger hair brushed back off his forehead and soft full lips, under the glow of the stained glass he seemed to be tearing up. She was remorseful for her critical, mistrusting thoughts. She did, she did feel his love.

The priest turned, his face worry worn, and motioned to Teréza and her father to approach.

The tranquility vanished when the priest informed her it was already past eleven. She humbly apologized, realizing only then she had arrived late. Her mind found others to blame: she couldn't get her father to walk any faster, Uncle János should have determined the walking routes the night before. She spun around. Where were Uncle János and her brother?

Men did everything half the speed of women. She had tired of pointing out their unfinished business. It made her want to scream: a cupboard door left open, a rag unwrung, a pail of water filled at the well but not carried inside. Why the hell couldn't men finish their business? And here she found herself again dependent on the pace of men. Had she idealized the males of her family? What confused her more was how she could swing so easily between adoration and hate. Her sister Klára was right. It happened on a dime. A mechanism she had no understanding of.

"Reverend Father, can we wait just another few moments for my brother and uncle?" She glanced at Hermina who forced a smile.

The Father nodded and shook his head here and there to mean yes and no.

Delays under a dictatorship never equated to good news. Teréza debated; Hermina couldn't go alone, and Teréza couldn't volunteer István to go find them. Visiting a church already presented a formidable risk for him. When he looked at her, his mouth about to form an apology, she placed her finger to her lips and said, "I understand."

Teréza smelled a waft of chicken soup; most likely from the church's kitchen where an old woman was cooking the priest's Easter lunch. She pulled her rosary from her purse and began to pray, discreetly, moving her fingertips along the beads.

"It's God's will that we begin," said the priest.

Resigned, Teréza looked to István, Hermina, and to her father. Everyone nodded reluctantly. Hermina arranged the twins, whose fingers were covered in dried wax – they'd been playing with the holy candles. They held their hands far from their bodies as if they'd had no part in this waxy business. One of the twins asked, her little voice echoing throughout the church, "Is this wax the same as ear wax?"

The only thing missing was a stray dog running up and down the aisle, barking at saints, thought Teréza miserably.

Gyuri tugged on his daughter's arm, pulled her aside. When he was out of earshot of the priest he said, "God's will, my ass. He cares more about his stomach than a wedding ceremony. He can smell his soup!" Walking at a snail's pace he led her back before the priest.

Standing there, Teréza realized she had no bouquet. The ordeal of getting to the church had pushed it from her mind. But she had not resigned herself to no bouquet.

She looked across the aisle at him. István fiddled with his wedding band and Teréza realized they hadn't swapped back their rings after the civil ceremony. She was too late, the priest opened his book and began to recite a prayer.

When Gyuri offered his daughter's hand to István, pride warmed his face. Teréza's fingers fumbled as István's pressed his ring into her hand.

"Pass me yours," he whispered.

He remembered. She smiled and reciprocated.

The priest asked when they had had their last confession.

Teréza answered dutifully, "Two days go."

"Years ago," István admitted, barely audible.

The priest gave István a hectoring look.

Hot shame coursed through Teréza. She couldn't believe it. How had he not thought of this? How could it be happening that on their wedding day, she would receive the Eucharist on her own?

"The rings," intoned the priest, dully moving through his routine.

The delicate gold bands slid easily on their fingers.

The priest made the sign of the cross. That was that.

They turned to each other, Teréza and István. Her fingers rested in his wide hands, and she looked up at him. She saw worry, regret and youthfulness. Hopefulness and caring too, in the fullness of his bottom lip and the warm brown of his eyes, the way they couldn't get enough of her. She searched for love. That came too, a few seconds later, in the form of a genial smile that broke into a gentle laugh. He lowered his mouth to hers. And they kissed deeply for a full, wondrous moment before the impatient priest cleared his throat.

Teréza dropped down to earth and looked back at her family. No sign of András or Uncle János.

Hermina had remained dignified throughout the entire ceremony. Teréza had not seen in her a single impulse to run and search for her husband. But soon afterwards Hermina's mood changed and Teréza felt guilty for the danger she'd put everyone in. She thanked the priest, who precipitously retired to the basement for his Easter meal.

★

István planned their return routes. His bride would be accompanied back to the house by her father. István would scout for Uncle János and András. As he exited, István noticed two men waiting near the church. He panicked and bolted, turned right, walked swiftly in the direction of the Sixth District, sensing one of them turn and follow him. He didn't know if he should slow down or speed up. He felt shattered. They'd been waiting outside the whole time; the bastards had probably been following him since he came down on the train.

"Not so fast," the voice called out.

István stopped. He felt the beginnings of outrage surging down his arms. What was he thinking agreeing to marry in a church? The footsteps approached, a hand touched his shoulder. The smoke of a cigarette wafted by his nostrils. Searching for his ID, he began to turn around.

"That won't be necessary." Uncle János sucked on his smoke.

István let out a laugh that verged on hysteria. "Shit, you scared the hell out of me."

"Wouldn't you know it? A goddamn police parade passed right by the church when we got here. I'm so sorry. By the time they cleared, we didn't dare enter. And one mustn't interrupt a church wedding."

"Let's keep walking. We can't stop here for long." István checked in all directions. Hermina was exiting the side door with Mrs. Stalin and the twins. She saw her husband and smiled in a way that transformed the air around her. It was a smile of relief and joy. It was the happiest István had seen anyone, István realized wistfully. Happier than Teréza on her wedding day.

★

After their wedding dinner, and before they parted for the night, István kissed Teréza long on the lips at the front entrance to Uncle János and Hermina's apartment. She surrendered her mouth completely for the first time and he felt her small teeth with his tongue as he got closer to all of her. Pressed together tightly, he could feel her breasts nestle into his ribs. His body tingled. He hoped hers did too. "Never stop doing that as long as I live." He held her tighter and gasped. "Can you feel it?"

She didn't answer for a long time. "I want to feel, but I can't always."

"Why can't you feel?"

She ducked her head; she wouldn't look in his eyes. Instead, she stroked his cheek. "See you at the station tomorrow at seven."

He nodded and stroked hers.

He circled nimbly down the circular staircase, light on his feet, and blew her a kiss up several flights. She caught it and waved goodbye.

István made his way to the Kilián army barracks near the Corvin Cinema where he would spend his wedding night.

In the register at the barracks, István entered his personal details, leaving another trail. He realized his ID booklet had been newly updated at City Hall: married. Another section of his private life was on file for the Interior Ministry.

He asked Csoki if he could eat something before he found his bunk.

Csoki shook his head. "Sorry, we're still on war rations."

"It's been six years!"

"Disasters repair slowly."

István's hunger extended beyond his stomach; it turned up between his legs as an intractable pulsing in his groin. Who or what could he blame for the fact that on his *second* wedding night, he was still not in the arms of his wife? Why was his body not on top of hers, finding its way between her perfect thighs, and gently, insistently, pushing its desire against the edges of her warmth? Why wasn't she wet and writhing, ready to receive him? Many were to blame, he mused. Whole generations.

István spent another lonely night wondering how this one yearning was denied him even now, and about all the decisions, seen and unseen, made for him by others.

AFRAID TO LOVE ANYTHING COMPLETELY

1951, March 26-31. Budapest, Hungary

Plenty of Russian soldiers got on and off the train. Each time, Teréza grew tense. István noticed a change come over her – she grew pale, her eyes glazed over – and he gently tapped the underside of her shoe with his. In no mood to be playful, she retracted hers, unwilling to reveal what troubled her. What had he done to annoy his bride a day after their wedding? Was she still perturbed about him missing confession and having to forgo receiving the Eucharist? He couldn't ask her, not here on the train, not with so many ears listening. He only hoped that she would have a change of spirit when she saw their new home. He fell silent, a habit-forming behaviour.

Changing trains in Szeged, he carried their suitcases to the next platform. Tired from the long ride, they spoke enough to indicate that one needed a toilet and the other would watch the suitcases. They'd already eaten the fried chicken, pickles and egg bread leftover from their wedding meal, but István was still hungry. His anxieties demanded fuel, his body consumed food as quickly as an engine burned gasoline.

"You don't need anything more," Teréza commented. "Why don't you wait until I make you something when we get home?"

He couldn't break it to her that their room had no kitchen and she'd be unable to cook for them.

The sun still shone when they arrived at the Makó Train Station after five, turning the sky lavender and blood orange.

The look on her face when she stepped into the room eased his famine.

"Very nice," she said, pleasantly surprised. Her hair was limned by the sunset framed in the window behind her; the velvety skin of her twenty-year-old complexion shined.

István had found a spacious room in an old house with high ceilings, sharing a bathroom with two other families. The owner of the house, a gentleman relieved of his wealth by the Germans, the Russians and then the Communists, did his best to let his rooms to decent people though he collected none of the rent. The Communists did.

István's training had taught him how to make the bed meticulously. Not a wrinkle. He'd bought cotton sheets with his meagre savings and an ecru eiderdown, handmade by a peasant woman who secretly earned money on the side. He'd repainted the walls the colour of chalk, hung off-white lace curtains to cover the single window, and hauled in a dark wood armoire and a small table with two chairs.

"How could you afford the furniture?" she asked.

István paused. "Small business owners who can't pay their taxes…"

Teréza finished his sentence, "...their furniture is taken away."

"And the state-owned store sells it for cheap."

She stared at the small polished table and chairs.

You profited off the misfortunes of others.

"If I didn't, we'd be sitting on the floor."

They didn't discuss it; the system compelled everyone to profit off the calamities of others, and everyone went after what scraps they could find.

Teréza sat on the mattress of the cast-iron bed and brushed her hand along the top of the eiderdown. "So soft." She spied a book open on one of the pillows, positioned quite purposefully. "What's that?"

"For you. Your wedding present." István felt a wave of emotion. "Read it."

She glanced at the cover and touched its pages. "Petőfi Love Poems."

"Will you read it to me?" István sat beside her on the bed. "I left it open on a specific page."

She read aloud.

" I'll be a tree, if you are its flower,
Or a flower, if you are the dew-
I'll be the dew, if you are the sunbeam,
Only to be united with you.
My lovely girl, if you are the Heaven,
I shall be a star above on high;
My darling, if you are hell-fire,
To unite us, damned I shall die. "

Teréza's voice dropped as her emotion rose. Her hardness gave way, her softness set free. "I'm sorry," she said to István as he gently guided her to lie down. He lay down beside her, wiped her tears away. "So little has gone right in this life. I'm afraid to love anything completely."

"Let me love you. Let's start there."

For a long time, he touched her only through her dress, and only when she was under the cover of the eiderdown, in the darkness of the room. Sometimes she did not move, and he wondered if she had fallen asleep or if her body had gone still under the watchful eye of the God of shame. He kept telling her how beautiful she was. When she did reply she said, "You can't see in the dark." They fell silent when he moved her dress higher and slipped off her underwear. He felt her head turn. Her body under the covers drove him wild. He could barely control himself. He wanted her drenched, he wanted in, but she was far away. So he took it, with every selfish unmet longing he'd ever felt, he pushed his way in and apologized with every breath and every thrust that released him from his torment.

"You're beautiful," he said again and again.

Next morning, István woke her at six, with kisses on her eyelids.

"I need to make us breakfast," she said, sitting up, rubbing sleep from her eyes as he pulled his pants on in a hurry.

"Get dressed. I have to get us to the barracks. We'll have breakfast there."

"Why can't I just make it here. For us, alone?"

"We don't have a kitchen." He buttoned his shirt.

Her heart sank. No job, no kitchen. "Is that where you eat every day?"

"Yes."

"They've done this on purpose, haven't they?" She shook her head in frustration. Opening her suitcase, she selected a cotton skirt and blouse, and a cardigan.

"Done what?" He pulled on his uniform jacket.

"Divided up homes, rented out meagre rooms without kitchens. The state has made it impossible for us to have independent lives. You're forced to eat where you work, in the state-run kitchens so they can always watch you. We live in a perpetual kindergarten." She pulled on her skirt, zipped it up on the side.

"Come."

"I'm not hungry."

"You need to eat something." His stomach growled loud enough for her to hear.

"I don't want to go."

"Please? I am dying to show off my beautiful wife." István leaned in and kissed her mouth. "Please, hurry."

"Breakfast, lunch and dinner?" She fastened her bra. Her nipples hurt. He'd sucked on them long and hard during the night.

"We can bring some meals home," István offered.

"And eat them cold?" she asked, skeptically.

"Can I button up your blouse in the back?"

"It won't make me go any faster."

"It's not because I want you to go any faster!" he blurted. "For God's sake!"

Teréza glared at him. "What's gotten into you?"

"What's gotten into you!?"

"There's nothing wrong with me. Look at yourself."

"I can't be late for the goddamn political talk, Teréza. They make us attend every bloody morning. Do you think I like it?"

"Stop swearing." She folded her arms and sat back down on the bed.

"And every bloody Monday afternoon. 'Further Political Training.' And once a month, another goddamn Production Meeting to praise the growth of the Soviet System. Do you think I like this?"

"When did your mouth get so foul?"

"I'll come back for you at lunch time." István bolted out the door.

Teréza felt lost. She didn't know what she'd been expecting. Had she just woken from some delusional state in which she believed that love would deliver her from life's afflictions? She berated herself for having been so utterly young and stupid.

She thought about the night before. She had held her legs tight, not because it pleasured him but because she needed to resist the carnal within. God was watching. Her flesh had been contaminated – not like Klára or her mother, or the fifty thousand other women in Hungary – but she'd fused with humiliation as well. She cried soundlessly, convinced this would only ever be a duty. No one had ever told her otherwise. And he only ever wanted to love her. She wished she had something to give.

When István came home to get her for lunch, he brought a *Szabad Nép* newspaper.

"Why did you bring me this? Every single word is a bloody lie." She tossed the paper on the floor.

He picked it up and handed it back to her. "Yes, it is.

We've known that forever. Now memorize a couple of news stories."

"Why would I do that?"

"You'll have to show up for the monthly meeting with me tonight, now that they know about you. There's no way around it. I'll be spoken to harshly if you don't show."

Teréza wouldn't look at it.

"Okay, I'll read to you. Let's see…the government's erected a new bronze statue in Budapest in honour of Captain Ilija Osztyapenkó who arrived with the Soviet Liberators at the end of 1944 and was brutally murdered by the Nazis."

Teréza fussed with a hole in her stocking. "Glad they did away with him."

"The statue stands in a median dividing Budaörsi Road. The four-hundred-and-thirty-five-centimetre bronze holds a flag in its hand."

"I'd vomit on it if I saw it."

"Can you learn the details? Please?" His eyes implored her, and she felt sorry for him. She didn't want to be a harridan.

"A bronze statue," she replied petulantly.

"How high?"

"Dwarfish." She was giggling now. She delighted in torturing him.

"It's four hundred and thirty-five centimetres."

He continued to drill her while she went for her first lunch at the barracks – still lamenting the lack of a kitchen. On the walk, István warned her never to say anything that could incriminate them. Over lunch – a starchy cottage cheese and noodle dish that bloated her – she smiled graciously and greeted the firemen and their wives. She knew that any of them could be informants.

That evening Teréza couldn't see for the cigarette smoke that clouded the meeting room. She couldn't tell the colour of the walls. Almost everyone smoked. Thankfully István hadn't picked up the disgusting habit.

She'd never had to frequent Party meetings before. Ordinary citizens could choose not to join. With that choice, however, came menial jobs with no hope of advancement and certified life-long poverty. Nonetheless, the majority of those who did join the Party still grovelled at factory jobs. At best they got slightly better apartments and a few other perks. Those in uniform, however, like István, had no choice. Their allegiance was expected.

Teréza cringed throughout the boring gathering. She focused on the black mole on the Party leader's nose; it stopped moving only when he dropped his notes. She clapped when someone praised the construction of a new factory somewhere in the country.

István elbowed her to say something. The higher-ups expected her participation. Reluctantly she raised her hand, forced herself to regurgitate what she had memorized.

"A four hundred and thirty-five centimetre bronze statue was erected in Budapest." She paused and waited.

The unctuous Party Leader expected her to say more. She said nothing more. A few claps began to ripple throughout the room. The firemen and their wives clapped in unison.

"Comments?" The Leader said to the assembled group.

Another wife added, "The statue stands in the centre of a median dividing Budaörsi Street."

We're all sheep, Teréza thought. Neither she nor the other woman mentioned whom the statue honoured, an omission that protected their last shred of dignity. Everyone clapped again.

István elbowed Teréza to join in. She clapped easily, because she was clapping for herself. She'd figure out how to resist without anyone having told her. Withholding. If someone reported something, they communicated it with an omission. From these omissions she could figure out whom she could trust by what they withheld from the report. She did however take note that none of the women complained about the lineups to buy cheap, shoddy goods that ran out before the line did or about the fact that feminine products had all but vanished.

At the end of the meeting she sang songs she didn't know the words to; tuneless, bulky, unrefined songs in Russian, abhorring every minute of it.

As they were leaving the smoke-filled room, the Chief Officer pulled István aside. Teréza kept a hold of his arm. Mészáros was ten years István's senior, with bushy black eyebrows – awnings over his eyeballs – his mouth stretched as wide as a frog's, and his upper lip was but a flap of skin. His wavy black hair receded only at the corners of his head. The rest poked forward in the middle of his forehead, like a cat's tongue. Mészáros made no secret that he considered István one of his best, and she had no doubt the display was for her benefit.

"A bright new wife I see." Mészáros squeezed István's arm.

"Yes, she's very bright."

"She could put her talents to use by learning Russian. It'll come in handy when she applies for a job. You know it's a civil offense not to work."

"I'm well aware. Your words are an encouragement to her, sir."

Late that night as they lay in bed, István stroked her cheek and told Teréza he was proud of her for being so smart at the meeting. He wished they could sleep naked, but she wore a nightgown, which forced him to wear his pyjamas.

"You figured it out," he said, as he touched her hair.

"It was my complete disdain of the subject that led me there."

"We need to find you something to do."

"I have no training. I never finished school. All I've ever done is work as a maid."

"You'll have to go back and finish." He lay on his back looking up at the ceiling.

"I haven't the foggiest idea what to study. What can I do in this country the way it is, other than work in a factory?"

"You could learn to be a typist. Get a job in an office."

"That's not a bad idea. I could absolutely do that."

She rolled over and nuzzled him.

"But you'll have to learn Russian before you can be a typist."

"Rubbish! I'll do no such thing. This is still Hungary."

He tickled her until she relented, and her nightgown slid off and his pyjamas did the same. Sweaty and bare, he tamed the colt and helped her feel something again.

The books thudded from desk to desk with the weight of sullied history. Teréza opened her fresh new textbook embossed with the red star and breathed in the smell of fresh ink. And there was Stalin on the very first page, smiling at her.

Teréza watched the Russian teacher's freckled, puffy hand scribbling on the chalkboard.

девушка

The stout woman in ugly flat shoes, her calves as large as loaves of bread, sounded out the word, "*Devushka.*" The imposing letters filled the chalkboard, stern and foreign. "*Devushka.*" The teacher punctuated the first syllable. "*Devushka,*" she pronounced staring through squinty, swollen eyes at a roomful of blank faces. She repeated it twice more when the overall response proved too slow for her liking.

Looks like she came straight from the pig farm, thought Teréza.

Within a week of their arrival, István had enrolled Teréza in night school. He offered his help with the galumphing Russian language. For the first time in her life, Teréza didn't care about her marks. She wanted to fail. Instead of studying, she entertained István with impersonations of the Soviet teacher, mimicking her speech patterns, showing him how the woman rose awkwardly on her toes when writing at the top of the blackboard, like a dog trying to balance on its hind legs. She demonstrated how the woman sat, unable to cross her legs, due to her tumescent calves. This made him laugh.

In return István mocked speeches of the Party Leaders, emulating their pontification. He gestured broadly, his arms stiff like wood planks. He overemphasized words in completely the wrong places and screwed up his face to look inordinately serious. Inevitably it would send them both into peels of laughter. And then, to her growing delight, to the bed where István never tired of her.

The teacher repeated, "*Devushka.*"

Teréza's mulish mouth refused to form the words. Twenty students, ranging from seventeen to forty, repeated *Devushka* like idiots, disorganized sounds dropping from their lips.

"*Devushka!*" The woman said again, this time louder, demanding compliance.

"*Devushka,*" Teréza joined in, her tone lethargic but she could barely suppress her guffaw.

"*Mal'chik! Mal'chik!*" The woman demanded, scanning the room for dissent. She wrote Мальчик on the board. "*Mal'chik!*" she repeated emphatically. The word hit the wall like a cork from a bottle of champagne. The students responded like fizz, glug-glug-glugging out of the bottle but strange sensations shot up in Teréza. Her bubbles erupted like lava and ash and moisture sprung from her pores like sulfur. It took only one word. The image of blood seeping under the bedroom door had her locked in a freeze frame of the past in which she was held captive by violence and death, not of her own making. Boy! Boy! Boy!

YOU TRY SPOUTING THAT
BULLSHIT

1953, March. Makó, Hungary

Teréza had barely returned from a lunch of sliced potatoes layered with cooked egg and sour cream at the office cafeteria when she heard the news.

On the other side of town, István had just finished taking apart a truck's engine while his colleagues completed fire drills. István was up to his arms in grease when Mészáros, the Chief Officer at the Fire Department, came in and made the annoucement. News like this spread as quickly as arrests.

In their separate locations, István and Teréza kept their mouths shut and listened to the chatter with contrived concern. Inwardly, they were ecstatic and could barely contain their glee.

Stalin was dead.

The dictator had suffered a stroke.

"The devil finally took him," Teréza said with a delectable

laugh as she welcomed István at the door that night. "But why not take Rákosi along with him?"

"Love me," he said with abandon and kissed her mouth.

Teréza blushed as he brushed his lips along her neck, her throat, her eyelids. That evening more shackles fell off, but her stockings stayed on. She laughed and gave herself to István's desires, keeping her eyes closed as he kissed his way down her abdomen, down towards her underwear. She contracted slightly with each kiss, a tortuous tickling sensation he tried to temper with softer wetter kisses. "Is this better?" he asked. She tried to answer but couldn't and didn't know why. With his teeth, he pulled at her underwear, and she helped with her fingertips. Then he brushed his lips along her leg, to the arch of her foot, where he breathed warmly through her stockings. Startled, she felt a quickening at her core. The way she felt when he stroked her nipples. He looked in her eyes as he kissed the sole of her foot, moved between her legs when she closed her eyes. When she squeezed her legs together he hardened between her thighs, then he moved closer, pushing ever so slightly. Her body gave way and welcomed him. He rocked against her for a long time, until he could contain himself no longer.

She warned him to pull out in time. "We're not ready for a child."

He groaned and ejaculated on the sheets. She invited him to place his head on her breast. His breathing slowed, and his head rose and fell with her breathing. Something had softened in them both. She wished Stalin could die every day.

The next morning over breakfast she said, "Maybe now that Stalin's dead…" She let the silence grow pregnant with possibility.

"Someone has to kill Rákosi first," István laughed as they parted for work.

Teréza's prospects had changed considerably in the two years since she married István. She'd graduated from high school, completed her typing course and she was seven months into working as a typist at the Guardian Authority where the state handled adoptions. She felt content with her first professional job, and her work rescued István from the agitation that overtook her when she had nothing to do. She could clean their tiny apartment only so many times a week before she was washing the same corner of floor. István had only so many pairs of underwear to iron.

She enjoyed pressing her blouse the night before work and hand-washing her pullover once a week, laying it flat to dry. She relished wearing a pencil skirt to the office paired with low heels, raw-liver toned, the latest Communist trend. Though cheap and mass-produced, these recent acquisitions made her feel guilty. She knew István couldn't afford much more than what they had to spend on rent and essentials.

Teréza had stumbled upon a small sense of importance typing up official documents that helped orphaned children. She worked long hours, but for the most part, her office environment was free of political meetings. Above all else though, she brought to the household a little extra money, and with it, a sense of pride and independence.

With her meagre earnings, she was on her way to the State Department Store where their slogan, "Small Store with Big Selection," blatantly lied. There she picked through dwarfed items designed with the intent to save fabric. Jackets that were sewn too short. Blouses showed up without collars. Pants without pockets. She managed to find one decent-looking, mass-produced V-neck pullover vest for István – the V not too large – and bought it for him as an anniversary present. Unable to wait, she handed it to him, still in its bag, when he got home that night.

"I hate the colour blue," he said, apologetically.

"Since when?"

"Since the ÁVO started wearing it."

She couldn't argue with that. "I'll see if András wants it."

"After they beat him?"

She threw the vest in the garbage.

Very little changed in Hungary after the dictator's demise.

A week after Stalin's death, István complained he would be leaving her for a month-long compulsory Communist training camp, to further his political education. He would leave the day after next.

"There's that word again," she said. "Compulsory. Why didn't you tell me sooner?"

"Don't be absurd," he protested. "They give us no notice on purpose."

She rolled her eyes at the lunacy; Communist governance was based in secrets and lies, on paranoia and control.

"They just told me today I have forty-eight hours to prepare. They've granted me tomorrow off, so I could spend it with you."

"I work tomorrow, like the rest of the country."

"How about you hop on the back of my motorcycle, and I'll take you for a ride out in the countryside. The light's beautiful right now." He'd managed to scrape together enough money to buy himself a motorcycle – another astounding luxury. He'd been dreaming of owning one since Germany had paved the roads in Hungary, an unexpected benefit of invasion. He tried to overlook the fact that it was a Soviet copy of a French moped, with a pitiful two-speed gearbox, a pedal gearshift and telescopic suspension. The whole bike weighed no more than forty-five kilos. A little less than Teréza. But he had something to hop on, to take corners with, to pick up speed on and feel the wind through his hair.

"It'll break holding the two of us." Teréza crossed her arms.

István shrugged.

She told István she feared falling off something that had only two tires. She didn't trust the sensation of being exposed. Truth be told, she didn't want the feeling of metal between her legs, but she didn't tell him that.

Several weeks living without her husband had Teréza savouring how easy it was to keep the house clean. How she could dawdle home on late afternoons like this, and it mattered not if she ate at the barracks or at the table in her bedroom. Duck fat on bread with a beer hit the spot. With some sliced raw onion on the side. She didn't need a kitchen to make a meal like this. A knife and a cutting board sufficed. She would eat the same thing until István returned.

The sun was shining pleasantly on her walk home when an enormous and ever-changing form filled the air overhead, like a giant paintbrush writing messages in the sky, erasing its black calligraphy as it went. She craned her neck. So captivated was she by the flock of starlings that she couldn't properly register what was in front of her when she looked ahead. She slowed her walk.

A man in a uniform. Though he was still just a speck in the distance, the sight unnerved her. In this police state, uniforms were enough to make Teréza moist in her armpits. She'd already broken a sweat from the heat. She wanted to turn, go down another street. Moments without fear were like an eclipse; keenly anticipated but over too soon. They moved too quickly to apprehend. The figure was approaching, steadily. She sensed something familiar about the gait, a recognizable lilt.

"István," she said to herself, half-talking, half-whispering. "Jesus Christ, István," she said a little louder. She sped up, not at all happy to see him. He was supposed to be gone for a month. Frantically, she counted the weeks on her fingers. One, two…two and a half weeks, not a month. He didn't wave or acknowledge her. Couldn't he recognize her? He walked with his head down.

She couldn't call out to him for fear of drawing attention to herself. Or to him. The last steps felt excruciating. Why wouldn't he look up? By the time he did, his face pale and expressionless, she was winded and his full lips had thinned into a seam.

"What happened?" she asked, fear pitting her voice.

"That's no welcome home. Can't you hug me?"

She gave him a feeble kiss, wheeled around and walked in the direction of their home. Once inside she couldn't wait for the explanation as accusations boiled inside her. "So what did you do this time?"

István flinched. "This time? Nothing."

She kicked off her shoes, shoved her feet into slippers and tried to block out the image of two young men, silhouetted by moonlight, shovels in hand. The memory rattled her coherence. "Don't say nothing! You're home for a reason."

"That's exactly it. I didn't do anything. I didn't want to do it."

"Are you crazy?"

"I couldn't do it." He dropped his head into his hands, combed his fingers through his hair and tried to soothe his frustration. He reached for her hand.

"Are you going to tell me what happened?" She tore off her sweat-soaked blouse and stood in her brassiere. She turned her back and put on another blouse.

"They sent me home."

"Because you weren't participating. Why do you always have to be so different?" With diligent jabs she tucked her fresh blouse into her skirt.

"They wanted me to praise that rotten, stinking Stalin!" he yelled.

"Why couldn't you just pretend like everyone else? Make small talk. It was only for a month!" she yelled back, walking away from him.

"You try spouting that bullshit all day, every day, for a month!" István pursued her.

She spun around. They stood nose to nose. "You didn't last a month. Only two weeks."

István tore off his jacket, threw it at the bed like he was trying to put out a fire, his movements a tangle of sleeve and fury.

"Hang up your coat," she called after him as he slammed the bathroom door.

"What are you doing?" She could hear him urinate. "Say something!"

The toilet flushed.

"Leave me in peace," István mumbled.

"There is no peace in this country! You could have given us some peace by going along with it!"

The door opened abruptly to reveal István fuming on the other side. "What about your fucking church? You *know* they're breathing down my neck about my church-going wife. But now it's *my* bloody fault for being different! You're such a hypocrite!"

"When did you lose your faith? Your God? At least you learned something in those two weeks you were away. How to be a Godless Communist."

"God damn it, woman!" He shoved past her, unable to get away from her in the small apartment. He slammed his body down on the chair, clamped his fingers around his skull.

The sound of a sonata drifted through the floorboards from the piano upstairs. The owner of the house never played during the day.

"They're going to fire you," she said, pacing the room.

"Maybe not, now that Stalin's dead."

"They will. The Jew will come for you."

He had to hold himself back from slapping her. "What the hell are you talking about?"

"Rákosi, the Jew. He'll come for you next," she said tilting her head.

He couldn't stand that look, that head tilt of certainty. "How the hell do you know Rákosi's Jewish?"

"Of course he's Jewish. It's common knowledge. All the Soviets are Jews."

"That's ridiculous." István said without looking at her. "Even if they are, it's no wonder, after how the Nazis treated them."

She ignored him. "Rákosi's punishing Hungarians for

what Hitler did to the Jews."

"God, you know everything, don't you?" István got up, shut all the open windows and locked the front door. "You can't say 'Hitler' out loud. Are you mad?"

"This isn't a life!"

"I know this isn't a life! What the fuck do you expect me to do about it?" He grabbed a chair and threw it against the wall.

"Bravo. You're as violent as the rest of the brutes out there. What's happened to you?"

"What's happened to you? You're supposed to help me through this rotten world. But when I try to hug you, you look at me with contempt in your eyes. What do you want me to do? Hatch an escape plan? Do you want to get killed?"

"Yes, you fucking coward!"

"Well, that's just great. Get killed then."

"I will. I'll kill myself." She grabbed her sweaty blouse and marched towards the bathroom.

"That's the spirit. You'd rather die than stick this out. You cowardly bitch."

"Thank you."

"Pray to your rotten God. Maybe he'll take you to heaven."

Teréza slammed the door in his face.

István and Teréza rose according to routine. They proceeded to their workplaces in silent agreement that the pretence of normalcy might stave off the punishment for István's actions. The few colleagues he still trusted seemed to concur and remained conspicuously uncurious about his sudden home-coming.

While István awaited his fate, he continued to take apart engines.

Faster than onions grow, Rákosi became unpopular, and within weeks, István heard that Nagy Imre's name circulated around the country as a possible replacement. Nagy served as Deputy Minister in Rákosi's government but was known to have a softer, more reformist stance. István liked Nagy's soft fatherly features and his round spectacles. The man had an air of decency about him. István viewed the prospect with optimism– a state he hadn't experienced in years – but he knew better than to weigh in at work after his recent transgressions. He was astonished that the ÁVO hadn't yet singled him out.

Before he punched the clock, István collected a voucher for two free movie tickets from the receptionist at work. The week before his two-year wedding anniversary, István had nothing more to offer his wife than a date at the cinema. He didn't even own a respectable suit anymore. He had only his officer's uniform.

He stopped in at the state-owned grocery store. The Hovel, he called it. The shelves, painted steel gray, matched the colour of everything else in the store, including the food. He bought two bottles of beer for the eve of his anniversary. The grim-faced checkout woman in her green uniform pitched the change on the counter, barely extending her arm.

No pleasantries here. Not in the state-owned shops.

"I'd avoid heavy lifting if I were you," István said.

She looked perplexed and returned to filing her nails.

István slammed the door on his way out.

Lucky she's got a goddamn nail file.

His mood sunk as he walked home with two lukewarm bottles in his hand. He was in no mood to convene with Pista, but the disembodied voice persisted like a bad smell.

The only escape is to do nothing.

The thought of nothing sat heavy like a rock in István's heart, a big, heavy rock of meaninglessness. "The reward for nothing is a work camp. I would only get away with nothing for so long."

Four weeks after Stalin's passing – like Christ, everything now was marked before and after his death – the silent celebration had worn off and István was called into the barrack's main office. His number was up.

Chief Officer Mészáros shook his head sadly. "Do you know the fable of the fox, the wolf and the rabbit?"

István glanced at the collection of sweet onions decorating the wall of Mészáros' office, their dried stalks tied with ribbons the colours of the Hungarian flag. In between them Rákosi grinned. "I told it to my brother while he was dying."

"I'm sorry about your brother. Did it happen recently?"

"No. After the war."

"How old?"

"Just a boy."

"And you told him this particular fable while he was dying?"

"Yes."

"Why?"

"So that he would be comforted by a familiar voice."

Mészáros offered István a cigarette and a shot of brandy. István declined both and sat stoically in the chair in front of the Chief Officer's desk.

Mészáros cleared his throat. "There's a bitter battle over in Budapest between Rákosi and Nagy. Nagy has replaced Rákosi as Prime Minister under orders from Moscow. Rákosi, as we know, will maintain his position as General Secretary of the Hungarian Communist Party." He flipped through a file on his desk. "Someone's done a thorough check on you."

István's stomach jumped to his throat.

"Arrow Cross." Mészáros paused for a long time. István's scalp grew hot.

Mészáros continued, speaking affectionately. "We all made bad decisions in our youth. It's worse when we make them when we're adults. You're Jewish? Really? Trying to hide in plain sight, eh?" He shook his head again.

István stayed silent and kept his hands tightly laced in his lap. Sweat rolled down his brow.

Mészáros shook his head again. "István?" He walked around, stood behind him.

István didn't budge. The truth was suffocating.

"I've always been proud of your work. I'd been keen on having you rise higher in the ranks, but now…"

Here it comes…

"…but now this is the ideal time to be relocated."

At first István didn't know how to interpret it, unsure of what "relocated" meant. To a work camp? *Recsk? Kistarcsa?* To prison? He sat emotionless as Mészáros walked around to face him.

"You're a very lucky man, István. Our new Prime Minister has announced that the Council of Ministers passed a resolution calling for the end of internment camps." Mészáros took a seat at his desk and leaned back in his chair. "You have the choice of where you'll go."

István nodded, utterly confused. The sun blinded him as it moved into his field of vision. He felt embarrassed and disgraced before his mentor.

Mészáros stood again, came around, leaned into István's ear and grabbed his collar. "I pulled a few strings on your behalf. I don't suggest Budapest. Go somewhere small where you're less likely to get into trouble. And keep your bloody mouth shut. Unless of course you need to repeat slogans. Then open it. Open it wide. Repeat the bloody slogans. They're watching you now."

"Thank you, sir." István's words caught in his throat.

"Don't mention it." Mészáros released István's collar. "Now get the hell out of here and talk it over with your wife. I want you out of here by the end of the week."

SO, YOU GOT YOURSELF IN TROUBLE

1953, April. Makó & Szombathely, Hungary

Teréza surveyed the layout of their new home in Szombathely, more spacious and brighter than their place in Makó. Her favourite feature was the archway that divided the sitting room from the kitchen. Its architecture reminded her of a church. The rooms had deep, thick windowsills onto which she placed doilies. She planned to add potted plants. Red geraniums. No one had painted over the wooden doors, and she liked that. Natural wood.

With the first day of April spinning around in her new kitchen, Teréza pulled out a cutting board and sharpened a knife, yanked a steel pot from the cupboard and placed it on the stove. She melted lard, grabbed an onion – she'd brought a bag of them from Makó – peeled it with precision and sliced it with accuracy. She slid the sliced onions off the cutting board into the pot and lit the gas flame. Tears streamed from her eyes. Onto the onions she sprinkled a generous amount of paprika, tossed in chopped pork and stirred, then she let it simmer. She gathered the ingredients for liver dumpling soup. The kitchen was cozy and well arranged with enough room for a square table and four chairs. The sun entered through the window over the sink. Teréza adored standing there in the beam of sunlight.

Soon she would see her family again: her mother, her father, Ági, Juli and Kati. She cherished the thought more than the new kitchen, unaware how starved she felt for the closeness of family. She was but a thirty-minute bus ride from Ják when the buses didn't break down. And yet Teréza viewed her return to the region with reluctance. Szombathely's ancient one-story houses appeared moldy and their facades were protected by large iron gates. Their yards were laid with flat rocks, not grass.

That afternoon, Pista rode his rusty bicycle to Szombathely. If nothing else, news travelled fast in Communism. Unlike progress.

István saw him arriving in the yard, stumbling when he dismounted his bike, hopping on one foot to save himself from falling, narrowly missing a lamppost.

"Whoa!" he yelled for everyone to hear. The smell of booze wafted off him. Pista grabbed István in a tight embrace.

"You stink, brother," said István.

From the look on her face, Teréza had little desire to receive him in this state, but she didn't object when Pista pulled out a chair and asked for brandy.

"Nice shoes, Teréza," Pista said.

István grabbed shot glasses from the kitchen cupboard, slammed them on the table and asked Teréza to slice a few pieces of sausage.

Self-conscious of her Oxfords, Teréza walked lightly on her feet as she moved about.

István sat facing Pista who lit a cigarette. Teréza opened the window.

"You still haven't given up that disgusting habit." István poured drinks. He hardly wanted to give Pista another, but it was bad luck to pour only for himself. István raised his glass. "Nagy has lifted some of Stalin's heavy-handed policies. Shall we drink to that?"

"He's a good man." Teréza showed enthusiasm to keep the conversation positive. She knew of Pista's tendency to provoke whenever politics came up.

"Teréza, Nagy could be your father," remarked Pista.

"Don't be ridiculous! I would never have a Communist father. My father is good man."

"You both have round faces. That's all I'm saying." Extending his arm, Pista placed his glass on the table, waiting for a refill.

Teréza served the liver dumpling soup seasoned with marjoram. They ate in silence with the speed of the famished. Before the men finished slurping she was already serving up the next course.

"So, you got yourself in trouble," Pista said, after swallowing his last bite, "I'm proud of you." He lit another smoke while the first one still burned on a saucer.

"So you said." István pushed his empty plate aside.

"When did I say that?"

"When I got sent home from the camp."

Teréza looked at her husband like she didn't know him.

Pista shook his head. "You're losing your mind, brother. I haven't talked to you."

István blushed. "Well, I resisted. That's more than you've been doing."

"Did I come here for you to insult me? I'm sawing through bones for the butcher so your wife can make soup and spread marrow on your bread."

"Admirable. I need some water," István said turning to Teréza. She slammed a glass of water on the table just out of his reach and brusquely stepped outside.

"What's she like in bed?"

"Catholic," István said quietly, fearful that Teréza might overhear them. "She's getting interested in having a baby."

"That should get you some for a while. So she's not a rollicking Jew like yourself? Too bad." Pista knocked back another brandy.

"I'm not a Jew." István glanced towards the door at the moment Teréza breezed back in.

Pista abruptly changed the subject. "I wonder if Hungary will ever build lenticular flying machines? You know, like Romania?"

"It's the only area in which Romania is ahead of Hungary."

"You two talk about strange things."

"Has István ever told you what we did on his eighteenth birthday, Teréza?"

"Tell me." Teréza pulled up a chair and leaned her elbows on the table.

"We'd purloined a bottle of booze. By sunset we were too drunk to cycle. István ditched his bike in the bushes."

"Somehow we had arrived at Varga's house," István added, remembering.

"You remember Varga?" Pista conducted with his cigarette.

Teréza shuddered. "Who can forget the Renaissance man? First a bully, then a soldier and then a Party Inspector."

"Exactly. We were weaving down the road, pissed out of our minds and we came upon a pile of bricks near Varga's house."

"Bricks for a shit house?" István reenacted their conversation.

"You thinking what I'm thinking?" Pista followed suit. "We waited for hours in the shadows for the last of the house lights to go out."

"Then we set to work –"

"– until we used up the entire pile of bricks to seal up the front entrance including two windows."

"And István, you stood back, admiring your handiwork. And the whole time you had an uncontrollable case of the hiccups. I kept telling you to keep it down. Your hiccupping was echoing throughout the county."

István was getting red with laughter. "I remember saying, 'Tomorrow morning, Varga's gonna wonder why it's so bloody dark in the house.'"

"The stupid fuck was wondering if it was still the middle of the night." Pista slapped the table, hysterical laughter convulsing from his belly.

"And when he opened the door to check –"

"– he smashed into a wall of bricks!"

"Remember how Varga's fat mother fainted when she discovered her front door completely sealed? She couldn't get to the shitter."

"You're making this up." Teréza shook her head. The two old friends were losing it, tears streaming down their faces as

Teréza watched them, giggling.

"When Varga figured out who'd done it," Pista explained to Teréza, "we narrowly escaped broken jaws. The church organist stumbled across the bloodletting and thwacked his thick bible on the side of Varga's head."

"Varga howled, cupping his ear and yelled at us, "You will pay forever!""

"And we have," Pista said, suddenly sombre.

After Pista left, Teréza and István sat at the side door of their new abode, facing the adjacent house, blankets over their knees, sharing a bottle of beer. The moon waned. The night air was damp. From behind the thick wall of the neighbour's house came the faint mutterings of the radio. Talking. More talking. Then singing. Women's voices.

"Shhh!" Teréza listened closely. "Radio Free Europe," she whispered.

The residents of Szombathely who owned radios could access the station because of the city's proximity to the Austrian border, and because censors, due to prohibitive costs, were unable to install enough jamming equipment to silence it.

Only crickets dared make a sound. Faintly audible, the quiet voice of dissent, considered seditious by the Soviets, made Teréza both elated and nervous at once.

"I'm not supposed to be hearing this." István looked down both ends of the narrow stretch of yard. Checking had become a reflex, like yawning.

Teréza cocked her head, straining to hear the voices of the escaped. Émigrés, political refugees, singing the banned songs of Hungary. Broadcasting from Munich, they sang to those stuck behind the Iron Curtain, sent them invitations to keep believing in freedom, to keep hope alive.

She hung on to the fragments and tones of muted discussions. Freedom, something, something. The crusade for freedom, something, something. Oppression. A musical interlude was followed by Stalin, something, something. Hope. Freedom. Occupying forces. Stalin and Rákosi imprisoned... thousand dissidents. Two escaped...western border. Shot.

"I can't hear it properly." István stood from the stoop, nervously. "Come to bed." He offered his hand.

He woke the next morning and watched her as she moved quietly throughout the room gathering her things. "Where are you going?"

"To church," she answered, avoiding his eyes.

"On our anniversary?"

"It's Sunday."

"It's dangerous."

Teréza pulled on a cream-coloured pencil skirt and an olive boat-neck pullover.

"I'll be back soon." She kept her head down as she placed her prayer book in her purse and clicked it shut.

"You'd rather go to church than spend this morning with me?"

"It's the last form of resistance I have left."

"You could get me in trouble," he said to the ceiling.

"I won't get you in trouble." She came and sat down beside him on the edge of the bed.

He combed his fingers through his hair, making himself presentable to the ceiling. "How do you know?"

"Because I know." She reached for his face.

He turned his cheek away. "I wish you wouldn't."

"It would do you some good to come with me."

"Don't even start. You know I can't," he said, exasperated.

"Why is teaching the Bible unacceptable to the Communists?"

"I don't know." István rolled away from her, positioned himself on his side.

"Because the Bible shows us that first there was chaos and through the help of God's plan, order prevailed. But Communism shows us that first there is a plan and afterwards comes the chaos."

István cracked a smile and sat up in bed. "Where the hell did you hear that?"

"From the priest at church back in Makó. I'll be back soon." She got up.

"You're so stubborn." His insides felt taut like the knotted end of a sausage.

She hurried out the door.

He lay back down feeling deserted, staring at the white ceiling, the white walls, the white door and the white sheets. He was dying to read a new book, but they had only three. He'd already read them many times, including his favourite, Sándor Márai's *Embers*, with its nostalgia for the Austro-Hungarian Empire. He kept that one hidden under a loose floorboard.

He endured the morning without Teréza, seething at her defiance. He got out of bed, took a shallow bath, shaved. He pressed small pieces of tissue on his shaving cuts, buttoned his shirt to the top of his neck. Then he punched the wall.

Rosy from her adventure, Teréza returned, managing once again to avoid arrest. "I made it," she said, placing her shoes neatly at the door.

István didn't acknowledge her. The anticipation of his anniversary faded with her departure in the morning. He sat in a chair, brooding.

"Shall we go to the movie?"

After maintaining a cool and punitive gap between them for a few blocks he relented and offered his arm. She took it and surveyed the budding trees along the main street as they made their way to the cinema.

Inside the theatre, Teréza looked around. She noticed the usual grim-faced ÁVO man stationed at the door. István read the disapproval on her face. She was incapable of hiding it. Smiling behind the glum cashier, on a poster inside the box office, a perennially happy woman in a bathing suit held up a fizzy soft drink – a *Bambi Orange* – ready to pour herself a tall glass.

"Want to try one?" István suggested.

Teréza shrugged.

"They're cheap enough," István said. "A Bambi Orange, please." The bottle glistened in the dark foyer of the cinema.

István poured the neon orange liquid into a glass, tasted it and nearly spit it out. "Tastes like petrol!" he scoffed. He searched for a place to deposit the vile stuff, but Teréza swiped the glass from him, embarrassed that he would rid himself of something he'd just paid for. She took a sip.

"You're right, this is ghastly," Teréza concurred, but drank it all back in one go.

István grinned at Teréza. "Your tongue's turned orange. It's glowing like a landing strip."

Only a handful of people were in the audience, someone

smoking a cigarette among them. The cinema fell into full darkness. The first film began to roll – a Russian language short with Hungarian subtitles on the topic of pig breeding. It followed a day on a pig farm from waking to feeding, from squealing to snorting, from mating to rolling about in the mud. Large swollen balls paraded in front of the camera, a snout dipped into a shallow puddle of water. Backsides wiggled. A farm dog chased a squealing baby-pink pig. When the film ended no one applauded.

Film number two, also in Russian, was called *How To Throw a Javelin* and was set in a gymnasium. A woman with powerful thighs lifted weights. She wore shorts with stripes down the sides that Teréza thought looked like underwear. The athlete marked the movements of throwing a javelin to the accompaniment of Soviet lounge music, without actually throwing the javelin and without an actual javelin in hand.

"She's looks like a man," Teréza whispered.

"What?" István leaned over.

"She's looks like a *maaaan*," Teréza said a little louder.

At the back of the theatre the ÁVO man cleared his throat.

"That was a great film," István said to Teréza without moving his lips, turning his head like a wooden doll.

She giggled. "Well done! I married a ventriloquist and his dummy."

"Thank you," he said, smoothly rotating his head towards the screen.

"Can we go now?" She attempted to stand, but István grabbed her arm.

"I promised I had a surprise for you. Don't you trust me?" he whispered in the dark, pulling her down into her seat. She slumped next to him and closed her eyes.

Music. Cheerful staccatoed opening notes of zithers and violins. One of Teréza's eyes sprang open. She sat on the edge of her seat, stunned. The frame filled with flowers, row upon row of bursting flowers, panning under the title, *Ecseri Lakodalmas*. The Wedding from Ecser. Teréza sat up. A chorus of women began to sing. A sumptuous sound, exultant, passionate, yet serious and minor. It travelled from major to minor in a single verse, within a single line and played a syncopated rhythm.

> *Beneath the gardens of Ecser*
> *Flows love's creek*
> *Whomever drinks too much of its waters*
> *Will bid farewell to their lover.*

Teréza lost herself in the bucolic setting. Villagers prepared for a country wedding; singing, dancing, baking bread, carving meat and hanging wreaths above doorways. Their modest homes looked just like the thatched adobe house she'd grown up in.

Each frame of film became an accretion and a painful reminder of how vigorously she'd been forced to change by the new regime. The music touched every corner of her being. It became her. She held on to every note, every change of key, every gesture, every swivel of the dancers' hips. She tingled each time a man slapped his leather boot.

It was her Hungary, her people, her music. Rich, winding, complex and mysterious. It was her reminder, her hope and her resolve to always remember her ancestors. First and foremost she was a Hungarian. Not a Soviet. Not a Russian.

As the movie drew to a close and the newlyweds stole a kiss, the other dancers twirled wildly throughout the tavern.

Teréza sat in exhilarating silence, tears streaming down her face. István looked at her and felt thankful. He'd brought her temporary peace.

SEPARATION

1957

I'M GLAD THERE IS YOU

1957, October 23. Winnipeg, Canada

Never in his wildest dreams would István have imagined that exactly a year after the outbreak of the uprising, he would be living in an icy Canadian prairie city.

On the anniversary of the Revolution – the first commemoration of any failed event had to be the worst, he thought – the pain that resurfaced after a year of bottling grew stronger, like the alcohol in brandy when it is heated.

He couldn't bring himself to untwine the emotional tangle nor to put it into writing, but Teréza was due a letter. He pulled on his chilled, rigid coveralls. Blue. He still hated ÁVO blue, and it stung to touch the zipper with his fingertips. He'd walked only seven minutes from the bus stop to Ackermann's Service Centre, but at six forty-five in the morning -9.4 Fahrenheit had turned his hands into useless stumps. Standing all day on cold cement penetrated his bones, and pumping gas in a Winnipeg winter was Canada's version of a work camp. Two months in Winnipeg felt like an eternity. What kind of an inhospitable place threatened blizzards in October? What was this part of the world paying penance for?

"Today is twenty-three October," he said.

"October twenty-third," Ackermann corrected, checking over his paperwork. The boss was prematurely grey. What could be so worrisome in Canada?

A small filthy sink affixed to the wall of the bay hung crooked to the level of the cement floor. Asymmetry troubled István, and more so this morning. The bone-chilling temperatures were making him feral. He turned on the tap and waited, but he really wanted to rip the sink off the wall.

"When your hands are frozen never put them under hot water. It'll hurt more," Ackermann advised, his specs perched on the end of his nose.

How strange it was to István that warmth could hurt in Canada. He closed the tap.

Half the time István still didn't fully understand what the boss was asking him to do and felt immediate discomfort upon hearing instructions. Ackermann was a correct man, but English was a problematic language that sounded like barking dogs. He communicated quickly even when István requested he slow down.

"Customers need their cars," Ackermann would say, "I don't have time to explain twice." Speedy service was valued in this country.

István managed to do the opposite of what Ackermann asked so often that the boss gave István the physically demanding chores, the crummy clean-up jobs, the tasks that left him feeling like a servant when all he wanted to do was get his hands on a North American engine and see how it differed from a German one. These grand, luxurious boats had comfortable, spacious interiors. More than once he stretched himself fully across the backseat of such a vehicle and snoozed while Ackermann was out on an errand.

István never wanted to concede to fatigue, though he'd been taking English classes every evening after a tiring, dirty day of work. He took a bus from his apartment to work and from work to class and then from class to home again, disliking the buses' ungainliness all the while. Three long lumbering trips in a day. He longed for his flimsy motorcycle back home.

"What is it my job today?" István asked the boss.

Ackermann filled out requisition forms. "First the washrooms need cleaning. Then I need you to do an oil change on that Buick. My wife's sick today; I have to leave early to drive my son to his hockey game. Can you lock up for me?"

István had informed the boss a week ago that he'd need to leave an hour early. He'd already put in the overtime. "I'm sorry. I can't do this," István said, following Ackermann to the Buick, his face turning red as he explained everything again.

Only a Hungarian understood what it meant to swing from victim to victor and back again within the span of thirteen days. A Canadian whose nation had never experienced such radical mood swings could never understand the need to commemorate the defeat of a revolution.

Before Ackermann could open his mouth to protest, István was already greeting the familiar-looking customer, Stan, a middle-aged car dealer, as he lumbered into the shop, letting the metal door clang behind him.

"Have you seen this, Steve?" asked Stan. "I brought it for you."

In English, István's name was Steve. He discovered he

liked the ring of it. "TIME Magazine," István pronounced flawlessly. The drawing on its cover, of a handsome and fierce looking man with a bloodied, bandaged hand, holding a rifle, looked exactly like Pista. The revolutionary Hungarian flag with the excised hammer and sickle flew behind the man. István read the words aloud, "Hungarian Freedom Fighter, Man of the Year, 1957."

"You Hungarians are in my good books, fighting the Russians like you did."

In spite of the warm welcome István and the 56ers received from the majority of Canadians, he had been sifting through feelings that he had failed. Hungarians who'd left right after WWII had been losers, who had fought on the wrong side, and they received no special welcome from Canada when they landed. When he was complimented for his bravery, he felt undeserving. His nod and smile were a lie. After all, what had he done for freedom? He'd managed to get out alive, without his wife and son. Was this any kind of triumph?

"You know this guy, Steve?" Stan asked.

"No," István said, staring at the rendering.

I show up everywhere, don't I?

István thought he was going to be sick. Pista's voice was back from the dead.

Even our hair looks the same, doesn't it? I could have been this hero, once. What happened to me? Hey István? István?

"Hey, Steve? Steve?"

Before István could reply, the door swung open again. An attenuate man presented himself; gaunt and unshaven, cane in one hand, sweat-stained fedora in the other.

"Good morning," István said, looking up.

"That's some accent. Let me guess, Polak? Kraut?"

István shook his head, almost imperceptibly, unsure if not answering was more appropriate than doing so. He couldn't guess what was coming next.

"You a Bohunk?" The man's arctic eyes glared at him.

"No."

"Out with it! Or do you only speak three words? 'Good' and 'morning' and 'no'?" The man was a confusing blend of embittered hobo and sophisticate.

Stan glanced at István, who put the magazine aside.

"Hungary," István said, feeling foolish. He'd meant to say Hungarian but got tongue-tied.

"Hungarian!" The man belted from his collapsed chest. "One of the Axis Powers in the Big One." The man tucked his cane under his arm and rolled up his sleeve to reveal a deformed, emaciated arm. "I was over there. Not conscripted. I volunteered. Gave up my university post. You were fascists. And when it looked like you were losing, you tried to change sides."

István felt bludgeoned and embarrassed though he missed most of what the man said.

What is it in a man that makes him despise what he recognizes in himself?

István moved his hand towards a wrench on the shelf, but Stan grabbed his arm.

"Don't pay him any mind, Steve."

Ackermann calmly entered from the bay. "What seems to be the problem here?"

"You've hired a Nazi sympathizer, is the problem. Don't know when he'll turn on you, but he will. Just his dirty, rotten nature. Is this what we want to let into our democratic country?"

"I'm going to ask you to leave right now." Ackerman

moved in front of István.

"You can ask me." The man sucked back rum.

"I'll call the cops if you don't leave in three seconds."

"Mark my words!" The man raised his cane. "This country will be overrun with immigrants in a decade and before you know it, we won't hear our own goddamn language."

István reddened, as Ackermann manhandled the erstwhile professor out the door, his cane waving in all directions.

"Are you okay?" asked Stan when István fell silent.

"Whatever doesn't solve itself isn't worth dealing with," István answered.

Ackermann returned and started filling out paperwork. "You can close up a few minutes before five tonight," he said to István without looking at him, "for that celebration. That's the best I can do."

At ten minutes to five István shivered at the bus stop. The cold brutalized him more now than it had in the morning. He looked at his watch and at five minutes to five, daylight leeched from the sky and the world plunged itself into a blackout.

"Whatever you do, don't look directly at the sun," Ackermann had advised him. "Use this." He handed him a small square of glass so dark it was almost black. "It will protect your eyes from the eclipse."

Why was it that the moon chose this day to slip between the earth and the sun, to cast him into total blackness? Was it some kind of a cruel joke? The darkness that engulfed him was the same the day two thousand tanks rolled toward Budapest. Should this darkness not have covered those who had put to end to that glorious moment in Hungary's history?

On the bus, his fingers thawed in time for him to remove from an envelope Teréza's most recent letter. It was short.

Dearest István,

András told me to tell you two things: he misses playing cards with you and secondly that the Soviet Union launched something called a "satellite" into the sky on October 4th. Apparently, this is incredible – and I don't know if you have heard of this in Canada, but I don't really understand what it is. András explained that it is a polished metal sphere the size of a very large ball, with four external radio antennas to broadcast radio pulses. It weighs 83 kg and it took 98 minutes for it to orbit the earth. He was sure this would change history. (I've memorized these facts like you taught me to, though I no longer attend "education" meetings. Can you believe that Kádár made them optional?) Isn't it amazing that a ball circling the earth can change history while so many lost lives made so very little impact? I think of you always. I don't know how to wait for something that has no predictable end. I pray to God for fortitude. All my love.

I kiss you, Teréza

He pocketed the letter and removed from another a small plastic packet. Subtle light was returning to the sky as remarkably as it left. He held the packet up to the window, so the slanting rays of the eclipsed sun emerging from behind the moon could shine through. The dark hair looked like black threads.

He was convinced he should be able to find an encoded message in the fibres of his son's hair, but he didn't know how to relate to these strong dark locks curled between the plastic and the cardboard.

He felt discomfited by his own reaction, as though he should have felt something. But he didn't. Nothing. Should these strands have evoked a longing to hold his son? *Should I feel love?* How was a man supposed to respond to his son's first lock of hair? Whose hair had his son inherited? Why was it so dark?

He neared the Hungarian Cultural Society on Selkirk Avenue still smelling of gasoline. A quick-tempered gust slipped in with him. He shoved closed the doors, but the wind shoved back. He'd made a raucous noise while the hundred or so assembled refugees chanted the famous *Petőfi* poem of 1848.

... We vow,
We vow, that we will be slaves
No longer!

Marika turned and winked. Bela tipped his hat. They turned back towards the priest and the Hungarian flag and continued to recite the words written against the Austrians.

We were slaves up til now,
Damned are our ancestors,
Who lived and died free,
Cannot rest in a slave land.
By the God of the Hungarians
We vow,
We vow, that we will be slaves
No longer!

The modest hall was decorated with Hungarian flags, hand-painted ceramic dishes, miniature flasks covered with cowhide, and hand-embroidered tablecloths nailed to the walls. A map of pre-Trianon Hungary hung on the largest of the walls. A zither and several violins were set up in one corner. This is where the passionate and the crestfallen gathered to soothe their homesickness, where they drank brandy, discussed politics in loud voices – something they could never do back home – retold escape stories, watched Hungarian dance ensembles, ate large cabbage rolls and pig's feet dinners and celebrated anniversaries of Hungarian battles and traditional Christian holidays. Here, the refugees maintained a semblance of their identity.

István stood with his back to the wall for the duration of the speeches. His mind drifting, a thought turned up like a dead body on a shore.

The term he'd learned in school had seemed so warm and comforting at the time: "land-taking" or "home reservation."

It took him all his life, up until this moment, to realize that the Hungarians had themselves been a brutal occupying force when they conquered the Carpathian Basin. Did everyone everywhere eventually take their homes by force? And was history simply rebalancing scales that had been too long tilted?

He was roused from his reverie; women wept as the priest spoke, their pain still fresh from the previous year.

After the priest finished his blessing, the food was served. No sooner had it been placed on the tables, than the peasant class were already stabbing their forks into the largest pieces of meat and István was squeezing himself into a spot between Bela and Marika.

"Boors," he said under his breath, watching the best

morsels get whisked away.

"What's up, you scoundrel?" Marika played footsies under the table. "Is work more important than your homeland?" She poured him a tall glass of red wine. *Egri Bikavér.*

"Don't you start in on me, I'm in no mood." István said through bloodshot eyes.

Bela leaned in. "We can make you feel better."

"When I was better I didn't need help."

"He'll need a few glasses tonight." Marika looked at him with her perfect pink lips and a pixie haircut. Her big blue eyes looked at him in wonderment.

After dinner Bela lit a cigar. Pint-sized girls ran around the hall in Hungarian costumes and little boys pretended to throw Molotov cocktails re-enacting the bloodbath they'd fled with their terrified parents. István munched on the cartilage of his chicken bone. Marika refilled his glass.

István adapted to the small grieving community that shared jokes, though the gossip irritated him. He knew they talked about him to everyone else, just as they talked about everyone else to him. Some women complained about the parents who spoke English with their children. Losing their mother tongue, these children were beginning to speak Hungarian with "Canadian" accents. "How deplorable," István heard them say. These same women threw English words into conversation to show how well they were picking it up. Or spliced the beginning of an English word onto the end of a Hungarian word, or spliced the two together randomly like *FRIGider* (refrigerator) or *megyünk NORdra* (we are going up north), or *ha FEELezd magad PHONEoj* (when you feel like it, phone me). What István and Bela called Hunglish.

"WORKölök as an engineer," Bela reported with an impish grin. "Imagine that. I'm making good money even if my English is still the pits. The only thing the Soviets gave me was a decent education."

István had nothing to add.

Marika held up a white Hudson's Bay wool coat with four horizontal stripes in green, red, yellow and black and a wide stylish belt with a large buckle. "I've been working in the clothing department. Look at my new purchase." She was the best dressed every time they met at the Hungarian Club, and tonight was no exception. István couldn't help himself. He desired her.

"Things are going well for the two of you here in Winnipeg."

"It's not European enough for me," Bela said, puffing on his cigar. "And it's impossibly cold. October last year we were still wearing light coats in Budapest."

"We're thinking of Montreal," Marika said, checking István's reaction.

He didn't respond. He couldn't bear the thought of Friday nights without his two friends. Neither the band nor the spirited conversation was enough to drown out his disappointment.

Dressed in black pants, vests and billowy-sleeved white shirts, the band started playing the *Csárdás* and old pre-war favourites. Soon the lonely exiles danced while fried meat, winter pickles and roast potatoes purled in their bellies.

"Why not a little fun?" Marika elbowed István. "You may be waiting years until you have your wife's arms hold you again."

"She's right." Bela tapped his foot in time with the music. "There is no hell, you know."

"He's right," said Marika, winking at István.

"That's not what the priests taught us."

"I never took you to be a Christian."

"We already lived hell back in Hungary, what could possibly be worse?" Bela offered his wife his hand. "Come, my beautiful."

István sat confined in his chair, his arms and legs crossed, wondering about the usefulness of loyalty.

Marika and Bela danced deliriously between the elderly and the young, amongst moustaches, curled hair and red boots and bows. Amongst billowy sleeves and sequined dresses, whilst István watched.

After his alarm went off each morning, István was beset with a feeling that grew stronger the longer he was away from Teréza. The troublesome sensation swirled in his gut as he rinsed the bathroom sink and touched his face after shaving. Looking in the mirror he saw a guilty man. István's rational mind responded. Nobody knows anything. But he was wired for vigilance, which had become as reflexive and unconscious as breathing. It was no longer the memory of a secret police force that promoted this unease, but his fixation with what had happened on the ship with Marika and Bela.

István's daily guilt passed around late morning when work put a temporary pause on his obsessive preoccupation. It returned again in the evenings and tormented him until he thought of Marika and masturbated. Then a blissful, ignorant sleep blanketed his mind only to awaken him by the mornings' recurring guilt.

Some days this cycle consumed him so fully that he re-read each letter he wrote to Teréza before sealing the envelope in case some unwitting part of him inadvertently made a confession without his conscious knowledge: the reckless part of him that wanted to be absolved of his guilt and forgiven for his act of desperate need and loneliness. By the Friday night, the guilt had transmuted into surges of excitement and an intoxicating sense of liberation that rushed to his head like wine. Under their friendly Friday night conversations at the Hungarian Club, Marika offered more with a playful tilt of her head, a twinkle in her eye, a re-crossing of her slender legs, all under the approving gaze of Bela.

A dead part of me comes to life when I imagine what is forbidden, thought István, in conversation with Pista. It pesters me with threats of eternal banishment to the land of the estranged. Help me, he almost said aloud. But his old trusted friend Pista was no longer responding.

Sweaty and sexy, Bela offered, "Why don't I get the car and you two meet me out front?"

"Come. You have only one life." Marika grabbed István's hand and pulled.

István stood reluctantly. "And one wife."

István sat in the middle of their couch while Bela mixed cocktails and Marika kicked off her heels. Her smoky voice soothed him while they bantered. Bela flirted in his usual way by velveting the tone of his voice. Their new apartment on Balmoral was small but well appointed. They had smart, low living room furniture, teal blue and wood and bark cloth curtains in white, grey and red. Through the open bedroom door, István saw Marika strip down to her satin slip. He tried to convince himself she was changing into a more comfortable dress, but he did a poor job of playing innocent. Over her shoulders she wrapped a light shawl and walked smoothly down the hardwood towards him. Her well-defined legs made him hard. But then she detoured to light several candles when from the kitchen came the racket of ice hitting metal for several seconds.

"Brother, have you ever tried a martini?" Bela yelled to István.

"Not yet," István blushed and crossed his legs.

"We bought a record player." She opened the lid. "Oscar Peterson," she said, and lowered the needle. She adjusted the volume to perfection.

"I don't know it," István remarked, breaking into soft laughter. He felt like the last half of a novel that didn't fit with its first half.

"Is something funny?" Marika sat down close beside him, smiling wryly.

"It's all very laughable," he said, unaware of why it was so.

Bela placed a full martini glass on the table and watched his wife unbutton István's shirt, caress his bare chest and press kisses to his sternum.

The radiators hissed and responsibility left István like steam, evaporating into nothingness. At first he felt his body loosen and his thoughts soften against the pillows. It felt so incredibly creamy, this feeling. Marika pushed him down and straddled him.

Sitting opposite them wearing nothing more than his underwear, swirling ice in his drink, Bela said, "It's really hot in here. Like a Budapest summer." And then he sang in his thick accent, "*I'm glad there is you.*"

Marika was tender as she hummed in István's ear. Her slip had moved down to her waist. István lips reached for hers.

"I love Budapest. I love Oscar Peterson," Bela said, "I love my wife, I love my friend." He let his head fall back against the lounge chair as he reached for a knob and turned up the volume. As Marika unbuttoned István's pants Bela moaned. "Go all the way this time my good friend."

In the moment that István caught sight of Bela's hand down his underwear, István's bliss turned to disgust, from desire to loathing. When he saw Bela's hand begin to work, he begged Marika to move aside. "I'm not made for this," István said, almost whimpering. A hole replaced the area around his heart. Marika gently moved off him and draped her breasts with her shawl.

"We'll make you up a bed right here, dear friend. We never meant any harm."

"I can't stay." István reached for his clothing.

Bela turned down the music. "I've only ever adored you. My sincere apologies."

Their camaraderie made István feel a hundred times lonelier than he'd felt all day. It didn't make sense. And then a minute later, one thing did: no matter how many adore you, thought István, if you can't accept love, the adoration means nothing.

He took the bus, declining a lift. When he got home after midnight he checked his mailbox. A letter had come! This time it was from András. István's heart skipped a thousand beats. Only now did he recall the affection he felt for his wife's brother. As his body flooded with warmth he tore open the envelope as he climbed the stairs, livened by feelings that could lay dormant for years then reignite in the time it took to register a rekindled communication.

István read at the door of his apartment:

Brother Dearest, you must be surprised to be hearing from me, as we have not put pen to paper, ever. And yet you must know how deeply embedded you are in my heart though much more than continents divide us. And I must admit how ashamed I am for leaving a lapse both in our correspondence and in what I am about to tell you. I wish not to waste your precious time any further with sentimentality. I have been told by Teréza how long you work a day in Canada with your new business. In fact I am just stalling to reveal the most unfortunate reason for which I write. I am deeply sorry to be the one to inform you that Pista is dead. He was found lying in a ditch between Ják and Szombathely. I am told the day was more beautiful than any spring had seen in the last decade. In fact Pista's body lay in the bulrushes and István, this is true, his face bore a smile. It is some miracle that he looked heavenward, his eyes and face smiling. Like the Pista we knew in the early days. Smiling like he had just told a joke. Peace came to him I assure you. He must have been thinking of you. I cannot say more. Love, András

Was there anything else for István to do than to drink alone in his room? A can of beer for each year he had been away from Pista. A can of beer for each time he foundered in cowardice, neglected the truth and destroyed his friend's life. István felt despicable. The pain he felt for the loss of his lifelong friend surpassed the ache he felt for his wife and son. He had betrayed each of them, but Pista most of all.

After Bela and Marika moved to Montreal, István didn't return their letters. He stopped going to the Hungarian Club. He didn't answer the phone when it rang on Friday nights.

VIOLATION

1946-1947

IT'S NOT YET REAL

1946, November. Hungary

Crammed full of passengers, the overnight train to Budapest trundled along the eastbound track. Facing her on the hard, wooden bench sat a man who had the bearing of someone waiting for instructions. Teréza sensed he'd been given a terrible choice to make. He was in his fifties with thinning hair; the outer corners of his eyes curved downward, like two large tears. Beside him sat a peasant woman, a shapeless grandmother wearing several layered long skirts, one over the other. Her lower face was crumpled. Teréza surmised that she had no teeth. On either thigh sat an underweight girl and boy no more than three or four. Her grandchildren. Teréza yearned to touch them. Her heartache always eased when she held her little sister Kati. From the souls of small children, Teréza could borrow the joy that came naturally to them.

At first, she didn't know where to look, the carriage held so many dejected people forced to witness each other's misery. Everyone was dirty, coated and caked with grime. Where did these people come from? she wondered. Every train in Hungary was packed full of people, dazed and disoriented, malnourished and rail thin, trying to get back home, whatever was left of it. Between avoiding faces and staring at them with morbid curiosity, Teréza's thoughts travelled back to István and the funeral, the way they had locked eyes in understanding. She didn't have the heart to tell him directly that she was going to Budapest, so András had mentioned it to István in passing, on her behalf.

For the first time in her life she'd left home. Sixteen years old. Her chest still rushed with the emotion of saying farewell to her father, her mother, to András, to Ági, Juli and Kati. Back at the station under the mottled moon, Teréza's father had cried and her mother had held herself still as a tombstone. András told a joke or two as the family waited for the train.

"When did the world have its first democratic elections?" András asked.

"I don't know," Teréza had answered impatiently, looking down the track, waiting for the oncoming light as passengers gathered.

"When God put Eve in front of Adam and said, 'Pick a wife.'"

Teréza laughed, despite herself. Underneath lay the sting of missing him before she'd even left. She'd never been on a train before and grew nervous.

"Did you remember your acorn?" András asked.

"Of course," Teréza said, reaching deep into her pocket. András had carved it for her. It was still there. She rolled it around in her palm, the ridges in the cap-shaped cupule, the body of the nut, perfectly precise, smooth and sturdy. She nodded again.

András reminded her, "It represents power and strength, perseverance and hard work. And brotherly protection and familial bonds. Never lose it."

"Did you make that up?"

"Which part?"

"The part about brotherly protection and familial bonds."

The train rattled into the station.

In a sudden change of spirit Ági placed her hands on Teréza's shoulders, kissed her on one cheek and said, "I'll miss you terribly," and then the other, "come home soon." Juli handed Teréza a picture she'd drawn of a perfect rose with the inscription *Remembrance* 1946. XI.I. And Kati's cherry red nose glowed when through sleepy eyes she tried to understand why Teréza was getting on the train and they were not. Kati clamped onto her and wouldn't let go.

When Teréza managed to pry her off and hand Kati back to their mother, she boarded the train with Birka Bandi, a young soldier and son of a family friend also headed to Budapest. Tears ran from her eyes to the corners of her mouth. Sadness coated her throat.

The young soldier squeezed next to her snored. Bandi's head lolled clumsily, too heavy for his body. How could he sleep so easily? She wanted to push his weight off of her but was too polite to intrude on his slumber. She counted passengers. Some rows held five to six people, when at one time four would have been snug. No one ate; there was no food to pack into a basket. Those who could afford cigarettes smoked. Most people's frames looked unnaturally diminished, most likely from concentration camps, labour camps or refugee camps. Some people were returning to flattened cities, charred villages or occupied homes, others to Budapest, to acres of twisted wire and rubble.

When during the fighting she'd imagined the end of war, Teréza only ever thought of the relief it would bring. What she hadn't foreseen was the lingering pain and deprivation once the initial relief had faded. Now came the hangover. She saw it in the faces before her. It had simply taken on another form. What would Klára look like? How long would it be till she could see her? She'd not seen her sister since she left home to work as a maid in the city, almost three years ago. Would she have the same soulless look in her eyes as these passengers on the train?

Teréza hadn't slept a wink when the train swayed and yanked itself to a screeching halt – again. This had occurred several times over the course of the night but still Bandi didn't wake. At various points, Russian soldiers carrying machine guns got on and off the train, crawling out of the foggy blackness of the sleeping villages. Their figures loomed at the doorway of each train car, their expressions smug.

The third time this happened they stayed on board. She heard them arguing. She kept her head down and tried to still her trembling hands. When Teréza looked up she saw four soldiers watching her. Once the train began moving again, two proceeded to the adjoining carriage, and the other two entered the one in which she travelled. She reached for the acorn in her pocket, rolled it around in her palm.

The train moved slowly. The boots of the Russian soldiers thumped down the aisle, nearly drowning out the click-clack of the wheels on the tracks. They paused. She recognized the stench of vodka; they wore it like cologne. She elbowed Bandi in the ribs to wake him.

The two soldiers stopped beside her. If she kept her head down, it suggested submission, so she raised it, looking straight ahead as if she saw something captivating. Her defiance couldn't withstand their smirks. She felt her cheeks redden as they chuckled at her silly game of resistance.

Bandi rubbed his eyes and noticed the soldiers for the first time.

The train keeled. One soldier jerked, pushing the other forward onto her. The Russian soldier pinned her to her seat. She felt a hand on her breast, another in her crotch, squeezing painfully. His face pressed against hers. "Slut," he snarled in Russian. She knew the word for that. She forced her legs together, but he tightened his grip. She pushed against him with her crumpled arms as he penetrated her with his fingers. Bandi tried pushing the soldier off, but the second soldier cocked his gun and held it to Bandi's temple. The train swayed and the brute bore inside her harder, until finally, she could stand the shameful pressure no longer. She urinated on him.

"Stupid girl!" He yanked his hand out and shook it off with distaste.

The train straightened itself on the track. No one other than her emasculated Hungarian soldier had come to her rescue. Everyone else knew there was no use.

She sat there in shock, wet and humiliated. The old lady across from her watched with an accusing eye, as if the assault were her own fault. She drew her grandchildren closer to her and tucked in her chin.

Teréza could only look down at her legs and the darkened fabric over which she neatly arranged her shabby coat. She felt shamed, dismissed, undone. She hated herself. The two soldiers laughed and swayed as they made their way down the aisle until they stood before another woman in her forties. They each grabbed a breast and twisted. She cried out.

Teréza covered her ears.

The Russian soldiers left the carriage.

The next six hours felt like days. She felt grimy and soiled. And though she wanted to get away from Bandi, Teréza felt pity for him and his pathetic attempt to protect her. The war was showing her a new side to men: their impotence to protect their women.

Teréza strained to make out other forms and images in the world beyond the train, but she could see little. A few scattered houses, some chickens, a lone figure. She managed to catch a glimpse of a sign marking the city limits. The word Budapest was crossed out and in its place its name rewritten in Cyrillic. The Russians had staked their ground. As the city grew thick with dwellings, the train huffed with fatigue. Bombed-out buildings cluttered the outskirts. The city was dark.

The fog had not yet lifted when the train halted and jerked metres from Nyugati Station. Bandi stirred. This time, the Russian soldiers waited outside the train while Hungarian policemen filed on. They checked IDs randomly, pulled a few people off. The situation made her insides burn, but she couldn't get to the squalid toilet again. She dared not call attention to herself. The humiliation was already a sticky film coating her skin.

Teréza watched from the corner of her eye as more people were pulled off the train and led away. She twisted her hands in her lap.

While she waited for the train to pull into the station, the first glimmers of daylight broke through the fog. She'd once marvelled at pictures of the great city – its spired Parliament Building, made with four million bricks, a half million precious stones and forty kilograms of gold. On its façade, proud statues of Hungarian rulers and Transylvanian leaders. She'd fantasized about visiting the Buda bank, climbing Castle Hill and taking in the view of Pest. Of seeing Gellért Hill and Margit Island from each of the seven towers of Fisherman's Bastion, and Mátyás Church, with its diamond-patterned roof tiles and gargoyle-laden spire.

What she saw outside of the train window was little comfort: endless rows of demolished buildings. Broken arches, crumbled columns, cracked facades. And mounds and mounds of earth and brick where houses once stood. Blasted bridges lay in the Danube, half submerged.

She'd heard that people had been living in cellars for months on end. It was real to her now. In that instant, as the fog lifted, she despised men and war all over again. With Hitler dead, why did the Russians have to stay?

Since leaving Ják, she'd eaten only one slice of bread spread with duck fat, saving the second slice for later. Now she was famished. She climbed down the steep steps, her bones aching and numb from the assault. Already her mind pursued whatever would block the pain and looked for beautiful distractions. The *Gerbaud Café*. It was a word she loved to say to herself because it made her feel like a princess – *Gerbaud*. The illustrious café was famous even in a village where a child would likely never darken its gilded doors. If only she could have settled into a plush upholstered chair with smoothly carved arms and ordered a piece of cake. Or, the *Dobos torte*, or the custard-filled *krémes*.

She took her leave of Bandi on the platform, assuring him she could make her own way. He tried to walk her to her relatives who were meeting her at the station, but she pulled away when he tried to touch her. She felt nauseated and weak from hunger. His touch made her queasier.

The air smelled of grease and dust, but also the baked goods from the vendors who lined the platform. More than anything, she needed fresh air. As she walked, Teréza searched for her relatives amongst the strange and worn-out characters. What did they look like? Without a photo, she hoped to find traces of her father's features in her uncle's face. Uncle János, a tailor, married Hermina. Hermina's mother lived with the couple along with the three-month-old twin girls she was coming to care for. Mercifully, their home on Eötvös Street had been spared in the siege. This was all Teréza knew.

As she passed a Russian soldier standing on the platform, his face severely pockmarked, she quickened her pace and regretted leaving Bandi. She breathed in air thick with soot and humidity, so unlike the clean country air she'd been accustomed to. Was anything green out there? Past the train station? Past the detritus? In the Buda Hills? What kind of a world had she stepped into? Then she saw them at the end of the platform. A couple with twins. A man with her father's smile.

"My beautiful niece." Uncle János began to cry as her father had done twelve hours before. But that life no longer existed, she reminded herself. Her uncle was the city version of Gyuri, sporting a well-tailored suit and an impeccably maintained moustache.

His wife Hermina had lost the natural curve bestowed upon a breastfeeding woman. War rations robbed her of the cushion that insulated the twins while they slept in her arms. An absence of flesh on her frame made Hermina's breasts look unnaturally large, and her lower legs like those of young girl. She reminded Teréza of the great bustard strutting around the *Fő* Square. Her brunette hair, parted on the side, reached her jaw line in loose waves that made her look glamorous, like she belonged on stage.

Aunt Hermina and Uncle János took turns kissing both her cheeks, their tenderness unexpected in this godforsaken place. Instantly, Teréza wanted to be like Aunt Hermina, refined and stylish and sweet.

"So, this is the peasant girl," said Hermina's mother, her voice as cold as tin on a winter's day. Her use of third person not only verged on rude, but was intended to degrade. Hermina went to the kitchen to make tea, and Uncle János scuttled away to the water closet.

Teréza stood at the door of the apartment. "*Csokolom, Hermus néni.*" She used the appropriate greeting for her respectable elder; Teréza's status was only slightly higher than the gypsy class. She tried to kiss her cheek, but the old woman pulled away.

"What's that?" said Hermus, reaching for the small cloth sack in Teréza's hand. She snatched it away.

Hermus walked to the kitchen, tearing open the brown paper that wrapped the slice of bread. She made a sound of disgust. Teréza watched her toss her duck fat on bread into the garbage. Rage surged up Teréza's spine, and she blinked back tears. Her mother never wasted food! Why hadn't the bomb fallen on this woman? Teréza let the thought come freely, and she didn't apologize to God for it afterward.

Hermus returned to her dayroom. Once Hermus was out of sight Uncle János returned to the hallway. He smiled at Teréza diffidently and whispered, "I'm glad you're here." He shrugged his shoulders and lowered his head. "Forgive me, I need to get to work." He returned to his sewing room.

Teréza had observed this behaviour in her own father when her mother yelled at him. Passive retreat. Teréza stood, waited for a cue, feeling awkward and out of sorts. Hermina came into the hallway. "Don't let my mother get to you. The war made her unhappy, but we're excited and grateful that you're here. You'll bring spirit back to this place."

Teréza barely managed a smile.

"Are you alright?" Hermina asked.

Teréza wrestled with the lie on her tongue.

Her idealized Budapest was gone, and with it her hopes of a life skirting the intellectual, aristocratic class and an elevated way of being. She could not accept that her sole purpose in life was to cook and clean for relatives. That her sole reward was her uncle's food, lodging and tailored clothing.

"Yes, thank you, Aunt Hermina. Everything will be better now."

Uncle János' apartment had high ceilings, simple furnishings and four rooms: the kitchen; the bedroom where her aunt and uncle and the twins slept; the workroom where her uncle sewed with two other tailors, and the small living room that doubled as a fitting room and where Hermus slept on a day bed. Her uncle's independent enterprise survived in spite of the Interior Ministry – the Communist wing of the government – that barely tolerated this sort of business.

The workroom served as Teréza's bedroom, a room that by day filled with the curling coils of cigarette smoke and the smell of men. Their sweat accumulated under the tape measures they wore around their necks. Earlier in the day, she peered into the room as her uncle worked. Watching him manipulate fabric with such precision gave her a new appreciation of what it took to make something. For the first time, Teréza had a sense of how hard István worked for his stepfather. She was surprised to feel desire for him, here in her Uncle János's apartment. Despite the bruises blooming on her thighs, she was surprised to discover him in the chambers of her heart.

That first night, after Teréza washed the kitchen floor, she entered the sewing room and coughed. The air felt used up and dried out from the hot irons that pressed clothing after adjustments were complete. She opened the windows wide and welcomed in the November air. Leaning over the pane, she looked out into the deserted sidewalk below. Only two streetlights shone in the entire street. From her fifth-floor perch, the ornate buildings of Eötvös Street were beautiful even in the dark. They were adorned with intricate mouldings: figures of naked babies with full heads of hair, poets with open books, voluptuous women with dresses off their shoulders, all looked down from the edges of rooftops. She heard a mourning dove, a sound of village life. A birdcall she had always loved. Something familiar.

The particles of the city air drifted in through the open window, descending on her face. All her life Teréza had been used to falling asleep in bed while talking to her siblings. She had only ever shared a bed with her sisters, and a bedroom with the rest of her family. Torn between autonomy and loneliness she contemplated her first sleep away from home. Solace came from knowing that Klára slept under the same stars somewhere close by. She looked out the window at her stone companions, but they could not speak. Two policemen turned the corner and entered the street. They were smoking. The click-clack of their shoes echoed up to her ears. She closed the windows without making a sound and looked at the small couch in the corner of her room. When she sat on it, she could still feel the motion of the train under her, disabling her. And the ache between her legs. She pushed the humiliation as far as it would go, but the despicable feelings returned to her. She would bear them like her mother had. And Klára. In silence. For what could anyone possibly do for her?

Each night from then on, before she made herself comfortable on the couch, Teréza threw open the windows to let in the night air of Budapest, blasted down to its foundations but still beautiful. She pretended to be an aristocrat addressing the masses, assured them she would listen to their needs and pleas. She visited with the figures of babies, poets and ladies alike, and she alleviated all their suffering.

After a week on Eötvös Street, Teréza craved the city air, though saturated with the dust of destruction, because it was more refreshing and optimistic than the cigarette smoke that coated every surface here. After her nightly "address" she crawled under the eiderdown and escaped to sweeter fantasies, if only for a few short hours.

The Grand Central Market was severely battered by the end of the war, so they travelled en mass to the makeshift local market which was windowless and poorly stocked with only eight vendors selling highly priced items: old onions, rubbery carrots, browning parsnips and bad cuts of meat thick with gristle. Teréza was unimpressed, Hermus sighed audibly and the stalls looked practically bare. So little was available. But they bought what they could, and Hermina was delighted to find shrivelled dill and sour cream to make potato soup.

At the end of dinner one night, when Hermina placed a plateful of simple homemade jam-filled *kifli* pastry on the table, Hermus repositioned the plate so that those pastries with the burnt ends were in front of Teréza. Like the inert passengers on the train, Uncle János and Hermina couldn't come to her defence. Hermus had the same effect on the family as the Russian soldiers had on the nation, Teréza thought wryly. If nothing else, the constant unease Teréza felt around this woman dulled the feelings that kept fighting for dominion. She had been expecting her body to break out in spots. She swallowed her pride and ate the burnt offerings.

During that first week, Teréza watched her uncle cower to Hermus who outright ran the show. Around her, his shoulders stooped more than they did in front of his sewing machine. It was astonishing that Hermus' gaze could transform another's posture. Teréza observed how the two hired tailors, even customers who came for fittings, went silent when Hermus entered their vicinity. It was as if their silence acted as a shield from Hermus' sharp tongue and her critical commentary. The less anyone said, the less it gave her to reprehend.

Hermus had become Teréza's tormentor. If the sadistic actions of the secret police operating on the streets below her window didn't send a chill down her spine, she got a dose of the cruelty from Hermus whose every comment carried a complaint and a jibe. Her glances at Teréza were contemptuous, her greetings nonexistent. Teréza's first week was hellish despite the joy the twins brought.

During her nightly address to Eötvös Street, Teréza

vowed to attend to Uncle János and Hermina, and not take personally their inability to prevent her maltreatment at the hands of Hermus. She would help raise the twins to be kind, intelligent citizens. Hermus, like Stalin, was the enemy. That was it! She would call her *Mrs. Stalin*. The revelation gave her strength. She laughed out loud in the darkness as the night air brushed her neck.

Now she had to see Klára.

The place looked like a glorified cafeteria with cold metal tables, drab olive walls and a scuffed floor of checkered tiles. Dim, diffuse light made a dreary establishment, with nary a smile to be seen, nor a laugh to be heard, sadder still. Strange people. All she could hear was the mumble of a dispirited drone. No music played. No one ate much, except for small shapeless pastries that looked dry even from where Teréza stood in the doorway. Men and women as young as twenty and as old as seventy wore overcoats, some, fingerless gloves. Others kept their hats on. She saw their breath mix with the steam from their coffees. She felt eyes on her the moment she entered.

The café appeared just as Hermina had described it.

"Since the Communists took over the Interior Ministry, all private coffee houses have been closed, including the Gerbaud. Sipping espressos and eating tortes is now considered a bourgeois activity. These bourgeois cafés run the risk of becoming meeting places for people to talk and discuss ideas. Heaven forbid."

Teréza had never set foot in such a café, had only ever stared longingly, through a café window at a display case, replete with cream-filled cakes during her one and only visit to Szombathely, accompanied by Klára.

Hermina had warned, "These cafés echo like caves. Smartly dressed informants lurk and listen. They've all been trained by the ÁVO. They take notes in back corners. Discussing anything is impossible, so intellectuals stay away. People are disappearing. It's not safe."

"My apologies for asking," Teréza had blushed, "but what is the ÁVO?"

"Let's talk about something else."

"Hermina, please."

Hermina took a breath. "State Protection Authority. I can't believe I'm telling you this." She lowered her voice. "The ÁVO's mission is to hunt, find, torture and kill all those who oppose the Soviet regime and Moscow's rule over Hungary. And those who supported the Germans during the war."

"Close the door, already." The command came from the woman at the café's front counter. Black close-cropped hair, very red lips and fake black eyebrows expertly drawn on her forehead, high above where she'd plucked the originals, gave her the look of a vampire.

The door closed with a thud. Teréza would have felt graceless – suspicious even – had she turned around and headed back out onto the street to wait for Klára.

Shocked by the admonishment, Teréza stepped gingerly over the threshold wondering what mistake she had made. "If the place is not to her liking, what on earth is she doing here?" Teréza heard the woman say to a waiter, so thin and tall, she mistook him for a coat rack. He was better dressed than the place deserved, in a clean white shirt, black vest and pants and neatly combed hair. He waited at the counter until the woman placed three espressos on his tray. Then he glided to a table, nose in the air. Walks like a woman, thought Teréza.

"For goodness sakes, can the princess not find a suitable seat?" The vampire glowered.

Teréza walked to the nearest table, sat with her back to the woman and to the door and waited. At once she noticed the grime collected in the corners where no one had bothered to sweep or mop. The grime of war remained long after the fighting ended. It settled into the places where no one wished to look. The café was called the *Muskátli* – geranium. The irony hadn't escaped her. The Soviets had a gift for deception. They chose an inviting name, the traditional Hungarian flower, to deceive those who approached the premises with the hope they might find something pleasing on the other side of the door.

The clock on the wall showed one minute to four. Teréza sat in a disadvantaged position, her back to the door. The woman with the black eyebrows had shamed her into sitting here, without a moment to decide. Changing seats now would look suspect.

Teréza didn't even know if Klára would come. When yesterday Teréza visited the residence where Klára lived and worked, four tram stops along Teréz Street, her sister had not yet returned from errands. Teréza's heart had pounded all the way up four flights of stairs. An old woman opened the door. Anikó, her very distant relative, many times removed, was nice enough. Anikó informed Teréza that she would have to come back if she wanted to see Klára. She'd invited Teréza in for tea, but Teréza politely declined, saying she couldn't stay, asking instead if she could leave a note.

"Absolutely, my sweet girl," the widow had said and waddled to her desk, searching for paper. She began opening mail and moving documents around, inspecting each item with a scrunched face. She was rummaging through a large, unruly pile; it looked like it hadn't been touched for a decade. This took a good five to six minutes and made Teréza testy. Though she did her best to conceal it, she could feel her ears getting warm. The woman stopped to read a couple of official-looking documents. She began to read haltingly and out loud.

"*Dear Dohány Tiborné.*" Pause. "*You are required to submit the exact dimensions.*" Pause. "*Of your dwelling by the 30th of this month.*" Pause. "*Please use the form below. Failing to.*" Pause, pause. She cleared her throat endlessly, phlegm rotating in her throat like a tire stuck in mud.

Teréza wanted to tear the documents from her hands and read it to the woman.

"*Failing to do so, the Ministry of the Interior shall assign.*" Pause. "*An inspector to your case.*" Pause. The old woman harrumphed. "They sure have a boorish way of offering renovations." She drooled, her chin glistening before she remembered she had a hanky. She held the letter out in front of her as if admiring a photo.

Oh, for God's sake. Teréza dug her fingernails into her palm; Anikó was senile. When finally she handed Teréza the document, its blank back page facing up, Teréza noticed the government had a new stamp bearing the red Soviet star. Teréza frowned, folded the paper and began to write, *Klára, Meet me at 4:00 pm tomorrow, at the Muskátli Café on the corner of Nagymező and Jokai. Kisses, Teréza.* She was unsure if the note would make it into her sister's hands, but left it nonetheless.

"Yes?" said the tall, thin waiter. He didn't look at Teréza. Instead, he looked at the wall, at the clock, at the room, impatient for an answer.

"An espresso, please." Teréza looked back down at her hands. The waiter pranced away. She realized with a start that *tomorrow* could have meant any day depending on when the old woman gave Klára the note. Distracted by the woman's slowness, Teréza forgot to write *Tuesday*.

The hands on the clock moved. The big hand was now biting into the other side of four o'clock. Teréza had a bad feeling. The coffee came black and watery. There was no sugar or milk on the table. She tried to get the waiter's attention, but he wouldn't give it to her. The door opened, a draft slapped the back of her neck. She swung around, charged with adrenaline. Two policemen, in brown uniforms, brown shoes. She felt embarrassed, put the black coffee to her lips, swallowed bitterness as the policemen's boots thumped to the counter. One spoke Hungarian, with a terrible accent. A Russian, no doubt. She heard them exchange profane jokes with the vampire. If she could hear it, everyone else could too. She watched two people get up, walk past her, out the door. Another slap of cold air. She took another sip, forced herself to drink what she'd paid for, growing angrier by the minute.

A hand touched her shoulder. Her bowels clenched, and she nearly spilled her coffee. The hand transmitted warmth throughout her chilled body. Teréza reached back, her fingertips sought contact, and without even turning around she knew and thanked God. Composing herself, she pulled her emotion into a tight bundle and secured it with string. She stood, turned around and gazed upon the beautiful face of her sister, embraced her long enough to feel her, but not long enough to draw the unwanted attention of the policemen. They kissed each other's cheeks. Their eyes reddened.

"It's not yet real." Klára said, seating herself in front of Teréza. She dabbed at her smiling eyes. Klára looked like a woman. Her hair had darkened. Her body was stocky like their mother's, but her smile was the same. Eyes like their father's, small and dark like the cupule of an acorn.

"This is not yet real," Teréza repeated. Was it a question or a statement? Confusion was her mind's way to defend against emotion.

"Look at you," said Klára, "you've grown so beautiful."

Teréza brushed the compliment away like she would a fly. The room turned misty. Her coffee was cold. She looked at everything as if through frosted glass. If she breathed on it, it would obscure the world forever. She blotted her tears with her scarf.

"What's going on, my little pastry?" Klára smiled quietly.

"Nothing." Teréza shook her head, ashamed to make a display of herself. "It's been a long time." She couldn't even begin to express all that that meant. "Please excuse me, you don't look...well."

Klára's frizzy haired disobeyed her chignon. "I don't look what?" She sounded insulted.

"That was so rude of me. Forgive me."

"You've seen better days yourself. How's mother? Father?"

Teréza felt foolish. "The end of the war has been hard on them."

"And Ági, Juli and Kati?"

"There are changes in the educational system," Teréza said softly, aware someone in a grimy corner might be taking notes.

Klára nodded, knowing she couldn't ask for details. "And our darling András?"

"András pulls us through. I don't know how he finds it in himself, but in spite of everything he can still tell a good joke."

Klára's eyes looked hollow and haunted as if she grew lonelier with the inquiry of each family member. Her skin had a more olive hue than Teréza remembered. More like their father's. Her smile looked pained.

What had Teréza been thinking? That her sister would come, break down and share the dreadful experience she'd left out of her letters? That she could ease Klára's pain? That she could save her sister from…from what? Teréza was crestfallen and ashamed. She'd set up a rendezvous, picked the most inhospitable environment and then expected vulnerability from her sister. What had she really wanted to know anyway? What difference would it make if she knew the details? Teréza felt disgusted with herself. She knew her mother would never talk about her own ugly hour. If Klára told her story would it make it easier for Teréza to tell hers?

The waiter reappeared at the side of their table, but still would not look at them.

"Linden tea," Klára said to the waiter, who dashed away sooner than she could say please. "Your mind is as busy as a hummingbird. I can see it in your eyes."

Teréza dropped her head. "The whole trip here was such an ordeal. I haven't been myself."

"A woman recognizes when another woman has been altered," said Klára. "What happened?"

Teréza felt ashamed. When she looked up again into Klára's eyes she saw the dullness, it was there. They shared that now.

"I walk by him everyday," said Klára.

A long uncomfortable silence passed between them. The droning in the room unnerved Teréza. Outside, the sky had darkened. She heard two pings on the glass, and then it started to rain heavily. A downpour. With the deluge came the memory of her mother's long loud scream from the house as her little sister Kati played with the chickens outside.

"It's what you wanted to know, isn't it?" Klára spoke through tight lips. A sign she was angry. Teréza recognized it well. A cup of steaming tea appeared on the table between them.

"I don't know what I wanted to know." Teréza grew morose. "I wanted to know you weren't going to –"

"– Kill myself?"

"Don't say that."

"Listen to me…" She grabbed Teréza's hand and squeezed it hard. "If you can't walk by them, you've let them win. You can't let them know they've gotten to you."

Klára's vehemence surprised her. It had never occurred to Teréza to thrive in the face of adversity. Only to endure, or to choose death. To thrive was counter intuitive, but it appealed to Teréza because it satisfied her desire for revenge. The idea of it was a balm to anger.

"It's not revenge," Klára said, looking into Teréza's eyes.

How could Klára read her every thought? "It's condoning it if it's not revenge."

"Wrong!" Klára answered her, forgetting where she was. Heads turned.

"What is it then?" Teréza wriggled her hand out from under Klára's grip.

"It's self-preservation."

"That's what I'm talking about too! We want the same

thing. There are different ways of getting it." They stared at the teacup between them.

"Have you no other news for me?" Klára asked after a while.

Teréza hesitated. "I'm fond of someone."

"Fond?" Klára almost laughed. Her face a blend of admiration and disbelief that Teréza had the audacity to fall in love while surrounded by rubble and an occupying force.

"I'm not going to tell you who it is if you laugh at me."

"I didn't laugh."

"You almost did."

"Tell me, who are you fond of?" Klára leaned in, resting her elbows onto the table.

Teréza hesitated again. "István."

"István. Which István?" Klára thought for a moment. "Kiss István?!"

"Why are you so surprised?" Teréza blanched and began to doubt her choice. Her sister was always her barometer.

"Because it's news," Klára replied. "All news is surprising."

"That's not true. Not all news is surprising."

"You looked embarrassed," Klára said, kindly.

"Well wouldn't you be nervous?" Teréza asked, with annoyance in her voice. "I've never dated anyone before. I'm looking for a little encouragement." That Teréza needed Klára to predict the future was only half the truth. The other half of her tension came from the worry that if István found out about the Russian solider he'd refuse her.

"I forgot how first love can be so intoxicating and unsettling."

"You felt the same way when you first fell in love?"

"Of course." Klára's face softened.

Teréza was relieved the conversation moved away from the brutal world of men. Each time she came close to divulging the incident, something inside stopped her. A verbal paralysis caused by shame.

"Can you point him out? You said you walk by him every day," Teréza blurted.

"Why? Will you spit at him on my behalf?"

"If you want me to."

Klára took Teréza for a walk. There was still adequate light in the sky. She walked her confidently past Russian soldiers wielding submachines guns in front of the Parliament Building in Kossuth Square so they could take a good look at "The One."

The one who'd raped Klára.

Teréza glared at him. "That's the filthy bastard?"

"Shhh! Yes, that's the one," said Klára and laced her arm through Teréza's, hurrying her along. "He's gained some weight since the war. Our good Hungarian cuisine is fattening him up."

Teréza took one quick glance at him. A machine gun was positioned across his chest and his neck was thick as a tree trunk. Within seconds her breathing got laboured, her knees jellied and she started to break out into a sweat. She was hyperventilating before her sister, walking ahead, realized Teréza was buckling at the knees.

"Teréza!" Klára rushed back to support her.

"I'm sorry, I'm sorry, I'm sorry." Teréza whispered.

Klára laced her arm through Teréza's, hurrying her away from the soldiers. "My darling, what's happening to you?"

"I feel like I might be sick."

Klára pulled a handkerchief from her purse, began to wipe her sister's forehead.

Teréza undid the top button of her coat, letting the cool air rush in. Fragmented images flashed through her mind – boots, a square face, hands on her mouth, the sound of a train, Bandi looking away, urinating. A crippling pelvic pain had her gripping Klára's hand as her sister guided her to a bench near the Danube. The river was high as the sunlight glinted off its surface. Black headed gulls flew overhead, their calls harsh and scolding.

"I don't know what's come over me."

"Teréza, what happened to you?" Klára took her hand.

"I don't know what you're asking." Teréza pulled her hand away and clutched her chest, trying to breathe.

WHAT DID YOU PUT IN THIS

1947, Summer. Budapest, Hungary

By the following summer, Teréza was finding ways to cope, and ten months gone from her village, her feelings for István were receding. It had occurred to her to write to him, to see if there was still something there, but like everyone else she was afraid to put pen to paper. Each correspondence was a gamble; what would inspectors glean from her letters? She wanted them to know as little as possible about her life. Somehow too she was a little annoyed that István had not written to her. Wasn't it a man's job to keep the courtship alive?

While preparing to leave the apartment late one afternoon, Teréza heard Mrs. Stalin complain, "Who gave the degenerate peasant girl the rest of the day off?"

"I did," Hermina replied in a tone that left no room for an appeal.

Teréza took a small sack of vegetables to Klára's where she intended to cook up a surprise. Something without baloney in it. And what a surprise it would be. As summer set in with searing temperatures, the tomatoes ripened and a vast array of peppers filled the markets: Hot Banana Wax, Super Sweet Banana, White Hungarian, tomato-shaped, hot, sweet, semi-hot, red, yellow, green.

There was a bounce in her walk as she headed to the tram.

For some time now, she couldn't walk down the street without someone shoving propaganda into her hand. She scrutinized the young comrade positioned in front of Nyugati Railway Station, his burlap bag full of flyers. Lean, no more than sixteen, he wore a grey cap with a red star in the centre. Another five-pointed star on the youth's forearm peeked out from under his rolled-up sleeves.

Teréza noticed a pair of city workers installing a new street sign on the side of the railway station: Marx Square. She thought she'd explode with rage. What the hell was wrong with the Hungarian name? Nyugati – *Western* Square? With a name like Marx Square how would anyone know what direction to go if they were lost? Emboldened by her new city skills, she headed towards the young man along Teréz Boulevard.

"Peace for Hungary!" yelled the youth.

Peace, my ass, Teréza thought, as she drew even with him.

He sliced the air with his flyers. "Here," he said, thrusting one into her hand.

A few weeks back, when the campaign to quell resistance first began, Teréza showed Hermina the flyers she'd brought home.

Hermina scoffed. "The church won't sign the peace petition."

"Why not?" Teréza asked.

"My darling, the church refuses to participate in this government sham. Now, of course, they accuse the priests of being warmongers."

Carelessly, Hermina tossed the flyer on the kitchen table. "Get more, will you? We'll find some use for the paper."

After that, in whichever district Teréza ran errands, she accepted flyers from enthusiastic comrades. Carefully tucking them in her purse or in her shopping bag, she took them home where her pile grew tall. The campaign went on for months.

Teréza stopped, smiled, and took a flyer from the young Communist in front of Nyugati Station and pretended to read it, like she did every time. She asked for extras, to which the youth answered, "Take some for your friends!" She knew the more he gave out, the more accolades he got at Party meetings. She stuffed the flyers in her purse and hurried along the pavement. She ran awkwardly for the tram. She'd tied the new laces on her Oxfords – the ones István had given her – too tight, and continued on her way to Klára's.

At Klára's she dropped the groceries at the front door, kissed her sister on the cheek, yelled a "good day" to Anikó, raced to the water closet, locked the door and sat. No toilet paper. Smiling, Teréza reached inside her purse.

First, she crumpled the paper into a tight little ball. Then she undid the ball and smoothed it out on her knee. She repeated the process a couple of times until the paper had softened adequately and didn't run the risk of grazing delicate skin. She sighed and finished the job. The peace flyers proved far better quality than the rough, unwieldy Soviet toilet paper she found in state-owned stores.

Just as she was flushing the toilet, she heard Klára

answering the door. In the cramped hallway Teréza came face to face with the two female government inspectors who announced that they were measuring apartments to ensure each apartment in the City of Budapest contained the "acceptable square metres per family."

"How many people live here?" asked the thinner inspector.

"Three!" Anikó bellowed as she shuffled down the hallway.

Teréza was tense. She'd heard rumours of the "eviction campaign," and now that Anikó was including her in the headcount it was dangerous to cause confusion by correcting the old lady in front of the inspectors. Eventually they would be visiting Uncle János' apartment as well, thereby recording Teréza's name twice.

The other inspector began to take notes and asked, "The lady and the two girls?"

"Of course not! My husband, my niece and I. This niece is visiting." She gestured towards Teréza. "My husband's out getting milk."

Teréza and Klára looked on, horrified. What Anikó said was strictly true; her husband had in fact gone out for milk, but it was over two years ago during the Siege. An air raid struck, and he never came back.

"My delinquent husband! He does this all the time. I send him on one task, and he's gone for hours. I know he's gallivanting with younger women. He won't admit to it. Who does he think I am? An old woman?" Anikó followed the inspectors around the apartment with her hands on her hips, raving. "I don't doubt that his girlfriends look a lot like the two of you!"

With relief on their faces to be finished with the old woman, the female inspectors wrote *Sikeres* on their clipboards.

When Teréza locked the door, they could barely contain their guffaws.

Klára led Anikó off for a nap. After she tucked her in, she joined Teréza in the kitchen. "She has no idea she's lying. If they knew they'd turn her apartment into a closet," Klára chortled.

Teréza pulled out the cutting board and put on an apron. "Look at these," she said, cutting up some well-formed, shiny banana peppers.

Klára peered over her shoulder. "How many of those are you putting in?"

"Don't worry, in a pot this size, the flavour will be lost."

Out of her sleep the old woman announced in a clear, loud voice, "Prepare tea and cakes, girls. I expect a visit from my favourite German officers in just under an hour. If my husband has girlfriends, then I can have liaisons too!"

In a panic, Klára dashed to the bedroom. The walls had ears. She must have covered Anikó's mouth because her loud instructions stopped abruptly.

Teréza convulsed, no longer able to stifle her laughter. She wiped the tears from her eyes and continued chopping a mix of peppers, tomatoes, Makó onions and Szegedi paprika. In a huge pot she fried the ingredients in smoked bacon fat and added sausage to the *lecsó* – a traditionally hair-raising spicy ragout.

Teréza told Klára about her innovative use of the Peace flyer.

"I bet between the two of us we could collect enough flyers to resell them on the black market as high quality toilet paper," Klára strategized.

"But first we'd need to put each flyer through the 'softening process.'"

"We could package them in stacks of twenty."

Teréza suggested they come up with a name to market their product. "How about *Peace Wipes My Ass*?"

Klára brayed like a donkey. They laughed until their stomachs hurt.

When the diversion of the *Peace Wipes* wore off and while the *lecsó* simmered, Klára read Teréza the news from *Szabad Nép*.

"Hungarian Collective Farms Benefit from Russian Model," Klára read.

"Communist bullshit," Teréza commented as she stirred the stew. Red splatters of sauce squirted from the pot, landing on her forearm. She sucked her skin.

Anikó waddled into the kitchen. "Are you making something special for my German commanders? I told them to come for dinner at seven after they finish fighting the Russians. One of them doesn't like spicy food. I usually make him schnitzel."

Teréza half laughed, half snorted. "It's not quite ready yet, but I promise it won't be too spicy for him." She motioned with her head towards the radio. Klára swiftly turned it on, loud enough to drown out any talk of Germans. The windows in the kitchen were wide open.

Teréza set the table and sliced large chunks of bread. "Which officer is it that can't eat anything spicy?" she asked Anikó, winking at Klára.

"Adolf," she said, batting her eyelids. "Don't tell my husband that I fancy him. Speaking of which, where the hell is that husband of mine? I asked him to go out and get milk, and the gallivant is taking forever."

Teréza raised her eyebrows. Klára did the same and

turned the volume even higher.

Anikó ventured a sniff under the lid and started sneezing fiercely. "What did you put in this? Poison?" she asked. "Are you trying to poison Adolf?"

"I guarantee, she's not trying to poison anyone," Klára said and took the old woman by the arm. She led her back to her armchair.

Teréza pried the lid from her arthritic fingers, grabbed the wooden spoon, and held it to her lips. The peppers lashed her tongue and tears sprang from her eyes. She turned away, faced the window and sucked in a bit of air. Oh my good God, she thought.

What could she do to repair the *lecsó*? "Do you have any sausage?" she called to Klára in the dining room. "It could use a little more smokiness."

They sat down to eat and Anikó toasted her imaginary guests with a splash of Tokai wine. It wasn't long before the three were coughing and turning red in the face. Teréza, determined to eat everything in her bowl, urged them to eat more bread. Tears streamed down her face as she stuffed huge chunks in her mouth with each spoonful of *lecsó*.

Klára coughed between bites and reached for water.

"I wouldn't drink any water," Teréza said calmly, "It'll only make it worse. Here, have another slice of bread."

"I'll explode if I eat more bread," Klára said fanning her open mouth.

"This is for the devil," said her old charge, slamming her spoon down. "Adolf is unwell, just look at him."

Klára and Teréza exchanged knowing glances. Klára kept fanning, trying not to laugh. "I don't know how you can go on eating this."

Sweat beaded Anikó's forehead. She looked like she might

faint from the heat of the *lecsó*; instead she began to choke. Teréza watched Klára slap her on the back until she spit the contents of her mouth back into her bowl.

"You can't fix this, Teréza," said Klára. "But you can kill a few Russians with it."

Teréza roared with laughter even as her mouth burned. "It's like I've fallen face first into a patch of netthles." Her tongue was swelling. She laughed too hard to even speak. She tried to say, "Let's send thith batch to Rákothi, and we'll thend another batch…to Thalin."

Anikó said she felt diarrhea coming on. Klára muscled the elderly woman to the bathroom.

Teréza laughed harder, and had to rest her forehead on the kitchen table.

"Don't worry, Anikó," Teréza could hear Klára say from the bathroom, "we'll make sure Adolf gets sour cherry soup for dessert to wash down the *lecsó*. No, my dear, Teréza isn't trying to poison Heinrich with the *lecsó*. She's on our side."

Later, after Klára put the old woman to bed, Teréza listened as she read a letter from their mother. "She writes that István was in Budapest for two weeks but decided factory work wasn't for him. He's returned to Ják."

Teréza couldn't understand why he hadn't looked her up. She sulked.

"Maybe he didn't want to start something he couldn't finish," Klára offered as Teréza turned to go.

"I have a feeling he's hiding something from me."

"Who isn't hiding something?"

Teréza wouldn't reveal – even to Klára – what she suspected István had done during the war. Somehow it was easier to charge István with what he wasn't confessing than to say it out loud herself.

They hugged instead of kissed in case they burned each other's cheeks from the residue on their lips. Teréza had already got some in her eye. As she walked to the tram, she wondered over her own reaction to István's avoidance. Did he have a girlfriend back in Ják? If so, who? She felt an intractable need to hear from him, to know something, though she knew not what. It was an altogether original feeling for her, this need to chase the affections of a man. She didn't like the feeling.

When she walked in the door that evening, she found Mrs. Stalin sitting in her chair. The woman mumbled something unintelligible, but her disdain was unmistakable. Teréza ignored her and headed to her room. Her guts were making a whining sound like a cat in heat. When her insides finally settled down, she wrote István, unleashing her one nagging desire. She wrote in the kitchen by the light of a single lamp while everyone else slept.

István, she began the letter, *my Sweet István…*

She described her fiery batch of *lecsó*, articulated in great detail the scene with the old lady and laughed herself into a better mood.

I thought of your little brother today. I don't know why Lali came to me. I pray I'm not upsetting you by bringing him up. Does it ever really heal when we lose our favourite people? It was how you cared for your brother that impressed me, that came to mind. I saw in you a selfless kindness when you were with him, the way you took him on your back or looked at him like something you never wanted to lose. Where in yourself did you find this? If only I could find the same in myself. You inspire me to find it within.

Life in Budapest changes daily. I remind myself every morning that the smell of a fine tomato can ease the strain of life. That it is important to admire the cherry blossoms in the spring or to observe flowing water to stay in touch with one's essential nature. I listen to the sound of my own footfalls on the sidewalk so I can remember to keep a bounce in my step.

I wonder how life is treating you in Ják. My days are full of cooking, cleaning, ironing and taking care of the twins. They cling to me. Their grandmother is a witch. Saturday nights I spend with Klára. While I am grateful for this opportunity to work, I long to return and finish school. Other men and women our age are finding mates and creating their futures.

She signed the letter, *Affectionately, Teréza.*

LEARN NOT TO SPEAK

1947, September. Budapest, Hungary

When István and Pista arrived at the Western train station in
Budapest they saw a sunken, starved city changing its
complexion. Its citizens, supervised by Russian soldiers, were
placed on mandatory work details, serving the reconstruction
effort. The façade of the residence where the two of them
reserved accommodations lay in waste. The room they'd
rented was in a disconsolate place: a subdivided apartment
with four families living in what was once a single-family
dwelling. One grimy bathroom served them all. Their room
was not much bigger than a larder. From the landings, old
women watched the comings and goings of everyone in the
building. Were they Communists or paranoid or bored?
István wondered as he listened to the gypsy kids thump up
and down the hallways. His first impression of Budapest was
disheartening. Or rather, his second. His first had been on
that heinous night, exactly three years ago, gathering the
shoes of Jews with Pista, watching bodies fall into the
Danube. He shuddered at the memories, unable to shake their

beckoning. The isolating shame of his involvement.

Pista hated Budapest. The Russians. The factory. Every-thing. They'd started at the factory two days after they arrived. The monotony, paltry pay and long hours – extended in the name of building Communism – were crushing. It would take a man working ten hours a day, six days a week for more than a year to buy a simple suit. And that was if he didn't have a family to feed.

"Comrades." The man was in his fifties, wiry, with pinched nostrils and a conceited delivery. He wore a gray suit modelled after Uncle Stalin's.

An ass-licking opportunist, thought István. He breathed deep and braced himself for the rhetoric while he glanced around a dismal windowless room at the hundred or so factory workers. Pista looked as bored as he felt. The clock on the wall said eight twenty-three. The bare light bulbs hurt his eyes.

"Comrades, how are you *seeing* things *change* for the better?" asked the wiry man, summoning István from his reverie.

An eager zealot raised her hand. "There is a new bronze statue on Gellért Hill."

"Well observed!"

Sheep. Most of those weary factory workers cared little about the goddamn statue of a Red Army soldier dominating the Buda skyline. And how exactly did it make things better? With its square jaw, clenched fist and a Russian flag, it threatened to leap down from the hills at the first sign of dissent. From István's perspective, on the Pest side, the statue

was gargantuan, standing surefooted next to the Freedom
Statue. Their collective presence was inescapable from any
unobstructed vantage point in Budapest. Lit with powerful
beams, it used more energy, he surmised, than all the
streetlights of Budapest combined. The beautiful Széchenyi
Chain Bridge lacked any electrical current at all; its energy
needs, by decree, had been diverted to light the Soviet
monument.

"We are still reeling from the *devastation* the Germans
left behind," the man continued. "Our *dear* friend, brother
Russia, came to our aid. And we are only still learning how to
build Communism. The great *Soviet* Union is versed in
Communism. Our Russian friends are here to give us
guidance. So that we, *its great proletariat,* will not have to live
like *slaves* like we did under our *filthy capitalist captors.*"

"We cannot put *all* our promises into place *all* at once,"
the wiry man continued, slowly. "We are still rebuilding
Hungary after the *devastation* caused by the *Fascists.* It takes
time. There is still much work to be done. We need to buckle
down and repair the damage."

István felt reprehensible every time he heard the words
"German" or "Fascists." In the two weeks István had spent in
Budapest, he couldn't bring himself to look up Teréza. He felt
too deflated to let her see his face, too guilty. His big move to
the city had amounted to nothing. István waited for
something to change, but he didn't know what.

Sitting next to him, Pista sighed heavily. István wouldn't
look at him. He felt Pista's elbow jabbing into the side of his
arm, trying to get his attention. István wouldn't respond.

He could sense Pista's rising ire. Pista was looking
increasingly demented these days, or asymmetrical, like
someone had grabbed his face and disfigured it.

"My dear comrades, go home *confident* this evening. The work you are doing here is *valuable*."

István stared straight ahead, unwilling to meet Pista's eyes. Pista jumped to his feet.

"Comrade Pista, we have not yet adjourned the meeting," the man said calmly.

"My *sincere* apologies…" Pista mocked the leader's pompous style. "But are we not in *need* of more time to go home and *think* about building the *future* of Communism?"

István wished he'd never been placed at the same workstation as Pista; he could get in trouble by mere association.

The wiry man smiled from one side of his mouth. "Our respected comrade is correct."

István blinked in surprise.

"We will have *many* more opportunities to gather together to *learn* about becoming the best we can become, as individuals, as a nation, as a worldwide *community* of Communists. We shall see you all tomorrow, *bright and early*."

István waited for workers clumped at the end of the row to clear out. He needed air. He bolted outside as soon as he saw an opportunity, taking the back exit.

The factory yard felt eerie and desolate. It was late, and he could hear Pista's distinct footsteps, his lopsided gallop, right behind him.

"They're making me fucking crazy. They tell us to buckle down and repair the country. Our country! That the Germans and the Russians destroyed! And then they fly their red fucking flags everywhere," Pista yelled into the darkness.

"Keep your voice down, Pista."

"Do you know where our food is going?"

"I don't know." István kept his head down, chin to chest, his hands shoved in his pockets.

"Of course you know. To fucking Russia! And our uranium?"

"I wouldn't know," said István, crossing the street. Pista followed tight behind.

"To Russia! We've been led to believe…" he puffed, out of breath, "that these exciting promises…made by the Soviet propaganda machine would benefit us all."

"I don't know," István snapped, and picked up his pace, again.

"Is that all you can say? *I don't know?* What's wrong with you? Let me guess. You don't know!" Pista cackled like a madman.

"Keep your voice down." István dashed ahead into a deserted park, tendrils of fog creeping around the tree trunks. Pista chased after him.

"I know you hate them as much as I do. I can see it in your eyes!"

István glanced back. Pista's arms flailed wildly, his legs kicking out at odd angles. It was uncanny; he looked like he was dancing the Csárdás in Teréza's kitchen.

When István reached the edge of the park he slowed his run to a brisk walk. Running looked suspicious. He headed towards a narrow street, avoiding the main boulevard. He kept his eyes fixated on anything that moved. Police. Soldiers. ÁVO. Anyone who could arrest them. He was about to dart around a corner when he ran headlong into Pista who was trying to cut him off. István grabbed him by the shoulders and shoved him into an empty doorway.

"Do you want to get us thrown in prison, you idiot?" István held his face so close to Pista's, his vision blurred.

Pista cackled and continued his rant. "Managers, advisors, ÁVO spies and party bosses, they get the goddamn vacations. They get automobiles! Their wives get fur coats! And their ugly bloated offspring get the chestnut purée!"

"Chestnut purée!? What the hell are you talking about?" István slammed him back into the door again. In the clutch of his fists, he felt Pista's bones. "Stop already!"

Pista's eyes bulged. István covered Pista's mouth. Pista bit his hand. István smacked his face. Pista laughed louder.

"There are four kinds of stores in our country. One for Russians, one for Hungarian officials and the ÁVO, one for minor Communist officials, and one for us lowly workers. The Russians get the best things Hungary produces. At an eighty percent deduction! The ÁVO for seventy percent. And we get the leftovers for inflated prices."

"What do you want me to do about it?" István implored, holding Pista by the throat. "What do you want me to do?"

"I want you to fight back with me, goddamnit. You owe me."

István clasped his hands hard around Pista's neck and felt powerful squeezing the life out of him. Pista was crazy enough to die for the truth, and István was not. He was lost in impulse until he heard Pista begging him to finish him off.

"Go ahead, do it." Pista choked. "Please! Kill me," he whispered. "Before this fucking system does. I beg you."

Horrified, István released his grip. Pista's body slid down the wall. They were both shaking.

István scrunched his face, trying to hold back a deluge of tears, but they poured out in heaving sobs. Snot stringing from his nose. He fell to his knees and cradled his friend, balled up in the corner of a doorway. Pista stared, his eyes dead, while István rocked him like a child.

"I'll put you on the train tomorrow," István consoled. "Back home. I need to stay and find Teréza. I'll come back to you as soon as I can."

The mist off the Danube soaked the city as István left the train station and the statues on Gellért Hill receded. He craved a bowl of hen soup like he always did when he felt anxious.

In the distance, positioned on a street corner, several Russian soldiers wielded "pe-pe-sha" submachine guns, their frames stockier and less refined than his. They looked like miniatures of the statues on the hill. He took a left to avoid them.

"Young man!" a caustic voice called out. István reached his front door and fumbled with his keys. They hit the cement, jangling. István swore.

"What's on the ground, young man?"

István didn't answer and didn't turn around. The question itself left István incredulous. What use was it to answer, *keys*?

"Unless the young man has committed some offence, he should answer the question." The man moved closer. "The young man should know by now to offer his identification papers."

István reached into his pocket.

"Well?" said the man.

Before catching the Budapest-bound train back in Ják, Feri had sat István down and spoke in a reflective, solemn tone. "I still don't understand why you're leaving us. There are other women."

"Not for me," said István.

"Then learn not to speak," Feri spoke forcefully. "There are only four ÁVO men who visit our village. How many thousands in the city?"

The ÁVO's numbers had been growing like maggots.

Since he arrived in Budapest, István had observed their behaviour, characteristics and mannerisms. On his nightly walk home, he took note of who lingered alone, who paced back and forth, who wore sturdy brown shoes provided to low-level bureaucrats. In the countryside, the ÁVO waited for people in ditches; in the city they appeared from behind lampposts or materialized from the shadows. István put himself in the path of such men despite Feri's warnings. He saw them waiting for him morning and evening, he felt them rise from their benches to follow him. He felt them turn corners with mechanical accuracy and soften their footsteps to elude notice. They timed their footfalls in sync with his and followed him at a distance that elicited an agonizing blend of self-consciousness and derangement. Their aim was to confuse and paralyze him.

István felt the pistons of his heart accelerate. He looked into the man's ruthless eyes and pulled his papers from his pocket.

The ÁVO man couldn't have been much older than István. Even in repose, his face wore a sneer. The thought reassured István in a strange way: the man was permanently flawed. And this made them equals.

"Name?" the man demanded.

István fixed on the ÁVO insignia sewn on the upper arm of the man's uniform.

He cuffed István on the side of the neck with his gloved hand. "Are you mute?"

"You know my name." Astonished by his own reply, István waited for the rebuke, but none came.

"How do you know Vidám Pista?"

"Pardon me?"

"Are you deaf too?" The ÁVO man raised his hand and cuffed him again. "I said, how do you know Vidám Pista?" He stepped on István's keys when he caught him looking towards the ground.

"I don't know Vidám Pista," István said.

"You must either be stupid, or lying."

István began to sweat.

"Don't lie. You nearly choked him last night."

István locked his knees to keep steady.

"There are many reasons to choke a man, but why a friend?" He folded István's papers but didn't hand them back.

"I don't know his last name. He's not my friend. I work with him at the factory."

"Since you arrived two weeks ago?"

István nodded.

"From the same village?"

István felt himself turning red. He coughed to mask his changing skin.

"Seems your friend Vidám Pista has quite a big mouth."

"He's not my friend."

"Why did you try to strangle him?"

"Over a woman."

"Is that why he left on a train this evening?" The man's face formed an indistinguishable expression.

"Yes." István hated himself. He wanted to grab the ÁVO man's gun and shoot himself.

The ÁVO man retrieved István's keys and dangled them in front of his nose. "Thank you, comrade. I don't believe you. I wouldn't be too eager to leave those meetings if I were you." The ÁVO man threw István's keys in his face.

★

István went into work the next morning and spent the day stacking munitions shells, trying to convince himself that the lies that began as a necessity were not becoming a full-blown character trait. He skipped lunch. At the end of the day he went to the foreman's office and reported his intention to quit, fabricating a story that his father had fallen ill and he needed to return home right away. "It's very serious," he said, unconvincingly. He was a poor liar; involving Feri made him feel worse.

The unsympathetic foreman told István he would not get paid before he left. Behind an even phonier smile, István pretended it was no inconvenience at all and said he'd return in some weeks to pick up his wages.

He had no intention of ever coming back.

LAUGH TODAY, CRY TOMORROW

1947, October. Budapest, Hungary

"Is your heart pounding too?" asked Klára, almost giggling.

"It's in its usual resting place. My throat."

Klára covered her mouth to muffle her laughter.

A month after the *lecsó* incident, Teréza and Klára walked nimbly down Andrássy Boulevard in their low heels. They turned the corner at Vörösmarty Street, an elegant ruin, crushed by the Siege. Klára was taking Teréza past the ÁVO Headquarters where lists were compiled, orders carried out and Hungarians were tortured. Teréza knew the street, though. She'd pushed the twins past this very building every day for a month. Teréza hadn't realized until today that victims lay bleeding, beaten and electrocuted mere steps away the whole time. She glimpsed a star, a hammer and a sickle on the double doors.

"Don't look directly at the building," Klára said quietly. "Is that number sixty?"

Without turning her head, Teréza strained her eyes until they hurt. "Yes." She looked back at the sidewalk in front of her. The late fall leaves smelled of cinnamon and black pepper.

"The only way to survive it," Klára said quietly, "is to look at what's really happening. Ignorance is not a solution."

Teréza's precept was to take a page from her uncle's book and stay off the streets unless absolutely necessary. She left the flat only to take the twins for a short walk, to shop at the market, to attend church or to visit Klára. Klára was dauntless. She confronted head on what she needed to conquer. She walked up to the threat, looked it in the face and neutralized it. Every day.

"You can't let them own our streets." Klára looked at Teréza with mischief in her eyes. "Ready for another lap?"

"Why not?" Teréza answered, admiring Klára's courage, wondering what István would think of her newfound bravery. She had a desire to write to him about it, but changed her mind when she realized that if she described how cleverly she visualized burying her resistance she was worried he would equate it with a veiled message – perhaps it would make him paranoid and want to reject her.

That night, Teréza ironed tea towels while Mrs. Stalin slept and Hermina read to the twins. She watched Uncle János smoking in the sewing room by the radio, a tape measure around his neck, one hand sunk in the pocket of his pleated pants. He looked like her father just then, his shirtsleeves rolled up to his elbows, sucking on a cigarette. His third in a row. Not one announcer on Magyar Rádió dared to utter the words *election fraud.*

No sooner had Teréza aired out her bedroom and

prepared for her nightly address to Eötvös Street then Uncle János came to her room, sat in his work chair and lit a smoke. She didn't have the heart to tell him not to light up. And though she'd spent a lifetime sharing her bedroom with family, somehow it felt too close with him in the room.

He didn't ask her any questions. He didn't say anything at all.

Teréza's mind raced. She wondered if now was a good time to ask the question she'd been dying to ask since Hermina told Teréza about the ÁVO. "Were you aligned with the Germans during the war?" She remembered her mother telling her, "The Germans are cultured. It's the Russians we have to fear. They're the real barbarians."

Uncle János didn't answer at first. Then, looking up from his feet he said, "I wasn't vocal."

"You know the ÁVO Headquarters? On Andrássy 60?" Teréza asked.

"Who doesn't?"

"What was it before?"

Uncle János paused. "Why are you asking?"

Teréza remained silent.

"The Arrow Cross tortured the opposition there during the war. Now the Communists torture their opponents at the same address."

Teréza let that roll around in her gut. What had always been a clear picture of two opposing sides was starting to run together like the juices of peppers and tomatoes in a *lecsó*. Same crimes, different uniforms.

"Not the best bedtime conversation." Her uncle butted out his cigarette, stood and gave her a hug. He felt like her father, only taller and with more meat on his bones.

Teréza didn't sleep. Her couch felt like a narrow box.

After facing down Andrássy Avenue 60, Teréza made a promise to herself never to think of her disgusting Russian perpetrators again. She'd unthink them. And by doing so, they'd untouch her. And the event would unhappen. Keeping busy staved off – for the most part – images that tried to intrude while she maintained a productive routine in the home of her uncle. Nightmares in which she couldn't find her clothing while Russian soldiers tried to break into her bedroom, woke her with revulsion and a pounding chest. She assuaged her guilt with ten Hail Marys, asking the gracious mother to cleanse her of impurity.

In the charcoal night, she imagined digging a deep hole. She poured her hatred for Soviets, for Russians, for all things Communist inside a wooden box and buried it in the ground, along with her newly formed disdain for the Arrow Cross torturers who'd taken lessons from the Nazis. She tamped down the earth, and swept it with twigs and leaves to leave no trace. She backed away, obscuring her footsteps. Only she knew where she kept her dissent. But when in her mind's eye she turned to leave, she was startled to find a young man with ginger hair watching her.

The next morning, on October eleventh, Teréza turned seventeen.

Hermina pulled Teréza aside, "Please, no cleaning today, or cooking. It's your birthday."

"Please forgive us," added Uncle János. "We're unable to throw you the kind of party a seventeen-year-old deserves, but allow us to invite you for dinner this evening in our dining room restaurant."

"That would be lovely. I accept," said Teréza. "But may I go the market? I love getting out."

"Ah…" Uncle János said, pressing several coins into her hand. "Get several lengths of spicy sausage and no Paris baloney. I can't stomach anymore of that artificial crap." He handed Teréza ten forints. "They grind everything from intestines to teeth into it." It had been a good year for business. He'd been begrudgingly sewing dress uniforms for Party officials. Now he could afford a few perks for the family.

"She ruined the Paris baloney last time by frying it," Mrs. Stalin yelled from the day room.

Teréza paid her no mind and bounded down three flights of the spiral staircase, singing to herself.

The city had recently re-opened the Central Market on the Pest side of the Liberty Bridge – the ground-level "chicken hall" was badly damaged during the war. Teréza's third visit to the impressive wrought iron, glass and brick building was still exciting for her. She heard old market folk complain that it lacked the splendour of the original – wounded buildings like wounded people gradually exposed their scars no matter how well they tried to dress them up or hastily get on with life – still when she stepped inside its cavernous structure, slender steel columns allowed for boundless daylight to flood the market. Teréza was buoyant. Sunlight was God's way of healing pain.

At seven in the morning the market was bustling. Teréza stood at the entrance to take it all in. Though three floors were open, congesting the central ground floor aisle were grumpy deliverymen and haggling old ladies, their thinning hair wrapped with headscarves and their breasts busting out from shrunken cardigans – their elbows thrice darned. She could smell hen soup on the second floor where the walls were still crumbling like sand. To Teréza the sights looked worn and wonderful between strings of dried red paprika and garlic, brown eggs, and slabs of meat for those who could afford it. Wrinkled faces examined wrinkled cabbage. The sound of falling coins competed with the laughter of children scampering to pick them up. She admired the sight of a white scale weighing a bag of poppy seeds, its needle moving up and then down as the vendor handed over the purchase to a woman with an attractive burgundy beret.

In the basement butcher shop, Teréza took a number – thirteen – on a piece of rough brown paper. Customers spoke in low tones, no joy in their conversations. Painted a shabby grey, the concrete shop gave the meat in the display case a decayed hue. The selection was paltry, the service brusque. The bored and surly workers behind the counter wore utilitarian green aprons, white shirts, and hairnets on their heads. They moved slowly, inconvenienced by the long line-up. A grimy fan sat idle with a frayed cord. Teréza wished she had chosen the other butcher shop a little farther down, but now she was in line and didn't want to start over.

As Teréza waited, her eyes wandered to the only thing on the wall apart from the chalkboard behind the counter. An outdated poster for the peace campaign. The font looked magisterial yet tried to be friendly. Her eyes were drawn to the muscled man on the poster wearing a green apron and white shirt with rolled up sleeves, his strong chest flush to the viewer and head in profile. One arm was extended high above his head with a clenched fist. In the other, he held a Hungarian flag with a new centre motif: a shaft of wheat under a blazing red star. Behind him stood a woman in the same stance, holding a solid red flag. With determined faces, the figures lunged into a future with flashy colours. In the background, factories spewed smoke.

Teréza had never seen an image so deliberate, so brutal. It lacked beauty and softness.

"Looks like the butcher, doesn't he?" An elderly man whispered in her ear.

Teréza gasped.

"Soviet art," the man said ever so quietly.

She turned slightly to take him in. He was thin with a head of grey hair. She smiled. He smiled back and winked.

"Those are lovely shoes," said the man looking for a moment towards her feet. "My neighbour had the very same pair."

The remark made Teréza uncomfortable. "What happened to her shoes?" she said in a whisper.

The man's expression turned heavy. "Where are you from?" he asked.

"Ják," she answered, almost apologetically. "What happened to the woman?"

He gently shook his head. "She's dead in the Danube."

"Thirteen!"

Teréza handed the butcher her slip. "Good day, sir. I hope my number is lucky today," she said brightly.

"Hurry it up," replied the butcher.

"Four lengths of sausage, please?" Teréza watched as the man pulled two small lengths from the hook and wrapped them in course paper. "I beg your pardon, sir, but would you kindly add in two more lengths?"

"We got an aristocrat here? If you take four lengths, what d'you imagine the workers are gonna eat at the end of the day?"

Teréza looked down. The elderly man touched her shoulder, leaned in closer to her ear. "You have to join the

Hungarian Working People's Party to get four lengths."

"Anything else?" the butcher asked.

"Soup bones, please," Teréza replied. Mrs. Stalin would never believe they wouldn't give Teréza four lengths of sausage. She would probably accuse her of eating the other two on the way home.

"How many?"

"How many am I allowed?"

The butcher looked offended and stacked several hefty bones onto brown paper and wrapped them tight.

As she climbed the stairs back to the ground floor, the mouth-watering scent of freshly baked bread and jam-stuffed pastries lured her off course. She wasn't ready to leave the market. While zigzagging between sack-laden shoppers – her own arms straining from the weight of bagged soup bones – she saw István. His red hair. Her heart rushed and she felt her body rise. She ran through the congested aisle like a hobbled horse, soup bones slamming at her shins, wending her way around shoppers. When she finally closed in on him – now only a metre away – a butcher pushed a dead pig prone on a dolly in front of her, cutting her off in full stride. Her passage blocked, she swore at the butcher, who turned and stared at her with his arms crossed.

She looked at the pig and then at him.

He looked at the pig and then at her.

It was a standoff.

It took everything in her not to attack, not to tear him to shreds. Through tightened jaws she said, "My sincere apologies, sir. I don't know what overtook me."

The man moved his pig from her path.

Teréza picked up her pursuit of István, but by then she'd missed her chance. There was no sign of him in the vast and humming market.

"Damn it!"

When she returned from the market, Mrs. Stalin blamed her for the loose threads that had migrated from the sewing room to the day room, plucking them disdainfully with her long translucent fingernails.

Teréza cried in the bathroom before dinner.

The old woman didn't bother to toast Teréza when Hermina placed a Napoleon cake on the table after the meal of *Gulyás* was served. "What on earth is the occasion?" Mrs. Stalin asked instead, reaching for the knife to cut the first slice.

Hermina wrestled the knife from her hand and initiated the first notes of the birthday song: *Long live Teréza.* The twins sang off key while Uncle János sang baritone.

Hermina handed her a weightless parcel wrapped in brown paper with a card made by the twins. Uncle János handed her a letter.

"It's in a gentleman's handwriting."

"Must be a mistake," said Mrs. Stalin.

"Go to bed, mother. Now." Hermina had finally lost her patience.

Tearing open the present Teréza found a lovely new dress – hazelnut satin with a lacy Peter Pan collar. Uncle János had made it for her.

"You can wear it in the spring. The satin's too delicate for this weather."

The card from the twins was covered in pink hearts. The letter she reserved for the privacy of bedtime.

István remembered, or else had inquired. His handwriting made her giddy. She studied it under a magnifying glass and caressed the ink on the page. She noted that he formed his characters with care and precision, yet they never lost their flow. Capital letters had grandness to them, and his lower case looked like precious pearls. He'd not made one mistake on the page. But what really impressed Teréza was the depth with which he expressed himself.

How kind you are to mention my little brother. You're right, my heartache is profound. It is with deep shame that I confess I was in the nation's capital for two long weeks, and I didn't arrive at your doorstep. If I explain my reasoning, I can only hope that you will rethink your opinion of me. The nature of my work did not match my spirit, and hence I could not be as useful as I know I can be. And without a life purpose, I cannot be useful to you. I want you to see the man you truly deserve, and that means I have more work to do. Mercifully, I now busy myself with that task. I realized on the train back to Ják, as I drifted ever farther from you, and deep snow mantled the countryside, that it's always darkest before dawn. Sure enough the light did come, in an instant, from my fair friend Pista. At first, the dimwit suggested I become a butcher. How is that different from making leather shoes I asked him? But recently he brought me news of a training program for firefighters.

I've been handpicked for officer training in the Firefighters' Academy in the capital. By next spring I'll be training in Budapest! And my darling Teréza, I can be around automobiles. I don't know if you know this about me, but I have a feel for metal and the way parts fit together and how they come apart, how they work as a whole to make something run. Not only can I save people from disasters, but I can also get under automobiles, my second love after you. Csók, István.

Csók, she'd whispered to herself. Not a childish *puszi*, but a mature kiss. A *csók*. She kissed the letter and tucked it under her pillow; the next morning she tucked it in her apron and carried it with her wherever she went, willing her dreams to manifest. She was aching to show it to Klára, but Anikó had fallen ill with whooping cough and Klára, unable to leave her bedside, adamantly warned off coming over.

Teréza wore the dress to church the next day, a day of rain and bluster. While still in her room, she threw her coat on over the dress so Mrs. Stalin wouldn't get a glimpse of it. Uncle János bid the ladies a safe journey and settled into his armchair with a cigarette.

Each outing to the church was a gamble, a public insult to Communism. When her husband asked the women to stop going, Hermina reprimanded him. "They're not taking this away from me."

Teréza agreed.

Uncle János declined the weekly mass, preferring instead to read the *Szabad Nép* newspaper. "It gives me a chance to stay on top of the lies."

Teréza could see his point. She winked at her uncle and pulled open her shabby brown woollen coat.

"Couldn't it wait till spring?" he chuckled into his newspaper.

"What's so amusing?" demanded Mrs. Stalin.

"Nothing that would interest you," Teréza answered, chuckling with her uncle.

"Laugh today, cry tomorrow." Mrs. Stalin pulled on her black leather gloves.

Out on Teréz Boulevard, Teréza felt the winds blow up under her dress. Mrs. Stalin was going to think she was such a fool. Hermina and the twins trailed behind.

Teréza no longer grew nauseated during the tram ride, but Mrs. Stalin still stood several metres away from her. On Teréza's first tram ride in the city, she held her hand over her mouth to quell her nausea. Mrs. Stalin had rolled her eyes and looked away in revulsion. Hermina mouthed to Teréza, "Ignore her."

But Mrs. Stalin's precaution didn't particularly bother Teréza today, drenched as she was in the blush of love.

The church was half empty; most people were too intimidated to keep attending. In this holy place, Teréza's fear vanished, and her strength renewed itself. The priest's words gave her hope. The frankincense lifted her spirit, elevated her mind and cleared her thinking. Here she trusted in God. She was beginning to realize that the ever-changing conditions in Hungary were nothing but more of the same. Stasis masquerading as change.

At the end of the mass, an altar boy handed the priest an envelope.

"Cardinal Mindszenty has a few words for us," the priest intoned, his manner grim, as he removed a carbon copy letter from the envelope.

Teréza straightened, eager to hear every single word written by the revered holy man. The priest cleared his throat as two men wearing brown shoes rose from the pews and walked to the back of the church. They stood against the wall.

The priest adjusted his glasses and read Cardinal Mindszenty's letter in a clear, loud voice. "*I do not wish that any Catholic should lose his livelihood because of me. If Catholic faithful sign letters of protest against me, they can do it in the knowledge that it is not done of their own free will. Let us pray for our beloved Church and our precious Hungary.*"

The priest slowly folded the letter and replaced it in the

envelope. An unnerving silence settled. The two men exited the church, and a cool breeze wafted up Teréza's skirt. She shivered. The smoke of extinguished candles filled her nostrils, reminding her of Christmas, when her father put them out on the tree before midnight mass. The front doors of the church opened, allowing in another chill gust of wind. They closed with a loud thud, sealing in the guilty. Teréza kept her eyes on the priest. He placed the envelope near the edge of the pulpit.

Four ÁVO men walked up the aisle to the altar and stood on either side of the pulpit to face the priest. They hadn't even made the sign of the cross, Teréza thought, shocked by their sacrilege. She felt the relief of déja vu, but it was tainted by fear. One ÁVO man removed the letter from the pulpit and passed it to the other, who placed it in a folder. They took the priest by each arm. A chilling hush descended as the ÁVO led the priest away. The congregation remained seated. No one raised a hand in protest. Four altar boys watched, dumb-founded. Their censers drooped in front of them.

"Where are those men taking the priest?" asked one of the twins.

Hermina blanched.

The other twin called out after the priest. The last of the four ÁVO men paused and looked back. Hermina struck her daughter hard across the cheek. The child sank back into the pew and began to wail. Teréza muffled the protestations of the second child by covering her mouth.

The ÁVO man smiled at them. "Such lovely girls. Twins, are they?" Without waiting for a reply, he turned sharply on his heel and walked out.

When finally they exited the church, Hermina told Teréza to stand watch while she dragged her twins into an alley behind the church. Teréza witnessed a frantic Hermina get to her knees, while Mrs. Stalin paced nervously in front of the tram stop. Hermina pulled the crying girls close. "Never, never, never, under any circumstance, ask any questions in public, ever again! Do you hear me?"

By the time they reached home Budapest was covered in an icy fog. The city slouched with the weight of foot-long icicles dripping relentlessly.

Tension and fear ate up all of Teréza's excitement over István's letter. Her insides felt ravenous for security. A constant need to keep moving, keep busy, staved off the terror of being caught doing something wrong, first in the eyes of God, second in the eyes of the state and third in the eyes of Mrs. Stalin. Only the rustling letter in her apron pocket gave her any faith in the strength of human love.

SEPARATION

1961

WHAT IS THE WOMAN WAITING FOR

1961, January & June. Szombathely & Budapest, Hungary

Five years to the day István had escaped, his son tapped a rhythm on the kitchen table in sync with the harsh January wind that rattled their window. Teréza celebrated in secret with Zolti. "Today is the anniversary of your father's success," she whispered as she placed a photo in front of Zolti's plate. "He got out."

She wondered what it was like for Zolti to know his father only from photographs. This was one of Zolti's favourites, taken in September 1958, showing his father leaning against a large handsome two-toned car with chrome bumpers. His father wore pressed pleated pants and a white shirt with the sleeves rolled neatly above his elbows. The grass was tall around his pant legs. She placed that photo on the table, propped up by the saltshaker.

"Canada is very far away," she explained, "and eventually

we'll follow your father there, but don't tell anyone." Teréza knew no avenues existed while Kádár's government busied itself with reforms and revenge.

"Why?" Zolti asked.

"Just don't," she answered, placing two sticky chicken feet on his plate. "Eat," she said, "You need the strength to get to Canada."

"Are we running too?"

"No. Eat."

"How will I get strong if the feet have no muscles?" Zolti replied. "Isn't this just skin, bones and tendons? I need meat if I'm to build muscle."

"My, my what a devilishly smart boy you've become! Now eat."

Meanwhile she swore at the stovepipe. Rusting away, it had cracks causing the whole flat to fill with smoke. Teréza threw open the front door and aggressively fanned the smoke with a dishtowel.

Zolti coughed between bites of chicken skin, and Teréza covered her mouth to keep from inhaling smoke. The kitchen quickly grew cold, forcing her to close the door. She cursed the stovepipe again and continued to fan the air.

Teréza watched as Zolti tried to lick his fingers clean. Instead, he transferred the gelatinous matter from his tongue to his fingertips. When he tried rubbing his mouth clean with a small square of rough brown toilet paper, he got paper bits and gelatin all over his face. In the end, he looked like a man who'd cut himself shaving.

"This isn't food," whined Zolti, his fingers sticking to his face. "It's glue! Like in Grandpa Feri's shop."

Teréza took his wrists and lead him to the kitchen sink where she scrubbed him clean. The two were firmly and anxiously bonded; their worlds revolved inward and outward from each other. István was only someone in Zolti's imagination, less substantial than chicken feet.

After dinner Zolti found a station from Vienna on the radio. He was determined to learn German from the radio host. "Guten Abend!" he crowed, marvelling at the thought of another language.

Teréza pressed her forefinger to her lips. "Shhhhhh. Only at home will we speak German. It's our code language. It never leaves these walls. You understand? Everything now is between you and me." She was entrusting secrets to her son that once she would have only shared with her husband.

As she did every second Saturday, she took Zolti on the bus to visit his grandparents in Ják. First she stopped in on Feri, visiting him at his shoe shop where she showed him István's letters from Canada. Feri grew sensitive, almost as though his heart had sprung a leak. Fast moving tears slid down to his chin, and he rocked. Teréza couldn't bear seeing him so inconsolable.

He'd fallen heartsick over István's departure and was unable to reconcile that he may never see his eldest son again. Moments like these she felt disappointed with István. How could he have left his stepfather without saying goodbye?

"Look at Zolti," said Feri, drying his face and chin. "He's already drawn to tools. Look at the way he picked up that awl. A natural. Zolti might even take over the family business someday. Who am I to pass it on to? Neither István nor Tamás were interested. I wanted to hire Pista after István left us. He was good with his hands but turned into a drunk. May the poor soul rest in peace. He was a loyal friend to István."

"Zolti shares István's love of machinery," Teréza said with a defensive edge noticeable enough for Feri to look at her with concern. She gazed at her son, evading Feri's curiosity. "When I was allowed to sign out the small washing machine from the County Council, I had to push it several kilometres home. Through downtown, up our street. It was on casters and made such a racket as it rolled over the cracks in the sidewalk, then over our gravel street."

"I helped push it out of the pothole in front of our house!" Zolti added.

Teréza's laughter ignited in small spurts.

"Yes you did! Neighbours stepped out into their yards. The noise was so terrible. I was embarrassed, but I didn't care. It was the only chance I had to wash our clothing properly." Teréza's laugh turned bittersweet. "Zolti fell in love with the apparatus right away. Didn't you sweetheart?"

Zolti nodded enthusiastically.

"Do you remember how you adored the burring and the droning?" Turning to Feri she continued, "He fixated on the motor like István obsessed over car engines. When it was time for me to push it back to work, Zolti threw his arms around its body, hugging it goodbye and crying. "Washy maching, washy washy. Please come back!"

Feri smiled broadly as Zolti looked up at him. Zolti's cheeks flushed; the boy was pleased to hear the adorable story about himself.

"I said to him, 'You'll have so much to cry about in life, my son, don't use up all your tears on the washing machine.'"

Zolti had stopped listening. His small hands were immersed in a shallow pot of glue, shirt cuffs just skimming the surface.

"Watch your clothes, Zolti, please don't get anything on them," Teréza said.

Teréza had long ago stopped visiting István's mother

Zsuzsa. The woman barely asked after István, and when she did, it was only to ask when István would write and send money from Canada. Her questions infuriated Teréza. Without answering, Teréza would gather Zolti up and give the excuse that she had to see her parents down the lane.

In her parents' yard the snow had packed down. Gyuri inspected the bottoms of Zolti's shoes to make sure he hadn't stepped in any frozen chicken shit, then took his grandson by the hand.

"It's time you learned to fetch water," he said to his grandson.

Zolti jumped up and down flapping his arms. She smiled as the two scuttled off, hand in hand towards the white adobe well. A great bustard swooped low, its neck outstretched, flying over the frozen pond at the edge of the property. Its deep grunt scared Zolti, who clung to Gyuri's leg. Teréza watched, remembering the bustard on the day of the drum, laughing aloud as her father stretched up like a bear, waving his fist at the crane.

"Stay away from my grandson, you lousy bird!" Gyuri pretended to be outraged as Zolti's fear turned to riotous giggles.

Anna came out of the house wearing a sheep vest, a pail in one hand, wiping the other on her apron. Teréza reached for her mother, pulled her stiff body in and hugged her tight. "Father's putting Zolti to work. No time to waste around here." Teréza caught sight of her father heaving Zolti onto the edge of the well, holding his waist as he cast the pail deep into the well. Teréza covered her mouth as Zolti's delighted shrieks were carried on the breeze.

"What are you doing, Gyuri?!" Anna yelled. "You're going to kill the boy!" The bustard flew away, and Anna turned to Teréza. "Have you thought about how you're going to join István? Hasn't it been five years now?"

"Five years yesterday," Teréza wiped a tear from her eye.

"Too long for a boy to be without his father."

"We're still waiting for the government to soften its stance. How much longer can they keep families separate? Something has to give at some point."

"I admire your optimism. I lost mine long ago." Anna stood. "I have to relieve the chickens of their eggs."

On the way home, the bus to Szombathely was full. Teréza and Zolti stood in the aisle. A caring young woman took Zolti onto her lap, and as soon as she did, he started to tell her, in a serious and pensive tone, what he'd dreamt last night. Teréza overheard him saying, "The cunning fox came into the yard and ate the hen. The peasant felt heart sick and died."

The next day, Teréza received news that Feri had died from a massive heart attack. Teréza wondered what part of her son picked up on what was communicated without words.

"We didn't use enough glue to make Grandpa stay," said Zolti, through tears.

Teréza could hardly bring herself to write of it to István.

István's letter expressed the depth of his anguish for Feri's sudden death, at not having said goodbye and gratitude for the man who chose to father him with kindness. His letter also contained a coded message. *There is a lovely walk we*

used to take near the British Legation in Budapest, he wrote, even though they'd never been near the building, and all their walks were in the Buda Hills. Still, Teréza dutifully made the trip to Budapest in mid-June and stayed with Klára, her husband and two toddlers.

Teréza woke early. At daybreak the fog hovered just a foot over the sidewalk and suspended in the trees like thinning white hair. Through the open kitchen window, a smell of garbage wafted up from the street. The rains had begun in Budapest. The moisture in the atmosphere troubled and unsettled her. It was like that feeling she got when the day started off amiss.

She gathered her clothing off a chair, neatly folded and laid out the night before. At the basin, she used a cloth to wash her face, her underarms and between her legs, then dressed herself. She backcombed and neatened her hair, applied pale coral lipstick. She took another look out the window. The scene had changed completely. Through long elegant tree branches, rays of sun cut through the fog.

She stepped out and breathed in the early morning air. What a lovely day, she thought. Look at the way the sun is at just the right angle to create a masterpiece of light on the sidewalk. She caught herself; enjoying the light would have constituted a betrayal to her inner opposition. Maintaining resistance meant keeping a fire under her anger and resentment. She could not let the glory of this scene outshine the heaviness of her soul.

As she rounded the corner onto Harmincad Street, she saw the gorgeous Art Nouveau building. The British Legation had been in the building since 1947. For the first time in five years, since the end of the Revolution, reunification of families became a remote possibility. With its high-pitched roof and colonnaded loggias, the Legation was the only gate to the West. All she needed was to make it inside without anyone stopping her.

She walked down the opposite side of the street and stopped in front of the state-run dry cleaning shop. She had heard rumours that the ÁVO hid a camera in the "O" of the *PATYOLAT* sign which promised sparkling clean sheets. She'd once taken sheets there for Hermina. "They came back grey. The lazy pricks," she said out loud. Teréza's habit of talking aloud when she felt outrage had not yet gotten her in trouble. She walked directly across the street towards the Legation with her back to the camera so they couldn't get a photo of her face.

Decorated with a Hungarian tulip design, the engraved doors were worn and chipped. Teréza's spirits lifted. She kept her head down and dashed up the steps. Pushing open the heavy doors, she was flustered to be received politely by a Hungarian staffer. She expected to be snubbed.

The receptionist already knew why Teréza was here. "Good morning. Please proceed to the fourth floor," the woman said warmly, pointing to the elevator. Inside the walls of the British Legation, Teréza encountered a civility that she'd not known in Hungary since before the war. There was only one reason a Hungarian visited the Legation. She proceeded to the lift and pressed the button for the fourth floor. She was met by another Hungarian staffer, this one also amicable, in her fifties with bright red hair and blue eye shadow. "Are you applying for an Exit Visa?"

At first Teréza couldn't answer. She'd not yet spoken of this to anyone. She nodded and listened carefully to the woman who directed her to a private doctor's clinic in another part of the city.

"You'll need to take a tuberculosis test. It's valid for six months. Do you understand? I'll call the doctor's office right away and book you an appointment for a few hours from now. Go there next, right after we start your application."

Start your application. The idea hardly seemed real. Teréza felt the first rush of achievement. "Yes, yes, I will go there," The thought made her lightheaded.

"Name?" asked the woman. Together they began to fill in the forms.

Teréza left her documents half filled in. She had more information to collect and promised to return after the doctors' appointment.

"Good luck," said the woman on the fourth floor.

"Until next time," said the receptionist on the main level.

Teréza's pointy shoes ushered her trippingly out the doors, in the direction of the doctor's office. In her single-minded pursuit, she was caught off guard.

"Your identification card."

The voice hit her ear abruptly and forcefully. It's tone hard and inflexible. His head was wide at the temples, his hair combed back and slippery, the lines in his forehead carved deep. His breath mixed with hers as her heart pumped recklessly. She felt rudderless.

Before her trembling hands could even undo the zipper on her purse, the AVÓ detective had already summoned a policeman. She fumbled for the card she kept in the same place, the card that never left its compartment. The worn identification card that went everywhere with every citizen wherever they travelled, even for a jaunt to the corner grocery.

Impatiently, the detective blew smoke at her and exchanged a smug look with the policeman. They grunted sarcastically in agreement.

"We haven't got all day," said the detective, his voice steelier than before.

Teréza's frantic hand found the familiar plastic covering, pulling with it tissues and photographs. Several items cascaded from her purse to the sidewalk. What miracle was it, that in that moment, a truck crashed into a microcar at the end of the block, prompting the two men to look over their shoulder? Teréza stuffed István back into her purse. She quickly scooped up her identification card, tissues and pen.

The two men made no move to assist the driver pinned inside the accordianed microcar while the truck driver swore a blue streak. Instead, the two rifled through Teréza's ID booklet while she kept her head down at a slight angle like an obedient horse. She'd learned that if you looked them in the eye you might be persuaded to confess something. One of the men made notations in his little black book. They said nothing to her. The threat of punishment lingered in the nothingness. They looked her up and down, admiring her figure.

"May I go?" she asked.

"What is the woman waiting for?" asked the detective.

"I am not waiting for anything if it means inconveniencing you."

"You'll need this. Next time you might want to find a more obvious place to keep it." The detective handed Teréza her ID.

"Yes, detective, sir," she replied and started walking in the opposite direction to the men.

She waited at home for a knock, though it never came. Her documents stayed at the Legation, incomplete, and the doctor's appointment came and went.

ENGAGEMENT

1949-1950

PROMISE ME TWO THINGS

1949, April. Budapest, Hungary

The wind blew tirelessly. Trees pitched, clinging to the ground – weather that István generally took to be a bad omen.

"It's me, István!" István had called out to Gyuri, waving in a friendly manner.

Teréza's father had been sitting under the veranda sharpening knives, his long apron, bloody as always. He wore a beat-up brown suit jacket and looked older, his moustache matted and unkempt. In contrast, István arrived clean-shaven, wearing his tidy uniform.

Gyuri didn't smile, nor did he look surprised to see him. Anyone in uniform was bad news.

"I hardly recognize you, boy," Gyuri said, standing up, putting down his knife.

"Good day, sir," István said extending his hand, noticing Gyuri eye the red stars on his epaulettes. "It's not what you think."

Gyuri shook it. "Good."

His hand felt chapped and misshapen from work. "May I

speak with you?"

"Come with me, out to the field, where it's safer." Gyuri ambled over to the house, disappeared for a moment and came out with a bottle of brandy. He motioned for István to follow.

István walked alongside Gyuri through the tall grass of the field adjacent to the Édes house. Upon seeing the outline of a lone house on the horizon and a sweep-pole well, he was drawn into the darling memory of Teréza dancing the *Csárdás* while Gyuri and András plucked the zithers in their kitchen. His reverie was interrupted by the sight of a handle-less pitchfork, its head lodged into the ground, teeth sticking heavenwards, grass grown up around it. Curious, he thought.

"That was a bad day," Gyuri chuckled.

Under the cover of the majestic apple tree just starting to bud, out of earshot of the world, István and Gyuri sat on the splintered grey rails of an ancient fence.

"I can see the entire world from here. It gives me time to figure out how to deal with it." Gyuri offered István a smoke.

"I don't smoke, but thanks." István raised his fingers to decline.

"I can't let Teréza's mother know," said Gyuri. "She'll baste me in my own juices. I promised I'd quit when Teréza still lived at home."

István observed Édes Gyuri's profile. He saw Teréza's impertinent nose, her pointed chin, her forehead. István watched as Gyuri positioned two glasses carefully between his legs on the fence, his filthy apron serving as a tablecloth, and poured two shots of brandy. Gyuri stirred melancholy in István, his weather-beaten skin, his fingernails thick with dirt, the smell of his decaying teeth.

Gyuri handed István a glass of brandy, raised the other,

and removed the cigarette from his lips. "To your health," he said and took a big sip. Gyuri let out a long satisfied, "Ahhhh," and smacked his lips. "Life would hardly be bearable without it."

"True," István said, contented by the burning sensation that travelled down his throat.

"Tell me," said Gyuri, pouring two more shots, "how is it that Hitler was over his head in shit but Stalin was only up to his waist?"

"I don't know," István replied. A smile grew on his lips. He crossed his legs.

"Because Stalin was standing on Lenin's shoulders."

The two men laughed. Gyuri shot back a second brandy. István followed, clocking that Gyuri had cracked a joke that could get him jailed. He was vetting István, testing him. Because he already knew why István had come.

István obliged him. "I would like to ask for your daughter's hand in marriage."

"How old are you boy?"

"Twenty-four. And a half, sir."

"My daughter is only nineteen." With chapped fingers, Gyuri brought a cigarette to his lips, took a long drag and blew the smoke into the sky. The sun had slipped behind a cloud and somewhere downwind a pig snorted.

István suddenly felt nervous, almost heartbroken, as though his dream of a life with Teréza might vanish into air like the smoke from Gyuri's cigarette.

"You have to promise me two things, István."

"Anything."

"That you will never become one of them," Gyuri said, looking at the star on István's collar.

"Never. I promise."

"And that you will never leave my daughter for any reason. Never."

Something like guilt shot through István's stomach. "Of course." He leaned forward, elbows on knees, and laced his fingers neatly into a ball, as though trying to find a container for the promise.

"Promise me," Gyuri said.

"On my honour," István replied.

Gyuri leaned in. István allowed, with a firm grip on his jaw, for Gyuri to bring István's face close to his.

"You have my blessing," he said and kissed István on the lips. And then he drew a handkerchief from his pocket, blowing his nose and sucking back tears.

The smell of manure infused the warm wind and carried tiny voices from the figures of Ági, Juli and Kati entering the far end of the yard. Their red scarves fell haphazardly off their necks. Their white ankle socks slouched. They carried school bags, kicked up dust and walked in zigzags, twirling their skirts. Following behind and looking pained under the burden of two heavy sacks was their mother, Anna.

"I love my little women," said Gyuri, suddenly wiping away tears.

István couldn't wait to learn from Teréza the feeling of loving a woman.

István ushered Teréza to the Buda Hills, via tram and bus, far up above the city, above the coursing, glittering Danube. The sun shone brilliantly in a blue sky, sunbeams burst through trees resplendent with glossy new leaves, every shade of green. Sycamores, black pines, old orange mulberries. He looked down at her pink cheek dappled with sunshine and felt deliverance.

As they strolled pathways under willows and ancient oaks, her thin but sturdy arm felt just right in his. The subtle curves of her compact body moved in rhythm with his long stride. He'd waited his whole life to experience this. He spoke softly to her, and she replied softly. They talked like lovers. But there was another reason why they kept their voices low as the wind blew over the hills, snatching snippets and depositing them elsewhere. They knew the rules of engagement in public places, in any place outside of home.

He caught her glancing at the red stars on his epaulette.

"Have you become a Communist?" she whispered.

István looked over his shoulder, his stomach lurching from the question. "Please, we can't talk about this here."

"I just need to know," she whispered back.

"Over there," he said quietly, cutting her off. She looked at him, impatient for an explanation. István looked out towards Pest and pulled her close. "Look to your left."

"What?"

He squeezed her shoulder, hard.

No less than ten metres away, the man appeared from behind a tree like an apparition. His timing was immaculate. The stranger stood stock-still and stared.

István looked at him squarely. "Good day."

He could practically feel the man bristle. Teréza touched her fingers to her lips.

The man nodded and flashed crooked teeth. He took a few steps towards them and then quickly veered off through the trees in a different direction.

"Come." István guided Teréza towards an enormous weeping willow where he removed his coat, smoothed it out for her by the tree's trunk. "Please," he said as he helped her sit. He lay on the ground close to her, on his side, his head propped up by his hand. Was it too suggestive? He didn't care. A sense of self-assurance arose from nowhere. The willow shaded them from the sun like a giant parasol. Only the sun managed to peak in and dapple István's face, illuminating one of the bronze buttons on his coat sleeve. Teréza played with it. "I haven't seen my father since I left for Budapest," she said, leaning against the trunk, idly touching each button one after the other.

Lying on his side, he beheld her ankles, followed her dress up over her thighs to her small waist, up over her shapely breasts to her lacy Peter Pan collar. He couldn't look at her face. In this position, she was too pretty for him to take in all at once. Perfectly clear skin, with a blush of pink showing up on her soft cheeks. Her fine hair cautiously held in place at the temples by two bobby pins. An impulse, animalistic, shot through him and he wanted to take her right there. "I'm sorry," he said absently.

"Sorry?" She looked at him confused.

"That you haven't seen your father. What a beautiful dress," he said.

"Uncle János made it for me. He feels sorry for all that his mother-in-law puts me through. She's just awful. I call her Mrs. Stalin."

István laughed, remembering that cantankerous voice.

"When he gave me the dress, János wrote on a slip of paper, *For the burnt ends.*"

"The burnt ends?"

"The shitty burnt ends of *kifli*. She turns the plate so I can only take the burnt ones. What are you chuckling about?" she asked.

"You're so pretty when you say the word shitty. I can't look at you." He ached to touch her. Her hand, her hair, anything. "What are you smiling about?" István asked.

"Your laugh. You burst like a grape. With a kind of astonishment, a kind of enchantment that nearly brings tears to your eyes. It's lovely."

"You're lovely."

"Don't be silly," she said with practical modesty.

"Am I silly to recognize real beauty?"

"You're silly because you think you see it."

"But there's something else I see." István propped himself on his elbow so he could look into her eyes. Green. They were green.

She smiled as she sat up and slipped out from under his gaze. His desire made her uneasy – he could see that plainly.

He repositioned himself, losing his nerve as he watched her smooth out the edges of her dress. She had a dainty habit of continually neatening herself. It appealed to István's predilection for order.

"Our future," he said.

She looked at him and gave nothing away.

István sat up, rose to his knees and took her hand in his. "You can say no now, and we can be done with it."

"Now you're being silly," Teréza teased unconvincingly.

"And now I've lost my nerve to say any more." István reached in his pocket, pulled out a tiny box wrapped in gold paper and handed it to Teréza. "This is why I visited your father. Please, open it."

The scent of young leaves infused the air.

He noticed goose bumps on her skin as she reached, with great care, for the tiny box. "If I am ever to marry, I only want you. No one else. I won't marry anyone else," he said. Her laugh changed in a thousand ways. He heard every note and tone, each having its own narrative and character. The last one was bittersweet, as if she knew love would also bring pain.

"I want to look at your green eyes every day. Your lips, your skin and your eyes, are the colours of the Hungarian flag. Red, white and green."

This time she didn't laugh but carefully unwrapped the gold paper and opened the box. He watched her small fingers stop moving, waited anxiously for her reaction.

She admired the fine gold band, hardly thicker than a thread. She reached for his hand. "My goodness," she said and laughed again, throwing her head back.

He felt calm for the first time in his life. "I only want you," he said again.

The trees rustled, the wind blew. The weeping willow swept the ground around them, playing with the hem of Teréza's skirt.

From nowhere the stern man reappeared, blocking the sunbeams, demanding their identification papers.

LOOK! LENIN'S FARTING

1949, May 1. Budapest, Hungary

The sound of a doorbell and someone pounding. At first Teréza thought she'd been dreaming. But in the early hours of May 1, she woke to the sound of a short, sonorous discussion on the other side of her wall and knew instantly.

"They took the Ferihegyi couple, the actor and his wife," Uncle János said the next morning lighting a cigarette while Teréza folded her blankets and converted her bed back into a couch. "He'd complained about having to act in propaganda films."

The doorbell rang. Teréza's hand shook as she approached to answer it.

"What's got a hold of you?" István asked, looking at Teréza's ashen face.

"Come in."

"We don't have time."

She peeked into the hallway. "Was anyone following you?"

"Not that I know of." István took her in his arms. She

bowed her head into his chest. For a moment it was comfort, the breath of heaven. When he reached for her chin to lift her lips to his she said, "Not right now." Her mind was unable to focus on the simple pleasure of kissing.

István thrust a small red flag into her hand. "Take this," he said, agitation in his voice.

"Phooey!" Teréza frowned and grabbed the flag like she would rather break it. She reached for her spring coat on the hallway hook, shoved the flag in her pocket and bellowed a farewell to Hermina and Uncle János. They bellowed back saying they would make their way in a while. In her chair in the dayroom, Mrs. Stalin scowled at the goings-on in the hallway. The twin girls came running to give Teréza a hug.

"Come, I'm going to be late." István grabbed Teréza's hand, and together they hurried down the spiral staircase, busting out into the bright morning, into a sea of red, their feet striding in unison. She held his hand tightly, like she wanted him.

Everywhere Teréza looked she saw red flags and ribbons dangling from balconies and lampposts. On moving and parked cars, red bows were tied to their side-view mirrors. Buildings, accustomed to looking dreary from soot and pollution, their crumbling facades riddled with bullet holes, put on their May Day best: gigantic red bows. Millions and millions of metres of red shiny fabric decorated Budapest.

The year before, Teréza vowed she'd never attend again. She'd hide in a cellar, jump into the Danube – knowing she couldn't swim – throw herself on the tram tracks, anything to avoid this bogus spectacle. She was attending only because of István.

"What new miracle is this?" Teréza had said when she'd first heard about May Day. Since the Soviets arrived in 1945,

May 1st was named to celebrate the Hungarian Working People's Party, the official "festival of work." "As if we don't work enough. Now we have to celebrate this relentless condition," she'd recalled her mother saying. The entire country was obligated to cease all activities and show up for the festivities. From the day Teréza saw the world saturated in Soviet red, she'd vowed never to wear a red dress.

The thin gold engagement band encircled Teréza's ring finger. She could feel István's fourth finger curling into her palm, checking for its presence as they walked hand in hand along Eötvös Street, out towards Andrássy Boulevard. Her acorn rolled easily around in her other palm, buried deep in her pocket. She still couldn't believe that István had made a man of himself and presented himself with such dignity. As she walked she vacillated between the joy of their engagement and repulsion against the world cloaked in Soviet artifice.

"You know how much I hate this day," Teréza said, resisting his momentum like a stubborn dog on leash. As her heel caught a dent in the sidewalk, her cream-coloured shoe came off. "Damn it!" She shook her hand free from István's grip and limped back towards the shoe. After jamming her foot back in, she stood for a moment, hands on her hips, and looked down at the pavement as people rushed by.

"The parade starts at eight. I really need to hurry. Please, we have to pick up our pace." István raised his voice over the cacophony and glanced back as he pulled her along.

"Kiss me," she said and raised her chin. He took it. She felt the gift in his touch. His hands were good and strong, and his lips warm and dedicated.

"Come. You look beautiful. Don't let go of my hand whatever you do." István led her around the corner onto Andrássy. At quarter to seven in the morning Budapest's streets were overflowing with people of all ages, walking and waving red flags. They headed in the direction of Heroes' Square.

As they pushed through the crowd, Teréza could hardly get a glance at the ÁVO Headquarters' double thick walls. Her mood grew prickly. The torture department, she figured, would be the only government office exempt from compulsory participation in May Day.

"I'll have to stand in a special area, but you'll be somewhere close by." István tugged on her arm.

Why was he always tugging at her?

They started into a light run, dodging other pedestrians, lampposts and bicycles. As she ran, Teréza kept her eyes high up on the cherry blossoms bursting above her, a canopy of pink shielding her from the red world. She let István lead the way and steer her from near collisions. Known at the academy for his unfailing punctuality, he was cutting it close. But her defiance of the system was greater than her charity to protect his reputation. Had he not come to retrieve her, she would not have come at all.

His pull grew more insistent, hurting her wrist, and inwardly she objected to the way he went along with Communist orders. Why wasn't he complaining about any of this?

"We have to pick up the pace, please!" he yelled above thousands of voices, and then stopped abruptly. Teréza smashed into him.

"What are you doing?"

He took her by both shoulders. "Smile, for god's sakes! We're nearing the square. You'll be watched. Please. Smile for me." She forced a phony smile.

"You can do better than that." He lifted the corners of her

mouth with his forefingers, then flubbed her lips.

She couldn't help but laugh.

"Think pink cherry blossoms." He offered his hand and they continued running. Red streamers brushed their heads.

Every street was in a festive mood. The multitudes filed towards Heroes' Square. Children wore their Sunday best. Crammed into the backs of lorries, factory workers sported their workweek overalls, held large red balloons and waved to pedestrians. Teréza didn't wave back. Had Hungarians really become sheep? Lorrie drivers sped along Andrássy, honking, sharply circumventing groups that spilled into the boulevard. They cut dangerously close to people on the road.

A group of workers yelled from a lorry, "Out of the way!"

"We all have rights!" Teréza yelled back.

István's jaw dropped. He stopped and pulled Teréza towards him. "Look," he said, pointing towards a display across the street. "Lenin," he whispered in her ear.

Parked in the middle of the road, waiting for the start of the parade – nine metres of grey papier-mâché Lenin crammed his thighs into the bed of a 1930s truck. His left arm pushed itself against the roof of the cab while his right hand suavely held the lapel of his long coat. A stern, unmoving Lenin-on-a-truck. Someone had expertly draped his coat over the sides of the truck bed while his body pitched forward. In a perfectly pressed shirt and tie, a button-up vest, his goatee cleanly trimmed and eyebrows perfectly peaked, he waited to lead the parade. Flanked on either side by a row of men and women, Lenin-on-a-truck waited patiently to be worshipped by the throngs.

Teréza noticed Lenin's escorts had folders tucked under their arms. "Blueprints for Communism." She chuckled, allowing herself to feel a little better.

"I can't imagine his balls are comfortable in that position," István whispered.

Teréza's chuckle loosened her ennui.

Papier-mâché-Lenin-on-a-truck lurched forward and stalled, teetering.

"The stupid driver forgot to undo the parking brake," István remarked. "They should have me driving that thing. They bring in a bunch of incompetent peasants that have never driven anything other than donkey carts."

Lenin made an awful grinding sound as the driver restarted the vehicle and pulled the truck out of first gear back into neutral. Black smoke spewed out from under Lenin's jacket.

István snorted in Teréza's ear, "Look! Lenin's farting!"

This time she laughed freely. She laughed so hard a tear coursed down her cheek. István's smile widened, and he offered his arm again.

When they arrived at Heroes' Square – Budapest's immense and most important gathering place – thousands had already assembled, packed in front of the Millennium Memorial, a towering column of the Archangel Gabriel holding the holy crown and the apostolic double cross in his hands. Gabriel, rising between two semi-circular sweeps of columns, leading the seven tribes who founded Hungary with Árpád at their helm. They too were draped with giant red sashes.

People closed in around them. He led her deeper into the centre of the press. Red flags flapped in a frenzy in front of her eyes. Her breath trapped itself somewhere between her lungs and throat in a hard, painful bubble. Try as she might to keep hold of István's hand, she was losing her grip as he snaked his way forward to his post. Slapped in the face by one of the little red flags, Teréza swore and couldn't get a breath. Her indignation became unbearable.

"Let go of me!" she yelled to István, but the immense crowd swallowed her voice. He kept moving forward. His focus infuriated her. She yanked back her hand and saw his quick and sudden desperation, a look she'd never forget. In seconds he was by her side, pulling her into a small opening.

"Are you alright?" he asked.

"When I was better I didn't complain."

István bit his lip. "We're almost there. Can you make it?"

"Do I have a choice?"

He brushed his lips against her cheek. They both felt its remoteness. She took note and decided one day she'd return the same weak kiss.

"Stay in line with the outer edge of the Museum of Fine Arts and Andrássy. Okay?" István waited. "Will I find you here again?" he asked.

"Maybe," she said as the crowd began to cheer. Officials emerged.

"Promise?"

Teréza looked away as though the whole mess was somehow his fault, this whole Soviet world. He turned and hurried toward his post.

István jostled and pushed without apology. Though Teréza tended to nervousness he'd never known her to be this edgy. He could feel so easily rejected around her. It left him wondering why those closest to him meted out the greatest punishment. Fear bred anger in delicate flowers. He had done his level best to make things better for her, but still she hadn't thanked him. He fumed, ready to call it quits.

He arrived at his assigned post in the nick of time, his first misstep. He'd never been the last to arrive, anywhere, ever. The slip enraged him. He filed in with his firefighting comrades, in a section cordoned off for all those in uniform. He could feel them watching him, judging him, turning their heads in his direction. Two and a half years he'd waited to see Teréza, to ask for her hand in marriage. For that whole time, he eyed no other girl. Almost none. He wanted skin. They were both virgins, and he didn't know how much longer he could wait for his Catholic bride. Sometimes the pressure got too great. Would it have been better to be raised a Jew? Could they fornicate more freely than Catholics?

He wanted more than anything to take Teréza out of here, to walk her through the Buda Hills. This farce of a parade was as loathsome to him as it was to her, but the Academy monitored with whom he associated. Couldn't she understand his predicament? To survive as lovers, she would need to learn how to be the wife of a man in uniform. Why couldn't she understand this? It took him a good five minutes staring straight ahead, ignoring his comrades, to figure out the nature of the grievous feeling. Hate and need entangled; a feeling he'd only ever experienced with his mother.

By turning his head slightly, he tried to get a glimpse but could no longer see her. All he could see was his Drill Commander looking at him disapprovingly. István nodded like he had the answer to some mystery and stood at attention, maintaining his view of the Museum of Fine Arts where lower rung Party Officials took their positions.

Teréza felt miserable. Rising up on her tiptoes she caught only slivers of faces: sunken eyes, protruding cheekbones, plump cheeks, workers' hats. She saw peasant faces worn with misgivings, and the peripatetics bused in from the countryside, the ones forced to join collectives and brought in to behold the loyal following in the big city.

She could see little but felt the energy of thousands. She softened at the sight of the chubby hands of waving toddlers. She heard the excitement in the voices of school children, saw the red bows in their hair, kerchiefs tied round their necks as they straddled the shoulders of their fathers. The pint-sized beauties waved their flags like speedy metronomes, and she thought of her sisters, Ági, Juli and Kati. Some parents in the crowd had tired eyes set in expressions of false enthusiasm. She knew that look. She'd seen it in her parents when they greeted new Socialist teachers back when her sisters were made to rip and discard pages of Hungarian history from their textbooks. What troubled her were the looks of genuine eagerness. Too many enjoyed the display.

Teréza recognized her people, those who never chose to be sheep but were terrorized into submission. She felt faint as bodies pressed into her, swaying, her face set at the level of armpits. She smelled the stench of cheap meat in their sweat. The new economy didn't include luxuries related to personal hygiene, like decent toilet paper or underarm deodorant. Because of Communism people stank.

István didn't stink. The realization livened her, made her miss him. Her behaviour this morning had been petulant and ungenerous. She felt a need to go to him, but the press of bodies grew suffocating. She gasped for breath. The thought that her cheek might rub up against a man's sweat-stained shirt was abhorrent to her. She felt close to fainting.

"What's wrong, princess?" said the young man next to her, his sleeves rolled up over his bulging biceps. "You must have woken up and eaten sour pickles for breakfast. None of us want to be here, so you better make the best of it and start waving your little flag." The young man reached down, lifted her unwilling arm and waved it for her.

She snatched it back.

The young man laughed at her. "You know what Communists do to a princess?"

She turned away and lifted her flag and promised herself to be better to István.

The red parade entered the square, organized, meticulous and high-spirited. István leaned to the left and saw Lenin leading the procession and farting black smoke, still in need of an oil change. Throngs of schoolgirls beamed and marched neatly past Rákosi on the thoroughfare below the balcony, waving their flags. István liked girls in crisp white shirts and pencil skirts but could have done without the red scarves tied round their necks.

Music blasted through loud speakers hung high on lampposts. Dancers from the Hungarian State Dance Ensemble followed; men slapping their black leather boots, their shirtsleeves full as sails. Their female counterparts twirled ahead of them, embroidered skirts bursting like flowers over their red knee-high boots. The very boots his stepfather made. The thought of Feri made István doleful. He grew sentimental over the slow melodic start of the *Csárdás* and then enlivened as the dancers drove its quickening pace. How ironic, he thought, that dancers retained their freedom in this new world order. The strength of their performance was their improvisation. How satisfying that they could employ spontaneity as a secret weapon, a rare freedom.

István leaned forward to get a better look at the crowd. The number of ÁVO unnerved him. He could identify them by their uncompromising stance. Their heads rotated like owls without the slightest echo of movement in their torsos. They all possessed identical trunks that looked like they'd been stuffed into their uniforms like ground meat into casings. Hundreds of them along with hundreds of plainclothes informants scoured the crowd, tracking, who waved to Rákosi, who didn't, who participated enthusiastically, who didn't.

If he leaned a little to the right István could see Party Officials gathering on a makeshift balcony erected high above the crowd in front of the Museum of Fine Arts, halfway up the building's columns. A banner draped across the front read: *Proletariat of the World Unite!* Along Andrássy Boulevard he heard the parade in full swing, nearing the square. Rákosi – along with Ministers Gerő, Farkas, Révai and Rajk – emerged on the balcony to thunderous applause. Reluctantly István joined the ovation. He felt like a puppet mindlessly slapping his hands together.

As the parade navigated past a smiling, waving Rákosi, István's entire body ached.

If you weren't so ambitious…you could have stayed in Ják. Learned to be a butcher…or something. It was as if Pista lurked there beside him, on cue, loud and clear in his head, berating.

At least in Ják you can go out into a field and lie in the grass.

István amused himself by positioning his hands so that

each clap smashed one of those leaders. First, Rákosi, the Moscow Communist, with his bald head and turgid body, the master of sadism, the butcher. Gerő, another Moscow Communist. And then there was Farkas, the third Moscow Communist, the Minister of Defence, the main culprit of terror. István's wooden puppet hands hurt as he clapped. He clapped even harder. He saw Révai, the fourth Moscow Communist, Chief Editor of *Szabad Nép* and responsible for lies and brainwashing. He had to lean forward to get beady-eyed Rajk, the only homegrown Communist in the bunch, who liquidated national, democrat and independent establishments. In his mind, István listed off their offences as he clapped so he could remind himself that he wasn't a dumb, compliant puppet after all.

Others around him had stopped clapping. István felt foolish. Lost in his litany he'd missed the cue to stop.

Adjusting his microphone, Rákosi swivelled his head from right to left. He talked of progress and a bright future, and reminded "fellow comrades" that enemies prowled among them, enemies who could threaten the future of the nation.

The enemy is you, thought István.

The enemy is you, thought Teréza.

University students in bright red shirts advanced down Andrássy Boulevard maintaining a perfect Soviet star as they walked. Hundreds of other students in white shirts created the background for the star and not once did they deviate from its impeccable form. Teréza couldn't help but be impressed: close to a thousand bodies moved in unison. On the VIP balcony, blond schoolgirls, bows in their hair, presented Rákosi with monstrous bouquets of carnations. They kissed his cheeks. He kissed theirs.

The massive crowd began to chant, "*Éljen Rákosi! Éljen Rákosi! Éljen Rákosi!*" Long live Rákosi.

"You have to chant too, princess." The sweaty young man nudged her.

"Leave me alone," she grunted. I'm not wishing long life to a man I would rather put to death, she thought.

Rákosi spoke into a microphone, extolling the virtues of labour and industry. The throng grew silent. Teréza willed herself deaf as Rákosi spewed a long, deliberate homily.

"In the first place," Rákosi swivelled his head, "the reason for the election is to ask the Hungarian working people if we have been travelling down the right road in the last two years." Teréza nearly shat herself in disbelief. "The last two years," Rákosi continued, "have brought enormous changes, and it's time to ask the nation if they approve these changes."

What a moron, she thought. Who on earth believed this doubletalk? "On election day, we consult the authority of the Hungarian workers, from the working peasants to white collar workers, if we should continue in our political endeavours."

Teréza imagined flying high above the captive masses, like a bird. She zeroed in on Rajk who did away with religion and organized the ÁVO. She imagined, in her birdlike form, shitting on his head. She shat on all their foreheads. Every single minister. On their noses, on their shoulders, on their polished shoes.

ALL YOUR LOVERS FLEE
THE COUNTRY

1949, July 25th. Ják, Hungary

István hated having to declare his destination to the authorities: by train to Szombathely and bus to Ják, with Édes Teréza and Édes Klára.

Three months after their engagement, István had a weekend break from his training to attend his hometown's annual summer dance, the Day of St. Jacob. Teréza and Klára would be spending the summer helping repair the thatched roof of their family home.

While they waited for the train, Klára recounted how her senile old lady had passed away earlier that week. "She had a fatal stroke while sitting on the toilet reaching for a sheet of *Peace Wipes.*"

It was hard for Teréza not to laugh.

"What a way to go," said István, with a little envy.

They found their seats, and István heaved Teréza's

suitcase overhead onto the rack.

From her basket, Klára pulled out a stick of two-forint sausage, bit off a good piece, started chewing and looked out the window.

István wanted to hold Teréza's hand, but she held them clasped in her lap. When he offered his open hand, she shook her head, as if his idea were entirely inappropriate in public. His need for affection was both painful and tender. He ached to give and receive and interpreted her physical distance as an intentional snub. Who would care if they held hands? It wasn't a sin under Communism.

Teréza and Klára spoke almost nonstop. István was still engaged in the conversation when somehow they got onto the topic of the number ninety-six. How the crowning of Árpád marked the beginning of the Hungarian state in 896. Since then every building in Budapest couldn't be higher than ninety-six feet.

Klára added, "If the anthem is sung at the correct tempo, it should be completed in ninety-six seconds."

István stopped listening after Teréza emphasized the right spirit in which to sing the athem. Instead, he stared out the window, pointed out the odd rare bird. The sunflower fields bloomed spectacular yellow. Teréza spotted a golden oriole but István missed it.

Disembarking from the train, István noted the increased security presence in this western part of the country. With its proximity to the Austrian border Szombathely was a heavily guarded city. Russian soldiers and other bulky forms monitored the streets. Their presence endured, as foreign and foreboding as always. It was now clear that Stalin had no intention of ordering them back home.

In Ják, Pista met them at the bus stop. He'd been holding

down the fort, surviving on odd menial jobs. His wavy dark hair looked fuller on the top, more rebellious in its volume, with a curl falling onto his forehead. The sides shaved close. Now that the Communist government had declared unemployment illegal he could work, but agents like Varga and his uncle Németh saw to it that he got the lowest of labour jobs. And they tormented him; they kept finding ways to fine him for infractions like wearing the wrong shirt to work.

"You couldn't be bothered to shave?" István grabbed Pista's hand and pulled him close with a half embrace.

"If I don't shave for the pope, why would I shave for you?"

"And that hair, my friend."

"Progressive, isn't it?" Pista beamed.

István and Pista bantered all the way to the Édes house.

András greeted them at the gate with a broad smile and a new lexicon of jokes. István's future brother-in-law leaned in close and remarked, "The only thing wrong with Stalin is that he was born alive."

István offered András one. "Stalin is in his office, and notices mice. He complains to President Kalinin. The President thinks for a moment and suggests, 'Why don't you put up a sign reading "Collective Farm"? Half the mice will die of hunger and the other half will run away.'"

István chuckled. András guffawed as he led them across the yard to the house.

András revealed, albeit apologetically, that he worked for the Ministry of Agricultural Economics – the same ministry that had ordered the confiscation of everyone's land. He still lived at home, commuting on bicycle back and forth from Szombathely. "Like everyone else, I take what work I can."

"What did you expect from this new Hungary. Freedom?" Pista said with mock astonishment.

"How long are you staying?" András asked, "Will you have time to see your family?"

István had debated stopping to see Feri but convinced himself that he was at the mercy of Teréza's plans. The truth was, he had no interest in seeing his mother or Tamás ever again. The origin of the break was Tamás. Their mother was so proud he could recite Petőfi's poems by heart, that he was exceptional at math, that he was picking up German, that he was a true Hungarian. Every compliment she gave Tamás was a blow to István. After his brother's birth, István was reviled and neglected by his mother, who saw in him a painful reminder of his biological father. "The Wandering Jew" was her acerbic nickname for him.

A warm homecoming shown by István's future in-laws only highlighted the divide.

"Everywhere is good, but home is best." András nudged him with his elbow.

"That may be true for whomever came up with that silly platitude. Life has taught me otherwise. 'Everywhere is good, just not home.'" István grew serious, looking away.

Around the dinner table, pangs of regret and loss dampened István's robust appetite, forcing him to put down his spoon. He thought of his deceased little brother and how time did not heal this wound.

Watching Kati, the youngest sister, nestle up to Teréza made his future wife look like a woman ripe for motherhood.

Kati drew out of Teréza her tenderness. The warmth of this family in the face of their loss was impressive. He remembered well the expanse of their former farm. It saddened him to imagine the young Édes girls, along with their brother, playing tag through apple orchards and lavender that now belonged to the Collective.

Once they'd eaten, everyone headed to the dance. This once, Gyuri took off his long bloody apron, wore a clean ecru shirt and styled his moustache.

The Gypsy band arrived last minute, like they did every year, already into the brandy. As the musicians tuned their well-worn instruments, the six of them, István, Pista, Teréza, Klára, András and Ági, stood in a small group. István noticed Varga, his nemesis, right away. Varga eyed Ági from the other end of the yard.

"Remember how his fat mother fainted when she discovered her front door completely sealed with bricks?" Pista's breath was fiery in István's ear. Like the band, he'd started celebrating early.

"What are you thinking about?" Teréza nudged István as the music started to play.

"Nothing at the moment." István felt suddenly remote.

Teréza grew serious. "I overheard what you said to András about home. We have such opposing views on family."

István lived for himself. He acted like an orphan, his mentality one of striving and loneliness. Could he ever learn to appreciate togetherness?

"Sometimes when I'm with you, you feel very far away.

Like you're on a deserted island losing hope of any help."

István knew the drill. This was a sign that Teréza's anxieties were spiralling out of control. One climbed over the other, like ants. He'd always sensed that she felt jealous of his friendship with Pista.

To his surprise she said as much under her breath. "The two of you may as well be holding hands."

"Dance with me, and I'll show you who I'm holding hands with," he said.

István offered his hand. Teréza took it. They set off towards the earthen dance floor. Teréza giggled as István spun her around.

"Are you coming?" she called to Klára.

Pista reached out to Klára and clicked his heels. A cigarette hung from his mouth.

Klára sprang up and followed him.

A gentle breeze cooled the sweaty night. Girls spun their tiny waists between the guiding hands of their male partners.

The *Csárdás* held the place of honour as the last dance before intermission. Played in 4/4 time, it began slowly. Mournful yet flirtatious, within a few bars a glimmer of optimism slid in on a major key then, after a turnabout, a slow descent into a cautious desire in a minor one. István and Teréza pressed close, pulled apart, spun. She surrendered to his lead, and he relished the heat and power of her lithe body. The feeling of her in his arms was incredible.

Then without a moment's notice, the song took a cheerful swing, followed by doubt, every bar describing a seductive melancholy, culminating in a virtuosic frenzy and a dead stop ending.

The band members dispersed for intermission and went on the prowl for a little romance between sets. Carafes of *Egri*

Bikavér wine sat on every table. Teréza and István drifted apart and branched off, finding seats next to András, Ági, Pista and Klára. Everyone was catching their breath, getting comfortable when István said, "I'm not young anymore," and blew through his lips.

"What are you talking about?" Teréza said. "Men twice your age dance the *Verbunkos.*"

István reached for a carafe of wine, filled everyone's glasses.

"What's troubling you so much?" Pista leaned in toward Teréza. "Something must be going on in that pretty little head of yours."

"Nothing's going on," Teréza said, taking a sip of wine and glancing at István.

"It has to do with me," Ági said, crossing one leg over the other. She'd grown slimmer and taller than Teréza, and spoke with a confidence that verged on arrogance. It wasn't lost on István how little patience Teréza had for her attractive younger sister with a few centimetres on her. Teréza was the shortest of the family, the most fiery. The two sisters frequently clashed, and Teréza's aversion to Ági began to infect István as well.

Ági cleared her voice as though she was about to begin a speech.

"I forbid you to talk about it," Teréza said firmly and turned away from everyone.

"She's concerned for our parents," Klára said, her cheeks red from wine. "The authorities might punish them."

"Isn't anyone going to tell me what's going on? I can't start a spark with the twigs you ladies are throwing me." István refilled his glass.

Teréza refused to speak.

"Tölgyesi Szilvér sent me a letter," Ági said, clearly enjoying the attention.

"Ági!" Teréza whipped her head around.

"It's my problem, not yours!" Ági straightened her back, then leaned in towards Pista, exposing her cleavage. István leaned in as well.

Teréza frowned at István. "And now it's our parents' problem too!"

"Ladies!" András chuckled.

"This conversation may as well be going on in Russian 'cause I can't understand a single plot point," István interjected.

"If I may interpret," Pista slurred, "Szilvér is the new headmaster at the school. Correct?"

"He *was* the headmaster. He escaped across the border to Austria some months ago. Please, let me finish," Ági said impatiently.

"By all means." With a flourish, Pista gestured towards Ági. "Why did he write you a letter?" he asked.

"To throw the authorities off track about his whereabouts," she answered.

"Criminal," Teréza spat, refusing to look at her sister.

"I suspect Somogyi was in on this too," András added. "He's been living in Austria, paying off border guards to get information, and letters. In this case, out and back into Hungary."

"Okay, back up," said István. "You Édeses never follow a direct line when it comes to telling a story. I feel like you're trying to throw me off."

"He wrote me a love letter," Ági explained.

"Oh for God's sake," Teréza muttered.

"A love letter..." prompted Pista, pulling out a smoke.

"He said in the letter how much he's been thinking about me, how I was his best and most intelligent pupil. And that he would like me to come to Austria to join him. He wants to court me." Ági re-crossed her legs.

"Tell them why he wrote this," Teréza said over her shoulder.

"I'm getting there," Ági said archly, who bloomed under the glow of their attention. "Rumour had it that Szilvér made it across the Austrian border, but that's not at all where he's been."

"Really?" Pista blew smoke rings. "Why don't I know about this?"

"Finally something you don't know. He's been hiding out here in Ják, hasn't he?" István prodded.

"Exactly!" Ági reached for Pista's smoke. He obliged.

Klára raised her eyebrows. Ági held a cigarette to her lips, pretending to take a drag. "It's not so easy to escape across that border," Ági said, swinging her foot.

"It's nothing but barbed wire, landmines and blood-thirsty Soviet-trained dogs and border guards," István agreed.

"Our country's a prison," Klára added.

"Unless you're Somogyi and you have money to pay off border guards," offered Pista.

"It turns out," Ági said, handing the cigarette back, her fingers lingering on his for a moment, "that Szilvér has been hiding out at his brother's house, in the basement!"

"And Somogyi was helping him out by taking the letter he wrote, smuggling it across the border and then mailing it to Ági from Austria," said András.

"To make it look like he's in Austria?" Klára asked.

Ági nodded triumphantly.

"Finally! A cohesive story out of the Édes family." Pista

wacked the table. The glasses tinkled. "So it wasn't about love at all."

"Excuse me? He could have chosen to write to someone else, but he chose me," Ági argued.

"Did he regale you with poetry? More wine, Teréza?" Pista was pouring another round.

Teréza shook her head. "Poetry is irrelevant. Szilvér put my parents in danger. They could get in trouble with the police. It was an irresponsible thing to do. Downright selfish. And Ági is pleased as punch."

István didn't understand the sisters' rivalry. "Why's Szilvér been hiding? Why do the Communists want him?"

"Because he's against Communism. A teacher. And he's been vocal about it," András said quietly, looking around. "A fellow at work, a good guy, told me that the ÁVO from Szombathely are watching Ják now. They're planting informants all over the place. He warned me not to talk to anyone I didn't know extremely well."

The band wrapped up the *karikázó* folk dance, which had women dancing in a large swift circle. András paused, aware of the hush between songs. "We have to be careful, even here."

István looked around. "That's old news in the city. You've had the luxury of talking for this long?"

"You probably don't know this, István," András began, "but Fodor Lajos made it across the border about two weeks ago. Around the time the letter came from Szilvér. Ági's been getting letters from Canada as well!"

"Lajos made it to Canada?" István asked with controlled curiosity.

Teréza clocked his interest.

"He now lives in a place called *Velland*, near the

enormous waterfall, *Niagara Fallsh.* He wants Ági to join him!"

"Enough," Teréza said to András.

On the makeshift stage on the grass, significantly more inebriated than before, the band began to play the punchy Hungarian foxtrot, "Jealous Eyes." Teréza walked with intention, over to her mother and father who'd recently arrived at the dance. She bounced gently to the music, from hip to hip, accenting the lively 4/4 rhythm and singing along.

"How did Lajos manage it without getting shot or arrested?" István asked. Something new had taken over his mind, the thought of escape. A fresh incentive resuscitated him. He urged András along, "So? Keep going, I need to hear more."

"Lajos went with another teacher in town. They set out in the middle of the night, each of them carrying a plank under their arm," András explained. "They propped one plank against the barbed wire, and then another across to the other side, over the landmines."

István listened with keenness, conceptualizing and internalizing the physical actions it took for the men to get to freedom. Then, unbidden, Gyuri's appeal rang in his ears: *Promise me you will never leave my daughter.* He looked towards Teréza.

"That takes guts," he said, imagining Teréza straddled on his back as he waded in the dark, through a marshy area, holding her up high so her t-strap shoes wouldn't get muddy. He didn't know what would happen next. There was a blank spot in his plan.

"Were you dating Lajos, too?" Pista asked Ági, listing dangerously in her direction.

"What do you mean, too?" Ági laughed and fanned

herself.

Pista winked. "Because all your lovers seem to flee the country."

István looked to the dance area. The gossip triggered a reaction in him: the regret of a missed opportunity, the anticipation of a failed future. Escape was a feat István was too cowardly to attempt. As the foxtrot picked up, the men smacked their black leather boots and spun about. Nice boots, he thought, forever the shoemaker's son.

As the dancing couples whooped and called, István, Pista, Klára, Ági and András grew quiet. Amidst the joyous bars of "Jealous Eyes," a sombre spirit passed through them all.

"You know, I've heard not everywhere along the border is rigged with land-mines." Pista offered. "There are pockets of possibility."

Varga loomed and cleared his throat. "Good evening."

István cringed. Despite his size the man had a knack for stealth.

Varga extended his hand to Pista first, who ignored him, then to István. István didn't offer his hand either, but replied, "Good evening," granting Varga the minimum of respect. Social decorum was even more important on a night like this, when any deviation from proper behaviour had many villagers wagging their tongues for weeks afterwards. Drunkenness was the only acceptable excuse.

Varga saddled up next to Pista like an old buddy.

"What can we do for you?" Pista lit up.

István recognized Pista's protective yet belligerent posture when he got drunk. He got more hunched, crossed his legs tighter, like someone had kicked him in the balls.

Varga took a long inhale on his smoke, smiled and looked at István. "We haven't seen you in Ják for some time."

"I've been away," István offered helpfully.

"I know. Officer training. You still finding time to court that fiery paprika?" Varga swivelled his head towards Teréza. István didn't answer.

"Isn't she living in Budapest now too?" Varga smiled, flashing a new golden tooth.

"And what's your business, Varga? You've been coming and going a fair bit." Pista was visibly impatient, working up to one of his irate outbursts.

"A little bit of this, and a little bit of that. A little import, export. Say Pista, why don't you dance with Ági? No one's danced with her all night. You gentlemen could both score big with those Édes girls. Ripe for the plucking, both of 'em."

Pista tossed his butt and nearly fell off the bench. He caught himself by balancing a finger on the ground.

Varga wouldn't relent. "I've heard she's interested in you. That's why she hasn't danced with anyone else; she's been waiting for you to ask her."

Pista noticed Ági looking their way.

"You're not going to let this tango go by without asking the lady for a dance are you? Fodor Lajos is gone," Varga said loud enough for Ági to hear. "But she was never interested in him anyways."

"What's it to you who I dance with?" Pista said too forcefully.

"Whoa! I'm just trying to do my village duties, help out an old pal. I know it's slim pickings in these parts, so I thought I'd give you a tip. Things get around, as you know."

"What things?" Pista asked, standing like the earth had moved beneath him. István righted him. "Come on István, it's time we walk. Teréza needs some attention. Excuse us ladies." Pista bowed gracelessly towards Klára and Ági, ignoring

Varga.

István dragged Pista away. When they got out of earshot Pista let out a string of expletives hot enough to light a fire.

"That ass-licking-mother-fucking asshole," Pista ranted. "That cum-sucking Communist. You know what he was trying to do, don't you?"

"Keep quiet."

"Get me to dance with Ági so that –"

"– So that after you danced with her, he would ask her to dance as well –"

"Right. And then she'd have to dance –"

"– With him."

"Because etiquette demands it. That motherfucking, douchebag!" Pista swayed dangerously.

István propped Pista against a tree and held a finger to his lips, but Pista kept ranting. "And then once Varga seduces her, he fills her head with Communist babble."

István nodded. He whispered, "You're right, so be quiet. Exactly. Recruitment. They won't stop at anything. This is complex stuff, Pista. It's amazing you can keep up. You've had enough booze to drink yourself smart."

"Import, export, my ass."

"Shut up already, Pista." István had humoured him long enough, but Pista had already thudded face first in the dirt. István gestured to András who rushed over to lend a hand. Together they heaved Pista to a table, dragging his toes in the dirt like they were plowing a field.

"He's like this most of the time," András said apologetically.

"I can hear, you know…" Pista clutched István's face in his hands and held him close. "Without you, I'm nothing." He planted a kiss on István's lips.

István didn't know how to respond. He felt an intense embarrassment for his once-proud friend. "I need to go to Teréza. She's upset with me for some reason."

"That woman's going to keep looking for your flaws," Pista said like a sage.

"More than you?"

Pista winked and guffawed.

The band broke into a lightning version of Teréza's favourite song, about a chickadee that lands on a reed rooftop. Teréza clapped spiritedly and István watched her lips. How could she sing so fast? The Gypsy violinists leaned their bodies into the delirious rhythm and the village children danced like keyed-up fowl. Juli and Kati flapped their arms, and their antics made Teréza laugh. The sight of her tossing her hair and her glorious smile made István love her all over again.

He'd taken several steps in Teréza's direction, when in the distance he saw his mother and Tamás arrive. He knew they'd come, and he'd been dreading this moment. Tamás had grown tall, thin and blonder; he had the beauty of a woman. His mother drifted where Tamás drifted. She looked heavier. István avoided her like he avoided the ÁVO. Then he caught a glimpse of Feri. Their eyes locked. István blinked and nodded his head. He tried to send a message from his heart, but this subtle action could not suitably explain his absence, nor console the heartbreak he saw reflected in the wrinkles on Feri's face. Feri began weaving through the crowd towards him. Changing his course, István eased himself between revellers, moving with nervous anticipation into the reassuring presence of his stepfather's embrace. It was only now, after this considerable separation that István realized his nervous-ness was caused by the part of him that never believed he was worthy of Feri's love.

"You vagabond!" Feri said playfully, kissing István's cheek, pulling him close.

"That's no joke, father." István held the back of Feri's head. The word slipped out of his mouth. Father.

"What did you say?" Feri pulled away, his face an array of expressions, like a flipbook changing from one feature to another in a fraction of a second.

"Father. I said father."

"There's a first for everything." Feri began to tear up.

The Gypsy music hovered over the dancers as István and Feri sat at edge of the dance field on two tree stumps, the high notes hitting their ears. The late afternoon sun warmed their shoulders.

"Your friend Pista is not doing so well," Feri began.

"I wake up every day with the feeling that it's my fault."

"He's had all the opportunities you had. He got the same marks you got in school. He has decent parents. He has a brain, but he's choosing the bottle. Laziness has seized his soul."

"I betrayed him."

"You can blame me for that. I drove you to do that."

"I have a reoccurring nightmare that I've *accidentally* murdered someone. And I'm covering my tracks. And I know the police are coming, and I'm trying to make up an alibi, trying to figure out who will lie for me. I feel guilty, but know I'm innocent. I wake up pleading that it was an accident and I had never intended for anyone to die. The only thing that brings consolation is working from morning to night."

"That, my son, works for most ailments in life. Contributing through work is the best penance. That's what I've done. It's kept me out of more trouble."

"What trouble?"

"If only you knew. This is not the place to tell you. Someday."

István wanted to say there wouldn't be a someday and that Feri had to tell him now. "I'm getting married," he said instead.

"I heard. News travels fast in this village."

"You sound bitter."

"I wanted to know firsthand and not hear it on the *Fő* Square. And now you're an officer as well. Congratulations."

"That too," István said with little enthusiasm.

"You have the weight of the world on your chest."

"I couldn't save my brother."

Feri winced. "For someone who gave up God and the Catholic church, you have enough guilt to start your own religion, boy."

They laughed together, but it was only a moment before István said, "Why do I feel everyone goes downhill around me?"

"Why do I feel like I'm failing you, István?" Feri's eyes were soft and kind.

"One parent gives the pain, the other tries to take it away." István stood, searching for Teréza. She was still singing.

Feri stood as well. "Or maybe the oldest child tries to carry their parents' pain."

"Sounds like another millennium of losing battles." István looked to the ground.

"Go to her, István, and remember, I'm proud of you."

István walked over to Teréza and gently caressed the back of her neck. She started and stood.

"I'm sorry," István said.

"I was afraid you were Varga," she said, turning around and placing her hand upon his chest.

"Has he threatened you in some way?"

"No, never. But he's up to no good. It's written all over his comportment. I can feel it in my bones that he wants to take over our village and turn all of us into Communists."

István clasped her hand to his heart, so that she might feel it beating. "The next dance?"

As they stood alone at the perimeter of the dance area, swaying to the music, the sunset began to fire up the edge of the world with saffron and magenta. The gentle summer evening wind blew the scent of sweet peas, transporting them to a garden paradise. István slipped his arms around Teréza's waist and kissed the flesh between her ear and her cheek. "Let's leave," he whispered.

She blushed. "Are you joking?" she asked calmly.

"No, I mean it. Let's leave Hungary."

WHAT'S THE SOUND OF
COMMUNISM

1950, January - February. Makó, Hungary

The Russian flag outside the Makó Fire Hall flapped noisily and stood out against the snow, bright red. Its yellow sickle, a sliver of sun.

István made his way to the Fire Hall. He'd hoped the situation would be friendlier here than in Budapest.

Who are you kidding?

István quickly suppressed Pista's voice, shoved it like a gopher back into its hole. Distracted, he stepped in dog shit.

Like every small city and town in Hungary, Makó had both paved and dirt sidewalks. The countryside bumped up against developed areas. Concrete and grass competed for supremacy.

Who the hell would want to escape from Makó? Where would they get to from here? Romania, Yugoslavia, Bulgaria? Any place south or east of here is just another prison.

"Shut up, Pista. I didn't invite you here."

István had been given only three weeks' notice before his deployment. He'd struggled with telling Teréza the news. They had walked to the Danube's edge one evening and settled on a bench. The water looked caliginous. The lights of the Széchenyi Chain Bridge had been off for years. The river no longer shimmered. Teréza had shuddered as a cool wind picked up and skimmed the surface, pushing the water along. They'd sat in a long silence that confused and unsettled her.

"I got high marks. I've been posted to Makó," István finally spoke.

Teréza stared straight ahead.

"It's the land of sweet onions. I'll bring you bags full and visit you on my days off."

Teréza didn't turn to face him.

"Aren't you going to congratulate me?"

"I congratulate you." Teréza crossed her arms tightly. "When do you start?"

"In January."

"You're leaving me." She looked skyward at the new moon.

"Only for a short while. You'll come join me before too long. I promise."

"I don't want to be left alone in this city teaming with ÁVO. You know I can't go for walks alone in the hills. And now what do I do with myself after a gruelling day with Mrs. Stalin?" She leaned forward, her crossed arms resting on her thighs. She looked into the black rushing river.

"You dream about me, touching your beautiful face. Your future handsome officer."

★

When the opportunity arose, István volunteered for extra circular activities, like fixing fire trucks. István learned how to do oil changes, inspect fluid levels: transmission, differential and brake. He loved the interconnectedness of it all. How checking tire pressure saved gas, how cleaning spark plugs made the truck run smoothly, how a new muffler made the truck quiet and how resurfacing the brakes allowed it a perfect stop. He changed fuel and air filters and savoured the smell of diesel fuel.

All the books he'd read and memorized in his childhood came back to him as he opened the hood and quieted Pista's voice. He could finally be alone with the complex beauty nestled beneath the hood of a powerful vehicle and spend as little time as possible with other people. István could trust trucks; he couldn't trust people.

But Pista's voice returned when István placed an order for parts and discovered new regulations, new forms and new procedures. Parts were available only after filling out reams of forms and requisitions. These forms, bearing his meticulous handwriting, travelled from department to department, stamped by bored government workers. And with each stamp in each department, a trail of István's activities were mapped. His daily movements recorded, the joy of industry waned as he waited months for a simple part and the truck stood, waiting, while he pressed another into service or scavenged for used parts. Someone somewhere knew what he did, every single day, what parts he ordered, where he installed them, what truck he drove, where and when.

He could have fixed the truck within hours, but now it would take months.

A simple part, a simple goddamn part! The Soviets have cunningly stolen, amongst other things, the brilliant bureaucratic infrastructure we Hungarians built with the Austrians.

As István lifted his head to wave Pista away, he banged it on the hood and swore. "Fuck you, Pista." He threw a wrench at the wall. A puffy-eyed colleague clicked his tongue at the door of the repair room. István glared at his colleague and moved to pick up the wrench.

The man lunged and grabbed it first. "You know it violates Socialist values to destroy communal property?" The man extended the wrench slowly towards István.

"Have you never dropped anything?" István tried grabbing the wrench. His colleague smiled and wouldn't let go.

"I've got tabs on you," said István's colleague, smiling. Finally, he let go and left.

An oversized photo of Rákosi observed István from the wall.

Within a month István needed to see Teréza. In the early hours of the second Saturday of February, the day of the new moon, he boarded a train to Budapest. He fancied the smell of the steam engine. By the time the brilliant sun appeared on the horizon the natural countryside displayed beauty and contentment. Neatly thatched roofs, horse-drawn carts, their riders urging their horses along wide dirt roads, nestled amid rolling hills. When the train pulled into Déli Station, Budapest cast itself in sparkling sunshine and a biting chill.

He found her waiting for him in front of the building on

Eötvös Street. She looked a little gaunt, but full of radiant expectation.

"*Szia*," István kissed her on both cheeks.

"*Szia*," Teréza kissed him back. Her eyes told him she was relieved to see him.

"Onions." He handed her the bag. "Sweet onions from Makó, as promised."

She laughed. "Thank you. I love a man who brings me onions!"

He felt hope stir in his heart and his pants. They headed upstairs.

He stood, silently, awkwardly, in the hallway while she gathered her things for a walk. He felt too constrained, too worn down from the daily dread to slide into any easy exchange.

"You look good." István gazed at her through the hallway mirror.

"My face is sunken."

"Still, you look good."

"The slog is showing on my face."

"As you like."

She couldn't accept his compliments without butchering them. He fought to avert his frustration. But it was true that the softness had waned from both of their faces. The winter had been hard.

Cognizant that Mrs. Stalin sat in the day room leaning forward in her chair, he motioned to Teréza with a nod of his head that they were being listened to. He thought he could smell *kalács* and wondered if Teréza had been baking. He was about to inquire when Teréza turned her back to Mrs. Stalin and removing her apron whispered, "Is it okay if András comes with us?"

"András?" István felt the smile drop off his face.

"András. My brother András. You remember him." Teréza fixed her hair in front of the mirror.

He spoke to her reflection. "Of course I remember him. What's he doing in Budapest?"

"He moved to the city last week and started working in the Ganz Radiator Factory, casting iron." She wrapped a scarf around her neck. Puckering her lips, she applied red lipstick and lowered her voice even further. "He was forced out of the village."

"Forced out?" István repeated, to make sure he'd heard correctly.

Teréza reached for her coat on the hallway hook. István beat her to it, opened the coat and offered her right sleeve, then her left.

"They wanted András to become one of them."

István adjusted her coat but kept his hands on her shoulders. He pressed himself into her back and leaned into her ear. He liked how they looked in the mirror together. They were young and beautiful. Looking at her green eyes, he felt something powerful again. His desire returned. He wanted to undress her.

"Stay close, tell me the rest of the story." István kept his lips near her ear, thankful for András' misfortune. It gave him a reason to be proximate to her body and feel her delicate sturdiness. But the embrace made Teréza antsy, and she pulled away again. István let his arms fall to his sides like flags on a windless day.

"We best get going. András's waiting for us."

Out on the boulevard, Teréza walked next to István, an adequate space between them.

Feeling empathy for her soft-hearted brother, who trailed far behind – András never led but always followed – she turned back to make sure he was still coming. Teréza had kept silent when earlier they'd stepped out of her building and István instructed András to walk thirty paces behind them. "Any more than two are considered by the police to be a group. We could be stopped and questioned," István had said.

Teréza wondered why István didn't mention that it was his uniform that put them under constant surveillance. Uniforms watched lesser uniforms. Like Rákosi watched Rajk.

In spite of breezy temperatures, they headed again to the Buda Hills. A decrepit bus carried them up the hillside, tossed them from side to side along winding, wet roads. Every passenger who got on or got off seemed vexed or preoccupied. The bus chugged out black smoke like Lenin at the parade. An old peasant woman, her face suspended in discontent, hauled her enormous package off the bus. It clucked a few times as she descended the steps. Hoarding food, thought Teréza, could cost her ten years.

She took in the city below. Through the drizzle and the dirt-covered window she could see the three metre tall red star on the Parliament Building. Half-repaired buildings, so many facades still ripped away. From a distance the emptiness of the city felt conspicuous, like everyone was on holiday. Ironically, no one was permitted to leave the country. The Freedom Statue on Teréza's right made her feel sullen and crabby.

When István pulled the cord for the stop, it made a worn-out choked sound. As they disembarked, the bus spewed black smoke in their direction. This time she and András tailed István as he led them across the road towards a secluded path in the hills.

Teréza walked close enough to András to hear him say, "I think someone's following us."

"How do you know?" Teréza said over her shoulder, her knees going weak.

"There's no one," István assured her. "I've been watching." He led the way while András kept checking. A nervous squirrel darted across the road, its tail signalling.

They sped up until they reached the mouth of the forest. When they entered the woods, Teréza bolted into the trees and waited, her breath rapid in her chest, until András and István caught up with her. Her heart felt as though it had been cooked in soup, tough and rubbery. "Why are you so sure we're being followed?" she asked András, trembling – a state that had become as habitual as thought.

"A man got on and off each bus we were on. Then at our last stop, he got off at the last minute, just as the doors were closing."

István's eyes widened. "Where is he now?"

"I didn't see where he went after the bus pulled away," András said, in the peasant accent Teréza used to have.

"You're sure you didn't see him coming after us?" Teréza asked, feeling the cold rush up under her satin hazelnut dress.

"No." András pulled his coat tight up to his neck.

István glanced behind. "We've been careful."

Teréza heard the doubt in his voice.

"I still feel him." András' breath mingled with István's, with Teréza's.

"Let's walk. We can't stand around for this long." István bent his arm, took Teréza's and linked it into his.

"Come," Teréza encouraged András.

The blue haze of the fir forest brought her an inadvertent and fleeting rush of wellbeing: its scent akin to rosemary, reminding her of her mother's kitchen garden. But a yellowy beige mist clung to their branches, giving them a soggy appearance, like clothes on a line that refused to dry. She imagined it was the exhaled breath of those tortured in the city below. The breath of anxiety and misery made it up into the hills and discoloured the particles of the atmosphere.

"The informant had been watching me for weeks," András volunteered. "He stopped me on my way home from work. The weasel crawled out of a ditch."

"I'm sure they thought that because you're so quiet and unassuming, you'd make a good informant. No one would suspect you," Teréza added.

"He pressured me over the course of about three weeks. He waited for me in that ditch every other day, wearing me down."

"What did he want to know?" István led them deeper into the woods.

"He wanted to know who in the village were *kulaks*. He also asked me what Fodor Lajos was doing."

"Fodor Lajos?"

"What the hell would you know about Fodor Lajos!? I told Ági these letters would come back to haunt us!" Teréza said too loudly. "Lajos escaped in the early summer. He's in Canada for all we know. What a completely absurd question. The idiots. What does he know about Fodor Lajos!?"

András stopped walking to look around the forest. "They kept offering me a 'better job' if I gave them information. I couldn't take it anymore. I quit my job in Szombathely and came here as soon as I could." András scanned the woods.

"Did you hear something?"

Teréza admired István's profile as he stood still and listened. Not a bird, not an animal. Just a cracking tree branch and the sound of wet wind. Moisture sprayed from the firs.

"What happened after you quit?"

"This is the most bizarre part of the story."

"I knew there had to be more…" István said.

"The night I refused for the last time, the informant leaked the information to Radio Free Europe. The next morning, on the radio, they announced that 'András from Ják' had been harassed by the ÁVO. I don't understand it."

"Simple. The asshole worked for both sides. He makes money by informing on his fellow countrymen and then reports on internal activities to the West."

Teréza sighed heavily. "What a despicable world we live in." She slipped on a patch of moss, wrenched her ankle and yanked her arm out from under István's. "Damn it!"

István jumped to her aid. "Let me help you."

"No!" Teréza rolled out her ankle. They paused. "I'm fine. Let's keep walking."

"They took another family from Ják." András' voice carried. Out here amongst the firs they forgot about censoring themselves.

"Who?" István asked.

"The Horváth family."

"My God," Teréza sucked in her breath.

"I don't remember them." István marched along.

"Of course you do," she said. "How can you not remember the Horváths? They owned the bakery."

"They sent the mother and the three children off to the middle of nowhere," András said, keeping step.

Sparked by the mention of a small, banished family,

Teréza, saw a brief flash of a figure's outline on the horizon with a shovel, digging a grave.

"What were they accused of?" István asked.

"The husband escaped. He left Hungary."

"So they punished the rest of the family," András said, looking up into the sky. "Dark clouds."

"It's a crippling thought," said István, "that one family member's freedom becomes a life sentence for the rest of the family."

"Yes, crippling." Teréza exhaled heavily.

They kept walking. Teréza's ankle began to throb. "Budapest is shrinking. I see fewer people on the streets every day. Certain faces have outright disappeared. I never thought I could keep track of so many faces in a city."

"I remember as a child," András began, "sneaking walnuts from a bowl. Mother had shelled them and told us not to touch them. When her back was turned, I took a few at a time, seeing how many I could sneak without her noticing."

"So it was you?" Teréza said, half amused, remembering.

"But someone always notices," András said, smiling. He found a fallen branch that would make a good walking stick as they began to climb uphill, handed it to Teréza.

Something moved in the forest ahead.

Teréza started.

"A small animal." István stopped and waited. "We must have scared it, whatever it was."

They listened again for footfalls. Looking behind, sideways, in all directions.

"What's the sound of Communism?" András whispered.

Neither István nor Teréza answered.

András grinned. "Receding footfalls."

They laughed uneasily.

"I don't get it," said István.

"Neither do I," Teréza complained.

András stepped backwards to demonstrate. "The system is following you and falling behind at the same time."

"Keep working on it." István looked ahead. "Let's keep going, a little farther."

"I don't know how much farther I want to go," Teréza said.

"Come on, just a little more. It's so peaceful here. We get so little of it." István reached for her hand.

Teréza hesitated, fighting the urge to run. She accepted his hand.

"Looks like it's going to rain pretty soon." András examined the sky again.

István led them through the forest as the drops began to fall. Teréza's mood had soured by the time István came upon a cave. "Will you look at that? Shelter, just in time."

Droplets of rain pelted their heads. Teréza hesitated as István proceeded to enter its mouth. Its height made it easy to stand. She watched uneasily as István ran his hand along the inside, its texture seemed to enthrall him. András followed István inside while Teréza brooded at the opening. She didn't like caves. They made her claustrophobic.

"Come inside, Teréza." István motioned to her.

"I don't want to."

"It won't bite." István headed deeper in.

"My ankle's hurting. I can see it from here," she called.

"It's not the same." István's voice already sounded distant.

"Please let's go back. I don't feel good about this. István? András?" No response. A crow cawed cruelly at the entrance. "Ugly bird." Teréza's discomfort doubled, and she leaned against a tree. She resented how men could carve out pockets of tranquility, seemingly able to set aside concerns in pursuit of adventure while she was forced to stay vigilant. She thought about peace, about how it had become a short-lived phenomenon. She checked her pockets, feeling around for András' acorn. Still there. She rolled it around in her fingers. It calmed her a little. She was starting to wonder if peace was a state unnatural to humans and their endeavours to find it were nothing but a foolhardy attempt to mimic the natural world.

"ID," the voice boomed.

Teréza jumped.

The thick, bull-faced ÁVO men were already questioning her before she could produce her ID booklet. They wore uniforms of loathsome blue. Beside them stood the man from the bus.

Teréza relinquished her documents like she had dozens of times before, glancing in the direction of the cave, fearing that István and András would come soon and fearing that they would not come soon enough. She cursed them for leaving her alone.

Flipping through the booklet, one ÁVO enquired about her waist size.

"My waist size?" she repeated, embarrassed.

"Yes. Take off your coat so I can see it."

Stunned, she was unable to protest. Systematically her fingers unbuttoned her coat, trained to respond to commands. "It's very cold here. I can't leave it off for long." She felt ridiculous, the whole situation surreal, as though their request was reasonable, even warranted.

"Toss your coat on the ground," said the other one.

Disgust shot up Teréza's throat. "The ground is dirty, and this is my only coat," she replied. Strategic files opened alongside haunting material. The front of the flashcard showed her mother's hair, her bun askew; the flip side taught *this will never ever be talked about.*

"Either you get your coat dirty or your dress dirty," said the man from the bus. "Which will it be?"

The three men wore oily smiles, prolonging their sadistic foreplay. Tears of shame pricked Teréza's eyes. She wondered how long she could forestall the inevitable, furious with István and András for exploring a cave. How could they be gone so long? She heard tree branches snap in the distance as a spray of moisture from a pine tree slapped her across the face as the wind picked up.

Positioned behind Teréza, the bull-faced ÁVO man pushed her to her knees. She dropped her coat and landed knees first on the dirt, ending on all fours, her hazelnut dress flying up over her underwear. "That's the way we want you," said other ÁVO man, snickering and slapped her buttocks.

A slow death, a feeling of drowning in tar was Teréza's preparation for the ensuing degradation.

"That's my fiancée!" István shouted from the cave opening, as András stumbled along behind him, clumsily keeping up.

Teréza pulled down her dress, crouching on her knees in dirt and leaves.

"That's my fiancée," he said again as he ran to her side.

"Your lovely fiancée had fallen when we found her. We were about to help her up," said one of the men.

Teréza wanted to scream *liar.* Instead she said. "I'm perfectly fine. Thank you. My brother and fiancé are here now. They can help me up."

István reached for her hand and picked up her coat. Shaking it out he offered the coats sleeves as she slid her arms and shoulders inside. She was shivering and disgraced.

"András from Ják," said the bull-faced ÁVO man as though he'd been waiting all day to say it. "Your identification."

István and András handed over their IDs.

"Makó Fire Department. Officer in training," he read aloud. He shoved the booklet back in István's hand. Through her terror, Teréza watched István conceal his contempt.

András stood smiling, his default position when he felt helpless. She wanted to smack him. How could he smile in a situation like this? The worst part was how little anyone said, all of them, the ÁVO included.

"Come with us," he said to András, the one with the glacial expression.

Teréza stifled tears as she caught sight of her brother's docile eyes. The ÁVO men shoved András along. She had been spared but her brother had not. The sky opened and emptied itself onto the earth. When they were out of earshot Teréza bore down on István, with the rain pummelling their bodies.

"I told you not to go in there! I told you I had a bad feeling!"

"I came out as soon as I heard something," said István, lifting his palms in surrender, attempting to shield himself from the onslaught, both from his wife and the sky.

"You left me alone."

"I invited you in."

"You knew I'd hurt my ankle. It wasn't safe. You left me out here all alone." She drew her coat up over her head and started to tremble.

"I came back for you."

"No! You left me vulnerable when I told you I had a bad

feeling. You saw what they were going to do to me." Earth turning to mud began to tether her sodden shoes.

"And they didn't because I rescued you."

"I was already on my knees, like an animal. Exposed. You try living with that!"

"I do live with that!"

She marched on ahead of him, back towards the trailhead as the wind lashed rain across her face.

The whole journey back to the Pest side, Teréza was drenched and unable to speak. István delivered her home and finally broke the silence by telling her he would sleep at the Kilián Barracks.

She nodded absently. She was still submerged in a feeling of disgrace.

"I'll see if I can find out anything about where they took András." István tried to console her, but in her heart she knew he could do nothing. They embraced numbly and she closed the door.

When Teréza heard a meek knock the next morning she hurried to the door, throwing it open. With blackened eyes, András collapsed in her arms. Straining, Teréza dragged him in and leaned him up against the wall. She bolted it shut.

"Who's there?" Hermina asked timidly from the kitchen.

"It's only András." Teréza realized the absurdity of what she'd said. His eyes were all but swollen shut, and he'd curled fetally, his knees against the wall.

Hermina came running while Teréza folded herself over her brother.

"My god." Hermina clutched her chest and ordered the

twins to stay in their rooms.

"They kept asking me…about István…" András stuttered between sobs. "Was he Jewish…had he ever worked with the Nazis or the Arrow Cross…but he never…never…never… he's not Jewish. I kept telling them. They wouldn't believe me."

Teréza pressed the acorn into András' hand. "Hold this," she said, "it will give you strength."

SEPARATION

1962

THIS IS WHAT HAPPENS TO
FATHERLESS BOYS

1962. Szombathely, Hungary

Sealed and soundproofed, the immutable grey room trapped her like a fly inside a glass jar. Teréza could hear herself sighing, if she dared sigh at all. The drab emptiness magnified everything. She could almost taste it in her mouth, the smell of iron. The thick walls of the Police Station were painted dark, glossy grey. Everything else matched: the desk, the chair, the ceiling. The lamp.

Ten months after the incident at the Legation in Budapest, Teréza had been ordered to report to the Police Station in Szombathely.

She'd been left sitting in a room for over an hour, facing an empty desk. Like a child waiting for the principal to arrive, made to think about her misdeed. She could only guess at her crime, imagine the severity of the punishment. She envisioned the worst, though the two policemen assigned to her case hadn't disclosed why they'd summoned her.

It couldn't have had to do with István's escape. That was over four years ago. It couldn't have had to do with her surreptitious sallies to church. They could have penalized her for those infractions a decade ago. Her mind raced, she was wet under the armpits and her hands were going white. Then it dawned on her; it was the wire.

She drafted her explanation, laid out the logic of her innocence: I needed money. My husband sent it. I received a wire from a law office in Budapest. I thanked the agency. I bought a coat for my son and fixed my stove and bought some sugar. I needed money. My husband sent it. I received a wire from a law office. I thanked the agency. I bought a coat for my son and fixed my stove and bought some sugar. I needed money.

What if the police threatened her as an enemy of the state? Accused her of being an unfit mother? What if they made her confess? To what? She rehearsed her reality again. I needed money. My husband sent it. I received a wire from a law office. I bought a coat for my son and fixed my stove and bought some sugar. I needed money. Please don't take my son away from me.

Two policemen entered the room. Their black boots squeaked around her as they moved into position. She could practically smell them, their breath toxic and sour. She assumed they'd been drinking. Didn't they all? One perched himself on a corner of the desk and glowered at Teréza. The shorter one stood to the side, blocking the exit. As they inspected her, she looked down at her knees.

"What did you buy with the money?" asked the one with a cleft chin, like Kádár's. *Róka*, read his name badge. Fox.

"I bought a coat for my son. He's only five. He didn't have a winter coat. And I fixed my stove. I live in a damp house."

Róka's profile darkened as he turned his head towards his partner. "I didn't ask her son's age nor how the woman lives." Rising from the corner of the desk, he turned his back and began pacing, an indication to Teréza that any further justification was useless, he'd heard it all before. He faced the wall. "How old are you?"

"Thirty-two, sir."

"You look twenty-two. Twenty-five at most." Róka turned around.

She was about to accept the compliment when she jumped at the chance to justify her story. "The stove was rusting, policeman sir, it had cracks…the whole apartment was filling with smoke. I hardly have any money left for food, I can barely feed –"

"Did I ask the woman a question?" Róka smirked at his partner.

Fighting a rising heat in her throat, Teréza answered, "No policeman sir. You did not ask me a question."

"That's right, I was asking my comrade."

"My apologies."

"Your husband left! He fled this country!" The short man shrieked at her.

"He was in uniform!" Róka blustered. "He's been sentenced to seventeen years. And now he has the gall to circumnavigate the system even as he hides his shameful face in Canada! And no doubt you have dreams of joining his side? Stupid woman."

Teréza's face burned, then paled. She'd been an accomplice since the day István escaped. Guilty for being a Catholic, guilty for being a self-determined citizen, guilty for being a Hungarian citizen in a Soviet world. Like a bird clinging to a branch in a storm, her toes curled inside her shoes.

"What did you buy with the money?" Róka wheeled around to face her.

"I already told the policeman, sir."

"How cheeky. Are we inconveniencing the woman by asking again?" the short one needled her.

Róka produced a grandiloquent smile. "What did you buy with the money?"

"I don't understand." Teréza looked at him.

"What's not to understand? Is the woman so witless that she doesn't *understand* that she's cheated the nation?" Róka moved in closer, caressed his gun with one hand. The short man stepped in to form a perfect triangle. Teréza read his name badge, *Farkas* – wolf.

Feigning incredulousness, Róka launched his rant. "The woman works at the County Council; you'd think she'd know what belongs to the nation and what belongs to her." He stopped to scowl. "Your cheating, fleeing husband sent money by a bogus route." He raised his voice again. "We cannot stop your deceiving, conniving husband, an enemy of the state."

He paused to let the ugly words reverberate against her face.

"But how are we to stop this kind of dishonest behaviour in his wife?" finished Farkas, repositioning his heels to stand wider, like he was ready to catapult himself at her.

"By informing the wife who informs the husband of the correct means by which to send money, policeman sir," Teréza spoke precisely.

"Ah, the woman's got half a brain," said Farkas, adjusting his holster.

She looked up as Farkas pulled a document from the top drawer of the desk and placed it front of her. He smelled like burnt baloney, hot metal and welding fumes.

"Your autograph here," he said, and handed her a pen.

"Please policeman, sir, may I read it first?" She left her hands on her knees.

Róka laughed at her.

She knew of the horrendous show trials of the past decade, the forced confessions. She knew her signature meant agreeing to misrepresentation or worse, a criminal offense, yet if she intimated distrust, she was putting herself in a precarious position.

"We haven't got all day," Róka huffed.

Farkas stretched out his arm like a worm, extending the pen towards her nose.

Her hands quivered on her lap. The font was miniscule and practically illegible, even with her good eyes. "Please… what does it say?"

"What does it say?" Róka sneered and began pacing. "I think the woman seems to be confused about who exactly committed the crime here."

"You'd think the woman would know what belongs to the nation and what belongs to her," Farkas parroted.

"Please don't hurt my son."

"Should we not be concerned about what you teach your son?" Farkas held the pen in front of her.

She was unable to take it. The pen, the silence, the crime.

He retracted the document and placed it in a file. "Write to your traitor husband. Tell him to send you the money again, the exact same amount. Then you'll come back here to pay your fine."

Teréza ran all the way home. A third of the way the heel of her shoe broke off. She threw off her shoes and ran the rest in her stocking feet, her shoes in her hands. Her stockings were torn by the time she reached home and rode up her ankles like short sleeves. She burst through the door of the divided house and climbed the stairs two at a time to Emi's flat on the top floor.

The neighbour woman had been babysitting Zolti for a year, and now that the boy was old enough to attend school, he returned everyday after class until Teréza could fetch him after work.

She heard the sound of her son crying inside the flat. Teréza knocked on the doorframe. There was no answer. She knocked again, stopping just short of pounding her fists against the door. When the neighbour's teenaged daughter finally answered, a sheepish look on her face, Teréza caught a glimpse of Zolti in a corner of the living room, kneeling on hard, uncooked beans. Teréza remembered suffering such a punishment herself as girl.

"Has he misbehaved?" Teréza asked, betraying herself with a question she knew was meant to appease and pacify the situation. "Where's your mother?"

"She's out," the girl answered. "Come along Zolti, your mother's here."

"Has he misbehaved?" Teréza asked again.

"Yes. Zolti hit me and called me a liar." The girl stepped aside as Zolti threw himself at his mother, ran around her legs and fled down the stairs.

Weary and frazzled, Teréza ran through the neighbourhood calling out his name, the neighbouring girl following close behind. Frost covered the trees and slipped into Teréza's lungs. When she finally found him, in the middle of a park, sitting in a mound of snow, his pants had soaked through to his bum.

"Why did you hit her? Why did you call her a liar?" Teréza

beseeched him.

"Because…because…" Zolti sputtered between sobs, "because…"

"Calm down sweetheart. Just get it out." Teréza stroked his cheeks, his chest, his forehead.

"Because when I told her I was going to Canada…" he sputtered some more.

"Yes?" Teréza coaxed him.

"She said my father is a bad man. And if he came home he would go to jail for seventeen years."

Teréza wiped his nose. "People will say such things out of ignorance, and you must learn not to react." She held him tightly, needing him more than he needed her, cementing their enmeshment. She smiled and kissed his nose.

One day when Teréza collected Zolti from Emi's she found him looking sullen. He didn't want to hug her. She suggested he play with a friend on the street, maybe that would cheer him up.

He went outside to the front yard. She watched him from the window. He looked from side to side and up and down the street, dejected. It wasn't long until Teréza heard shouting and crying. The doorbell rang. A neighbouring mother delivered a repentant Zolti to the doorstep. She told Teréza that he'd instigated a fight with her son. "This is what happens to fatherless boys."

Teréza felt disgraced and outraged. "Communist bitch," she said after she shut the door. "Zolti, write a letter to your father."

Dear St. Nicholas
wishes you a festive season
your little son Zolti.

Together they dropped the letter off at the post office on a blustery November afternoon. She encouraged him to seal the envelope with a kiss.

After six years apart, all they had were letters.

She let Zolti hand the envelope to the clerk.

Zolti pulled down the red velvet curtains at school the next day. They separated the seating area from the stage in the makeshift theatre the teachers had created in a small auditorium for the coming year-end pageant. He was upset that he'd not been cast in the role of the foreman in the socialist play *Singing a Beautiful Life*. Teréza disdained the play. Mercifully, her son still led the class with his marks. As long as he excelled at school, her son would find his way in life.

Within two weeks, the cash arrived in a brown envelope. István had wrapped the bills in newspaper. It broke Teréza's heart to be taking the same amount again to the Police Station. Fifty Canadian dollars. They didn't want it in forints. Which meant the fox and the wolf were sure to pocket it for themselves. She could barely conceal the daggers in her eyes as she handed it over to Róka.

"Policeman sir, you have not informed me of the correct means by which my husband can send money to help feed our child. I have no instructions."

Róka paused. Farkas bridled and stepped forward. Róka stopped him with a gesture. In his most instructive voice he explained that from now on she could avoid any unpleasantness if her husband sent the money directly to any *IKA* store where she could then receive a voucher to shop.

"This way, the People's Republic will benefit," said Róka, licking his thumb, counting the cash. He stopped to inspect the foreign currency, blue bank notes in denominations of five, with Queen Elizabeth II on the front and a country scene on the back.

The *IKA* shops were exclusively export stores where only the best, most superior grade Hungarian items could be found. Rum, chocolate, fancy cigarettes, high quality towels and linens, handicrafts and hand embroidery could be purchased with foreign currency. Nothing in these shops was made available for purchase by ordinary citizens, unless one had connections. Party members slept on silky linens while the rest of the population slept on starched cotton.

Teréza chafed at the injunction. While the vouchers gave her access to goods, she needed hard cash to obtain food, clothing and shoes from the considerably cheaper state-run shops. Prohibited from spending her money elsewhere, the "state" benefited, not her. Reminded again that the welfare of the state took precedence over her having a decent stovepipe, she felt the punishments extend to every corner of her life. Nothing was exempt. Even toilet paper colluded with the state, punitive as it had always been. She stood, waiting for Róka to slip the cash in his pocket. She wanted to see it for herself.

"You can go now," Róka said, grinning.

As she faced the entrance of *IKA*, her initial consternation turned to confidence. At home, she wrote to István and asked him to send his dollars to the *IKA* store, trying her best to explain as obliquely as possible. She got to know the items for sale at the fancy shop and took orders from colleagues at work. With her vouchers she bought what they could not acquire by ordinary means and turned a marginal profit by selling them for a slightly inflated price. Her colleagues marvelled at the quality of the merchandise, and Teréza used the profit to save up for her departure. If the system screwed her, she would screw the system.

OPPRESSION

1945-1946

MANOEUVRE AROUND THE EVIL
SIDE OF MEN

1945, Spring. Ják, Hungary

"*Devushka!*" Teréza repeated.

Seated next to Ági on the wrap-around bench in the kitchen, Teréza faced two young, strapping soldiers. She had figured out which soldier she could befriend. His name was Yvan.

Teréza's mother had gone to market, and Juli and Kati were playing in the adjacent bedroom. "If there's anything to buy…" Anna had said skeptically as she left. She had just said that morning that the war had been over for three months but neither peace nor food were available. Gyuri and András were sharpening knives in the stable while a Russian officer stood watch.

"*Devushka!*" Yvan, the Ukranian soldier, repeated with emphasis. He swung his index finger back and forth at the two girls like he was conducting a choir.

Teréza counted four wristwatches on his forearm. "*Devushka!*" she chimed, and swung her index finger, pointing back and forth between herself and her sister.

"*Devushka!*" Yvan said again, clapping his hands and laughing.

Teréza was surprised she liked the Ukranian soldier. His presence drew out of her both a girlish charm and an adolescent infatuation. She'd seen Russian soldiers go about the business of occupying her village, looting, shooting and intimidating. She overheard her mother and the village women whispering that "horrendous things were being done to women." Though Teréza was only fifteen she could not fully comprehend the nature of these horrendous things; her body was not a territory that knew the land of intimacy nor her mind a topography that could fathom the extent to which men could brutalize the female body.

Did the men promise to marry these women and then call off the wedding? Did they get them pregnant and then leave them? When she thought of "horrendous things" her mind drew a blank, though she thought of Klára in Budapest and the sadness in her letters.

This Ukrainian soldier seemed different. The cuter of the two, Yvan was a pleasing redhead with full cheeks. She noticed that he sweat easily. His disposition was calmer, gentler, more polite, his hands more refined than the others. He was her choir conductor. She wanted to believe that not all men were the same. Up until now, only her father and her brother counted as the exceptions to the rule. And priests. And maybe István, though she wasn't sure. Maybe Yvan fit into this category too. Sweet men don't rape, she told herself.

The sound of Russian was so remote to Teréza's ears, the pronunciation so harsh, that she couldn't help but ridicule their mother tongue. She leaned in close to Ági, winked at Yvan and said, "Sounds like a cross between a drugged cat and frying gravel."

The two girls howled with laughter.

Teréza noticed Yvan blushing. "What is boy?" she said in Hungarian pointing at the picture of András on the wall.

"*Mal'chik!*" barked Bolochka, the other soldier, the dark one.

"*Mal'chik!*" Teréza and Ági repeated in unison, mocking his seriousness. Teréza pointed first at Bolochka, indicating he was the boy, and then at Yvan indicating he was the man. "*Chelovek*," she said, remembering the first word she'd learned from the officer who'd ordered her mother to serve food to his soldiers. *Chelovek* – man.

"*Mal'chik! Mal'chik!*" Yvan pointed at Bolochka. His laugh was so deep he gurgled with phlegm. "*Chelovek! Chelovek!*" Yvan puffed himself up like a bear on its hind legs, making himself larger than Bolochka.

Teréza laughed hard for the first time in weeks. She melded her laugh with Yvan's, and the fear of the past weeks fell away for a moment.

They'd invaded Teréza's home three weeks earlier, at the beginning of spring on a cloudy afternoon. She'd been feeding the pig; she heard the Russians before she saw them. As the awful grinding sound of the vehicle grew near, barrelling down the long dirt driveway, she froze in the yard. As long as she had lived, only one other vehicle had ever driven down their dirt road.

It felt useless to run, but when she finally saw the green

truck, she tore across the yard screaming to her family, "Stay inside! Stay inside!" as she made for the outhouse. She latched the door shut and peered through the lace curtain, her heart pounding in her ears. The pig wandered from its pen – she forgot to latch the gate – and was running amuck in the yard, squealing as the truck veered out of its way. The truck skidded to a halt a metre from the house. Teréza could see four men in the back and two in the cab. She could no longer see the pig, but she could hear grunting and squealing.

In seconds the Russians had entered her home and were hauling her parents out onto the yard at gunpoint. Little Kati ran out after them, crying, while three other guns were trained on her family. Where was Ági and Juli? Where was the sixth Russian? Where was her brother? Just then, András emerged from the stable, jostled by a rifle-toting soldier.

Teréza sighed with relief. The soldiers were accounted for; none were in the house with her sisters.

When the Red Army soldiers kicked her father and brother to their knees, she screamed in the outhouse. Heavy boots in their backs pinned them face first on the ground as her mother pleaded for mercy. "We'll give you whatever you need," Anna yelled.

They turned to her and spoke among themselves. Two older soldiers escorted Anna into the house. Then everything went silent. Thirty minutes felt like thirty years. A long loud scream shook Teréza from her stupor.

Kati was playing with the chickens when Anna exited the kitchen with her bun askew and a look on her face that said, *This will never ever be talked about.*

After the pause that would never ever be talked about, the soldiers wanted food and horses. And wristwatches. As many as they could wear at once.

Teréza heard the soldiers muttering, "*Velosiped*," as they scanned the yard and spotted András' rusty bicycle. The soldiers wore expressions of surprise and envy. They made exclamatory sounds, inspecting it like a specimen. Teréza had heard the gossip that poverty was worse in the Soviet Union. As they trampled their way across her homeland, she wondered if the soldiers were jealous of Hungary's stunning churches and neat peasant villages. Even Teréza's family had a couple of chickens, a pig, a cow and a rusty bicycle. Father Stalin, it was rumoured, let his own family of peasants go hungry.

Stealthily she emerged from the outhouse and made eye contact with her mother, just as the soldiers were pulling her father and brother up off the ground and were leading them to the stable. While her mother stood motionless, her eyes focused on the ground, Teréza feared they were being taken away to be shot. When four soldiers returned from the stable with nothing, Anna was ordered to cook for them. Teréza helped. Anna slaughtered the chicken she'd been saving for Easter and made *Chicken Paprikás*, minus the sour cream. Teréza watched the soldiers gobble the succulent dish, sucking every bone clean, cartilage and all. Yvan chewed off the soft end of the bone and sucked out the marrow.

"Those too," said the middle-aged commandant, pointing at the meagre plate of morsels, the heart and the giblets her mother had set aside for her children. His cheeks had sunken, like soft, warm mud. Deep furrows travelled from either side of his nostrils to either side of his mouth. His complexion was olive under his five o'clock shadow. His wrist up to his forearms decorated with nine watches of various shapes and widths. The ninth a woman's watch, the black leather band narrow and delicate, done up on the last notch. A conquest?

Teréza had shuddered at the thought. But he put the brakes on his wild troupe of twenty-year-olds who eyed fifteen-year-old Teréza with lust in their eyes. Teréza noticed he chewed with his mouth closed. It meant he was civilized. The combination confused her.

The commandant kept asking her father where he kept his horses.

Teréza listened to everything, following the thread of news and demands that threatened their little existence here, as though her presence in the kitchen could somehow mitigate the harm that could come to her family. She'd looked to the handsome redhead with round cheeks who smiled at her, reassuringly. She smiled back, feeling for the first time in her life a strange prickle, the difference between innocence and seduction.

"*YA ne yest,'*" her father insisted. He had no horses.

Teréza had never heard him speak a word of Russian before. She searched her mother's face for an explanation. Her mother's face gave nothing away.

The commandant scowled, replying, "*YA poydu smotret.*"

The officer ordered Bolochka and Yvan to search again. Yvan winked at Teréza as he set out to scour their yard.

The officer asked her father to hand over any jewellery. Again her father answered, "*YA ne yest.'*"

In crude Hungarian, he faced her father and said, "Please don't hate us. I am a father with small children like you. I am but a finger on the hand of the government. I have to do what I am told."

Her father motioned to the officer to take a seat.

Their mandate was to mete out retribution and carry out revenge for their own heavy losses at the hands of the

Germans and Hungarians. But first, they had to rest.

Failing to find any horses, the Russian soldiers had settled in the stable adjacent to the house and slept on straw. They snored with impunity.

That first evening, after the soldiers had turned in, her father gathered Teréza and András by his side at the hearth. She learned a family secret: that her father had been a political prisoner after WWI, when Kun Béla's Hungarian Soviet Republic was briefly in power after the Great War. He'd learned Russian in detention. In that moment her father changed in her eyes. Her family wasn't as protected by God as she once thought, and this was the first time she really understood how truly vulnerable she was, even under the protection of her father. And to learn that her father had been hurt by the Red Army budded her hatred for all things Russian.

In fact, Teréza learned more than she cared to know. This was the first time she heard the name Rákosi.

"Rákosi Mátyas was in bed with Kun!" Gyuri's voice grew loud from the third brandy warming his blood. "And now he's back, with these…these Russians."

"Please Gyuri, keep your voice down," Anna said, looking worried.

But Gyuri's intensity didn't waiver. "Rákosi was the one who formed the Red Guard. They ran the camp that killed my father. The evil sons of bitches did nothing but spread terror! It was a deadly scourge. I thought we were rid of him. How did he set foot on our soil again?"

Teréza gripped the sides of her chair as if by her discomfort she could telepathically quiet her father down by doing so. She was terrified his loud voice would awaken and anger the soldiers, leading them to throw their entire family out into the cold, or worse. When she could no longer bear the tension, she leaned in towards her father and matched his volume with a long, "Sssssshhhhhh!"

He looked at her as if he'd seen a ghost, his eyes wide open.

"Teréza's right, father, please keep your voice down," András whispered.

Anna placed her forefinger to her upper lip, "Please Gyuri."

He replied with a grunt and continued.

Teréza listened to her father's whispered rant under the light of a single oil lamp.

"They made my beloved father dig a ditch with his own hands. Then they made him jump off a table with a noose tied around his neck! And they made the entire family watch." Her father heaved with grief as Anna held him by the shoulders.

Teréza had never heard this story before. Never knew how her grandfather had died.

She didn't move a muscle though her foot itched something fierce.

"They came in red trains out to the countryside. The Communists hammered nails into their skulls." Teréza moved her hand to her forehead. Her stomach jumped to her throat. "They sewed their tongues to their noses." Her father fell off his chair to his knees on the floor, and let Anna rock him.

Like a candle that went out, pitching a room in darkness, Gyuri fell into a sudden intense sleep, snoring like a beast.

Teréza and András looked at each other in disbelief, bearing witness to a truth too stark to comprehend all at once.

Anna asked András, "Please son, help me drag your father

to bed. The misery has him out cold."

That same night, the soldiers sonorous sleep roused Teréza into vigilant wakefulness. Her mind conjured lurid images of women being forced to undress at gunpoint. By transposing it on other women, she could forget it happened to her own mother.

Teréza snuck back into the kitchen. She carefully removed a small folded letter from its resting place beneath the foil wrappers saved from last year's Christmas candies. The mail service had started up again, sporadically, and a brief note finally arrived from Klára in Budapest. Teréza watched for subtle changes in expression when her mother read it to herself.

"What does it say?" Teréza had asked impatiently.

"She's alive," her mother said and placed the note in the top drawer of the hutch.

As Teréza skimmed the letter in the semi-dark kitchen she was struck by the change in Klára's handwriting. She'd always admired her sister's longhand. Perfectly formed and aesthetic. Now the letters moved unsteadily. Some looked like shrivelled grapes. She finished sentences carelessly. Teréza didn't need to know more; her sister had been defiled like her mother.

As the soldiers slept, Teréza made a plan to manoeuvre around the evil side of men: *charm them with laughter and make sure they eat well.* Ever since the Red Army soldiers settled in their home, she entertained herself by getting them to teach her Russian. Teréza had somehow adapted to the brusque, clammy soldiers. If Teréza welcomed them, talked to them, cajoled them she reckoned she could prevent them from carrying out evil actions. If she could tap into kindness, could kindness prevail? If this was naive on her part, she didn't care. She had the virginity of herself and her sisters to protect.

"Poselok. Gorod. Strana." The Russian lesson came to a halt and the light-hearted atmosphere abruptly turned serious. Sun vanished from the kitchen and slipped into the adjacent room. In an instant, Teréza saw something change in Bolochka's face.

The soldiers began to speak forcefully, discussing something in harsh tones. The expression on Bolochka's face belonged to a distant and unreachable man. His charming brown irises had turned darker, and shrunk to the size of dried currants.

Yvan's mood had also switched. She couldn't locate the sweetness in him. He'd turned quarrelsome and unrefined, his body rocking back and forth. His arms sliced the air with hifalutin gestures.

She couldn't fathom why everything had changed so quickly.

She needed to understand what they were talking about. Maybe she could intervene. But how? She'd only banked five Russian words. She felt Ági slip off the bench and tiptoe towards the bedroom, but Teréza felt obligated to stay. Her plan had backfired. Guilt overwhelmed her. She hadn't flirted enough with Bolochka. She'd mocked him. She smiled too much at Yvan. Something. She'd ruined everything, somehow.

In her periphery, Teréza noticed two inquisitive noses peaking out from behind the bedroom door, Juli and Kati, precious with worry. The soldiers yelled louder, more aggressively. All around her the room bleached white, the resulting colour when shame and fear blended together. She moved off the bench, over to her siblings, quickly shutting the bedroom door. She slipped on the safety chain, the one her father had quietly installed on the bedroom door the day after the soldiers arrived.

"What are they arguing about?" Ági whispered.

"How would I know? I can't speak Russian," Teréza snapped.

Ági demanded more information. Teréza balked. A chair crashed to the ground and Teréza froze. She heard a scuffle. Juli and Kati began to whimper. Kati cried out for her mother and Teréza cupped her mouth. Another thud. More yelling in Russian.

The gunshot exploded an arm's length away. Someone fell heavy against the bedroom door, and then a chilling silence engulfed the house. Teréza nearly called out his name. Yvan!

Blood seeped under the door and reached toward Teréza's toes.

"The window!" she whispered, gathering her sisters. She pushed them, one by one, through the small opening, across the wide ledge out into the muted light. She heaved herself through the window to meet Yvan's eyes on the other side, wild-eyed and panic-stricken as he exited the kitchen, the pistol in his hand.

"You shot Bolochka?" Teréza sucked in air. She clutched Kati to her chest, as Juli and Ági clung to her body. Yvan's wristwatches all read three minutes past eleven.

"*Devushka,*" he said, and flung the gun into the field.

She watched him run down the dirt driveway, zigzagging like a drunk. Weeping. Cursing. Beseeching the sky. When Yvan had completely receded from her view, she called out to her father who was already running in from the field, a stricken look on his face and burs stuck to his jacket.

"What the devil is going on here?" Gyuri demanded.

"Yvan shot Bolochka. He's on the floor in the kitchen."

She watched her father scramble to the house and bust through the door. She heard him curse God. Teréza marched her trembling sisters to a patch of wildflowers where she made them kneel. She found two sticks, placed them on the ground to form a cross. She pressed her sisters' palms together, dropped to her knees and made the sign of the cross.

"Close your eyes," she barked at her sisters, "and pray with me."

"Teréza, what are we praying for?" Juli asked.

"To give me a son."

"I thought you wanted a daughter," Ági said accusingly.

"I've changed my mind." In that moment, Teréza knew she would raise a son to teach him something different.

Bolochka had been dead ten days when Teréza passed by a small group of men, standing in front of the pub on the *Fő* Square, drinking black coffee out of small glasses.

"Hitler's committed suicide."

"What? When?" Teréza blurted.

The men turned out of their huddle, eyebrows raised, inconvenienced by the intrusion. They answered in unison, "Yesterday."

"Pardon me," she said, "I didn't mean to interrupt. I thought only Hungarians committed suicide. I didn't expect it of Germans."

The three men looked at her contemptuously.

"Peasants," Teréza said under her breath. Though she was one herself, she had aspirations and felt superior to these men, and all peasants who failed to improve themselves.

When she returned home later, Teréza found the first blooming rose in her mother's garden. She dedicated it to Anna and to Klára, and for all women who'd been broken. In a gesture of rare and defiant optimism, she plucked a rose and placed it in a vase on the kitchen table.

Nine days after Hitler died, Teréza heard that the Red Army soldiers hoisted their flag on the balcony of Hotel Adlon in Berlin.

All at once nothing felt right in Teréza's domain. She felt an inexplicable lack of control. Invisible forces were at work. All she could see were imperfections. Dust and dirt. Uneven surfaces. Grease marks on pots. Cracks that looked like creeping blood. She felt it all, overwhelming her. She could see spiders and other creeping insects that had never bothered her before. Things that could crawl over her without her consent. She wanted to iron, to fold, to patch up the cracks.

"Get up," she said to Ági and András.

"Get up?" Ági sneered.

"Why?" András asked, bemused.

"I'm cleaning the kitchen. I need you to get out of those chairs."

"But the kitchen's already clean," said András. "Are you waiting for the Saints to arrive?"

"Please leave," said Teréza. Her chest felt compressed.

"Have you suddenly gone crazy?" Ági chided her.

"Just get out and leave me alone."

She pushed Ági out onto the porch. András followed, looking confused and worried. She shoved the door closed behind them. Privacy had to be fought for in their two-room house. "She's insane," she heard Ági say from outside.

No sooner had Teréza finished than she started at a loud bang on the door. Had it not been for her experience with Russian men, she would have hid under the bed, the force of the knock was so disturbing.

When she swung open the door, she discovered Varga Ferenc standing there.

Varga had a serious, ugly face, with eyebrows thick like fur and and a chin that looked like a sledgehammer. Crowning his head was an "official" cap, with a visor. Everyone knew the village bully.

"Where is your father?" Varga asked.

Teréza was astonished by his rudeness. Could he not even start with good day? What had become of the world since the occupation? Had etiquette eroded to this?

"He's out," she said primly.

"Where out?"

"Out, out." She'd never liked the stories she'd heard about Varga, and she was in no mood to cooperate with him.

Varga sighed, childishly. "Give him this." He handed her a small, pale pink piece of paper.

"Is it a party invitation?" she asked.

"Of a sort."

She snatched the paper from Varga's thick fingers, and before he got to the gate, she attempted to stop him with her demand. "What is this about our well being in the wrong place? My grandfather dug it over sixty years ago."

"The slip explains how to pay the fine. The well should be visible from the front of the house." Varga was already trotting down the long dirt road towards *Fő* Square.

"To make it impossible to fetch water when the house is burning?" she yelled after him. "What kind of new hell is this?"

THE FOX AND THE WOLF
ARE BORED

1945, Summer. Ják, Hungary

By mid-summer, the Russian soldiers who had pushed on towards Berlin returned to the countryside. Teréza saw them coming and going in their vehicles. They arrived like honoured guests, eating the chicken, crunching the cartilage, finishing the heart and the giblets like they had done before. Together with her mother, Teréza served their meals and washed their plates, obediently filled their glasses with apricot brandy, offering a few words in Russian. Fearing for his daughters, her father watched the soldiers like a hawk.

Teréza watched the soldiers take everything they could. Pigs and bicycles. Paprika, poppy seeds and brandy. She heard they'd dismantled entire factories and packed them up to take home. They'd even developed a unique system to collect cherries: they took the entire trees out by the roots, threw them in the back of their trucks and ate the cherries right off the tree.

András gave Teréza the statistics over bread and coffee as the two of them sat alone in the kitchen.

"One in every four houses in Hungary is damaged. Half of the country's livestock is gone. And a half of our industrial plants are demolished. Our currency is worthless."

"Is this what you woke up thinking about, András? Couldn't you think of something more pleasant to regale me with?"

"Sister, there is nothing else to think about. There is nothing else to talk about."

"The Russians have already taken everything." Teréza swallowed. In the name of reparations, they *had* taken practically everything. Hungarian soldiers were dying in Siberian work camps alongside suspected Fascists. Teréza heard the rumours of police violence against citizens and of the random arrests of priests and parishioners. Women everywhere lived with stories of rape.

András looked at her. "What do you want me to say? How pleasant that we can still afford coffee?"

"It's not real coffee. It's toasted barley." Teréza poured boiling water over the grinds. The scalding water splashed on the back of her hand. She yelped and slammed the kettle down. "For god sakes, don't just sit there, András! Do something! Make your own goddamn breakfast. You're old enough." András had just turned eighteen.

When he tried to help, she pulled the kettle from his hand, and shoved him out of the way. András left his coffee, shut the flimsy screen door behind him and retreated to the yard.

Teréza had looked to him for consolation, but there was none to be had. If her brother could not find false hope in himself, he would not offer it to his sister. This absence of reassurance thrust Teréza's heart into a reckless and unanticipated longing in István's direction, though other parts of her resisted him. This resistance was so primal only her guts could articulate it by a nervous flutter that accompanied the pining.

In a fit, Teréza grabbed the coffee cup and expelled it and its contents out the door in András' direction. "Our money is worthless," she yelled at a scrawny chicken pecking curiously at the cup. "Eat while you can."

She hated herself but couldn't stop it. When she wanted to show love she reacted with anger. When anyone came too close, she lashed out.

Teréza was home alone ironing in the kitchen when she heard it. A drum beat. Steady. Insistent. She had no idea what it was, but it filled her with dread. Ears of corn sat in baskets on the floor waiting to be husked in the evening. Ági, Juli and Kati had left for school hours ago. András and her parents worked out in the field digging up potatoes and root vegetables. The first of the summer harvest.

Who was beating a drum at eleven in the morning? Was it István? Pista? Trying to get her attention? She refused to fall for that. Had they gotten so bored with their stupid lives that they had to disturb the whole damn village? She kept ironing, slamming the scorching flatiron down on the dishtowels. Pushing, pulling, straightening. The drumbeat wouldn't let her be.

"For heaven's sakes!" She shoved her feet into her shoes and marched down the driveway towards *Fő* Square, towards the sound. Why hadn't someone shut them up yet?

By the time Teréza got to the street, the entire village had migrated to *Fő* Square. Men and women drifted in from the fields, looking confused, disrupted, fatigued. Irritated workers came out of shops with befuddled expressions. Teachers led hungry children out of classrooms, straightened their zig-zagging lines by yelling orders. She saw Ági, Juli and Kati.

A few hundred people had gathered in the square by City Hall. Teréza searched for the faces of her parents, for András. Where were they? She saw István standing nearby with his stepfather Feri, and youngest brother, Lali. It wasn't István beating the drum after all. Who was it then? A cold drop landed on her nose. She looked up. Funereal clouds. It began to drizzle.

The drumbeat persisted.

From the corner of her eye she spied a rust-coloured bird walking the perimeter of the *Fő* Square. "What the devil is a great bustard doing here?" she heard a male voice asking.

Teréza turned, surprised to see István with Lali standing next to him.

She turned back to observe the bird. It had quickened its steps to avoid detection.

Teréza had learned in school that the great bustard was Hungary's national bird. A gregarious thing that preferred group gatherings, this solitary intruder was out of its natural habitat. Perturbed, the bird puffed itself up twice its normal size and strutted handsomely. "He's lost," said Teréza. "Like everyone in Hungary."

"Except you." István smiled.

Teréza looked at him. At nineteen István was insultingly handsome.

"I've found you."

Teréza blushed, looked away only to encounter Lali hopping from leg to leg in an irregular rhythm while he popped a pastry in his mouth.

Teréza cocked her head; stopped herself from commenting.

"He does that when he gets excited," István explained.

The wind picked up and elevated the bustard's feathers, giving it the look of a tousled aristocrat.

"Someone found food during this wretched war. The bird's as fat as Rákosi," István said.

Half-chewed pastry sprayed from Lali's laughing mouth. It landed on Teréza's dress.

István belted Lali. "I apologize for my retarded brother. Can I clean that off for you?"

Teréza brushed the mess off her plain summer dress. "I can do it myself." She scowled at Lali, excused herself and squeezed her way through the crowd, trying to get a better look at the source of the noise.

The drum hung securely around the thick neck of a brutish young man. Varga. Again! Two policemen dressed in starched green uniforms flanked him. A man in a sand-coloured suit stood farther back. Teréza thought he looked vaguely familiar, but she couldn't place him. She noticed his shoes immediately. Chestnut brown, brand new.

Varga stopped drumming. *Thank God.* Teréza waited and watched. She scanned the crowd for her parents, for András. She still couldn't see them, but she could still see István. His eyes were trained on Varga, who removed a document from his satchel. Teréza's stomach fluttered. What was going on? Nothing like this had happened before. She couldn't find a confident face in the crowd.

Varga read the declaration. "Each home is to bring four baskets of corn to the town centre by four o'clock this afternoon. By tomorrow, each home is required to bring six baskets of potatoes, again by four o'clock. With these reparations we thank our liberators, the great Soviet Union. You will be paid 100,000 *pengő*."

"Per basket?" someone yelled.

"Per delivery," Varga corrected.

Complaints murmured through the crowd. "The *pengő* is nearly worthless," an old man protested. "Six baskets of potatoes is surely worth more than that measly sum."

The man in brown shoes took notes. The police repositioned themselves with even sturdier stances, and Teréza started to tremble inside. She still couldn't see her parents, or András. She watched her other three siblings huddled together with their teacher. Teréza didn't dare walk over to them.

She noticed the bustard tittuping out from between her siblings' feet. Lali was hopping again, from foot to foot, in amongst the other children.

The bird marched up to the front, half a metre from Varga and watched him with a scornful eye.

"Get out of here!" A policeman tried to shoo the bird, but it stayed put, as if demanding to know what Varga was doing on its territory.

The other policeman threw a stone at the bustard, but it hit Lali who started to cry. István grabbed Lali and jostled him back into the crowd.

Varga began calling out names, and the mood of the crowd shifted abruptly.

With each name, Teréza's gut twisted. She tried to discern a pattern. Members of families, and their relatives. The adults and their children. The wealthiest of the village. Landowners who would have voted for the Smallholders Party. Varga called these people forward and ordered them to the waiting truck. The unsmiling policemen escorted them. As the adults were led away, Teréza recognized on their faces the legacy of history and a contempt for fate. She searched the faces of their children and found a mixture of excitement and dismay. They were going somewhere different. Children's untainted optimism gave them an advantage of resilience.

The drizzle turned to a summer rain as if it too had been asked to obey an ordinance to produce more. No one could take shelter in the open square.

The truck carrying the families, thirty-seven people in total, drove off. The man in the sand suit and brown shoes opened an umbrella, covering Varga and his drum, then shoved his notebook in his pocket.

Varga informed the crowd that the beating of the drum, from now on, indicated that everyone must cease their work immediately and come to the *Fő* Square for new decrees. He ordered everyone back to work, back to their shops, back to school.

"The beast," someone uttered.

The villagers talked amongst themselves, incapable of leaving the camaraderie of commiseration, even as the sky ripped open, drenching them. As the villagers lingered, Teréza caught a glimpse of István again, looking as forlorn as she felt. István turned away, placed his hand on his father's shoulder, grabbed Lali's hand as they moved away. Something softened in her for him.

Teréza finally spotted her family. She pushed herself through the crowd towards her parents who were gathering her sisters.

"We're going home," said her mother when Teréza finally reached her.

"What about the quota by four o'clock? Teréza asked.

"Over my dead body," Anna replied. "Let's go."

They walked in silence, around potholes filled with water. Teréza was a changed person. She'd heard of the advancing Russians and felt the poverty of their declining currency; she'd seen a soldier dead on the floor and lost touch with her eldest and closest sister; but it was the drumbeat that wired her for fear. From this moment forth, her body would shake at the thud of a drum. She had witnessed thirty-seven people taken away that day. She shuddered to think her parents might be next.

Teréza's body broke out in spots. Hundreds of tiny little red stars.

István's mind worked as quickly as the sewing machine's needle. The man who stood in the back and wrote down the names of the dissenters, the one in the sand-coloured suit with chestnut-brown shoes was Németh, a former Arrow Cross officer, and Varga's uncle. Németh had altered his appearance, lost several kilos, shaved his head and his moustache, but István recognized him nonetheless. More importantly, István had made his shoes. They were part of a purchase order from the brand new State Protection Authority, or *ÁVO*. The shovel-faced bastard and his nephew Varga had switched sides.

István was sure he'd never see those families again. *Kulaks* – a new term (another gift from the Russians) – were wealthy, prosperous peasants with land. In other words, targets. István had gone to school with two of the young men hauled off. Good, solid chaps. He'd watched as their fathers diligently boarded the truck, helping their children on. Subjugated men holding their shocked, shaken wives. The whole incident had sent a chill up his spine. Varga's monotone voice calling names, his sledgehammer chin. How the truck coughed black smoke, burning oil. How the families, the boys he knew, would likely never come back.

When the truck drove off, the fear went straight to István's bladder. He had wanted to relieve himself but had forced himself to hold it until the gathering adjourned, until it ached. Németh in his brown shoes, scribbled every time someone grumbled or walked away, so István made himself wait, adhering to the unspoken understanding that it was safer to comply. Two villagers that demanded an explanation, a man in his thirties, and another in his fifties were apprehended to be beaten. Afterwards when Isvtán had gone with Feri for a quick drink – an *Unicum* to calm their nerves – he saw the two men in the pub drinking heavily. Even from across the room, he could see the fresh wounds on their faces.

"Varga's the new Renaissance man," István said quietly, leaning in towards Feri. "What else is he capable of doing?"

Feri shook and nodded his head simultaneously.

Late in the afternoon Pista slammed the door of Feri's shoe shop.

István looked up from his stitching, bleary-eyed. In front of him a mess of shoes, wooden lasts, glues, leathers, dyes and brushes. He'd been daydreaming about Teréza. "What the hell happened to you?" István asked.

"Weren't you at the goddamn drum circle?" Pista scowled.

Pista made István nervous. Since the war ended, he demonstrated unpredictable moments of irascibility. His reactions were always on the dramatic side, but lately he'd looked like he'd swallowed undetonated explosives. Officially dissolved and banned, the members of the Arrow Cross – scores of village Christians who had volunteered to serve the right-wing party – were still being hunted. Maybe Pista was as fearful as István that their small part in it would soon be discovered. The police station in Szombathely had István's statement that his birth-father was Jewish. He would not be linked to the Christians, but Pista could be. István thought for sure that Pista had found out about his self-serving act. István's shame grew more debilitating each day.

"You look like you want to murder someone," István remarked.

Pista's nostrils were stiff and flaring. "If I could, I would murder a Communist, but then I wouldn't be around to keep you in line. I'd be rotting in a jail somewhere."

"Any Communist, or one in particular?"

"Two in particular."

"Of course."

Pista lit up and drew on his smoke like a vampire sucking blood. Puffs of smoke, short and long, punctuated the sentences forming in Pista's mind. István knew the demeanour well. Fuse for the explosives.

Feri motioned to István. "Close the windows."

"I'll drop dead from the heat," István objected.

"I said, close them." Feri raised his voice.

Lately, Feri suffered episodes of paranoia. Everyone did. Overreactions spread like a virus. Now even Feri comported himself like a nervous dog, ready to attack.

István closed the windows.

Feri checked to see who idled on *Fő* Square.

Pista drew hard on his cigarette. "Those police out there patrolling *Fő* Square. These are not normal police. Oh no.

They've been sent from Russia. Listen to how they speak Hungarian."

"Keep your voice down, Pista," Feri urged. "Turn on the sewing machine!" he barked at István.

István flipped the switch. The machine hummed and rattled without a shoe to sew, poking holes into nothing, yet it barely drowned out Pista's rant.

"We're going to have to start sucking up to Varga and Németh now that they're with the Reds."

"Like hell we do." István poked his finger with a needle drawing blood.

Pista grinned. "Our new Commies are sniffing out ex-Arrow Cross members."

"But Németh was Arrow Cross himself," Feri said. With his palm, his wiped his forehead of beaded sweat. "Everyone knows that."

"Doesn't matter. The Red Army gave the Hungarian Communists a quota," Pista said with a calm that was now alarming István.

István's head began to pound. Pista never gave him a break. István looked up from his stitching; he'd barely unzipped Teréza's dress.

Feri breathed heavily as he kept watch, pawing for a handkerchief in his pocket.

The door swung open and nearly hit Pista in the face.

István didn't look up, but he could tell by the sound of the shoe that entered – with a purposeful stride – that this was no ordinary customer.

Varga stood in the doorway. Behind him, Pista raised his eyebrows and mouthed the word *rat* and Feri nodded.

"Hot day to have all the windows closed," Varga said with a smile like melting wax.

"It must only be hot for you," István said. Cold sweat crept down his back. "I'm feeling quite a chill myself."

Varga looked at the sewing machine sewing nothing. "In capitalism wasting electricity is acceptable. Leftovers of the evil West."

István was about to say something – he didn't know what – but Pista cut in. "Capitalism has taught Communism a thing or two about industrialization. Before the war Russia's factories were pathetic. Stalin owes Churchill a bottle of vodka."

Before Varga could respond, Feri pounced. "What do you need done this time? Your shoes look fine to me."

"I'll take a pair of shoelaces," Varga said, while rummaging for something in his satchel.

"Get him some laces," Feri said, visibly seething as Varga transferred his weight to his other leg, and thumped with his foot.

He had brand new laces in his brown shoes. István moved slowly against the air, the sweat, the sound, Pista's smoke and the contempt, sealed tightly in the shop. He lifted a pair of laces off a hook behind the display cabinet and placed them on the counter.

Varga handled them as if they were made of fine fabric. "I'm offering an opportunity to join the Party," he said with a disturbing repose. "Then we don't ever have to bring those shovels up. Do we? I will personally sponsor you if you –"

István cut him off. "100,000 pengő for the laces."

Varga swiped the laces into his bag. "Run a tab. I have no money on me." He slapped a slip on the counter. Varga turned swiftly and thrust open the door, narrowly missing Pista's face again.

István yelled after Varga, "Is your parents' dairy also

receiving these pink slips?"

Feri shut the door hard and unleashed a torrent of invectives. He leaned against the wall, breathless and faint, clutching his heart.

"Just watch," said István, "the asshole's going to come after me."

"Worse." Pista held up the slip of paper. The lettering was uppercase, thick and belligerent. "He's going to come after your father. The asshole's not only a turncoat; he's a Party Inspector too. Look at this, all sorts of fabricated fees." He was about to crumple the slip when István yelled, "Don't do that!"

Feri slapped his hands on his ears.

"What the hell's the problem?" Pista shouted. "This belongs in the garbage!"

"I don't argue with that. Feri's ears are sensitive to paper," explained István.

Pista looked intrigued.

"Don't ask."

"Give me that pink piece of shit." Feri grabbed the slip from Pista's hand. "There's a tax for private business. A fee for owning machinery. And look at this! A fine for a fifty-year old well that's been dug in the wrong place on my property. I don't even have a well!"

As István ate dinner that evening, he could see two dogs through the kitchen window, going at each other in the yard. A third barked helplessly, pacing around the periphery, unable to get in on the fight. The two big dogs clamped down on each other, growling, barking, hoisting their front legs up on each other's necks. One dog yowled as the other bared his fangs and went in for the attack.

"Hungary and Russia," said Feri, glancing out the window.

Lali jumped out of his seat, pointing to the pacing pup. "And that one's Germany!"

István laughed and Tamás scrunched his nose in confusion.

Outside the dogs continued to growl.

"You don't get it, do you?" István said to Tamás, dodging his mother Zsuzsa's dirty look.

By birthright, Tamás had usurped István's place in the family because he was the first son born in wedlock. István baited his mother to prove the extent to which she spurned him. He waited until Zsuzsa was in a foul enough mood in order to intensify the results of his experiment.

István ran another test. "For some peculiar reason your hair looks curlier when you wear those black-rimmed glasses. You look like a cross between a secretary and a dairymaid."

Tamás raised his eyebrows. Feri was about to put István in his place when Lali yelled, "The dogs are bleeding!"

"*Az anyád Istenét*!" Zsuzsa cursed her mother's God, and leapt to her feet, bumping the kitchen table. Soup sloshed. Everyone grabbed their bowls. She stomped out into the yard, rabid as a raccoon.

Through the sheer yellow curtains of the kitchen window István watched the dogs disperse as his mother chased them with a wooden spoon. She stood in the chicken shit and mud of the yard in leather slippers, her grey knee socks sagging by her ankles, hands on her wide hips. It would be Feri who would clean and polish the filthy leather slippers, but when she marched back into the house, she complained, "Of course, I'm the one who has to get rid of those goddamn dogs." Zsuzsa grabbed the salt and shook a snowstorm into her soup.

István assumed her comment was directed at him. She deliberately avoided his eyes. Her focus moved from salt to table, spoon to soup, Tamás to Feri, from Lali to the window. Lali ate like he was in a race to finish first.

"For the love of God, slow down, Lali," Zsuzsa scolded.

She cleared the bowls and stacked them noisily. István watched her like a spy, resenting the way she moved about, as though each of her gestures were a violation. She placed a platter of *Chicken Paprikás* and egg noodles on the table, served the drumsticks to Feri and to Tamás and the wings to Lali. She gave István the back.

"I'd be gone by now if I could," he said under his breath.

"What's that?" his mother said, glaring at him.

"Another piece of chicken? More sauce?" His mother offered seconds to Tamás.

István could sense Lali fuming, crunching on cartilage and gnawing on bone, like the dogs. He gave him a don't-bother-it-won't-do-any-good look and resumed stabbing his egg noodles until he'd eaten every last bit and scraped the plate clean with the side of his fork.

He got up without a word, left the plate on the table, and let the door slam. He hadn't touched the chicken back.

"Come back and clear your goddamn plate," she yelled after him.

He skulked to the bathhouse where he could see his breath in the night air. Dogs bayed in the distance. He wet his shaving brush, swirled it around in the soap and painted his stubble with the moist, white lather. He shaved, splashed his skin with water and towel-dried his face.

In the mirror, he saw traces of a man he would never

know.

He withdrew into the seclusion of his bedroom, wondering why even his simplest desires could not be met. It was past midnight, and he lay in bed lamenting his virginity. The world outside stood still. The rain couldn't decide whether or not to fall. István realized that his chances at a respectable life were marginal; living in his own home, supporting a wife and child doing a job he loved all seemed impossibly out of reach. He would soon turn twenty.

His manly body no longer derived pleasure from executing stunts on his bicycle, from kicking a ball at a soccer game, or from seeing who could piss farther in the snow. Nor could his mind rest given the changing situation around him. In a second it could plunge into melancholy, triggered by any random thought, and then just as quickly bubble back up into delusional optimism.

István climbed out of bed, removed the crucifix from the wall and put it in the top drawer of his desk. He should have done that long ago, but his mother would have cursed him if she noticed it missing.

His bedroom window was backlit by the moon. A shiver ran up his spine; his adobe room felt clammy. He laid back down, on top of his covers this time, and when he reached down under his pajamas, his three middle fingers were cool.

He started slowly, awkwardly, stroking himself. He listened for any movement in the house and turned his ear towards his door.

He pulled his pyjama bottoms farther down, just far enough to expose himself. His cock bounced out, eagerly, expectantly. He rubbed his hands together until they felt warm on his skin. He spit in his hand and started again slowly, gripping and sliding. The need for emotional release bore deeper than the need for sexual satisfaction. He stroked up and down, fought with disturbing, worrisome thoughts.

He gripped harder to quell his fear. Sliding up and down along his erection. Spit into his hand again. *Teréza. Teréza. Teréza.* He pointed himself upward like an antenna.

He slowed down. He lost it again. Guilt, shame, Pista. His breath heaved with frustration. Fucking Varga. Teréza! His desire for her felt confusing. The more she appeared disinterested in him, the more determined István got.

He stopped. Tried to breathe calmly. His need for this release was profound. The tension had accumulated in his pelvis. His groin had been taut since his first encounter with the informants last week, as though his body had braced itself to be kicked in the balls. He'd stepped out of his father's shop for a visit to the outhouse and there they were, the *Spicli* – informants. They'd asked who his friends were and how he felt about Communism. The questions came quickly from men with little or no education. He could hear it in their dialects. They spoke with elisions, they dropped ends of words, used the wrong vowel.

István answered their questions with calculated restraint. Yes, Pista and he knew each other. Communism? Communism is a party with seventy elected seats. His life philosophy? Go from failure to failure without losing enthusiasm. He was wise enough to mention that Churchill had said that. The two *Spicli* nodded blankly.

István laughed out loud as he remembered, and his penis bounced in appreciation. He stroked himself vigorously. He thought of bare breasts. Nipples, buttocks, navels. Teréza. Teréza should be on a calendar, he thought, the kind soldiers pin up in the barracks. He undressed her from the waist up. Teréza's breasts popped out at him, plump and suckable.

Desires that priests told him were despicable swelled in his balls. They accumulated, stole his breath, reddened his face and liberated him. Release. It came with fear and despair, the finale to his lonely act, just as Lali cracked open the door and poked his head in.

"What are you doing?"

"Fucking hell!" István yanked the covers up. The wet seeped through the fabric. He balled up his blanket in front of his belly and turned to face his scrawny brother. "What are you doing out of bed?"

"I'm sleep walking, like father," Lali said, hopping from leg to leg in an irregular rhythm.

"For Christ's sake, Lali. You can't sleepwalk and still talk to me. Cut out that stupid hopping."

Lali stilled himself and grinned. "Why are your covers all balled up like that? What's that smell?"

"A cat died," István explained.

He stopped hopping. "Why won't father let me join the boy scouts?" Lali asked, picking his nose in the doorway.

"It's not a good idea to be in any group right now."

"But you are."

"I quit."

István was unable to protest when Lali crawled into his bed, felt the wetness with his hand and pulled a face. He wiggled a little closer to István.

"Let me tell you a story," István said. "I want you to listen closely, Lali. You're sharp. You know how to read between the lines. Please don't make me tell you why you can't go to boy scouts. Just listen to my story, okay?"

Lali nodded. His boyish frame was pressed against him. He began in a whisper, "The fox and the wolf are bored."

"Why are they bored?" Lali asked without missing a beat.

"They just are. Don't interrupt me. So the wolf says to the

fox, 'Let's go beat up the rabbit.' The fox doesn't want to and asks, 'Why should we beat up the rabbit?' The wolf replies, 'We'll beat him up because he's wearing a hat.' The fox asks, 'What do we do if he is not wearing a hat?' 'Then we'll beat him up because he's *not* wearing a hat.' So the fox and the wolf go find the rabbit. The poor little rabbit is afraid of them and crouches low to the ground. 'Look!' says the wolf, 'the rabbit's *not* wearing a hat!' And the wolf and the fox give the rabbit a good beating."

István felt Lali's legs wince under the covers as his brother kneaded the wool blanket under his tiny fists.

"Is the rabbit bleeding all over?"

"Not all over, but he's bleeding. Now keep listening, Lali. You need to get this. The next day the wolf says to the fox, 'Let's go beat up the rabbit.' The fox doesn't want to and says, 'We beat him up yesterday. Why should we beat him up again today?' The wolf replies, 'Let's ask him for cigarettes. If he doesn't have any, we'll beat him up.' So the fox and wolf go find the rabbit again. The poor little rabbit is shaking with fear when the wolf asks him, 'Hey rabbit, do you have any cigarettes?' The rabbit asks the wolf, his teeth chattering with fear, 'Do you want them with filter or without filter?' To this the wolf says, 'Fox, check it out, the rabbit is still not wearing a hat.' So they give the rabbit another good beating. Then next day when the wolf and the fox come looking for the rabbit, the poor little rabbit has a hat and cigarettes but no shoes."

István and Lali lay in silence. The wind outside picked up.

Lali sniffled. "Did they –"

"Yeah. They beat him up again." István wanted to hug Lali, but he still held the wet ball of sheets in front of him.

"It's terrible what they did to the little rabbit," Lali said in a small voice. "The wolf is the ÁVO, and the fox is the policeman and the rabbit is…us?"

"How do you know about the ÁVO?" István asked, alarmed.

"Everybody knows about the ÁVO. They supply the *Spicli* with cigarettes."

"I knew you were smart," István said fondly. "Remember that story, Lali."

"The rabbit should get a gun to protect himself."

"Where would the rabbit get a gun? He can't afford one."

"They're all over the place. I found one in the field near Édes Teréza's house."

"Leave those guns alone," said István. He knew the war left behind weapons, scattered about in fields for boys to find. Some empty, some with a single bullet waiting for a skull.

"When are you leaving us?"

"Why would you ask such a question?"

"Because that's what older brothers do. And you and mother never look at each other anymore."

"I'm not leaving you."

"Not even when you get married?"

"I'm not getting married. Who could I ever get married to?"

"Édes Teréza. You like her. But she doesn't like me, after I spit my pastry on her dress. Do you think she can learn to love me?"

"I don't know yet, Lali. I really don't know. Now don't ask me any more questions I can't answer."

"How do I know beforehand that you can't answer them?"

"Let's just say we now live in a world where the answer to any question can put you in danger, so best if you keep all questions to yourself."

"I'll miss you," said Lali.

"Don't say that," said István, choking up. His little brother was the only pure being left in his life.

I'LL GO WITH YOU, WHEREVER YOU'RE GOING

1946, January. Ják, Hungary

Her red spots came and went without warning, just like Varga's drum. Sometimes they hurt, sometimes they didn't, some had jagged edges like misshapen stars, and some didn't. But they were all irritating. Without the money to visit a doctor, Teréza had watched the spots come and go on her breasts, stomach, and inner thighs since the summer.

She covered affected areas with plantain poultices, supplying a measure of relief for a short while. She didn't talk of the discomfort to her mother and took to dressing in the kitchen while her sisters slept, in case they woke and saw her speckled body. When the spots didn't hurt, her heart raced inexplicably, fluttered in her throat as swiftly as a dragonfly appeared on the breeze.

One day in early January she went covert and inspected the spots in the safety of the frosty outhouse, shivering as she undressed partway. Teréza's underwear, hand sewn by her mother, needed taking in. Winter brought gnawing hunger when the stash of seed potatoes in the barn could no longer fend off mold and stink, and her family's dinner plates held little nourishment. Now, as the ice melted from the willow boughs and dropped from the eaves, the modest coverings were slipping off Teréza's adolescent hips.

She touched the spots with the delicacy of a paintbrush. What were they trying to communicate to her? Her shame turned to curiosity. They seemed to render unclear messages, impressions only, but she surmised that they served a function. As she stared in the mirror she was thankful that the spots had spared her face. Today they started to itch, and her stomach ached as though someone had punched her there. New symptoms. Why today? She wondered if her stomach and the red spots were connected.

She saw in the mirror that her arms were well developed from the daily labour that replaced her schooling. Institutions were open again – her sisters, Ági and Juli had resumed school, and Kati had started kindergarten – but her parents had to pay. They barely had enough to cover for the little ones. They couldn't pay for Teréza too.

She touched herself between her legs just briefly, before shame and guilt separated her from such corporeal urges. She had to make her underwear last till Sunday when her mother would give her a clean pair. All of her was red from the cold, and she returned to the house sneezing, ready to warm up at the fire before her sisters returned from school.

Squatting at the hearth, she thought of her eldest sister. Teréza had given up hope that Klára might come home to Ják upon receiving another note written in the same unsteady handwriting as before. The characters looked even more compressed, but Klára remained in Budapest living in the reconstruction zone. Teréza could see that nothing was altered in her sister's letter. Even in her small village, letters frequently arrived with blacked out sentences, confirming the rumblings that the Central Post Office in Budapest steamed open mail to "weed out fascist elements" or uncover "plots to destroy peace and freedom."

Ági, Juli and Kati burst into the house. The biting January winds chased them indoors.

"Come, come." Teréza helped Kati with her coat, while Juli and Ági undressed themselves. The sudden bustle snapped Teréza out of her malaise; menial tasks were a temporary cure for her lack of hope, her lack of direction.

She wiped the snot from Kati's nose and removed her shoes. She warmed her cheeks and feet, rubbed them like trying to spark a fire from two sticks and shoved her tiny feet into threadbare slippers. "Kati will soon leave bare footprints in the snow," she said to her mother. "The fox will know where she lives."

"I don't want the fox to find me." Kati's eyes began to redden; her lips became puffy.

"Drop her shoes off at Feri's shop. You could visit with István while you're at it," said her father.

"I'm not interested," Teréza said, dismissively.

"Objection means the opposite is stirring in the depths," Gyuri said winking, twirling the tip of his moustache.

Teréza failed to understand how her father could be in such good spirits since most of his produce was going towards reparations. Was he sneakily coercing her to secure a husband so he'd have one less mouth to feed? She would have none of it. She'd find a way to earn her keep until she felt ready to marry.

"The more we avoid someone, the more they mean to us," Anna said, smiling.

Ági and Juli pitched their schoolbooks on the table.

"Do you need help with your homework?" Teréza said, ignoring her parents.

"You need to start thinking about a husband," Gyuri persisted.

"No I don't." Teréza reached for her sisters' textbooks. She noticed her father elbow András, grinning and winking. She hated the assumptions heaped on girls her age. How did anyone know what she needed?

"Our books are getting lighter," Ági said.

"What do you mean they're getting lighter?" Anna asked. She held a tin bowl in one hand and kneaded sticky, elastic dough with the other. A rhythmic squishy sound filled the silence.

Teréza opened a textbook. "What on earth happened to these pages?" She flipped through the book with agitation. Pages had been removed. She grabbed another textbook. More squishy sounds as her mother kneaded furiously. More pages were missing, torn away at the binding. Whole sections of Hungarian history. Gone. "Ági! What have you done to your book?"

Teréza looked up to see Ági standing with her hands on her hips, defiant, her mouth mangled into a sour, surly expression. "Why don't you look at Juli's book before you jump down my throat?"

Teréza grabbed another book. There were dozens of missing pages in Juli's books too. The section on religion, on Hungarian history. In the second grade textbook, the same thing. Teréza remembered these texts. She had studied from the very same ones.

"Well, well, who shall you blame now," taunted Ági. "Me or Juli?"

"No need to get sarcastic," Gyuri intervened.

"Alright girls, who's responsible for this?" Anna pounded her dough.

Juli looked worried and wouldn't speak.

Teréza waited for the answer already forming in her mind, a sinister shape to things. The scent of yeast tickled her nose. She pinched her nostrils. She didn't want another new discovery to form an unpleasant memory associated with a smell she loved.

"They *made* us tear them out," Ági explained.

"Who did?" asked Gyuri, frowning.

"The teachers. Everyday, we rip out one page," Juli said quietly.

"Why didn't you tell us sooner?" When crucial information reached her too late, or when it raced ahead of her, Teréza felt paranoid and defenseless. Effectiveness resided in knowing.

"Anything relating to religion," Ági said, her eyes tight with intensity, "the teachers burn after school."

Teréza scrutinized the remaining pages. "History… anything relating to our victories, gone. *Rise Up, Magyar* is completely gone." She grew up reciting the famous *Petőfi* revolutionary poem. Its removal shocked her.

"So are the words to the Second Anthem," Ági added.

"My God!" Teréza crossed her hands over her heart.

"It's the rotten Communists in the government!" Anna slammed the dough on the cutting board.

"The Soviet scum." Gyuri pounded his fist on the table.

Teréza watched her mother pinch off morsels of dough one by one, making dents in the sticky mass. She dropped each severed piece into boiling water on the stove.

"And our school play is cancelled too, the one we started rehearsing before Christmas," Ági said with a kind of self-satisfaction that perturbed Teréza.

Anna was sweating over top of the boiling water. Bits of dough made a plopping, then sizzling sound as they hit the water.

She glanced at Ági. "You look like you're pleased about this." Teréza waited for her parents to say something. They didn't intervene.

"Don't be an idiot. Of course it doesn't please me." Ági plunked herself down on the small three-legged stool and crossed her legs. "I had the lead. I played Mariska, the young woman who borrows clothes to make herself more attractive to the wealthy mayor's son."

"Of course you had the lead. You always need to show off. Then what's with the grin?" Teréza said, growing more and more incensed.

"Did your teacher say why it's being cancelled?" András asked.

"The material is 'unsympathetic to Communist ideology,'" Ági answered, each word measured with a newfound intellectual maturity.

"Why do you doubt your sister?" Gyuri asked. He reached for a textbook, began to look for himself. "Isn't this proof enough?"

"She's always exaggerating. It's probably just postponed." Teréza rose from the table. Her mind whirled. She wondered what else the censors imposed on schoolteachers. She knew Ági was telling the truth, but she couldn't admit it out loud.

"Denying what's happening won't make it go away." András shook his head.

"Good then." Teréza marched out of the kitchen into the bedroom and slammed the door on her family.

"This is exactly what they want out of us," Teréza heard her mother say from the kitchen.

She wept into her pillow, a few short heaves, and then vowed to contain the rest.

István was walking on the *Fő* Square when he spotted her, heading towards the brand new "state-controlled" post office. It was a day after he had climaxed to the vision of her bare breasts.

A damp chill and a large cloud hung in the air.

He paused by a lamppost that did little to hide him and felt a blush rise to his cheeks. His secret came alive in his pants.

Wearing an oversized sheepskin hat, Teréza's head looked too big for her body, but István didn't mind. It charmed him.

On this very early Saturday morning, István had been making his way to Feri's shop to get a head start on things. Next to the already large order to repair the boots of the Hungarian State Dance Ensemble – they were up and twirling again after the war, and Feri was one of the best cobblers in the region – the "State Protection Authority" tripled its standing order for men's shoes. Not an order Feri could decline, because it covered the continual increase in taxes he was forced to pay to the state, but demoralizingly, the shoes supplied the very uniformed thugs who harassed István, his family and the rest of the population. István had offered to make them himself to ease Feri's outrage.

"You're a good son," Feri had said, shaking his head, "but we'll bear this cross together."

István resisted where he could, making the shoes slightly uncomfortable, a smidge too narrow in the toe and left a few discreet nails pointing in the wrong direction. He had actually woken in a cheerful mood, anticipating the rebellious mischief he was about to partake in, so that by the time he spotted Teréza he was fully primed.

He watched her enter the post office, an adorable bundle, spying on her like a *Spicli*. He stood with his hands deep in his pockets. His shoulders up around his ears, he tried to think up some excuse as to why he stood shivering outside of the post office.

He ignored the old ladies walking by on the way to the market, scrutinizing him with their thorny eyebrows. He kept looking skyward at the grey blotch overhead. To his surprise, he noticed that the Hungarian coat of arms positioned to the right of the post office door – the same place on all government buildings – was covered in a black cloth. Like Hungary had died.

The door swung open.

Out she came, walking right past him. She was halfway across the viscous, muddy road, her shoes making squishy sounds as she walked, when he called out to her.

"Teréza!" His voice caught in his throat, stopped by a dam of phlegm.

"István?" She laughed. The tone had a hint of irony to it. "What are you doing here at this hour?" she asked.

"Waiting for Pista," he said. Of course, waiting for Pista. He was always waiting for Pista. He had only seconds to come up with something else.

"Do you see what's leapt off the printing presses?" he

said, feeling like Pista's puppet.

"What?" she said annoyed and confused.

"I'm sorry, I've given you the impression that something's afoot. I just wanted to point out *Szabad Nép.*"

"The newspaper?" she asked.

"Yes, the newspaper."

She came a little closer. Thank God. He didn't want to keep yelling at this ungodly hour. The *Spicli* started early, and he'd already attracted more attention than he wanted to from the peasant women waddling past with large baskets of freshly baked bread.

"The newspaper destroyed by the Arrow Cross?" Teréza asked.

Why did she have to mention the Arrow Cross? Just the thought of it made him uneasy. "Yes. That's the one," he said, wondering where he could steer this discourse next. She edged closer. He smiled broadly, counting every second as a marvel of luck. It was like taming a wild filly.

"Look. It's up and running again. 'The free people of Hungary are grateful for a new Soviet friendship.' I've never read such bullshit in my life." István held the paper up for her. He had never before realized just how small she was. Childlike yet prickly.

"András read me the same line yesterday," Teréza said.

"You don't say!" he said, excitedly. Tone it down, he thought to himself. Too much enthusiasm will ruin everything.

"The Smallholders *Kis Ujság* is still the most popular newspaper in the country," Teréza said with conviction.

"That has no bearing. No matter how influential *Kis Ujság* may appear, Communists are infiltrating every corner of society. Popularity is not enough to withstand the effect of the Soviet system."

"The Communists now have an office here," she whispered leaning in. "They're showing up everywhere."

"I know."

"In schools, in churches."

"In youth groups."

"Post offices."

"Yes."

"Did you notice the coat of arms?" she said, indicating with her head.

"The death of Hungary."

He didn't know what to say next. He'd burdened their interaction with his talk. How could he seduce her now that they were both feeling suspicious and wary?

"I should go," she said, "I don't know what to think." She rubbed her forehead as though her thoughts hurt her brow bone.

He didn't know if she meant she had to go back home or wherever she was headed. He wanted to blurt out, *I'll go with you, wherever you're going.* Instead he said, "My apologies for keeping you."

He reached for her hand. She offered it. He kissed it tenderly.

"Please, take care, István," she said letting him hold her hand a little longer.

Inside, he glowed like he had swallowed a million fireflies.

PLEASE STAY WITH ME

1946, Fall. Ják, Hungary

Sometimes István wished that Varga had turned him in. It might have been preferable to this half-life – the executioner's ax poised delicately over his exposed neck. István staved off the melancholy induced by this consistent low-grade threat, by studying his automotive books. He derived temporary satisfaction from the fact that hydraulic braking systems were becoming relatively standard in vehicles, allowing for more consistent force distribution. He managed to push dark thoughts from his mind by memorizing diagrams on brake assembly for passenger cars, but making shoes for the secret police wore away at his conscience. Thinking of Teréza was the only thing that gave him pleasure.

Pista wasn't working, and it wasn't because he had no real skills. It was because the Communists were aware of his big mouth. He ranted at the tavern on weekends and now also on weekdays. The Commies – aka Németh and Varga – were making sure no one would hire him.

One afternoon, while István loitered on the *Fő* Square

with Pista, Teréza appeared out of the blue and invited them to the upcoming "zither night" at her home.

Teréza's invitation had seemed so calculated and rehearsed that István couldn't help but entertain the possibility that it had been a planned overture.

"Come on Saturday," she said cheerfully.

"How can I last until Saturday?" István said to Pista as Teréza bounced away.

István, Pista and Lali approached the Édes house with curiosity. A lively racket lit up the small abode. Candles in the windowsill flickered in time with the music, and a faint melody rode the wisps of fog that descended on the village. István had never stepped foot in Teréza's yard before.

In good form, Pista walked beside him, without a care, smoking. Lali tagged along, his pockets bulging with salty pastries. He asked, "Are you going to marry Teréza? And leave me once and for all?"

"Of course he is, he's going to leave us both." Pista smacked István on the back.

"Christ almighty, both of you. Shut up." István swatted at Pista's head. "I don't want either of you to botch this night for me. I want no talk of Stalin or Rákosi. No Németh or Varga. No Communists. And the ÁVO is off limits. And under absolutely no circumstances will you be going on about how Hungary is disintegrating. I have only one goal for the evening."

There was a silence.

"You raaaaaaaaat fiiiiiiiiiiiink!" Lali exploded. "You don't love me anymore! You only ever play with Pista! And now you're deserting us two for a stupid giiiiiiiiiiiirl!"

He threw himself against István, pummelling him with small fists.

"Okay, that's enough." István picked up his skinny, rabid brother, hoisted him on the side of his hip and carried him with one arm. Lali screamed louder. When Lali got like this it could go on for an hour. A few hundred metres away István tossed him across a fence into a darkened field of tall grass. He heard Lali grunt and whimper.

"That was efficient," Pista remarked, grinning.

"Sometimes it's got to be done."

Teréza's mother Anna opened the door, greeting the two young men with kisses on their cheeks. She made room for István and Pista in the corner of the wrap-around bench. Still wearing their long, white work aprons stained with animal blood, Gyuri and András played their homemade tabletop zithers. With picks on their right thumbs and wide smiles on their faces, they plucked and hit the vibrating strings like seasoned musicians.

Song after song, Gyuri and András played without stopping. Vibrations resonated from the zithers, ricocheted over the tabletop, travelled along its length, through its wooden legs and enlivened István's right foot. It wanted to stamp in time with the beat. He permitted his fingertips to tap in time with the music instead. Pervasive guilt kept in him check. Only one show of expression at a time.

István watched Teréza swirling around the Édes kitchen, her hands on her hips. Ági, Juli, Kati and two other neighbourhood girls were also dancing, but his eyes transfixed on Teréza, who sang the loudest. He was enchanted by her aliveness. The heels of her flat shoes hovered off the ground. He admired how Teréza never let them touch throughout the entire dance. She kept everyone on tune and in tempo. She had joy. She was a peppercorn, small and potent, bubbling at the bottom of a pot of soup. Her clear, young voice rose like a bird's above everyone else's.

Her skin glowed, blushed pink from the heat of the cast iron stove which her mother stoked with coal. Even in this abject country, the Édes remembered how to revel. What was in the fabric of this family that they could still enjoy themselves?

Already he felt more emotion than he was capable of containing at once. He couldn't take his eyes off Teréza. She had revealed another side of herself to him. It wasn't only István's right foot that wanted to come to life. He concealed his growing desire beneath the table. Her shapely calves teased him, flexed with each step of the *Csárdás*, and now she danced for him. She was beguiling.

"Sing!" Teréza shouted at him, over the call of the two zithers. István's pale face reddened. Clapping roisterously, Anna encouraged him.

"I can't!" István sat on his hands.

The girls danced rings around the dog nestled without a care in the middle of the floor. Pista elbowed István in the ribs, belting out the words to the song.

István scowled.

"I'm enjoying myself, brother, like you'd instructed me to," Pista warbled in a low-barrelled voice.

"That's it!" Teréza winked at Pista. Insistently, she clapped her hands together pushing the musicians and dancers into a frenzied rhythm. "Faster," she yelled.

István clammed up.

Gyuri and András picked up the momentum. The girls danced faster. The dog started barking. Pista sang louder. The dishes rattled. Teréza's hips shimmied. She tossed István the kerchief she'd pulled from her skirt pocket. It landed on his chest. Pista howled with laughter. István turned paprika-red.

My future wife, István thought, enthralled with his sudden discovery.

András plunked himself down beside István, put his arm around his shoulder. "I'm tired out," he said. Now only one zither maintained the euphoria.

The warmth of András' body next to him filled István with a sense of family.

"Sweaty work," András pulled István close.

"I can't play, I can't sing," István said, crossing his fingers into a clump on the table.

"Just listen and enjoy," András said, keeping the beat.

István spun around, glimpsing Pista up with the girls, dancing like a buffoon, slapping his boots. Arms and legs flailed in every direction. Anna laughed hysterically. And finally, Teréza rolled her hips and let a smile tug at the corner of her lips.

"She's leaving us to go to Budapest," András said, slapping his thighs in time with the beat. "Our tailor uncle and his wife have new twins. They need her help."

István's mind raced. Everything was lost. When was she leaving? How did she dare do what he couldn't? Why had she invited him here tonight if she knew she was going away? Of course, she'd eventually meet someone in Budapest. It was inevitable. His heart hurt. How could life do this to him? All at once the simplest fantasy of companionship seemed unattainable. He had only one solution. Conviction coursed throughout his veins. He was going to Budapest.

A gunshot rang out, crisp and clear. When the music stopped, the dancing stopped, and the laughter petered out leaving a thick eerie silence, like the fog outside the door.

Suddenly István knew.

"Lali!" István cried. He burst out the door and ran between the birch trees in the forest past Teréza's yard. He threw himself on his knees when he saw the wounded body of his little brother in the moonlight. The pistol lay next to him on the ground. Blood pooled in the injured cavity. The bullet had pierced his abdomen.

"Jesus Christ, Lali!" he screamed. "What have you done!?"

The autumn leaves surrounding Lali's body turned from gold to crimson. The sound of the gun still reverberated in István's ears.

"Jesus Christ, Lali! I told you not to play with guns! Fuck!" His flesh prickled with panic. István ran his desperate hands through his brother's hair. He held his brother's bloodied hand.

"There wasn't...there wasn't...supposed to be...any bullets left." Lali could barely speak. His eyes rolled back in his head. "I can't feel...my legs." He groaned.

"Fuck, fuck, fuck!" István got to his feet. "What are you looking at?" he yelled at no one in particular and everyone at once.

"Get someone. Fast!" Teréza yelled. "Someone with a cart! I'll stay with István. Run!" Her three little sisters and their two friends ran off towards the nearest house. András tore off his apron.

On his knees, István searched for the entry wound in the pool of blood. He balled up András' apron and pressed it into Lali's abdomen. "Please don't die. Please don't die."

Pista covered Lali's shaking body with his coat as Teréza promised István that God would watch over Lali.

István shook her off. "Lali, Lali, stay here. Stay with me,"

he repeated. "The doctor will help you. Please stay with me."
He leaned in towards Lali's mouth. The apron had turned
completely red. He stroked Lali's anguished face. His
eyebrows were lowered, no longer curious.

Lali shivered and his body went cold. Only one of Lali's
eyes stayed open, staring skyward. István pressed his mouth
to his brother's ear. "The fox and the wolf are bored. The wolf
said to the fox, 'Let's go beat up the rabbit.'"

"Why should we…" Lali's voice trailed away.

"Yes, Lali! You know what comes next. Say it. Say it, say
it, dear little brother. Why should we beat up the…say it, Lali!
Why should we beat up the…rabbit? Say rabbit, please say
rabbit."

Lali took his last breath and died. István, who didn't
believe in God, felt the instant his brother's soul left the earth.

Teréza stroked István's back, consoling him. Agony and
comfort together.

Teréza watched the coffin descend into its hole beside a
thicket at the edge of the church cemetery thinking that in
Hungarian, the word for *cry* was the same word for grave –
sír.

Teréza felt crushed by the death of this boy. Her first
impulse – to condemn fate – had mellowed. Some things fell
outside of God's jurisdiction. She sought to come to terms
with the notion that not everything fell into the category of
right or wrong, that things sometimes fit into indefinable
areas. Old sorrows could find new meaning in her mind. The
death of a child was harder to grapple with.

Teréza watched István lower his brother's coffin into the

earth. His expression was shattered, his eyes colourless. His full lips had a brushing of blue from the cold. He wore no hat. Together with the women of the village, Teréza sang a ceremonial lament. She sang it to István's heart. She sang it to his pain.

When István lifted his eyes and looked at her, she deliberately closed her own, left them closed for a pause, and then opened them. It was a commiseration of sorrow. He nodded in gentle agreement and looked back towards the coffin, showered with fresh earth and cedar bows.

After the funeral, István sat for a long time in the pale light of his bedroom. The single bulb above his head had fizzled out.

Lali had been the one in the family that showed István love. A brotherly love different from what he had with Pista. Different from the care and concern of Feri. It did not need earning or proving. It was wordless, complete acceptance. István ruined it all by telling Lali the true story of the rabbit. He forgot that Lali, just a child in this oppressive world, still needed lies.

"It should have been me," István said to the bare wall.

István dared to greet his mother as he came into the kitchen to take his seat for dinner. Usually, he averted his eyes.

"Good evening, mother," he said, using the occasion of shared sorrow to offer an olive branch.

Feri was washing his hands in an enamel bowl when Zsuzsa hissed her reply. "What's good about it? Have you no shame?"

Before István could formulate a rebuttal, his mother

pitched the next assault.

"If I had been able to choose, it would have been you who'd have died!"

Zsuzsi's hands had barely reached the soup pot when Feri smacked her face, sending the scalding cabbage soup crashing to the floor.

Her wail was István's sole comfort.

SEPARATION

1963

AT THIS TIME YOUR REQUEST
CANNOT BE GRANTED

1963. Hungary

For two years her documents had been gathering dust at the British Legation, half filled out, when Teréza heard of the general amnesty for the 1956 revolutionaries. The announcement came in March, two days before her twelfth wedding anniversary. She could hardly believe that they'd spent more of their marriage apart than together.

István's letters encouraged Teréza to start her application process anew. She caught his enthusiasm and made her return trip to Budapest in early April, this time taking Zolti along. She would again stay with Klára.

When Teréza arrived, Klára came to the door with an expanded waistline. Her family was well fed. Teréza was pleased to be in Klára's company and Klára in hers, but her husband Elek – a Kádár partisan who excelled in his workplace, making a little over the average salary – could not leave his political aspirations out of the conversation.

Over dinner, Elek made a point of emphasizing to Teréza that since coming to power, Kádár fought an ongoing battle in the government against the hardline Stalinists.

"But only after executing Nagy, his predecessor and former colleague," Teréza protested. "He's still employing the services of his former ÁVO torturers."

Elek spread his arms wide, like a gracious and benevolent priest, ceding the point. "The same men who once tortured him. Maybe that's why he hasn't yet resurrected a force under that name. We've become the only country in the Warsaw Pact without a formal intelligence service."

"How evolved of us," Teréza said, sarcastically. The standard by which her country celebrated was dismally low. She could no longer keep her mouth shut. "What about you, Elek? You hide behind a grand show of acceptance. 'Look at me! I'm so adaptable to the changing times. I even profit from it. I get the best jobs.'"

"Teréza, please." Klára tried to stay calm. "We need not add more paprika to the stew."

"Don't *Teréza please,* me. The stew is hot, and there's no fixing it. I'm sick of passivity masquerading as adaptation. To hell with this nonsense. I'm not going to compromise my integrity for a minute longer to find some redeeming quality in this regime that's been foisted on me since I was a teenager. How can you live with yourselves?"

"Very easily," Klára replied and ripped into a loaf of bread.

It was the first time she felt a rift between herself and her sister. How could Klára fall in love with someone on the other side? How was love even possible on the other side? Surely she knew of his associations when they married.

The next morning, Teréza left Zolti to play with his cousins and returned to the British Legation, which had recently been granted embassy status.

Consoled to see the same receptionist two years after her first visit, Teréza nodded to the woman who directed her to the fourth floor, where the second clerk told her that she'd been saving her file. A miracle, thought Teréza, everything augured well. Eagerly, she handed over the required doctor's note with a six-month expiry date clearing her of tuberculosis. This time departing the embassy, Teréza didn't encounter the greasy-haired undercover detective.

By the middle of the summer, a letter arrived from the Ministry of the Interior, in charge of granting passports. She tore open the envelope and read the words with confused astonishment.

"*Kérelme ez idő szerint nem teljeshitthető.*"– At this time your request cannot be granted. Certain she had misread it, she read aloud again, aghast. She had been denied a Hungarian passport and couldn't leave the country. No reason was given.

Klára suggested they travel to Lake Balaton. Elek's work provided vacation homes for employees to use for weeks at a time. In spite of her malaise and her distaste for Elek's lectures on the virtues of Kádárism, Teréza conceded, and for a week their sons splashed in the warm waters. With camps speckled about the famous lake, Elek made it clear it was the children who had the most to gain from "Kádár Papa's" system.

"All you can do is keep reapplying," Klára consoled Teréza. They lay on a towel on the beach.

A ball rolled up beside Teréza. "For how long? How many

more times? At what point does it become a sign?" Teréza tossed the ball out to her son and nephews who were throwing sand at each other and splashing on the shore.

"A sign for what?"

"That it's not worth it?"

"Worth what?"

"More grief." Teréza squinted against the sun. "Is this when I author fate, or does it author me?"

After seven years, she'd searched her heart wondering if she and István still knew each other, or if love had become an obligatory exercise. Both of them harboured these thoughts, unbeknownst to the other, but neither of them voiced their doubt.

"Let's eat something," suggested Klára.

They ate fried fish with pickles and peppery fish soup, walked along the sand and lapped at melting raspberry ice cream. One night they drank beer. Teréza had never been on holiday anywhere in her life, and she revelled in it. As she watched the ripples on the lake, she took inventory of all she had denied herself waiting to leave. Lunch at the office cafeteria, makeup, jewellery, books and movies; imagining other possible futures and the companionship of another man. She had to feed and dress her son instead.

In late summer the same form letters continued to arrive in Teréza's mailbox from the Interior Ministry. *"Kérelme ez idő szerint nem teljeshitthető."* At this time your request cannot be granted. No passport. The third, fourth, and fifth applications were denied, each with no explanation. She was determined to wear down the powers with her persistence.

She immediately reapplied. Under an amnesty, how many times could they deny her a passport? She would find out they could do it as many times as they wished.

In a fit of anxiety she started cleaning out drawers trying to make order out of chaos. Swinging open the wardrobe doors she hunted for items that held her back – a green cardigan, its elbows darned one too many times. A blue wool dress once tasteful now looked ugly. A burgundy beret formerly all the rage. She'd give it away. From the back of the wardrobe she fished out her brown Oxfords – well worn but beautifully holding up – and a wave of desire came over her.

She slipped them on, took two steps, and at once her face flushed and she felt indecent. The contact between her feet and the arches of her shoes sent heat to her pelvis; it made her want to masturbate. The need was so base, so unlike her, the urge so intense and outside of her that it pushed her down onto her bed and completely took over. She stroked herself fiercely, breaking into a sweat. When the forces were done, they moved her to discharge something demonic, unsaintly and inhuman onto the pillow between her legs. She cleaned herself quickly and got ready for work again.

She placed her Oxfords in the very back of the wardrobe.

What history was it that made it impossible for her to step into the future?

At first, István didn't notice the change in the frequency of Teréza's letters. He'd buried himself in work. By July, he'd saved enough money to open a B/A Service Station of his own on the corner of Kevin and Martin. At thirty-eight he owned his first business. Canada made that possible. Unlike

Ackerman's station, this one was a modern streamlined building, painted bright white with red trim, and had two bays and lots of glass to bring in the sunlight. He hired one employee, a young mechanic he trusted who looked at girly magazines on his lunch-break and greeted customers with, "What can I do for y'all?"

Now that he was an entrepreneur, István worked longer hours and didn't feel like writing letters. He skimmed over those written by his son. What he most loved reading were his customer evaluations written on postcard sized forms.

Service is always excellent, station clean, fully equipped, impressed by the honesty of manager re: repair work.

A remarkable station to do business with.

One of the best washrooms I've seen in Manitoba, and I've lived here all my life.

I have stopped here very frequently, and I find the attendants very polite and considerate.

As fall turned to winter with its frigid temperatures and mountains of snow, he felt heavy and joyless upon waking. He bought a tractor for the station with a front-mounted snowplow and drove around the lot, wind lashing his face, satisfied to clear the fresh fallen snow. Anything that gave him a sense of completion was worth doing. At night, when it was time to lock the station doors, he took in a meal at the local Hungarian restaurant, *The Csárda*. At home, he sat on a chrome diner chair he'd bought second hand, in front of his tiny new black and white TV. Only Wayne and Shuster, the Canadian comedy duo, could pull István out of the doldrums. He idolized the two men as much as he worshipped the automobile. They were willing to be idiots, and they genuinely enjoyed themselves. Hungarian comics, as astute as they were, had always been political; they needed a moral imperative. But these Canadians seemed carefree, like they had nothing to prove. With them, István discovered that he could laugh alone, never before having registered the sound of his own guffaw. The four walls created a container for his release.

He educated himself through the program, *The Sixties*, which presented newsworthy topics and subjects with an international scope, such as foreign assistance and the situation within the East Bloc. The segments on life in East and West Berlin riveted him. The Berlin Wall intrigued him. He didn't know why he found it so shocking that a wall could be built only five years after the Hungarians had so loudly protested the Soviet occupation.

He watched war documentaries every night to ease his homesickness. Peace unsettled him. The need to dissect and understand that which had shaped him became an obsession. It was only after he turned off the television that he felt his insignificance and a deep ache spread through his muscles like the stomach flu. He was an exile waiting for a reunion that might never occur.

WAR

1944-1945

THE LIE WAS TOO THICK ALREADY

1944, March – July. Ják & Szombathely, Hungary

"István! Come! Help me!" His stepfather yelled from the kitchen.

In the kitchen István's middle brother Tamás sat next to their mother by the radio. István's youngest brother Lali sat at the table too, drawing a gun in his notebook instead of his original school assignment: a tree with leaves. The radio was loud. István caught the announcer's last strained and urgent words before he signed off, "German forces are now reported to be at the Austrian border. At last count, eleven divisions."

István looked at Feri from the doorway. How big was a division? What was the horsepower of a Tiger tank? Their village lay five kilometres from the Austrian border. How long would it take for the tanks to get to their door?

"Here," Feri said, handing him large sheets of black paper, "*you* have to cover all the windows. Take these from me."

"What for?" István asked, noting the apprehension on Feri's face.

"In case they bomb the village at night." Feri answered. "You know I can't help you with this. Good luck." Feri left the house.

István had never understood his stepfather's papyrophobia, his aversion to the sound of paper: rustling, crumpling, dropping. Not even the texture was tolerable to Feri.

Once István affixed the paper onto the windows in the kitchen, two bedrooms and a day room, the adobe house felt stifling.

"You're lucky you're not yet of conscription age," Feri said to István, returning to the house.

István didn't feel particularly lucky.

"It would do István some good to join the army," his mother countered. "He's got broken promises in his bones."

"That's enough, Zsuzsa," Feri muttered.

István had stopped speaking with his mother some time ago, a necessary choice arrived at through accumulative cause. The silent treatment wasn't remedying his pain. István retreated to his bedroom.

The following day, István sat at Feri's crowded worktable at the shoe shop. By late afternoon the grey sky was overcast. The light in the shop turned murky with the influx of thicker clouds from the east.

His stepfather sat on a stool, staring at the floorboards, listening to the latest reports out of Budapest. His solid, dexterous hands rested on his work apron. "The Germans have wasted no time setting up a collaborationist government," he announced.

István felt oddly detached, even numb, as news floated in and out of his ears. His eyes strained under the dim light. He switched on a lamp. He was mending a woman's shoe – the eyelet had grown too large from overuse and threatened to tear the delicate strap in two.

"Szálasi is our new prime minister installed to head the government," Feri said. "His first act is to legalize the Arrow Cross Party. Unbelievable." He turned off the radio. "Horthy, our moth-eaten Regent will soon be ousted. Because he's not hard enough on the Jews." He shook his head.

István glanced at Feri. Though the head of state had been critical of the Jews, Horthy had banned the rightist Arrow Cross Party with the outbreak of the war.

"István, in times like these, when regimes change so quickly, it is best to keep your counsel. Don't get involved." Feri spoke as though he'd read every thought in István's head.

They locked eyes in agreement, but István remained silent. He pressed the leather between his fingers until he felt the glue hold.

István was on edge. A week before, as he and Pista were walking across Fő Square the early buds had troubled István. "It's as if the trees are rushing to bloom. What if we get a heavy frost? They'll die." István stopped to catch his breath and stared up at the clear sky. "It's not normal. Nothing's normal."

"You're too goddamn sensitive," Pista said. "Only you would take the weather personally."

A hulking man emerged from a dark street into the square catching István's eye. He walked towards them. Right away István saw the armband on the man's left sleeve. White with a black cross with ends like arrows, like fishhooks. The man brushed by István roughly. "Jew nose." He kept walking.

"Don't let it bother you." Pista had said, flinging his cigarette butt on the road and punching István's shoulder playfully before turning down his street. "I'll see you tomorrow," he called over his shoulder.

The jibe still shook István to the core, filling him with shame and bowel-clenching panic. It had to have been Varga, spreading rumours about István's birth father again. As long as István could remember Varga had been hurling the insult "Jew nose" at him, at school, in the playground and even during soccer games. Theirs had been a lifelong animosity; since kindergarten, Varga had been a bully sniffing out weakness and fear like a dog, tracking István in his weakest moments.

And now it was March and the Germans had invaded Budapest.

István's legs couldn't peddle fast enough. He crashed his bike into Pista's front gate.

Pista watched from a rickety bench outside his parents' adobe house, smoking. He'd been heckling the chickens when he first caught site of István hurtling down the path. "You need brakes on that thing. What's up, brother?"

"Your parents home?" István asked, dismounting.

"My father's in the field, and my mother's at the market." Pista flicked his cigarette at a chicken. It squawked and fled. "Come in." Pista sauntered casually towards his house and shot another barb at the chickens.

István gave him a good shove from behind.

The kitchen was snug. Old hand-embroidered pillow-cases with a tulip design decorated the walls, sagging from their nails. On the stove, chicken feet simmered in a pot. István and Pista sat on two sturdy stools, face-to-face.

"What does your birth certificate say?" Pista asked, once István had finally come out with it.

"Father unknown. Born out of wedlock."

"Then why is it a problem?" Pista picked dirt from under his fingernails.

"Because I was born in Vasvár."

"That doesn't mean anything. Lots of Christians worked on Jewish estates."

"But not all of the servants fucked their masters. For Christ's sake, Pista. Varga's been spreading rumours about me for years. I need your help."

"You don't take that animal seriously, do you?"

Pista routinely dismissed István's concerns, so István reciprocated. He filled his head with useless trivia just for these occasions. "Did you know there were only one hundred and thirty-nine vehicles built in Hungary this year due to the production freeze?"

Pista grabbed his balls in an obscene gesture.

Sweat trickled down István's neck. He undid the top button of his shirt.

Pista got up and lifted the lid of the pot. Chicken feet poked out like bayonets. The soup had stopped simmering. He threw more coal in the stove. "I can break your nose and make it look less Jewish."

"You're so useless sometimes. For fuck's sake, listen to me. I have an idea." István rolled up his shirtsleeves. "I want to join the Arrow Cross."

"You're that scared?"

"Only the *suspicion* of being Jewish can get you hauled off right now. I need you to join with me."

Pista rocked back on his stool. "Why the hell would I do that? We're safe. Everyone's knows we're Catholics."

István shook his head. "*Compliant* Catholics. We stick out enough already."

"This is a bad idea. I don't want to be anywhere near Varga. Or the rest of those bullies."

"I *need* to be near Varga if he's spreading rumours." István wiped his face with a hanky. "All we have to do is show up for a couple of meetings, nod our heads, look interested."

"I don't want to be affiliated with these crusading Christians." Pista got up and started to pace.

"If I join and you don't, it will look suspect. We've been joined at the hip since the first day of school."

Water from the simmering chicken feet spewed out from under the lid and made a hissing sound on the cast iron stove.

Two weeks later an unexpected cold front moved in with the equinox and István caught the flu, but he knew he couldn't miss the meeting. Not at this stage.

The Arrow Cross assembled in a barn adjacent to the cemetery. Since they had joined, István and Pista had attended the clandestine gatherings consisting mainly of long fulminations targeted at Jews, while eulogizing Hungarism and agriculture. István's bowels kinked and moaned throughout the meeting. His head throbbed. The Arrow Cross thug who'd commented on his "Jew nose" eyed István with suspicion. István did his best to ignore him. Considered young recruits, neither he nor Pista had yet been conscripted for any of the dirty work. "Soon," Commander Németh assured them. He moved his substantial limbs gracelessly, like a lumbering bear.

After the meeting was adjourned, István ran to the

outhouse. Upon exiting, he noticed Commander Németh in discussion with two gendarmes. Their faces looked minatory under the glow of a torch. The two gendarmes twirled their moustaches between their fingers. The long, black, feathers pinned to the side of their hats reminded István of a rooster's comb. On the opposite side they sported the Hungarian coat of arms, as big as a bar of soap. István had always wanted a hat like that. He saw the gendarmes nod several times, collectively inspecting a document handed to them by Németh.

In the dark, the woman's name caught István's ear, the headmaster's wife. István knew her. He had helped Feri repair the couple's shoes since he was a child. At first, he only polished and buffed the footwear; as he grew older he resoled them. The woman had small feet with high arches. She collected classy t-strap shoes and wore nude stockings made of silk, with a line up the back. She brought István desserts from patisseries in Szombathely. When he got old enough to get erections, he found her magnetically attractive. He'd fantasized about touching her in a satin slip.

István squelched a sneeze.

Németh turned, smiled benignly and wished him good health.

On their long walk home, István couldn't tell Pista what he'd heard. Already he felt damned for dragging his friend into this collection of thugs. By the time he got home, he was dry heaving.

István and Pista wrote nonstop with cramped and aching hands. They wrote April 15th, 1944, over and over again.

Németh had set them up with a desk and chair each, side by side in front of the doors of the grandiose Moorish-style Synagogue in Szombathely fourteen kilometres from Ják. The clouds were heavy overhead, but a break at the horizon showed the setting sun sinking into twilight hues of violet and orange. Soon it would be dark. István could scarcely read his own handwriting but didn't dare suggest they stop. Németh held a flashlight over István's page. Arrow Cross men handled the Jews and intimidated those who complained of fatigue by sending them to the back of the line.

Throughout the protracted days, István and Pista caught each other's eyes from time to time. István didn't like what Pista reflected back at him, but it was better than looking into the faces of the fearful fathers who obediently relinquished their details. Today's date. First and last names, address, place and date of birth, name of mother, name of spouse, names of children, occupation, and subscription number of radio and telephone. The Jews of Szombathely underwent obligatory registration.

For István the days were painfully long. The guards grew ornery and volatile, and the lineups seemed to get longer rather than shorter. It would take a few more days to account for the entire three thousand one hundred and sixteen Jews who were being rounded up from this city, the oldest in Hungary. The men recited their particulars, with their wives by their sides, silently clutching their children, pressing their bodies close. Two days now and István had barely lifted his head, his heart alternating between dread and dead as he heard the shakiness in their voices. He kept his hand firmly pressed to the pages when the spring winds blew violently, heralding an April rainstorm. Thunder rumbled nearby.

What would Feri think if he knew István was here in this

horror?

A drop of rain fell on his ledger. There was no way to finish before the light disappeared. He knew the families would be sent away only to be corralled again tomorrow, though the ones nearing the front of the line had been standing for close to six hours.

István calculated that with forty rows and nine columns per page, he and Pista had already recorded roughly one thousand and forty-four names. At least two thousand or more to go.

"You have impeccable handwriting, István," Németh had remarked the day before yesterday. "But this doesn't have to be a commemorative work of art. You on the other hand," he'd said, inspecting Pista's handiwork, "could try harder to make it legible. Looks like we stuck a pen in a dog's paw."

István glanced briefly at the sliver of sunset on the horizon, underneath purple storm clouds. Day three and his hand was almost useless as another drop of rain landed on his forefinger. Németh stepped away for a moment, sticking the flashlight in István's left hand.

"I'll be right back," he said as he went to investigate a kerfuffle between a guard and a young Jewish man.

"István."

A familiar voice lured his head from his work. The headmaster's wife. She had vanished from Ják a month ago. Her face still glowed but had grown thinner. Her nose and cheeks looked more pronounced. The sight of her brought him back to his humanity. Her chestnut hair was handsomely styled with a side roll. Robust waves cascaded down the back of her camel hair coat. Her gloved hand held a leather clutch and a single suitcase in the other. But now sewn on her soiled coat, was a yellow Star of David.

"Please tell my husband I'm still alive," the headmaster's wife whispered. She smiled at István through weary eyes and clasped her gloved hands tightly to her belly as though it hurt. "They've moved me to the Szombathely ghetto."

István nodded. "Maybe I could –"

"There is nothing you can do single-handedly. Just please, tell him I'll always love him."

"Name?" István asked, his throat choked with sorrow and entered everything he already knew about her. As the Arrow Cross guard led her away István's eyes followed the path of her feet in filthy t-strap shoes.

It wasn't too late to volunteer to take her place. István was about to rise from his chair when Németh lay a hand on his shoulder, "Good work for today," while Arrow Cross men barked instructions for the families to leave and come back again by eight tomorrow morning.

After István and Pista rode their bikes home to Ják in the pouring rain, Pista brought out a bottle of brandy. They threw it back on Pista's front porch in the dark. Rain trammelled the earth.

"You can thank your lucky fucking stars that the murderers are too busy to train us," Pista muttered. The end of Pista's cigarette glowed red in the dark like a one-eyed creature.

István didn't answer. The booze was only beginning to thaw his frozen heart. The Jews were being rounded up and taken to a ghetto, and he and Pista were helping. That much he knew. The guilt was exhausting his conscience and the self-loathing was knotting up his gut. He was beginning to see that life was one impossible predicament after another. "Let's revoke our memberships," he blurted out.

The rain fell hard. Pista laughed in his face, spraying brandy across István's cheeks. "Do you think they'll let us off that easily? Are you so naive?"

István felt embarrassed and morose. The alcohol soured his belly. "I don't know which is worse. You and me, moving up in the ranks, or what happens next to –"

"The Jews?"

In his quiet panic, István began to make excuses. "We're junior members. We're doing grunt work. All we have is membership cards. We haven't even earned uniforms. We've killed no one."

"Grunt work? Do you call recording thousands of names grunt work? Are you out of your fucking mind?!" Pista dropped his cigarette.

István calmed himself with the justifications he fell back on in times like these. He knew very few people in Ják who disagreed with the Hungarian cause; everyone in the village wanted the Germans to win if only so Hungary could claim back her lost territories. He took another sip of brandy. And while some people stood by merely watching the village Jews flee, others tipped off the Arrow Cross and the gendarmes. The shame was a cold hand wrapped around his heart, and the brandy was the only thing that warmed it. How despicable he felt saving his own hide. His fear of death trumped what could have been the honorable thing to do: turn himself in for the father who seeded him.

★

By late spring, the village was in full bloom with bursting Hungarian oaks and fields of red poppies. White storks nested in the marshes, alongside hovering dragonflies. Butterflies chased each other in the rye fields and along the rutted rural roads.

After months spent cycling to Arrow Cross meetings, István and Pista bickered constantly. Their lies to their families had isolated them. The stress of István's secret left the pair enmeshed and István at the mercy of Pista's increasing pressure to revolt against political, societal and religious constructs.

By mid-July, all of Ják's Jews had vanished. As the peaches ripened, Németh grew cheerful and was often away "on business" in Szombathely. István wondered if Németh was on the brink of a promotion. He was of two minds when it came to Németh. The leader seemed not to presume anything regarding István's parentage and Varga stopped spreading rumours, but why? And Németh had apologized more than once for being too preoccupied to adequately train István and Pista. At the same time, the Arrow Cross meetings grew increasingly chilling, not because of what was discussed but because of what was purposefully omitted. Had it not been for Feri running out of black leather, István would not have seen the loading of the cars.

He'd been heading out of Szombathely's town centre, the back of his bike piled with wrapped leather, when he decided to take a different route home. He thought he caught a glimpse of the headmaster's wife in her filthy t-strap shoes in a column shuffling towards the train station. Instinctively he knew not to show his face. He found the end of an alley partitioned from the scene by a fence where he parked himself. The tableau was awe inspiring and confusing all at once. All those people wearing coats in the sweltering heat, yellow stars on their chests. Why did that upset him so much? That they wore coats? He recognized many of those whose names he'd recorded climbing into cattle cars. Thousands piling in, squeezing in, some crying out, others silent. German soldiers wore wide, red armbands bearing a black, hooked cross in the centre of a white circle. They worked in tandem with Arrow Cross men, their demeanours stoney and detached.

Back in March, when he'd heard that the Germans invaded Hungary, István had been both expectant and fearful. The soldiers had barrelled through Szombathely bypassing Ják, enroute to Budapest, but now here they were in Szombathely shouting orders. Tall and unfazed by the heat, they commanded the events while the Arrow Cross men skirted about like border collies herding sheep.

Németh, bayonet in hand, shoved, pushed, and shouted orders at the men, women and children. Even the babies. The elderly were close to collapse and crying, but still he berated them. They had nothing but the coats on their backs and the shoes on their feet.

Jews stood in windowless cattle cars at full capacity while the Nazis and the Arrow Cross forced more inside. István felt his breath stuck in his chest. Sweat sucked his shirt to his back. If Varga had his way, István would be one of these unfortunate souls. Where on earth were they taking them? He had lost sight of the headmaster's wife. He hadn't gotten up the nerve to visit the headmaster to tell him he'd seen his wife. The lie was too thick already. How could he explain how he had seen her? István felt even more loathsome knowing he had helped put her there. It was better that the headmaster didn't know.

István felt the limp-limbed weakness of his cowardice. He'd done nothing to rescue this woman and wondered if now his own life was worth living.

THEY COLLAPSED LIKE NOODLES

1944, October. Ják, Hungary

Teréza skipped home in the moist autumn air and breathed in the sweet smell of turning leaves. Smoke rose from neighbours' chimneys like in the fairy tales she'd read in school, but their doors stayed shut against the late afternoon drafts. Leaf-green doors, pepper-red doors, dark-wood doors. She was a week shy of her fourteenth birthday, and her romantic hormones were stirring. Precisely in the moment she thought about the cute boy István from school, a shot rang out so close she wondered if it had been intended for her. She ducked behind a bush. The sound had come from the cemetery. With the next two shots, she watched a small family fall to the ground like paper dolls. Only the trees remained standing. Overcome with fright, Teréza tasted bile.

While the two Arrow Cross men laughed and slapped each other on the back, Teréza's callow mind processed what she had seen. Swigging brandy, they admired the bodies. A mother, her teenage daughter and her young son were now but a pile of death and yellow stars. Teréza began to shake.

Should she run or stay still? The men turned and noticed her behind the bush. One pointed his gun at her in jest. The other placed his hand on his crotch and sniggered.

She couldn't think. She couldn't move.

To her astonishment, they didn't shoot at her or try to prevent her from running. It seemed no one really cared she was a witness, so certain were they of their orders. Trembling behind the bush, Teréza watched the two Arrow Cross men greet two younger men in plainclothes, so close she could see their breath. They had the build of teenagers. As they stood by the bodies and leaned on their shovels, the Arrow Cross men offered them a bottle of booze. She strained to capture an identifying profile, but her eyes became lakes and the light was quickly changing. The figures took on a blurry outline, suspended on a two-dimensional horizon, with the world behind them turning charcoal grey. One of the teenagers noticed her. She felt sick. Was she was seeing things? She turned and ran on legs that felt like aspic. She could smell farm animals and hay on the wind.

To István's relief it didn't take long to dig the deep grave in the soft earth. He wanted this horrible assignment to be over. The three bodies would fit into the space of one trench quite easily. The teenage girl and the little boy had grown painfully thin, as had the mother. Their skin was a translucent white-blue.

"Just pile them on top of each other." Németh's breath smelled rancid, and it lingered like a cloud over István's shoulder. "They can kiss each other good night. I'm off. I still have a long night ahead of me."

In the village, Arrow Cross men were on the hunt for hidden Jews.

In the pitch-black, under the gentle glow of the young moon, István helped Pista. He positioned his feet wide, laced his fingers and offered his palms to his friend. "Put your hand on my shoulder. Use me as a step."

Pista grabbed the edges of the trench and hoisted himself up and out.

István reached his arms upward, clasped them around Pista's forearms and let himself be lifted. Scraping his body against the inner wall, moist soil dirtied István's clothing. He brushed at it vigorously when he got to the top.

"You didn't expect to stay clean, did you?" said Pista. His sarcasm had a punishing tone. "Let's get the bodies."

István nodded and followed.

"I wouldn't be able to do this in daylight," said István. He accidentally stepped on the girl's hand. He jumped back, horrified at the cushion of her fingers.

"She's dead," Pista said.

István's heart thumped in his chest. "Which one do we bury first?"

"Don't you fucking cry now." Pista pulled a smoke from his pack. "I can't do this if you're going to cry." The flame of his match illuminated the woman's face; her eyes stared up at them in stunned anguish.

István knelt down by the woman, took her hand. It was cold. "I didn't know that death had an expression."

"For Christ's sake, grab the boy's legs. He's the easiest to get to. I don't know how they got twisted up like pretzels." Pista puffed furiously on the cigarette clenched between his teeth and grabbed hold of two small arms. "I'm not here to manage your sympathies. You fucking dragged me into this.

Hurry up so we can go get drunk."

After they piled the three bodies into the narrow grave, István suggested they cover up their faces first. They had debated whether or not the bodies should be put face down or face up. Face up afforded them a little more dignity, Pista had suggested. The teenage girl's expression was the hardest for István to take. Her cheekbones shone with each match that Pista lit. Was it forgiveness István saw on her adolescent face? Or relief? He despised himself the more he looked at her.

"You do the honours." Pista handed István a shovel full of dirt. "You're not making me throw the first heap."

István tossed dirt over the girl's face hitting her eyeballs, nostrils, cheeks and teeth. Her hair curled towards life above ground, so he targeted that next. Still, tendrils pushed and sprang against the dark earth, as if it continued to grow. He shovelled until his arms ached and his hands cramped but still her hair refused to be covered. He swore. Shovelled faster until his back seized and all that hair disappeared from sight. István grunted with the last toss. The animal in his chest yammered a justification for an act that would spare its own life.

By the time he had filled the grave, István felt the claws of madness and the black dog of depression stealing in. When he finally broke down and wept by the side of it, his tears returned his sanity.

"I would have helped you," Pista said, kneeling down to examine the bloody blisters on István's hands.

István couldn't look at him. "We can't ever talk about this."

When he crawled into his bed that night István prayed – for the third time in his life – that no Jew would ever come through the village again. And he reminded himself why he had joined the Arrow Cross party: because something inside him still wanted to live.

★

When Teréza arrived home shortly after dusk her mother Anna was pacing the kitchen. She was late. She had taken the long way home, stopping to vomit.

"Where were you?" Anna asked with equal parts concern and blame.

Teréza tried to tell her mother what she had seen, but Anna was busy giving her an earful, not even waiting for an answer to her questions. Teréza reached for the potatoes with shaky hands and began peeling.

"We're having noodles for dinner," said Anna curtly. "Why on earth are you peeling potatoes?"

Teréza closed her eyes and took a deep breath before setting the table.

The noodles went down her throat in clumps. Her brother András observed her curiously. He could read her every mood. He didn't inquire, sensing perhaps that whatever had happened had left Teréza rattled. Her family ate quietly without much discussion. Like vapours, the events of the external world seeped through the cracks of their walls and poisoned everyone's frame of mind. Even her littlest sister Kati, who routinely milked András for stories and jokes, preferred instead to kick the leg of the table, causing their father Gyuri to snap at her.

Like noodles. They collapsed like noodles. Teréza pushed the noodles around on her plate, unable to swallow the lump rising in her throat. When everyone but her mother left the kitchen, Teréza worked up the courage to speak while she helped Anna wash dishes. Teréza closed her eyes, shook her head, felt her throat close. "…A little boy, Juli's age. And a teenaged girl…my age…" A tear spilled down her cheek, and she smeared it away. "And a mother. They were shot – at the cemetery."

Anna hung her large pot on a hook high above the stove. "They'd been here in the village for a few days – hiding. Someone must have turned them in," Anna said matter-of-factly. "I saw them at the market, then later, walking the streets."

"You knew about them?"

Her mother didn't answer.

"Why were they turned in?"

"They were Jews," said Anna, wiping a large pot dry.

"Why didn't you warn them?"

Her mother's silence confused Teréza. Did her mother think they deserved to die? Was Teréza supposed to agree with her?

Anna looked at her closely. "The Jews were behind the Red Terror. Your grandfather died at their hands. We lived through hell."

The colour drained from Teréza's face. Contempt for Jews permeated village life; there were good ones she was told, but they were few and far between. Still, she'd never before seen the lethal consequences of this hatred. All she could turn over in her head was the family's fatal mistake: why had they so freely wandered the streets? What were they thinking? How could they have been so careless?

When she tired of trying to reimagine their circumstances, another niggling fear intruded: in the echo of the fields she recognized the voices of the gravediggers.

The next assignment was worse than István had imagined. The wind was whipping up along the Danube's bank between the Chain and Árpád Bridges. The lights of the two bridges were off, and eight o'clock felt more like midnight. The air hung dense and black. István felt tired and tense. His malaise squashed any anticipation he had of visiting Budapest for the first time.

The prisoners, close to forty of them, shivered, lined up along the embankment wall. The youngest looked about four, the eldest, a man over eighty. Patrol dogs growled at the ends of their leashes, baring their teeth as their Nazi masters grew impatient. The Germans shone spotlights on the detained at random, blinding their eyes. Arrow Cross men escorted families down the ramp in a show of pompous cordiality as István and Pista moved along the line, holding open their sacks for the wallets, watches, broaches, earrings, and gold necklaces hung with the Star of David. István's sack grew heavy.

István and Pista had seen none of the capital since arriving at the Nyugati train station. They'd been whisked away in the back of an army truck, fed in a "headquarters room" István knew not where, and then briefed on their assignment. He was becoming skilled at subterfuge; he had explained his absence to "confidential activity in support of Hungarian soldiers that would take them away overnight." Even so, Feri had been hesitant to agree, and István sensed Feri knew more than he was willing to admit.

The only two without uniforms, István and Pista kept their heads down as they went from person to person.

When István stopped and bent down in front of a small

boy, the boy shook his head, meaning he had nothing to drop in the sack. István saw the child's shoelace was undone. He set down the sack and began to tie it up for him. The boy gently grabbed István's collar with his hands. "All those mans in the river, why aren't they wearing bathing suits?"

He pointed to five naked bodies floating face down in the river, their fingertips reaching for each other.

"If my fingers get cold," the boy insisted, "I can't practice my piano."

"Ádám!" scolded his mother.

Before István could answer, Németh shouted, "No talking to the prisoners!"

István stiffened. Dogs barked and strained forward on their leashes. The Nazis yanked them back. An officer trained a light on István.

Németh marched up to István and Pista. "Look, we haven't got all night. We're not polishing jewellery or tying goddamn shoelaces. Get to the end of this line. Fast. You'll collect their shoes and clothing afterwards."

István had hoped that the grave-digging incident was the worst of it, and that he had convinced Németh and Varga that he was one of them. He was wrong. Varga had resumed taunting him with whispers, "J-eeeee-wish."

Only yesterday, Németh had summoned István and Pista to his new office on the *Fő* Square, though the windowless room had nothing more than a wooden table, two chairs, a bare bulb and a bench along one wall. And now here they were on the edge of the Danube of Death.

"You've both been occupying my mind," Németh had

begun rather solemnly, adjusting his tie and cap.

The encumbered pair had sat side-by-side, convinced that their covers had been blown.

"I asked you both to keep a watch for fleeing Jews," Németh said, his expression devoid of its usual warmth.

Neither István nor Pista answered.

"They're very slippery those Jews. They hide under floorboards and in cellars. Under straw."

Pista cut in. "Commander, Sir, I'm sure you can appreciate how many jobs we fulfill as junior members of the Arrow Cross. We're active church goers which keeps us in good standing with the Catholics and the peasants. And István here works full time for his father –"

Németh cut him off. "Have you been drinking again, Pista?" He looked perturbed. He continued when Pista didn't answer.

"But now we've got good news. Things are getting hairy up in Budapest, and the Germans need our help. The Russians are closing in, and there really isn't any money left in the capital to get you up there, but I've pulled some strings. So you can feel like you're contributing to the greater cause. You did admirable work in Szombathely."

It was the worst compliment István had ever received. He adjusted himself in the chair. His insides were cramping.

"Be at the Szombathely train station by noon tomorrow."

That evening, they sat on Pista's porch watching the lightly falling rain. István prohibited Pista from drinking. "You can't show up useless," he said, knowing it could trigger an explosion.

Catching raindrops on his tongue, Pista had asked, "Why, what do you think they'll make us do?"

"How the hell would I know?" István snapped.

"Guess." Pista tapped out a smoke from his cigarette pack.

"Remind me again why we're in this fucking position?" István asked rhetorically.

"Because you're fucking Jewish."

"Keep your voice down," István whispered. "I'm not fucking Jewish!"

"You *might* be fucking Jewish," Pista said in a stage whisper.

"But there's absolutely no proof of that."

Pista sighed. "Why don't you tell Németh and Varga that?"

If Pista had been belligerent, István would have felt better, but his passivity terrified him. It was never good news when Pista quit fighting.

The women and girls stripped naked, shaking and shamed, crumpling inwardly to cover themselves before their families. Children were left shivering in their underwear. The naked men looked away from their wives' shrunken breasts, preferring to look down the barrels of rifles pointing at them. In the dark, the prisoners looked blue and white, already taking on the hue of carcasses. István couldn't fathom what he was witnessing.

Pista picked up bras and underwear, slacks, skirts and shirts, leggings, socks, dresses and blouses and coats with yellow stars. Delegated to the shoes, István collected them in a heap off to the side, a mountain a metre and a half high. He slipped behind the pile, shielding himself from view. He stared at a pair of women's Oxford leather shoes. With a wooden heel. He had them in his hand. Size five. He could tell just by holding them. They belonged to the mother of the boy who played piano. Good quality. They would eventually fit Teréza, but not yet. He'd have to wait a while. Pista arrived beside him, depositing a busting sack of clothing beside the shoe pile. He saw the shoes in István's hands and gave him a don't-you-dare shake of his head.

István shoved the shoes into his deep pockets, hiding them under his overcoat.

"That's a new low," Pista said, motioning for István to follow him to their designated posts.

The dogs barked as a Nazi soldier instructed the group of Arrow Cross men to "finish off the Jews." Ten Germans marched up the ramp, leaving their Hungarian counterparts to complete the killings.

An Arrow Cross man hollered at the naked and trembling Jews: "Face the river!"

"Point blank range!" Németh shouted at the firing squad.

They lifted their rifles and moved in closer, towards the prisoners. Catching István's eye, Németh smiled and called out to Varga. They conferred for a few moments, and then Németh waved István over.

"My nephew here is willing to let you have the honours." Németh placed his hand on István's shoulder. "Do me proud."

"But sir," István said, "I don't know how to fire a gun."

"Varga, will you give István a quick lesson?" Németh smiled wide. Turning to István he said, "The boy. He's all yours."

István couldn't see anything but the small naked backside of the boy in front of him. He was holding his mother's hand and crying. István could hear the whimpers. Németh and Varga stood on either side of István, waiting for him to take the rifle Varga offered. István's palms were slick with sweat, and his hands went cold as they touched the metal. Then István saw Pista, looking at him with an inscrutable expression.

His body burned from his penis to his throat as he lifted the gun and looked down its barrel, his vision blurry from wind and fear. He was about to murder a child.

"Not the boy! Or his mother." An authoritative voice rang out in the blackness.

István thanked God. One of the few times in his life.

An Arrow Cross Commander István didn't recognize motioned for the firing squad to lower their rifles.

"This boy's a prodigy. He'll grow up to be a famous pianist," the Commander yelled. He pulled the boy and the mother from the line-up and instructed Pista to dig through the pile to find their clothing.

I have her shoes, István realized. His hands shook so violently he dropped the rifle. Varga sneered, rescued his discarded weapon and shoved István gruffly out of the way. Németh shook his head in disgust and hollered, "Fire!"

Within seconds, the firing squad executed the fifty or so human beings standing at the edge. They dropped effortlessly into the black water of the Danube. Then up they bobbed.

István fell to his knees.

A week later, István faced Németh's empty desk as he had several times in past months, in the same windowless room. On all previous occasions, Pista had occupied the adjacent chair. Why hadn't Pista been called in with him this time? If only he'd been able to confer with Pista before coming here.

But Pista wasn't home when István went looking for him. While he waited and worried in Németh's office, he turned his attention to his recurring daydream: caressing Teréza's instep, then slipping the sturdy Oxfords onto her feet. He slides the other Oxford onto Teréza's foot and then touches her knees. She smiles.

István was startled from his reverie by a vile smell. One so subtle he had to sniff a few times to see if he was imagining it. The more he tried to block it, the more it irritated his nose. A barely audible thud came from somewhere beneath him. Had he imagined it? He couldn't always trust his senses these days; a few times his fear had got the better of him, and his bowels. He looked around but couldn't see a trap door or hidden exit. It had never before occurred to him to look.

Németh shoved open the door, bringing with him a refreshing gust of wind. He slammed it shut, and with a snap pulled off his leather gloves. He tossed them on his desk. "There is nothing more glorious and life-affirming than a day like this. The wind whips the leaves as if the giant, invisible hand of God carries them along. My goodness I love it. And it's brilliantly sunny!"

István stood. "Yes, sir."

"Please sit."

István obeyed.

Németh seated himself on the corner of his desk. "I've always believed in rewarding great work. In fact, great work is the way to my heart. For some men, it is their wives' cooking, but I am of a different ilk. For me, hard work is a virtue, something so deeply felt. I develop a fondness, beyond reason, for anyone with the same trait."

"Yes, sir."

"You can't possibly understand how crestfallen I was in

Budapest when you were so inept with the rifle. The thought won't leave me."

István's face stung as though he'd been slapped. "Yes, sir."

"I can only imagine it was due to my lack of instruction." István swallowed. "Yes, sir." The jig was up. He would be put on a train and sent away, of that he was certain.

"You would never take me for a sensitive man," Németh said. He began to sing a German lullaby, looking heavenward. Abruptly he stopped. "There is one more thing that I have always admired more than hard work. Loyalty. Loyalty between friends." He sang again. "*Morgen früh, wenn Gott will, Wirst du wieder geweckt.*"

"Tomorrow, if it is God's will, will you wake again," István translated.

"You know it?" Németh looked genuinely pleased.

"German comes easily to me," István said, his voice cracking.

"Spoken like a good Hungarian. You know, István, I'm not only embarrassed by how you and Pista behaved in Budapest, but my superiors at headquarters are breathing down my neck. They want to make sure we clean up any dirty corners in this country. You must know how hard I've worked these past months?"

István was running out of replies. Németh wasn't waiting for one.

"I am not an evil man, István." Németh sounded almost as if he was confessing to a priest. "But I pride myself in completing tasks."

István heard ringing in his ears, and another ominous thud somewhere below him.

Németh removed a document from inside his coat pocket. He unfolded it before István's eyes. "You know what rigamarole I went through trying to obtain this birth certificate from the public records office? The peasants in Vasvár region are incredibly lethargic. Read."

"Kiss István. Father unknown," István sputtered.

"I can see that," Németh said, impatiently, "but it's the estate that troubles me. Vasvár. A *Jewish* estate."

István could barely control the shaking in his legs. It was a good thing he was sitting.

"When we run the risk of Jews infiltrating the ranks, this kind of document makes me very unhappy." Németh's tone changed like the weather. "Things are getting a little tense for them as you can imagine. You've seen it for yourself. And amongst every group there are the mutinous few who don't understand compliance."

"What do you want from me?"

"Who's your father?"

"Kiss Feri." István's voice was level and even. "My parents were working together on the estate in Vasvár when Feri got my mother pregnant. When the Jew landowner found out, he kicked him off the estate. Feri married my mother years later in Ják."

"So, you were raised by this Jew landowner?"

"No. By my maternal grandmother, in Pothe, until I was five," István corrected.

Németh stared at István. "My little girl has been painting watercolours of our countryside in fall. She is an excellent artist, gifted with a steady hand and observant eye. Two talents my young friends István and Pista are not endowed with. Who's your real father?" Németh demanded.

"Kiss Feri."

Németh stood and crossed to the door. He opened it ceremoniously and waited, unnerving István. After a moment István stood uncertainly and began to exit.

"There's only one goddamn reason I have no more time for your lies. If it wasn't for the goddamn Russians advancing on Budapest, I'd put you on a train heading west myself."

István felt the jarring thud of the door behind his back. That smell again.

The next day, Pista barged into Feri's shop looking haggard. Feri was out. István didn't look up until Pista said, "Get me a drink of brandy, I have a bad taste in my mouth."

"It's too early to drink."

"Not today," Pista said.

"I hope you have a good excuse," István said, frowning and pulling a bottle from Feri's drawer.

"You'll never know the cost of loyalty."

"What's that supposed to mean?" István poured a glass and handed it to Pista. There was that word again. Loyalty. Németh used it yesterday. Twice.

Pista threw back the shot and breathed deep. "It means I've given myself permission to feed my demons. This way I can live life fully before the war takes me."

THE WEIGHT OF HISTORY
ON HER FEET

1945, January 3 – February 13. Ják, Hungary

The Siege of Budapest saved István and Pista from participating in any more Arrow Cross activities. The Russians were
clobbering the Germans in Budapest, and after nursing a New
Year's Eve hangover for over a day – István had tied one on
with Pista – he was back at the workbench in Feri's shop
repairing the battle-worn boots of Hungarian soldiers who
were backing the Germans.

Varga entered the shop, late afternoon, dressed in a well-
worn soldier's uniform. István had been relived to learn that
Varga, a few years his senior, had been conscripted, so he was
surprised to see him home. At first glance he appeared to be
genial, which in itself was troublesome, but still István kept
his back turned.

"Good afternoon," Varga boomed, in a tone that
suggested he had some sort of a pronouncement to make but

wanted to draw it out as long as possible.

Looking up from a job requiring a steady hand, Feri instructed him to sit down, that he would be with him in a moment. From where he sat, István could see Feri's shoulders getting more hunched. Even good-natured Feri despised Varga.

Varga screwed up his face, squinting in István's direction as though trying to place someone he might have recognized from a long way back. A stupid exhibition, thought István. Varga never missed an occasion to assert his manipulations.

Varga removed his boots and placed them on the workbench right in front of István's nose. István refused to look up. Varga sat down, reclined with a contented sigh, put his feet up on another chair and crossed them at the ankles. His woollen socks were darned beyond repair.

Feri mustered, "Any news from the Front?"

"Stalin and the Red Army are out to conquer Hitler on our soil. They've already overrun the entire eastern portion of Hungary. The Arrow Cross has taken up a rearguard action here in the west. And our soldiers in Budapest are so hungry now, they are eating their own horses."

István picked up the boots and began work, but avoided eye contact while Varga spoke, even though he ached to know everything he could about the siege in Budapest. Magyar Rádió had stopped reporting, and news was now spreading through word of mouth.

"We're giving cover for the retreating German army. They're rounding up Jews at lighting speed, carting them off." Varga sat very still, tapping a toe to a silent beat, silhouetted by the light pouring in through the windows of the shop.

István snuck a glance. He didn't dare bring up the fact that only months ago Varga was still part of the Arrow Cross. István's desire to destabilize Varga with exposure, would only backfire – it didn't take a genius to know that with the Russians advancing across Hungary, bloodthirsty for Germans, they were *both* targets as former members.

His blue eyes stinging from the toxic glue – István had never grown accustomed to the odour – he rubbed them and stayed focused on the job of keeping Varga's feet as comfortable as possible as he marched towards the Front. István would never compromise the skill he'd mastered, not even for this conceited bastard, though the smell of Varga's boot made him queasy. These boots had been marched through mud and dust, over dead bodies and rubble, made to stand in pooling blood. István fell into a new region of disquiet.

"Goddamn Germans dragged us into this," said Feri, aggressively buffing another pair of boots. He slammed down one boot, picked up another and started buffing it fiercely.

"The whole northeast of Hungary is already under the control of the Russians," Varga said, flexing and stretching his neck. "They're killing civilians, taking men, boys, anybody right off the street. Carting them off to Siberia. They're executing Arrow Cross members on the spot. In village squares."

István kept his head down. Terror shot from his gut in two directions. One to his sphincter and another up to his esophagus, like he was going to shit and puke all at once. How could Varga so easily erase his involvement with the Arrow Cross and flaunt this information like he was immune?

"If you have a watch, hide it," Varga said, yawning, stretching his massive body.

"Why?" István asked, in spite of himself.

"The Russians are taking whatever they can." Varga cracked his knuckles. "They have some sort of bizarre fascination with watches. Don't have any in Russia, I guess. They want to collect as many of them as they can. And they love screwing our bitches."

Feri glowered at him. "I won't have that kind of language in my shop! You can take your boots and leave if you keep that up."

Varga straightened himself in the chair.

"They're done." István hurled the boots onto the floor.

Varga stood, walked across the shop in his darned woollen socks, snatched his boots off the floor and shoved his feet into them. "My uncle Németh tells me you and Pista have been dismissed. Something about incompetency in Budapest…" Varga coaxed.

István busied himself with another shoe, trying not to add to the fire.

"What is this about?!" Feri interjected.

"It's been a while since we've seen each other, István and I." Varga continued. "When my uncle talked so highly of your son, it reminded me to stop in on my old colleague."

Feri stood. "What need would you have to stop in on my son?"

"See you around, István," Varga smiled broadly in the doorway.

"I wish you a fine day," Feri said, automatically.

"Many finer ones to come," Varga tipped his cap and closed the door.

The afternoon light turned charcoal grey. Through the shop window István saw snow clouds threatening. The ensuing silence may have been the greatest gift Feri had ever given him.

★

Some months had passed since the executions in Budapest, and still Feri hadn't inquired about István's absences. István was acutely aware of Feri's preoccupation; he didn't want the Germans in Hungary, nor did he want the Russians. Feri wanted Hungary for Hungarians. As long as trouble brewed in the capital, his stepfather seemed oblivious to the dangers closer to home, but István had seen firsthand what was little talked about and mostly avoided by village folk. Only a handful of people mentioned what they'd heard, that Jews in Budapest were being marched to the Austrian border. Hundreds of thousands of them.

Teréza heard, in her half-sleep, *It's all over. The Russians won. Victory belongs to the Allies.* When she opened her eyes, she thought for a moment that someone was standing over her holding a Hungarian flag, like an accusation. But the room was empty.

She climbed carefully out of bed so as not to disturb her siblings. An empty kitchen greeted her, the door ajar. The stove belted heat, but without the usual sight of her parents drinking their morning coffee and eating a chunk of rye bread, the kitchen held a chill. Two speckled enamel cups sat on the table. One was still half full. She checked the wall calendar. February 13. She stepped out into the yard, wearing only her flannel nightgown and socks, and saw her mother walking down the lane towards the market. A light sprinkling of snow covered the muddy world – it always comforted her – but this dusting left Teréza feeling exposed.

She looked around. Standing in the middle of the muddy field holding a pitchfork, her father wore his shabby coat and

no hat. He lowered his head as if speaking to the ground, but
Teréza couldn't see anything in front of him. Lunging
towards an imaginary foe, he began stabbing the mud with
the pitchfork with such fury that the handle broke after a few
blows. He swore. He ran a few steps, took a manic lunge
toward the south and threw what remained of the pitchfork –
an ungovernable javelin. It landed as haphazardly as a
plunging kite.

Perplexed, Teréza watched as her father began stomping
in a wide semicircle. He stopped, yelled towards eastern Hungary. Toward Budapest. Nothing intelligible. It unnerved her
to see him so erratic.

"Father?" she called out to him, shivering in her nightgown.

His moustache, the best indicator of his mental state,
drooped the lowest Teréza could remember. Gyuri didn't
respond. He was talking to southern Hungary now, that or to
the fence twenty metres away. She wasn't sure which.

"Father?"

He looked at her like he didn't recognize her. Even from
afar she could see that he had the look of a starving wolf.

"Father!" She called out with more force. She was trying
not to cry.

"What?" he croaked.

"You didn't finish your coffee."

He didn't respond. Had he gone mad? Had she? Why was
she yelling about a half-drunk cup of coffee? She returned to
the house. If her mother had abandoned the family and her
father had gone mad, then it was up to her to get her brother
and sisters up and fed. But her body felt uncooperative, like it
was being swallowed by quicksand. Hungary's loss sapped
her motivation. All this for what? This was the second war her

father had lost.

When next she checked on her father, he was looking into the well again.

"Father!" she called out from the kitchen door.

"What?" he barked into the well.

"What about your coffee?"

"It's not real coffee," he answered her, shaking his head. "It's nothing but toasted barley."

He was right. What he said made sense, and that reassured her. But he was no closer to doing anything useful; he kept staring into the well.

Back inside, she dragged herself from chore to chore, overwhelmed by this new parental role. She snapped at her sisters when they wanted to play. "It's no time to frolic. We have a country to rebuild. Where the hell is András anyways? Why isn't he helping?" She marched out into the yard. No sign of her brother András. Why were men so useless?

"What does rebuild mean?" asked Kati, the littlest traipsing behind. Ági followed casually while Juli skipped along to catch up. The sprinkling of snow was already melting, making the yard look shit-brown.

"It means work. Labour. Effort. Don't just stand there. Do something." Her sisters were becoming a bother to her; too young to understand the gravity of life, too innocent to care. Teréza handed them pails. "Ági, Juli, Kati. Take these. We need water from the well. At least we have water. Our very own. Come on."

"I don't want to work," said Juli, her mouth swelling into a pout.

"Neither do I." Ági tossed her pail to the ground and kicked it clear across the yard. Little Kati did the same.

"Grow up! You have no choice!" Teréza tramped toward

the pail. She could no longer see her father at the well.

Teréza grabbed the stray pail, marched up to Ági and pushed it against her chest. Ági winced and coughed. Kati covered her mouth in astonishment.

"We have to do something. We can't just get sucked into lethargy!" Teréza hollered.

"What's lethargy?" asked Juli.

"Look! Look at father. That! That is lethargy." She nodded towards the veranda where father sat, staring. His heart so heavy Teréza could practically see it sagging in his chest.

"Will father be alright?" Juli furrowed her brow.

Teréza shrugged.

"I want mama." Kati began to sob.

Ági dropped her pail and stood with her arms crossed.

Teréza began to pace. Chicken shit squished and flattened beneath the soles of her shoes. A curious rooster approached. He clucked a few times until Teréza swatted him. Squawking, the rooster alighted. Teréza managed to kick his outstretched wing but lost her balance. She squelched in fresh chicken shit.

Juli and Kati dared not laugh but Ági let out a huge guffaw.

"We're all going to have to grow up now. And you!" Teréza stared at Ági before kicking the pail back at her, hard. "All you ever do is contradict me. You always have to have the last word. Well, you know what?" She shoved her sister in the chest. "The Russians will put you in your place!" She knew as soon as she said it, it was the worst thing she could say to her sister who had only just learned of what men can do to women. Especially Russian men.

Ági slapped Teréza's face.

Teréza slapped her back.

Teréza walked a few paces and then turned back. She

looked up to the sky where a raven flew low and fast. She
could hear the beat of its wings, feel deep, ancient energies
swirling in her, whispering to punish those who stood in her
way.

Teréza walked away from her unmanageable family. If
her mother could do it, so could she. She'd only reached the
end of her dirt road when she saw the village priest, the
organist and postmaster running towards the village limits.
For a brief instant, she was stunned by the vision: the
postmaster held high a white sheet tied to a wooden pole. Ják
was raising a flag of surrender. It was a plea to the Russians:
don't burn our homes, don't kill our men, and don't take our
women. Have mercy on us.

Flustered and panic-stricken, Teréza took a deep breath.
She looked around and noticed István on his bicycle, leaning
dangerously into the sharp curve down the main street. The
curve straightened, and he righted himself on the bicycle
before narrowly missing the short fat woman crossing at the
post office. "Don't go to Szombathely," the priest shouted
after him, "the Russians are already there!"

István had been driving nails into the heel of a boot when Feri
hollered, "Come look!"

István stopped what he was doing.

"Jesus," Feri said, pushing open the shop window. Icy air
rushed in. "Get over here."

The cool air came as a relief.

István caught the tail end of a white makeshift flag before
it disappeared around a corner. He didn't catch who was
waving it. A straggle of distressed men grabbed tight to their

reins as their horses reared and changed directions. They yelled to all compass points: "Don't go to Szombathely, the Russians are already there!"

Just as István glimpsed Teréza on the other side of the square – looking pretty but harried – Feri slammed shut the window, turned to István and said, "Go to Szombathely. Now."

"What for?" István shoved his hands into his pockets like he could hide his deeds.

Feri grabbed him by the arms. "Go to the Police Station right away and tell them you're Jewish. You'll be protected when the Russians start executing Arrow Cross members."

A heavy fog enveloped István's head. He couldn't see straight. Tears swam in his eyes. His shame wouldn't let him look Feri in the eye.

In that embarrassing pause lived the confusion he'd encountered the day he decided he could no longer ask for Feri's help, the day Feri had said to István, "You're a man now." Whether it was because István thought he should be old enough or smart enough to solve his problems on his own, or whether he wanted to believe he had some measure of autonomy, the result of his going at it alone was dragging his best friend with him into the undertow.

His stepfather's nonpartisanship revealed his nature. Could this man who'd raised him possibly understand István's slapdash choice to join the Arrow Cross for protection? Would he disown him if he knew that he'd been part of the deportations? The thought made him desperate.

By cupping István's face, Feri demanded his eyes. "I don't care what you've done, son. Just go. All that matters is that you survive."

"What about Pista?"

"He's in this too, is he?" Feri released István's face and looked towards the floorboards.

"I'm the one who put him at risk. I was trying to hide in plain sight." István's eyes swam with tears.

"Let's just hope the Russians will be too busy over-throwing municipal governments to come after a harmless drunkard."

"What are you saying?"

"I didn't adopt you to lose you," Feri said gruffly. "Now, get the hell out of here." He returned to his workbench.

István paused at the door.

"No matter how bad it gets, you are going to be alright," Feri said, and began sorting shoes for resoling.

István hopped on his bicycle, riding the current of his own misadventures. He coasted down the hill, hugging the curve. Why was the fat woman always crossing the road when he was in a hurry? Though he swerved in time, he gave her a scare, and she cursed his mother for bringing him into the world. When he glanced back and saw Teréza wearing a green cardigan; his heart punched his sternum. What he wouldn't give to scoop her up on his handlebars and steal away with her to Austria.

Teréza watched István, the shoemaker's son, barrel down the street, peddling manically. There was something in the way he looked back, like he'd forgotten something or someone, that felt upsettingly familiar. And in that very moment an uncanny feeling crept down her arms and legs and tingled like icicles on her skin. She'd had the very same feeling when she saw the two young men with shovels digging a grave in the twilight. He veered towards the road to Szombathely, the only person travelling in the forbidden direction. She wanted to call out to him, but she couldn't find her voice.

She watched him turn into a tiny speck and then transform into a thousand pellets of snow. A flurry brushed her eyelashes and lips and cheeks and ears.

As he rode his bicycle through the blanched, wintery country-side, István practiced the story he'd cobbled together in his head, reciting it over and over. The frigid air lashed his face; his hands were white and freezing. At least his thumb no longer hurt. Soon his mind lost the threads of his fictitious facts.

The trip to Szombathely took thirty minutes by bicycle over a jagged and slippery road. In the town centre, he passed by the recently bombed Baroque cathedral and the damaged *Hótel Kovács*. Russian soldiers were everywhere, their movements brisk and defiant; nothing was standing in the way of their invasion. Soldiers dragged men from their homes, pulled husbands from their wives, and stuck rifles to their backs.

Gargoyles with bat wings sneered from the rooftops of Szombathely's three-storey buildings. How had he not noticed them before? He wasn't superstitious, but he felt like they were cursing him.

He glanced at the synagogue as he sped by, where he'd recorded thousands of names. He darted between horse-drawn carts, Russian army vehicles, pedestrians and other cyclists, avoided getting his wheels stuck in the tram tracks. He rode against a fierce wind. The trees along the boulevard bent like bows. His thighs burned, his heart throbbed, his eyes watered, and the wool of his pants rubbed harshly against his legs. Had István fully engaged with his self-loathing, it would have been enough for him to stop at the side at the road and ask a Russian soldier to shoot him on the spot. But István found a brief respite by blaming Varga for the very source of his travails.

Up ahead, he saw the Szombathely Police Station. A red flag flapped next to the Hungarian one by the door. He slowed, hopped off his bike and stashed it in the centre of an anemic bush, directly underneath the Russian flag.

He was out of breath. As he approached the heavy old doors of the building he fumbled his first lines in his head. He rewrote his script with each step up the stairs. He forgot his opening line.

The long hallway to the receptionist was an echo chamber for his footsteps; farther back in the vestibule, police and Red Army soldiers consulted with each other in a flurry of activity. Their voices grew louder, more forceful, the closer István got. He removed his cap, brushed his fingers through his hair and walked slowly and cautiously, unsure of his ingress. He passed stern-looking portraits on the walls. Police officers.

István greeted the receptionist with an honorific; she was a middle-aged woman with a head the size of a horse's. Stuttering and stammering he blurted, "My father was Jewish."

The receptionist looked at him in disbelief. "That's no longer a crime," she said snidely.

A peevish young officer intervened and asked what István wanted to report.

"The young man has come in to tell us that he's Jewish," the receptionist said, gazing over the frames of her glasses with an inflection on *Jewish*, suggesting that before the Russians arrived, she may have sided with the Arrow Cross.

István felt like an idiot. "My father. I said...my father was Jewish."

"Not your mother?" asked the young officer.

"No, just my father."

"That makes you Jewish too," said the horse-faced receptionist.

"Yes," said István.

"And?" the officer interjected strenuously, leaning his body over the counter like he'd finally caught someone red-handed. "Is there a moral to this story?"

István focused on the dark mole protruding from the officer's left eyebrow. Four Red Army soldiers hustled two handcuffed men in black uniforms through the front door. Their faces were bleeding and battered. One man's mouth looked like a smashed tomato and an Arrow Cross insignia hung off the left sleeve of his jacket. István looked away. Thankfully Németh's eyes were swollen shut. His old commander couldn't see him.

"Look, we haven't got all day. If you're here to report the disappearance of your father, there's nothing we can do to help you," said the officer.

The Red Army soldiers pushed their captives noisily down the hallway towards the rear of the station.

The horse-headed receptionist raised her eyebrows and rolled her eyes. István half-expected her to whinny.

"If you could just write down my name and that my father was Jewish, maybe some information will come forward," István improvised.

The woman reached for a file. "What good will that do?"

The officer didn't answer. He was distracted by the ruckus in the back.

"Name?" said the receptionist.

"Kiss István." He watched her write *Jewish descent* beside his name.

Then she asked him his birthdate, birthplace, address and occupation. "Father's name?" she asked.

István trembled. "He disappeared."

"Look." The perturbed officer walked around the counter and grabbed István by the shoulder. He led him down the hall towards the front door. "It's been a terrible time for Jews, I understand. But right now we have our hands full." The officer pushed open the door and a strong wind gust blew in. "See down there?" he said, squeezing István's arm. "That's the road to the mental hospital, over there, take a right. They'll be better able to help you. Good luck."

István peered in the direction the officer pointed. "Will you notify me if you find my father?"

The officer closed the door.

On the steps of the police station, his body vibrated. He felt delirious and buoyant, like he might break into spontaneous laughter. He bolted towards his bicycle, pulled it from the bush and rode with the zeal of someone starting life anew. A newborn. He vowed to take care of Pista, and from now on he would say as little as possible, anything to safeguard his luck. The less he spoke, the fewer mistakes he would make.

The whole thing had gone in a bizarrely different direction than the one István had imagined. He hadn't even been given a chance to invent a name for his Jewish father. He hadn't confessed to being a member of the Arrow Cross. He hadn't betrayed Pista.

On the way back to Ják, with snow pelting his face and cooling his hot tears, István had a vision. The girl in the grave appeared before him. She lived in the landscape, engulfed in perpetual nightfall. Her hair hadn't stopped growing, and neither would his guilt.

Back in Ják late that afternoon, he saw Ági furtively crossing the road in front of the Post Office. He asked her to deliver a note to Teréza. The young girl bristled at being conscripted for the task when more exciting things were unfolding, but agreed when she read the note.

> *Hi Teréza. Meet me behind the stand of trees at the edge of the field by your house. In an hour. I'll be waiting. I have something important to deliver to you. P.s. It's István, from school and the shoe shop. Kiss Feri's son.*

István stood near the end of the field, panting. His body already fleeing the impending rejection. Would Teréza and her sister Ági make a mockery of his note and burn it in the stove? The sun had crept closer to the western horizon and burnished the winter woods. The snow had stopped falling.

"István?" Teréza said breathlessly, pink-cheeked and lovely.

István startled.

"What is it?" She said almost impatiently, forgetting any pleasantries. "I'm sorry I startled you. It was hard to make up an excuse to get out of the house. I'm too young to meet like this."

"Thank you for meeting me," István held the gift behind his back. "I assure you it will be worth your while."

"I must say the suspense is killing me."

"I brought you these," he said. He presented her with a buffed pair of brown women's Oxfords, perforated, with a wooden heel. In mint condition. "Size five."

She covered her mouth with her mittened hands. "How did you know?"

"Know what?"

"My size."

"I'm a cobbler's son. I can tell by looking."

"But I've only just started wearing size five."

"I've been waiting to give them to you." He held them out to her.

"Where did you get them?" She reached for them, and he retracted them just slightly.

"May I put them on for you?" He pulled out of his satchel a tiny folding stool, and planted it in the snow. She sat. He kneeled. When he pulled off her lace-up boots he saw that her stockings had been darned many times. He felt a stirring in his groin. He carefully folded back the tongues, slipped the shoes on her feet, and laced them.

Teréza's smile grew wide and satisfied. "They're a perfect fit. I feel like Cinderella."

"I guess that would make me your Prince," he said, still holding her foot.

She laughed. He blushed and sat back on his heels, looking down at the ground. After an awkward silence, he noticed she looked nervously towards home and the smoke rising from the chimney.

"Did you make them for me?" she asked. He had made her feel special, in a way no one ever had. The shoe fit. Not only had he taken an interest in her details, but he had the means to transport her away from here, to a new place.

He was about to say that he had made them himself, when Teréza's mother stepped out of the house and called for her, an impatient edge to her voice.

"I have to go." Teréza hopped up from the stool, and István grabbed her arm.

"I forgot to thank you," she said, blushing from his contact.

"Can I see you again? Please." He leaned in close and felt her breath against his cheek in the morning air. She represented a fresh start for him. Beauty and innocence, a balm that would wash away his sins.

"I'd like that." Teréza ran towards her mother with her first kiss buzzing upon her lips and the weight of history on her feet.

SEPARATION

1964

DON'T GO, DON'T GO, DON'T GO

1964, January – February 28. Hungary

The envelope arrived with wind gusts and soggy days that persisted throughout January like an ill-fated flu. Like a gentleman charmer, nothing about it looked any different from the ones she'd previously received from the Ministry of the Interior. She let it sit for a couple of days, staring at it over breakfast. It elicited no response in her whatsoever, neither hope nor despair. One morning Zolti asked her, "Why don't you open that letter, mama? Are you afraid of what it says?"

How did he know that the longer the years, the more fear she had of leaving? Reaching for the envelope she was not aware that it was January 30th, exactly seven years to the day István fled. Her clumsy fingers tore open the flap. Zolti said nothing, as if he knew that in this world of theirs, his life was not his own.

The proclamation came straight from the government. Families separated during the Revolution were to be reunited. The feeling, when it came, was unintelligable. The world lay in front of her; the gates were thrown wide open. She wanted to feel excited.

On her last and final visit to Ják, all her siblings came: Klára, András, Ági, Juli and Kati. They ate spaghetti squash stew with dill and sour cream and fresh baked bread. Singing like sailors, they celebrated their reunion as though Teréza wasn't leaving.

Teréza pushed open the door and stood in the frosty twilight, brushing her hair. As she stood under the setting sky, she looked around the yard where she spent so much of her life, feeding chickens, doing chores, carrying well water, and playing with her siblings. She loved this place, its birds, flowers and soil. Cleaning her brush, she let her hair fall to the earth so that the birds could find it and build a nest in spring.

"Zolti!" she cried out, "Please come back. Canada is calling."

"What if I don't answer?" Zolti said, coming out from behind the barn.

The Édes family slept in the beds they once occupied as children, crammed together three to a mattress, Zolti on a little cushion on the floor. Teréza lay beside Kati, who curled into her and giggled while whispering in her ear, "Don't go, don't go, don't go."

WHEN I WAS BETTER

On his last day of school, Zolti's classmates made a circle around him, all of them wearing red scarves around their necks. Looking dazed and confused, they held hands while Teréza watched on.

"Why is your father in Canada?" asked one of his classmates, a girl with miniature teeth. Teréza liked this petite girl but was concerned by her question.

Before Zolti could answer, another classmate, a pudgy boy with bottle-thick glasses piped up, "Why doesn't he come back to Hungary? Kádár Papa will take care of him."

"We have summer camps and sports and culture and education, and we go to the doctor when we have tummy aches, and we are all comrades, and why are you leaving now when school's just started?" The girl's miniature teeth sparkled.

Teréza was surprised by the children's bold questions, especially the girl's. She wanted to intervene when she heard Zolti struggle with his answer. "Because Canada is calling," he said.

The children mumbled amongst themselves wondering what phone he'd used to answer the call.

"My father has a big, new car, twice the size of a Trabant," Zolti continued breathlessly, "and there's a place with eleven different flavours of ice cream, and I'll learn English from the radio like I learned German from Radio Vienna. Also, we can say anything we want when we get there because Canadians are free people, and no one goes to jail because they want to slaughter their pig."

Teréza turned all shades of the Hungarian flag. Before she could say anything to fill the stunned silence, the pudgy boy did it for her. "Your father's a traitor," he said.

Zolti pushed the pudgy boy and followed him to the

ground, tiny fists flailing. "Your father's a communist pig!" he yelled at the top of his lungs.

Teréza and the teacher pulled the boys to their feet and quickly restored order. In a corner of the classroom, Teréza spoke sternly to Zolti who huffed like a little bull. When he calmed down, she placed foil-wrapped chocolates in his hand. "Go." She gently urged him forward. Begrudgingly he handed each classmate a "Zolti chocolate" so they could remember how sweet he was.

He cried as Teréza led him away. She listened to his confession that he wasn't excited to go to Canada. "How do I know that the photos are of a real man?" he sniffed.

"Don't be silly, Zolti, your father is real." She was still reeling from her son's earlier unguarded disclosure at school. Good thing she'd already handed in her notice at work.

When she entered Szombathely Station to catch the noon train, Gyuri was already waiting, flanked by two officials, one of them a familiar yet unwelcome face. Varga's sledgehammer chin contradicted his aging, droopy eyelids.

"You are forbidden to leave with your birth or marriage certificates," he said. Varga gave no explanation and confiscated her documents, handing her an envelope in return. "Make sure you give this to your husband."

On the platform before she boarded, Varga searched through every item in her suitcase, lifting her copy of *Petőfi Love Poems*, the pristinely preserved volume István had gifted her for their wedding. He slipped it in his satchel.

"I never took you to be the romantic type." She picked up

her suitcase and turned on her heels.

Teréza waited until the train got moving and both Zolti and her father were asleep, before she read the contents of the envelope.

> *Kiss István. Sentenced in absentia for treason, destruction of government property, destruction of political material, aiding and abetting counter-revolutionaries, supplying arms to rebels. Seventeen years.*

It finally sunk in: neither she nor István could ever come back.

István flew from Winnipeg to Montreal the day before Teréza's arrival. He was met at the airport by his two loyal friends who looked dapper as always. Marika and Bela drove István around the French city, Marika's arm draped over Bela's shoulder as he commanded the steering wheel of their shiny new car.

"Impressive," István said, stroking the seat. He could see that the couple had settled well in Montreal. They fancied the glamour of the burgeoning metropolis, its European sensibility. They'd found work they could be content with, and Marika was pregnant a second time. She looked radiant, thought István, and his heart stirred all over again.

They stopped in at Montreal Hebrew Delicatessen on Saint-Laurent where István ordered a liver steak sprinkled with smoked meat pickling spices. "Sensational," he said, as he swallowed his last bite, well before Bela and Marika finished their plates.

István admired Montreal's sites. A metro was two years in the making, and the city was in a construction boom, erecting skyscrapers, superhighways, bridges, tunnels and express lanes in preparation for Expo 67.

"Isn't it ironic," said István, "that Moscow cancelled and we got the gig?"

"And now the world is looking to us to deliver on time," said Bela, abruptly righting the vehicle after it skidded on slush. Marika grabbed the dash.

"We're in a country where you can look to the future and feel optimistic," István said, gazing out the window in the backseat of the car. Deep snow bordered sidewalks and roads. Snow walls, he thought.

"And what do you see when you look in the future?" Marika said, turning around, her smile as seductive as always.

"I don't carry the gene for optimism," István joked.

"What gene do you carry?" Bela asked.

"One for getting away with things that I should be held accountable for."

"A guilty conscience?" Marika examined him through the side-view mirror.

In Bela and Marika's second floor walk-up, the three were listening to the Beatles' recently released album, *Beatlemania! With the Beatles*, for the third time when Marika fell asleep on the couch. Her belly was just starting to show.

István was feeling the third martini. "I can't finish this," he said, placing it on the coffee table.

"Don't worry my friend, I'll finish it for you." Bela was

about to play *It Won't Be Long* for a fourth time when István said, "I've had enough of this modern music. I'm almost forty."

"Old man!" Bela said, "You're looking so worried. Not like a man who's over the moon about seeing his wife and son in less than twenty-four hours."

István resented Bela's comment. "Do you keep secrets from your wife?"

"No."

"None?"

"None."

"Well isn't that just great for you."

Bela shifted uncomfortably. "I'm sorry. I pushed you into–"

"Forget it. What's done is done." István picked up his martini again. "I've changed my mind." He took a sip. "This is a terrible drink. Why do you have to ruin the vodka like this? I don't know why I'm even drinking it."

"Hard to know why we do things, sometimes."

"Why is it so agonizing to be truthful?" István asked, not expecting an answer.

"It depends on what truth you're about to reveal. And how you expect it to be received. If you're expecting an execution, you have two choices. Die for what you believe in or lie to save your life."

"So in the end, it all comes down to values." István reached for the martini, took another sip.

Bela smiled. "Without truth, there's no real connection. The truth hurts, but love eventually heals what hurts."

"You sound like a Beatles song. Teréza's hurt is a bottomless well of hurt. It might kill me."

"Do you want me to tell you it's futile to confess to

Teréza?"

"The truth is only useful when beliefs are flexible."

"That's a whole other matter now. So if she were flexible about monogamy your life would stand a chance?"

"My wife's not like the two of you."

"Or like you, István? You've been living alone for too long, my friend. You think too much. Can't you just meet her with love?"

István felt remorse, hostility and affection. His lucky friend had the luxury to act on his predilections and even thrive. But when István came close to revealing himself, another part of him locked him in tighter. "I need to sleep off the last seven years," he said. "I'm going to bed."

In Budapest, they stayed at Klára's for two days.

The night before the international flight, Teréza had set out her most stylish outfit on a chair in Klára and Elek's bedroom. For Zolti, she assembled an impeccable white shirt, a green V-neck vest and grey wool pants. She wanted them to look like cultured Westerners, not bedraggled Eastern Europeans.

In the morning before any others awoke, Teréza locked herself in Klára's bathroom and washed. She looked at her breasts. They hadn't changed much since István left and retained their fullness. She was still nursing the day he fled. She'd denied him a last viewing, tucked them back into her bra, quickly, after she had finished feeding Zolti. In seven years, she had given them only to her son. Turning sideways the cups of her flesh-toned satin bra pointed upward. She pulled her stomach in easily. Her body had been untouched for so long she couldn't imagine being exposed. Her sexual desire went dormant as though it never had a chance to fully wake.

Softly closing the washroom door Teréza tiptoed back to Klára's bedroom. Her small brown suitcase, lid open, sat on a chair and Klára was taking Teréza's items out of her own drawer and neatly placing them inside.

"What are you doing?" Teréza asked.

"Packing your suitcase," Klára replied.

"I can see that."

"Someone was sleep walking last night."

"Who?" Teréza looked towards Zolti who stirred.

"You! My darling. You! You got up some time after three. I thought you were heading to the bathroom, but then you started unpacking your suitcase, putting all your belongings into my drawers. It's amazing you managed to squeeze everything in there. And so neatly."

"Why didn't you say anything?"

"I did! But you were in some other realm, and you couldn't hear me. They say, never rouse a sleepwalker unless they're about to hurt themselves."

"Am I about to hurt myself?"

Klára closed the suitcase. She patted the edge of the bed. The two sisters sat down together, close to Elek's feet.

Teréza whispered, "I made a commitment to my husband the day I married him."

"This is your chance."

"Is it worth taking a chance if you can't be assured of a peaceful future?"

"If we learned nothing else from our Revolution, we learned that," Klára whispered in her ear.

They sat in silence for a time, listening to the morning,

listening to their boys breathing, Elek and Gyuri snoring. Finally, Klára crossed to her nightstand. "Come to the kitchen," she whispered.

In the soft light streaming in from the courtyard, she held up a delicate watch. "This is the watch I kept from the Russians during the Siege. Isn't it amazing it managed to survive the looting? It was by pure chance they didn't find it. It's yours," Klára pressed it into Teréza's hand, "so you recognize the significance of this moment in time."

Tears filled Teréza's eyes.

"Don't say anything," Klára said, her eyes growing bloodshot. They held each other tight.

"Don't say anything." Teréza placed her head onto Klára's chest.

Gyuri had never been to an airport. When Teréza saw just how out of place her peasant father looked in the modern facility, she was overwhelmed with sorrow. She disliked the regret she felt for his appearance.

"Don't say anything," Gyuri said as he held her.

"That's exactly what Klára said," Teréza's face was slick with tears.

"That's why we're a family. Because we don't talk about heartache, unless I'm drunk."

Few planes took off or landed at the Budapest airport. When an Aeroflot aircraft taxied in, Zolti pressed his nose to the glass and pointed excitedly at the engines. In the inhospitable boarding lounge, airport security pulled Teréza aside. She'd not yet been permitted to check her luggage, though all others passengers had. A man and a woman, red stars on their caps, ordered her to open her suitcase yet again and with stone-faced expressions told her to empty it.

"Is there not a table onto which I can place my items?" she asked.

Without a word the woman overturned her suitcase, spilling its contents onto the floor, right there at the gate.

The woman rifled through Teréza's belongings while others watched. It may as well have been a strip search as the woman touched every last pair of underwear. Teréza felt disgusted. After checking the bra size, the flat-chested rake of a woman relieved Teréza of her newly purchased brassieres, leaving her with only the one she wore.

"I'm not sure they'll fit," said Teréza, under her breath.

In retaliation, the woman also seized an exquisitely hand-embroidered pillowcase that Anna had made as a parting gift, then shoved everything back into Teréza's suitcase in a disorganized heap like dirty laundry, and clicked closed its latches.

Teréza fixed her gaze off into the distance, eyes red and vacant, to a point on the grey concrete wall and pretended not to see the male security officer pocket her forints. Why these acts of disrespect devastated her more now than the last thirty-four years she would never know.

By her side Zolti asked, "Why did the woman mess up your suitcase? Didn't it look better before?"

At twenty-three minutes after two they began boarding the *Malév* flight to Brussels. Teréza checked her watch.

Squeezing his mother's hand so hard it hurt, Zolti mounted the stairs to the plane, right in step with his mother. Under his arm, he held his scrapbook stuffed with photos of his father.

"I don't think I'll know my father's voice when I hear it,"

he said.

"Of course you will," Teréza replied. "You heard it in the womb."

"No. Father didn't like talking much," he said, as he found his seat.

"How do you know this Zolti?

"A feeling inside me knows."

Teréza shoved her purse under the seat ahead of her. The smell of the aircraft nauseated her, and the enclosed space felt suffocating. She felt panic in her chest. Juli had told Teréza about motion sickness and had given her some pills. Teréza scrambled for the container and choked back two without water.

"But I remember the washing machine always liked talking to me." Zolti fastened his seatbelt, dazzled with the closing mechanism. He snapped the latch open and closed, open and closed, open and closed.

"Please stop!" Teréza snapped at him and instantly regretted it. "I'm sorry." She kissed him. "Be a good boy." She fumbled with her own, unable to relate to the apparatus. A stewardess roughly closed Teréza's belt around her belly. Teréza raised her eyebrows like it would help get rid of the woman. Socialist service standards had followed her on the plane.

She waited for take off. The sound of the engines unnerved her. As the aircraft accelerated, Teréza gripped Zolti's hand. Their backs pushed into their seat as the plane picked up speed, tilted and lifted into the air. Soon the sky looked knocked on its side. Within seconds a woman across the aisle, in the row in front began to gag. The sound of the gagging woman, together with the sky on its side did Teréza in. She barely got the bag under her mouth before the pink pills came up.

Zolti pleaded with his mother, "Mother are you dying? Please don't die! Are you dying mother? Are you dying? Please don't die!"

REUNIFICATION

1964 (1955)

EVERYTHING CAME WITH ME

1964, February 29 – March 3. Montreal & Winnipeg, Canada

In a small windowless room, Teréza and Zolti sat quietly, still shaking from the turbulent flight. It was happening all over again. She'd already broken some arbitrary rule, and she didn't dare speak to her son. When a familiar face peered around the door, she burst out laughing with relief and joy. "Here I am," was all she could think to say.

"It can't be true," István answered, his smile sublime.

She wore beige pumps; he noticed those first. Then her A-line brown skirt with tiny pale squares woven into its threads. Her fitted, azure blue pullover accentuated her green eyes and her perfect breasts.

"Pretty," he said, breaking into tears. He held his wife for the first time on the other side of disconnection. They felt tiny to each other, thin from separation, their bodies unpracticed in contact.

Teréza remembered his full ginger hair, strong and plentiful. Now she felt the skin on the top of his scalp. "Your hair," she said to him, her heart pounding in her throat.

"I hope this will be the only thing that troubles you."

She laughed apologetically. "Who ironed your shirt?" she asked breathing in the scent of his collar.

"Someone who doesn't do it as well as you," he said. They loosened their embrace, and he handed her carnations. "These are for you, and I got us a beautiful room in a hotel."

She blushed and reached for their son. Nudged him forward.

"Mama was throwing up on the plane," said Zolti.

István looked at his son. The boy was short but well fed and smartly dressed. His eyes turned into slits when he smiled. Like Pista's. The likeness was brief and striking. How could his son's eyes look like Pista's?

"Zolti." István opened his arms.

"Father!" His son pitched his dense body against his father's legs, grabbing them in a reckless hug.

The Immigration Official arrived and spoke to István. "Can you tell her that her tuberculosis examination has expired?"

"*Mitt mond?*" Teréza asked István, her voice quivering. A flush of pride washed over her. She had never heard her husband speak English.

"Everything's fine," he reassured her and explained that they wouldn't let her enter Canada until a doctor examined her. She was led off to another room.

"You stay here beside me," István said to his son, touching his arm and holding him back from climbing off the chair. And then István drew a blank. He didn't know what to say to him. The boy was a stranger. When he did get something out, it sounded like the voice coming from the other side of the wall. Disembodied, emotionless and uninteresting. "How was the plane ride?" he asked.

"I was afraid," Zolti said, picking his nose. "I screamed a lot. Mother threw up."

"Yes, that's right, you told me that." István felt stuck again. "Tell me something else."

Zolti began telling him about his dream the night before they left Hungary. "Someone stole the wings off the plane, and we had to row across the ocean to Canada. A big fish like this," he demonstrated with his hands and arms, "stole our sausage."

István had no practice conversing with a child. A new discomfort ambushed him. He searched for topics, coming up dry. Something finally came to him. He started telling Zolti what he knew about Winnipeg. That Winnipeg meant "muddy waters" in Cree and that Canada meant "settlement" or "village," in Iroquois. He asked his son if he could speak any English.

Embarrassedly Zolti answered, "*Nem tudok.*"

"I can't," said István. "*Mondjad,* I can't."

"I can't," repeated Zolti. His face went red.

István encouraged Zolti to learn English as soon as he could so he wouldn't fall behind in his studies. "You can become something here," István said to his son, though he didn't entirely believe it himself. "Just please not a fireman or a policeman."

Zolti looked at him quizzically.

In another room, Teréza removed her gold chain, preparing for the examination. Presented to her by her colleagues back in Szombathely, the gift was accompanied by a card and an additional handwritten note: *If you don't like it there, come*

back. She knew it was her Communist colleagues who added the special note to the card. They always assumed the West had it worse off, that capitalism didn't care for people.

Already Teréza felt her respectability preserved. She had assumed she would disrobe entirely but the doctor motioned for her to remove only her sweater and keep on her bra. She stood behind the X-ray machine thinking about how in a Hungarian socialist hospital she would have been ordered to strip naked right in front of the doctor. The system had no regard for dignity.

An hour later, István opened the passenger door of the '49 Chevy while his son scampered into the back.

"Why is it so wide?" Teréza asked laughing and climbed into the front seat. "This car is so huge! Why do you need this much car?" Though she'd sat in a vehicle only once before, Klára's Trabant, she didn't feel swallowed up by the diminutive East German automobile. In the Chevy's bench seat she sat so low she could barely see over the dash. So she looked out the side window, out at the lights. István didn't reply to her question.

He whisked them off to the hotel in downtown Montreal while Zolti, wide-eyed, stared up at the buildings and counted the number of different automobiles he saw.

The speed, the passing cars, the wide roadways and the merging lanes made Teréza jumpy. Something was poking into her side. She cracked up the minute she reached into her pocket. She held up her stash when István stopped at the light. "Three forks, three knives and three spoons. A set!"

"You took those off the plane?" István asked.

"Yes!" she said, grinning.

Zolti kicked the back of the seat.

"How did you get three?" István asked, entertained.
"Zolti, don't kick the seat. It's not my car." The light turned
green.

Chortling, she could barely answer, "I stole the neighbours' set while they were sleeping!" She laughed uncontrollably, her forehead against the dash.

"Will you laugh like that until the end of our days?" he
asked. "It's remarkable." Though he'd caught her laughter
and had trouble focusing on the road – he had tears running
down his face – István couldn't help but chastise her. "You
know you can't do that here. We don't steal in Canada."

She shrugged it off. "I'm not stealing. No one said I
couldn't take them."

"Please don't steal anything from the hotel," István
ribbed.

Teréza shrugged him off.

At the Queen Elizabeth Hotel, István handed their
passports to the concierge. Gazing about, Teréza was struck
by the opulence of the hotel lobby. The carved wooden
panels, stained glass murals, colourful wall hangings, ceramic
tiles, the brass elevator doors and the arching ceilings.

"Gigantic!" Zolti said, hopping up and down.

Teréza leaned into István and asked in a quiet voice,
"How much is this costing?"

"It doesn't matter," he replied. "We can afford it just this
once."

Practiced at suppressing desires, Teréza's self-restraint
kicked in automatically, preventing her from experiencing
ease. "Please, can I look?" she insisted.

"No," István said, tucking the invoice inside his coat

pocket. The concierge looked at him curiously. "I'm sorry, sir, I was talking to my wife. Come," he said, turning to his family.

"How about some champagne?" he said, as the three of them walked to the elevator. Teréza looked at him as if he'd said, "The Russians are invading."

"That's not necessary," she said. "It'll cost a fortune. We can drink water."

"But water isn't champagne."

"You sound hurt, my love."

Zolti continued hopping from foot to foot in an irregular rhythm as they waited for the elevator. "Zolti, would you stop that!" István said a little too forcefully.

"What's wrong with you?" Teréza looked surprised.

István got on his knees and took Zolti in his arms. "I'm sorry, son. It's been a long seven years." Zolti lowered his head onto his father's shoulder. István was able to soften for an instant.

Tears filled Teréza's eyes. "My apologies," she said regretfully. "It's true, I've never had champagne before. I don't know why I was afraid. Please, order some."

Teréza placed the white carnations in an ice bucket and added water from the bathtub faucet, arranging them as best she could. The opening of the ice bucket too large to hold them erect; she fussed some more and left them splayed in multiple directions, unsatisfied. Instead, she admired the sheets on the bed, snow white and expertly pressed. Chocolates lay on the pillows. Only two.

Zolti reached for the treat, opening one without asking.

"Wait." Teréza stopped him from putting it in his mouth. "We'll share it and give your father the other one."

"I don't need one," István said, watching with an unexplainable inquietude as Teréza broke the chocolate in half, clumsily.

He wrapped his arms around her waist and kissed her neck, her lips.

"Not, now." She pulled her head away. "Not in front of him."

Then when, István wondered.

Zolti bounced around the room inspecting every corner. István bristled at the sound of a rambunctious young boy. He watched his son grab his mother's hand and lead her to the bathroom.

"Look at the size of the bathtub!" he heard him say. "Can I take a bath?" Zolti's voice echoed from the ceramic tiled room. While Teréza washed her son's back, István sat reading *The Globe and Mail.* Later when he heard the tub draining, Zolti ran into the main room and catapulted himself onto the bed, landing heavily like a large slab of meat. Teréza had dressed him in pale blue pajamas with cuffs. As he lay linking his big toes, staring at the high ceiling, István asked him, "What are you thinking about, my son?"

At first, Zolti blushed, then said through a giggle, "How come penises don't gain weight but other body parts do?"

"That's a really good question," István replied, though he had no intention of explaining. He got up, walked over to his son and kissed him on his cheek. Zolti recoiled, wiped the moisture from his face and said, "Yuck," while turning his head away from his father. He covered his face with his hands. As if someone had thrown hot water at István's chest, his forehead grew moist and the room went white. István couldn't have explained the ensuing feeling to anyone, not to Teréza, not to himself. Nor could he understand its depths or the turmoil it stirred. His son had rejected him. István felt repugnant.

"He's asleep now," István said an hour later, clumsily reaching for his wife in the dark. "We could…you know…"

"It doesn't feel right in front of him. I don't want to scare him."

The first of March in Montreal sparkled with morning sun. Bela and Marika met them at the hotel. Marika took over at the wheel of her Chevy, while István and Teréza sat in the back, Zolti between them. Bela lit a cigar. Teréza coughed from time to time. István spoke very little, his hands laced in his lap.

Marika drove expertly, impressing Teréza, as she spoke, "When we arrived in Canada, Bela and I were taken to a rooming house. It was so dirty."

Teréza listened.

"Every time I used the bathroom, I had to wash it entirely, from top to bottom." Marika turned onto a busy shopping street. "One day, you'll never believe it, but I found a fifty dollar bill under the tub. Never in my life had I seen that much money all at once."

With one hand, Bela smoothed his black hair and pitched the remains of his cigar out the window with the other. "There were hookers working in the rooming house," he said.

"Disgusting." Teréza made a face. István remained silent.

"What is a hooker?" Zolti asked, without missing a beat.

"Nothing Zolti," Teréza replied, pulling him close.

"Why is a hooker disgusting?" Zolti demanded.

"Quiet, Zolti, and let her tell the story." Teréza felt annoyed by Marika's candidness. Clearly she had no experience raising a child. She put her finger to her lips to silence her son.

"Can we choose our words more carefully?"

"Of course," said Marika and carried on. "So I went to István and said, 'What the hell do I do with fifty bucks?' By early afternoon he'd found us this gorgeous used Chevy. We had a down payment! By the late afternoon," she said, gesturing to István, "this brilliant man was teaching me how to drive!" Teréza not only noticed how tastefully Marika dressed but how her face glowed as she praised István, leaving Teréza feeling uncomfortable.

The five of them had lunch at a Hungarian restaurant, the *Tokay*, then walked to Montreal's shopping district. Teréza was taken with the refined shops, connected through a network of underground galleries. Though below ground, they looked elegant and welcoming. Everything in the city gleamed. She declined when István offered to buy her a better watch. "This one will do," said Teréza.

"When it stops working I'll buy you a better one," István said.

"That's a long ways away."

While Marika and Bela walked arm and arm, Teréza held Zolti's hand and István walked on his own. His life secrets pressed down on him, rendering him speechless.

The following day the new family flew to Winnipeg. The city looked dull and less developed, and István could see it left Teréza unimpressed. He wished he knew a way to lighten her spirits, but no words came. He wanted his wife to feel assured she had made the right decision. Small relief when he watched her mood change, when he opened the door to their one-bedroom apartment. The two-story rental unit was simple yet friendly. István had repainted every room in anticipation of their arrival.

"It's darling," said Teréza, smiling, removing her shoes. The kitchen was ample in size. István had bought a chrome kitchen set, upholstered with yellow vinyl and grey piping. Zolti got the bedroom while Teréza and István would sleep on the pullout couch in the living room. On the hard wood floors, Teréza walked about on her tiptoes. The suite had large windows letting in the brilliant prairie light. "Splendid," she said. Outside the sun glinted off several feet of snow. She admired the handsome living room furniture – wood with simple lines, its fabric pistachio green – running her hands over the upholstery.

"This was all your doing?" Teréza asked.

"Yes," István replied.

"Thank you. Thank you very much."

He felt better now that they'd arrived home. He loosened with Teréza's approval, playfully got down on his knees and pretended to plead with her. With great hyperbole he said, "Please, please, please, whatever you cook it doesn't matter to me, but please, please, I ask of the heavens, please don't make layered potatoes with cabbage, meat hash with cabbage, or stew cabbage for at least a year! The wretched woman I boarded with made nothing but these three dishes in rotation. I can't eat them anymore."

Teréza laughed heartily. "I'll make you wonderful food," she said.

He kissed her hands, her face, her lips, and she laughed some more.

Their first morning together in their new home, István woke early, kissed Teréza on the cheek and went off to work like it was their first morning together in Makó, fourteen years earlier after they were wed. He'd snored throughout the night, and Teréza couldn't sleep until well after four. She woke as if drowning and blind, as though someone had placed a giant wet cotton swab over her head. No matter how she tried to extricate herself from its soggy threads, they kept sticking to her eyelids. Her irritability accompanied extreme fatigue and a dizziness she'd never before encountered. She'd brought with her a small packet of ground coffee and an aluminum stovetop coffee maker. A strong espresso reoriented her a bit.

István had left his dirty socks and underwear on the floor beside the sofa bed. When Teréza used the bathroom that morning she noticed urine on the toilet. She wiped off the bowl and picked up his laundry. Why did this upset her so much?

She wanted to go out but realized she had no money and didn't know where to find a grocery store. In any case, she couldn't speak English to ask for anything, and she was not up for pointing like a child. She washed her one bra and István's underwear and socks by hand. To her relief, István returned at lunch with bags of groceries so Teréza could set to work cooking. She made *Chicken Paprikás* with noodles and cucumber salad.

During dinner that night, she reminded István not to eat so quickly. "You're not waiting for us to serve ourselves, and you're already eating. All those years of bachelor life…"

He paused before shovelling a forkful of noodles into his

mouth. She could see her reprimand stung, but she did not now how to unsay it. He feigned patience with his son when Zolti expressed fear about going to school not knowing the language.

"Let's wait until next week to take him to school," Teréza suggested.

"He'll only learn English by going," István said between mouthfuls. "I read your reports cards from Hungary, my son. You've been at the top of your class. I'm proud of you. There's no reason why you can't pick up English quickly."

Teréza looked at her son with concern. "How is he to speak to anyone? He doesn't know a word."

"My name is Zolti," István said, putting down his knife and fork, turning his face towards his son. "Say it with me. Watch my lips. My name is Zolti." Already he felt like an inept father.

Zolti hesitated.

"My name is Zolti. Say it with me, my son."

"My name is Zolti," István and his son said in unison.

"Excellent!" István said. "You see? He's a fast learner. My name is Zolti, what's yours?"

Zolti broke his new train set the following day. The boy took after his mother, thought István. She was clumsy when she got nervous.

"Why hasn't this boy learned how to use his hands?" István shook his head trying to discover the cause of the mechanical failure. Zolti got down beside his father and watched intently.

"He had no one to teach him. Because you left without

him," Teréza said, her arms folded like crossing gates.

István replied to her dig with a non-sequiter, in the manner he used to answer Pista. "Eight years ago today, on March 3rd, 1956, Elvis Presley's first hit, 'Heartbreak Hotel' reached top ten."

She glared at him. "Don't treat me like an idiot."

That night, Zolti curled into his mother's arms as she read to him in his room. István stood at the doorway watching them.

"I'm going to watch a movie on television. It starts in a few minutes." István waited by the door. He asked Teréza, "Do you want to join me?"

She paused her reading. "What's the movie about?"

"An American war movie with Gregory Peck called *Twelve O'Clock High.*"

"I've had enough war, and the Americans can go to hell. Besides, I won't understand a thing."

"I'll translate."

She didn't respond.

"Come give me a hug," István said to his son.

Zolti vigorously shook his head.

"Blow your father a kiss," Teréza said to her son.

Zolti hid his head under the covers.

István couldn't bear their closeness. He retreated to the living room, opened a can of beer and switched on the television.

Some time later, Teréza emerged from Zolti's bedroom, looking placid. István remained riveted on the action on screen. Without turning his head, István said softly, "Come, sit with me."

"I told you, I've had enough war. I'm going to busy myself

in the kitchen."

He had several empty cans of Black Label beer lined up on the coffee table by the time the movie ended. After the credits rolled another show started. István didn't move from the sofa.

Teréza turned off the television, plunging the room in darkness. Only the streetlights outside gave them silhouettes.

"Zolti doesn't look anything like me," István said, his voice dark and resigned. "Why doesn't he look like me?"

"Because for a time children look more like one parent than the other. It's natural."

"For God's sake Teréza! Do you take me for stupid?"

"Keep your voice down."

"Why is there nothing of me in my son?"

Teréza brightened her voice, "He's attracted to machinery, just like you. He loved the washing machine I brought home from –"

"God damn it, answer me!" István's face reddened.

"Mind your language, we have a child in the house." Teréza moved towards the hallway when István grabbed her arm.

"You're hurting me." She tried to pull her arm away, but he held on harder.

"I want the truth," he said, his jaw tight, "tell me why he doesn't look like me!"

Teréza looked directly at István. "Because Pista never wanted you to forget what he did for you."

István's body lost function, like a dead battery.

All these years István had been held aloft by the hope that Pista had forgiven him before he died. Now, as István registered her words, he felt like he was falling through the sky, tugging on a ripcord; his parachute failing him. A painless moment of shock before the panic set in, then an instinct to flail his limbs. The impending terror of the impact filled István with rage.

He let go her arm, curled his fingers and dug his fingernails into his palms. He stared blankly at the wall as if a grenade had just blinded him. He didn't know who to blame. The humiliation was paralyzing. Pista's revenge had become a living, breathing reality. His pain drove him to say things even he didn't believe.

"You made yourself attractive to him."

"How idiotic. I don't even make myself attractive to you."

Spite, fury and self-disgust flashed through István's mind like multiple lightening strikes. He was about to ask her if she enjoyed it, but she abruptly left the room. Her exit as empty as the last eight years.

GOD COULDN'T HELP ME

1955, August. Szombathely, Hungary

Pista bust into their home without knocking. "I have a present for you, brother."

Teréza gasped.

István placed his hand on her back, whispered in her ear, "It's alright Teréza, he's as harmless as a fish in this condition. He'll pass out, even before I ask him to leave."

"Happy birthday!" Pista had on his maniacal look, his Sunday best. "The big thirty!"

István felt nonplussed by the prospect of a gift. Every time he saw Pista in the last two years since they had moved to Szombathely, he presented István with either riddles or booze. István hated riddles, and Pista ended up drinking all the booze. This time Pista brought both.

"It's got legs but no hands. A back but no stomach. What is it?" Pista asked, already teetering between heaven and hell, a bottle in a bag tucked under his arm. His hair was a matted tangle and thinner than when he'd seen him last.

"I don't know and I don't care." At least he's shaven,

thought István.

"A chair!" Teréza exclaimed.

"Speaking of chairs, can you make it to one?"

"All these years, I survived just fine without you brother. I don't need your watchfulness." His bum nearly missed the stool as Pista presented István with the bag under his arm. "Peach brandy. Warms you from the inside."

István watched Teréza throw a freshly ironed tablecloth over the kitchen table, smooth it with her palms and place cheese and caraway pastries in the centre. "What's for dinner?" he asked.

"Layered potato casserole with mushrooms, tomato salad and cherry strudel," she said, checking on food in the oven.

"A fine birthday meal." István sounded like he was pretending to enjoy himself. He knew it sounded fake, and he no longer felt real in front of his lifelong friend. Facing him, Pista grinned. Waiting. István could feel something coming.

"Four of my favourite foods on earth. And all of them deadly, if you partake of the wrong part. Potatoes if you eat the leaves, mushrooms if you eat the wrong one, tomatoes if you eat the stem and cherries if you eat the pit."

"Like friendship."

"Precisely. Like friendship."

István knew that look on Teréza's face. The one that conveyed: I can't take this. I have to improve this situation.

She regaled him with a birthday song as she set the table. Pista looked her up and down as she moved about the kitchen, István watching him like a hawk. She ended the last note with a kiss on István's cheek. He turned red, Pista clapped, and Teréza apologized for not singing perfectly. The three ate quietly and ravenously like they always did when they were angry or uncomfortable. Sound intruded on the silence with the clanging of cutlery.

Pista belched.

István shook his head, set down his cutlery and shoved his plate away. Teréza got up and started clearing the table. István looked in her direction, away from Pista, anger and heartbreak marinating his soul like the leftover tomatoes swimming in white vinegar.

"Before you judge my unseemly condition, brother," Pista began, "you must understand the anatomy of my state."

"I don't know why you think I judge you," István replied.

"I see the look in your eyes. I know you too well. I've brought a story for your 30th birthday. I've practiced for years to recall the details. I fight to hold on to them so I can remember the truth. And those same details haunt me with nightmares."

"What are you talking about? You're not making any sense."

"They tortured me."

"Who?"

"Our commanding officer and his nephew. They tortured me instead of you."

Teréza was washing the dishes. István wanted her gone.

István blinked, swallowed. His scalp began to sweat. He felt encircled by a wall of flames, ignited by shame. In defence, he squinted his eyes and protected his hands by sitting on them. "Why didn't you tell me?"

"Because I'm telling you now. For years it was a block of ice inside me, and now miraculously, it's melting." Pista's body swayed on his stool.

"What happened?" István sat forward and felt sick anticipating the answer to the question.

"Where do I start?" Pista lit another smoke.

"Teréza, best you leave those dishes for later." István turned in her direction.

"I'm almost done."

"Please Teréza. The sun is setting outside. I know how much you love sunsets."

"They're more beautiful than my story," Pista wiped his forehead with his shirtsleeve.

"Thank you." István tried to take hold of Teréza's hand before she exited, but she pulled it away before he could reach it. Everyone, including him, was bracing, in anticipation.

The door shut with a bang behind Teréza. The tomatoes were wrinkling in vinegar in a bowl on the counter and István suddenly felt bittersweet love for Pista again. "Go ahead and tell your story if you're going to. The sunset will take a while."

"First, I'm made to think I'm being dined. In the cellar below Németh's office no less. Varga feeds me liverwurst sausage made with extra, extra, *extra* hot *Szegedi* paprika. He encourages me to eat every last bite until my mouth burns like a campfire. Even my dog wouldn't be able to stomach it. When I ask for water, he says the meal doesn't come with drinks. Thank goodness, I think, because I remember that water simply swirls the poison around in one's mouth, makes it cover more territory. Water and heat, not a good mix.

"It's not long after that that my guts begin to rattle. The liverwurst wants to move through me like organs in a meat grinder. That's when I realize there's no washroom and they're putting a gun to my head."

István knew he owed it to Pista to hear every atrocious detail but wanted him to hurry it up so he could burble his useless apology.

"So, just as I regurgitate the fiery mash, Németh comes in. I've been having such a jolly time with his nephew that I'm taken aback."

"Why reduce your story with sarcasm?"

"Can't have that! More brandy, please." Pista extended his glass. István filled it, and Pista tossed it back.

"When Németh produces your birth certificate I insist you aren't Jewish." Pista looked István squarely in his eyes until István was forced to look away. "I tell him straight up that Feri's your birth father and that he was kicked off the Vasvár estate after he knocked up your mother. I think to myself, there's no way your story's going to match mine. We hadn't even discussed what we would say in case of torture – we really dropped the ball on that, brother. But no matter, I had it covered. So much so, that Németh was furious with me and left me overnight with Varga."

Sympathy felt pitiful coming out of István's mouth. "I'm sorry," he said.

"Are you?"

"How can you think I'm not?"

"He makes me stand on a metal plinth in a sunken broom closet in the cellar, as narrow as a child's coffin. Standing room only. Surrounding the plinth is old well water. It's pitch black and suffocating. After only a few hours I'm in excruciating pain, and exhausted. When I fall asleep, I lose my balance and plunge into the icy water, which I'm then forced to stand in for the next – I'm guessing – roughly seven hours, unable to right the plinth with my frozen feet. They learned these techniques up at headquarters in Budapest, and I was the first test subject in Ják.

"When Varga finally lets me out, I can no longer feel my feet. When I try to take a step they're as useful as clubs and I fall into the centre of the room, just managing not to break my handsome face. Instead my shoulder takes the blow.

"That's when I finally take a shit. And this is where the details start to get fuzzy because I'm shaking on the floor and losing consciousness while Varga keeps kicking me in the kidneys to keep me awake. I don't exactly know when Németh comes in, but that's when I discover I'm stark naked, with my arms behind my back and my ankles chained to metal rings in the floor. I'm lying in my own watery feces with a sack over my head and a revolver pressing against my temple."

István cradled his head in his hands.

"Németh, sensitive man that he is, says in his sing songy voice, 'Wouldn't it be wonderful to get out into that fresh morning air, my young recruit? It stinks terribly in here. It's even a bit spicy.' I could feel him almost breathing on me."

István shook his head, trying to hide from himself what he was suddenly beginning to remember. That vile smell in Németh's office. On a morning nine years ago, István had been sitting in a chair above the cellar, listening to his best friend being tortured. Pista's horror in the cellar had saved István's life, and all István could feel was a caustic and ever widening gap between them.

"God couldn't help me. When for a second time, Németh produces your birth certificate, I know that this is the test. I have to remember exactly what I said the night before or else they'll kill me. But I'm delirious. As the words come out of my mouth, I can't even hear myself. Remember when the headmaster had us memorize Petőfi? *Rise up, Magyar, the country calls! It's 'now or never' what fate befalls...Shall we live as slaves or free men?* If only they had taught us to memorize poems while sitting in shit with a burlap sack over our heads. I may have had more of a mind for detail. The only hope I have is that somehow our minds are one."

This time István poured himself another brandy.

"So Varga keeps going at my kidneys. And then at my balls. I think that's when I vomit into the sack over my head."

"That's enough, Pista," István said, pushing away from the table.

"Enough?" Pista said, incredulous. "Enough? *I've* had enough when Varga manhandles me onto a chair, yanks my head back by the hood and proceeds to pour water down my throat while I sputter, gurgle and convulse. The water rushes into my lungs. I feel like I'm drowning." Pista levelled István with his eyes. "You know, it would have taken only my signature on a form to end the torture? A signature that would condemn my best friend to death?"

"Why didn't you sign?"

Pista reached for the bottle and saw it was empty. "You fuck. You're out of brandy." He draws his hands down his face and continues his story. "As I'm semi-conscious, Németh demands that I confess to you being a Jew. All I can say is "Kiss István is the son of Kiss Feri. Kiss István is the son of Kiss Feri." That's all I could say over and over and over again."

Pista pulled his chair closer to István. Uncomfortably close. "So Németh leaves again. His pit bull nephew is just getting warmed up."

A feverish feeling spread throughout István's body. The most sickening feeling of his life. Unsummoned, he recalled the sound of those muted thuds coming from somewhere below that office, while sitting across from Németh. The ones he thought he'd imagined.

István and Pista sat in silence. István couldn't look him in the eye.

"Do you want to hear more?"

István neither nodded nor shook his head. He owed it to Pista to hear every last detail. "Please hurry, before Teréza returns."

"We wouldn't want her pretty little ears to hear this would we? This is man-to-man. So Németh returns again, furious. He orders his nephew to remove my hood, and push me to my knees. Varga positions his cock right at my mouth. I opened wide, and waited. That's when he urinated. In my mouth, István. And then it was all over. I'll never forget Németh's parting words: 'Not only the thirsty seek the water, the water as well seeks the thirsty.' Did our headmaster ask us to memorize Rumi in school?"

István held his forehead as disgust and disbelief flooded his mind. "Did our stories match?"

"It's like we have one mind, István, you and I." Pista leaned his elbows on the table. "It's like our minds fused in childhood, and I knew every word to speak." Then Pista leaned back on his chair. "But if we have one mind, you and I, why is my life shit, and yours so successful? You know how much I get paid gutting pigs? They'll never promote me. Not with my record. Not like some people. The kind that get away with everything."

"You fucking son of a bitch!" István lunged at Pista, pulled him up by the scruff, and started manhandling him backwards toward the front door, causing Pista to lose his balance and clutch at furniture. Chairs overturned and banged to the ground just as Teréza re-entered the kitchen through the back.

"Enough!" she screamed. "Animals are for the barn. Not for my kitchen!"

István dragged his drunken friend out the door and pushed him to the ground. Pista lay sprawled, belly up cackling to the sky. "You owe me. Your beautiful life, your beautiful wife, all this that you have. You owe it all to me."

István shut the door.

"Did this have to happen on your birthday?" Teréza said, her arms folded, elbows sticking out sideways at sharp angles.

"It's always my fault, isn't it?" István grabbed his uniform jacket.

"Where are you going?"

"To work."

"You said you had the night off!" Teréza shrieked.

"I've changed my mind." István threw off his slippers and shoved his feet into his shoes.

"Why do you have to ruin your birthday?"

"There you go again. I ruin everything." István slammed the door.

She watched through the window as his figure receded, and her shock intensified. She had listened by an open window as she watched the setting sun. She knew everything.

When the figure crawled in through the side window, under the cover of darkness, Teréza was fast asleep. She woke only when her mouth was covered and she couldn't scream. She tasted dirt on his hand, and she bit down on his flesh. He then slapped her head to keep her tame.

"I only want a little of his comfort for my pain," he whispered.

She pulled in all her muscles towards her ribs, her pelvis and her spine. Like a casement of protection against what was to come. He forced his way in quickly, rammed her, whimpered his agony on her chest and cried.

She stared into the darkness at an untouchable ceiling.

When István came home the next morning, Teréza was gathering the bedding in the laundry hamper. "Why are you changing the bedding again?" Hadn't Teréza washed the sheets the previous day?

"Because someone has to do the laundry around here." She left the room in a huff, walking past István without a hint of eye contact.

He watched her through the kitchen window washing the sheets by hand in the outdoor sink. The sun was bright and the wind was up, sweeping branches and leaves from side to side. Red apples were ready on the tree. He grabbed a woven basket.

"How about I pick some apples?" he said to her, his voice carrying on the wind.

"That would be nice," she said.

He watched her hands scrubbing hard then wringing the cloth with might.

"How about we lay out on a blanket in the sun and stare up at the moving clouds?" he said, his invitation a guilty overture for walking out on her last night. "It's Saturday. We could rest a little, together."

"We could do that," she said, with indifference, as she hung the sheets on the line to dry.

"I'd like to make it up to you," István said.

"Give me a child to bring me joy. That might make things better."

He offered her an apple. She bit into it.

IS IT POSSIBLE...
THAT YOU COULD HOLD ME

1964, March 3. Winnipeg, Canada

Stone-faced, Teréza returned to the living room some time later.

It was clear to István she had been crying.

She brought with her a pair of shoes. Brown women's Oxfords with a wooden heel, well worn but beautifully polished. She threw them on the coffee table in front of István. The sight of them was horrifying and pleasing.

"You buried one family; don't bury another."

István's guts clenched.

"What else are you keeping from me?" she asked.

Decades were unravelling in seconds.

"I was following orders. I was young. I was scared. I didn't kill anyone. I only gathered their clothing."

"You wooed me with a dead woman's shoes?" Teréza's back stiffened.

"She didn't die. They spared her and her son. But I was never able to return the shoes to her so I gave them to you. I wanted some good to come out of that inhumane night."

"How many inhumane nights were there?"

"Too many. There was no one to turn to. Except Pista. My whole life feels fake. What I would give for a little dignity." István hung his head. "He's not my boy, and it's not too late for you to go back."

"Bravo."

Snowflakes the size of quarters began to fall outside their living room window. The streetlamps illuminated their crystalline forms in shafts of light.

Teréza watched as István dropped his head. His back began to shake. She realized he was crying. She recognized the very same condition in herself. She remembered all those years, hearing sounds through walls, neighbours dragged away to be tortured and exiled. Now their own minds dragged them away, to painful, tormenting places. She was as lost as he was.

She could feel their impasse constructed of pain that acted like repelling magnets. She wanted to reach out, but she burrowed inwards. She could feel him do the same. Would they be there forever, with an invisible barrier threatening to keep them separate? What price would she pay to open just a little to see if there was anything left? Like a child, allowing a parent a peek at its fresh wound, she attempted a small opening. "What's happened to us?"

For a long time he didn't respond.

A tremendous bitterness held her in place. She needed it as much as she hated it. Teréza held her heart, holding back all she could. She thought about how in Hungarian, the word for anger was the same word for poison – *méreg.*

She was about to turn away when he said, "I don't even know how to begin to answer that." The tear trickled so slowly down his cheek to his chin, she thought it might stay there suspended, forever.

"Everything came with me, not just the clothing on my back. Memories cling, and I can't rid myself of them." He spoke slowly, as if every thought tore tissue as it left his mind.

"What if memories are not to be gotten rid of?" She also spoke slowly, discovering her thoughts as she went, taking the pain and turning it over like a stone. "What if they are to be confessed to a trusted other, cried over, stroked, regretted and sworn never to be repeated?"

Teréza touched the shoes. An ache under the unrelenting hardness – the pain's origin so remote she could hardly touch its source. For centuries they'd carried it. As she yielded to its legacy, touched its core, she softened just a little. She imagined floating in something soothing and felt a whisper of liberation.

She sat down, removed her slippers and slipped her feet into the shoes. Tied the laces. When she looked up, it appeared as though István was returning to life again.

"Is it possible...that you could hold me?" István asked. "I'm so disgusted with myself."

She couldn't move towards him or answer right away. "It's possible," she said, feeling his remorse.

He came to her side, perched himself on the edge of the chair against her body. She felt his sadness as she drew him into her arms. She stroked the side of his face then laid her head against him. He needed one person to know how lost and scared he had been his whole life. "The war changed me," he said.

"Wars begin at home," Teréza said, feeling his beating chest.

"And the wars at home are the wars inside us," István said, breathing heavily.

István looked out the window, desperate to escape again. He wanted to freeze to death in a snowbank outside. Oppressive guilt weighed on his chest. Sobered by it, he wanted to see its end. What would it take?

Raise my son the way you once loved me. He's your second chance.

"Then will you forgive me?" István said aloud. "I wish I could remember when I was innocent."

"Let Zolti teach you. Our child is innocent," Teréza responded.

Our child. Our child. István's throat hurt from the truth.

"We've spent our entire lives hiding. I want to bare my heart, just once, without fear."

She reached over and placed his hand on her chest.

Bathed by the light of a streetlamp that flooded through the living room, they were overcome by a torrent of emotion. How familiar and strange it was to feel their bodies together after she had grown accustomed to touching nothing but the small hand of her son. István's body felt his sins, now more than ever. He lost himself in her skin, her breasts, while she hovered on the ceiling, watching herself as he consumed her and found his way into her, and she loved and unloved herself with waves of feeling and unfeeling. An intense coolness came over her and all she could say was, "Please, keep me warm."

Skin to skin, they pressed all their secrets together.

All that they had lost had found a place to be held.

Outside the window a rapidly falling curtain of snow was turning their world white.

END

ACKNOWLEDGEMENTS

Without my family, without my ancestors, this story would not exist. I am humbled and honoured to be in the lineage of strong, passionate people who had to survive brutality and still maintain a sense of humour and connectedness. My family endured conditions I will never have to know. And they have shared their stories with me through tears, with generosity and courage, cringing through memories that accelerated their heart rates. To the immense openness of my mother who shared horrid secrets and relived inhumane memories, in helping me piece together what happened in Hungary. To my father as he sat across from me, his feet on tiptoes, his mind ravaged by dementia asking me over and over again, "What are you writing about?" To the memory of my cheerful and joke-telling uncle Joska, who broke down and cried in my arms when he finally told someone his story. To my dear late aunt Irénke who without fail greeted me in Budapest, made me my favourite soup and gave me a home in the old country. To my aunt Cila who always brought vitality and optimism to my darker, more serious outlook.

She helped me see the light in the story.

Without the daily care, dedication, love, attunement and companionship of my beloved husband, I would have thrown in the towel. Ken Cameron has a beautiful and fertile mind and is a gifted playwright with a flare for comedy and smart dramaturgy. There is no way in hell that I could have tackled editors' notes without Ken sorting me out when I got overwhelmed. He blazed the trail to organize my thoughts and catalyze the conversations and strategies that would help me get underneath what felt at times like impossible tasks. He has been with me through thick and thin, cutting and pasting and reordering until we could make this historical tale a modern cinematic story of a broken family. He taught me how to start on action, cut what slowed things down and he affectionately read to me the passages that moved him. When we were exhausted from another round of edits, he never gave up and continued to do the dishes while he put his own work aside. This book would not have been possible without Ken by my side. His brilliance shines between the lines.

To the inimitable award-winning independent editor Adrienne Kerr who spent two years lovingly supporting me through the ups and downs of editing this beast of a novel. She stood by me as I despaired, collapsed and rebirthed the novel from its ashes. Adrienne left no stone unturned and passionately dove into each and every crevice of psychology, intention and motivation of the characters. She meticulously asked every question possible. She ached with me, cried with me and rejoiced with me. Adrienne Kerr, you are one of a kind.

Fellegi Ádám, the great Hungarian pianist, who shared his horrifying story of being a young Jewish child rounded up by the Nazis. Thank you for listening with interest and for your captivating house concerts where my creativity could germinate while your hands glided across piano keys.

To dear Lorinda Stewart, who inexhaustibly told me never to stop. She knows from her own life what perseverance is necessary to overcome the greatest adversity and to beat all odds. She counted with me the many rejections I received, 50 from agents and another 25 from publishers. And she still reminded me, to "never give up."

To Lara Tambacopoulou, a dear fierce friend who used all her connections to try to open doors for me. Thank you, Lara!

To my dear friends who listened to my many sorrows, when I thought I had come to the end of the road with this novel: Diane Stinson, Steve Schroeder, Susan Faulkner, Deirdre Young, Sandi Somers and Mel Parsons.

Thank you to Nicole Lerner (Nicoletta) for believing in "every word" and for knowing and feeling the care I take with them. Love you always.

To my lifelong friend Liza Kovacs, a dear Hungarian sister who kept my earliest writings and completed the final read before submission.

To Linda Jaeger and Eric Paetkau who braved reading the whole book.

Gratefully to Andras Bereznay whose maps of Hungary and of Budapest grace the front of this book. You can find his work at: www.historyonmaps.com.

Deep thanks to Liza Morrison, Tania Therien and my new champions at Atmosphere Press: Kyle McCord, Nick Courtright, Alex Kale and Ronaldo Alves. Thank you for being the ones to see that this novel can have a life. You don't know how much this means to me.

To the many sources that inspired me...

Books:

James Michener's *The Bridge at Andau*; Tamas Dobozy's *Seige 13*; Slavenka Drakulić's *Balkan Express* and *A Guided Tour Through the Museum of Communism: Fables from a Mouse, a Parrot, a Bear, a Cat, a Mole, a Pig, a Dog, & a Raven*; Sofie Oksanen's *Purge*; Victor Sebestyen's *Twelve Days: The Story of the 1956 Hungarian Revolution*; Erwin A. Schmidl and László Ritter's *The Hungarian Revolution 1956*; Anne Applebaum's *Iron Curtain: The Crushing of Eastern Europe, 1944 – 1956*.

Films and Documentaries:

Whooping Cough by Péter Gárdos and András Osvát; *Freedom's Fury* written and directed by Colin Keith Gray; *Sunshine* by István Szabó, *The Witness* by Péter Bacsó; *Gloomy Sunday* by Ruth Toma and Rolf Schübel and *In the Land of Blood and Honey* by Angelina Jolie.

To the talented writers who mentored, supported and inspired me: Dennis Bock, Esi Edugyan, Joseph Kertes, Guðrún Eva Mínervudóttir and Lee Kvern. Thanks to Humber College.

I am deeply indebted to the insanely gifted and powerful women who have motivated me to do it my way and to fearlessly carve a path outside of the mainstream:

Patti Smith and Marina Abramovic.
Angela Jolie and her humanitarian work.
Malala Yousafzai, Greta Thunberg and the band Pussy Riot.

I want to acknowledge the work of Amnesty International.

Thank you to the plant medicine Ayahuasca which was a companion in processing my own and my family's trauma and in developing compassion towards our collective multigenerational trauma.

I want to remember the largest humanitarian crisis we have witnessed on this planet and refugees everywhere that want what we all want: safety, security, freedom, liberation and their loving families, gathered together.

And most importantly, the freedom fighters of the 1956 Hungarian Revolution.

ABOUT ATMOSPHERE PRESS

Atmosphere Press is an independent, full-service publisher for excellent books in all genres and for all audiences. Learn more about what we do at atmospherepress.com.

We encourage you to check out some of Atmosphere's latest releases, which are available at Amazon.com and via order from your local bookstore:

Dying to Live, a novel by Barbara Macpherson Reyelts

Looking for Lawson, a novel by Mark Kirby

Surrogate Colony, a novel by Boshra Rasti

Á Deux, a novel by Alexey L. Kovalev

What If It Were True, a novel by Eileen Wesel

Sunflowers Beneath the Snow, a novel by Teri M. Brown

Solitario: The Lonely One, a novel by John Manuel

The Fourth Wall, a novel by Scott Petty

Rx, a novel by Garin Cycholl

Knights of the Air: Book 1: Rage!, a novel by Iain Stewart

Heartheaded, a novel by Constantina Pappas

The Aquamarine Surfboard, a novel by Kellye Abernathy

ABOUT THE AUTHOR

Raised by Hungarian refugees, Rita is a Somatic Relational trauma and psychedelic-informed therapist, a multi-disciplinary creator, playwright and retired professional actor and dancer. For 25 years, her co-written play *52 Pick Up* was staged in Canada, the US, England, Australia, France, Iceland and New Zealand and translated into French and Icelandic. Rita has been published in *The New Quarterly, FFWD Weekly, WritingRaw.com, Unlikely 2.0* and *Pages of Stories. THIS Magazine* awarded her 3rd prize in their Great Canadian Literary Hunt in 2012. Her travel stories have been broadcast on CBC Radio Calgary. She is an alumna of The Humber School for Writers. Her life practice is kindness and her life partner is Ken Cameron.

CPSIA information can be obtained
at www.ICGtesting.com
Printed in the USA
BVHW061440090522
636461BV00002B/12